ROTHERHAM LIBRARIES AND NEIGHBOURHOOD HUBS

RAO

R4

Juliette H

Juliette can be found spending time with her
daughters and giant dogs, or sewing uneven stitches with
her sewing machine.

Sue MacKay lives with her husband in New Zealand's
beautiful Marlborough Sounds, with the water on her
doorstep and the birds and the trees at her back door.
It is the perfect setting to indulge her passions of
entertaining friends by cooking them sumptuous meals,
drinking fabulous wine, going for hill walks or kayaking
around the bay—and, of course, writing stories.

Discover more at millsandboon.co.uk.

RULES OF THEIR FAKE FLORIDA FLING

JULIETTE HYLAND

SINGLE MUM'S NEW YEAR WISH

SUE MacKAY

MILLS & BOON

All rights reserved including the right of reproduction
in whole or in part in any form. This edition is published
by arrangement with Harlequin Enterprises ULC.

This is a work of fiction. Names, characters, places, locations
and incidents are purely fictional and bear no relationship to
any real life individuals, living or dead, or to any actual places,
business establishments, locations, events or incidents.
Any resemblance is entirely coincidental.

This book is sold subject to the condition that it
shall not, by way of trade or otherwise, be lent, resold, hired out
or otherwise circulated without the prior consent of the publisher
in any form of binding or cover other than that in which it is published
and without a similar condition including this condition
being imposed on the subsequent purchaser.

® and TM are trademarks owned and used by the trademark owner
and/or its licensee. Trademarks marked with ® are registered with the
United Kingdom Patent Office and/or the Office for Harmonisation
in the Internal Market and in other countries.

First published in Great Britain 2022
by Mills & Boon, an imprint of HarperCollins*Publishers* Ltd,
1 London Bridge Street, London, SE1 9GF

www.harpercollins.co.uk

HarperCollins*Publishers*
1st Floor, Watermarque Building,
Ringsend Road, Dublin 4, Ireland

Rules of Their Fake Florida Fling © 2022 Juliette Hyland

Single Mum's New Year Wish © 2022 Sue MacKay

ISBN: 978-0-263-30147-2

12/22

MIX
Paper | Supporting
responsible forestry
FSC™ C007454

This book is produced from independently certified FSC™ paper
to ensure responsible forest management.
For more information visit: www.harpercollins.co.uk/green.

Printed and Bound in Spain using 100% Renewable Electricity
at CPI Black Print, Barcelona

RULES OF THEIR FAKE FLORIDA FLING

JULIETTE HYLAND

MILLS & BOON

For Jenn.

For years of friendship, support and introducing me
to TikTok…though you probably regret that one.

Rotherham MBC	
B54 063 685 7	
Askews & Holts	19-Dec-2022
AF	£6.99
RTRAW	

CHAPTER ONE

"You realize three other surgeons have turned this case away?"

"They weren't me." Dr. Asher Parks shrugged as he looked at the head of the surgery department, Dr. Levern. Asher wasn't bragging—not really. Just being honest.

He was the best neurosurgeon at Mercy General. The best in Orlando, Florida…one of the best in the nation. He knew his skill set.

He'd chosen neurosurgery because it was complicated. In the academic world nearly everything had come easily…again not a brag, just a fact. Neurosurgery offered a challenge so many other things didn't. And Asher loved a challenge.

This surgery was difficult…some had said impossible. An operation most neurosurgeons wouldn't touch, and this was a competitive field. But it was a challenge Asher could meet; he was certain of it.

"A tumor in the spinal cavity. Definition of unlucky." Dr. Levern flipped through the images on the tablet, clicking his tongue at the results.

Asher felt his nose scrunch and intentionally leaned back. It was unlucky. Statistically, nearly impossible. He understood this line of work required at least some compartmentalization of emotions. Dr. Levern didn't mean anything by the throwaway comment, but there was a person on the other end of that "unlucky."

Jason Mendez. Twenty, barely more than a teenager, with a full life in front of him. He should be worrying about college, or starting a career, or dating. There were so many things one looked forward to at twenty, before adult realities sneaked in. A tumor had ripped that "normal" away.

Unlucky indeed.

"It's grown by three centimeters in the last six months." Asher rocked back on his heels, trying to keep the frustration at bay. A tumor in the spinal cavity was dangerous. The surgery would take at least six hours, assuming everything went well. Three other surgeons had looked at the location of the tumor and told the patient to prepare for the end.

But Asher wasn't ready to concede to the fates. Jason knew the risks, knew that a single slip could paralyze him. Knew that if the tumor had any attachments not currently seen on the images, removing it completely might not be possible. Since it was cancerous, that would buy him time, but not forever.

Jason understood he might not make it through the surgery. That was always a risk, but, when dealing with neurosurgery, the risks were even higher. Still, as Jason had told him, he was already under a death sentence. May as well give it a go.

And Dr. Asher Parks was more than willing to give it a go. In fact he planned to do this flawlessly. Perfection!

Dr. Levern clicked his tongue again. It was a tell every surgeon in the hospital knew. It meant the head of surgery was leaning toward yes and trying to convince himself it was the right choice.

"Think of the prestige the hospital will get for doing

this." Asher kept his voice upbeat even though the words tasted like dirt. He hated it that hospitals took prestige into their calculation matrix for high-risk cases. He may have chosen medicine because it was a challenge, but saving lives was supposed to be the purpose.

And it was for most doctors. But hospital administration was a different beast. All spreadsheets, profit margins and dividends. Unfortunately that was the beast Dr. Levern had to answer to.

"You'll write a paper? Answer any questions, if they're asked? Interviews, if necessary."

"Of course." Asher could see the mental calculations of at least a hospital-organized local press release and a medical journal publication coalescing into the affirmative. It shouldn't matter, but that wasn't the way life worked. And for his patients, he'd do anything.

"And you'll have to have the best team for this. They'll need to sign off on participating." He tapped a pen against his desk. "It's high risk and…"

"Understood." Asher wanted to pump his fist, but he kept his pose professional. This was going to be approved. Jason would get the surgery, and Asher would wield the scalpel. If anyone balked, well, most of the hospital owed him at least one favor for stepping out on a limb for them.

"That includes Dr. Miller." Dr. Levern handed him back the tablet.

"Of course." This reply was more subdued, but Asher kept the smile on his face. "Dr. Miller and I get along fine." That was a bit of a stretch, but Dr. Levern didn't push him on it.

Leaving Dr. Levern's office, Asher went in search of Rory Miller. Better to talk to her before word trickled out. He might need a bit of time to get her on his side.

He and Rory tolerated each other. They worked well together, but their personalities were diametrically opposed. He was a jokester, had to find some way to expel the stress, while she was commonly called the Rock of Mercy. She was great at her job, cared about her patients. Listened.

And the woman never flinched, never worried in surgery, never showed any emotion.

Unless it was annoyance with Dr. Parks! They'd lived next to each other for almost five years, worked together for six, and yet he wasn't sure he'd ever seen the woman smile.

Not that he hadn't tried. It was his secret personal project. Six years with no success, every attempt expertly rebuffed. All work and no play for the Rock. But Asher was persistent. One day he'd find the crack…

He'd met the anesthesiologist at the new-employee orientation. Sitting next to the fiery redhead with piercing green eyes should have been the highlight of his morning. Their safety presentation had been drier than dry. The monotone of the instructor made most of the assembled employees yawn.

He'd leaned over and made some joke…something lost to the fog of time now. And Rory had looked horrified; that he hadn't forgotten. Her jade eyes flashing as she shook her head. The drop of his stomach as the beautiful doctor judged him…and found him lacking.

He still recalled her explanation regarding safety and patient care that had tumbled from her lips. All of which he'd agreed with! It was the delivery he was poking fun at, but the damage was done.

He enjoyed the laugh, enjoyed making people smile. But sometimes jokes fell flat, and you moved on. He was fun, easy to get along with, according to the rest of the staff, but around Dr. Rory Miller he put his foot his mouth. All his jokes, his smiles, had no effect on the Rock of Mercy.

If Rory had her way, the operating theater would be quiet. Formal. Sterile in attitude not just germ-free.

They simply had different ideas of what *professional* meant. Rory was stoic. Asher, over-the-top expressive. She made quiet remarks about a patient's status. He joked about the day and chatted sports. And he enjoyed hard rock in the theater. It relaxed him.

Sure, most of the surgeons chose something a little less heavy. Dr. Stevens loved Vivaldi...classical. Asher personally hated when he controlled the music. Dr. Trent preferred country music. Asher was pretty sure she'd wear leather boots in the theater if she could get away with it.

But it was his attitude: "flippant" was the description Rory used. And she was right. Asher was chatty, jovial even, in the OR. No matter the case.

He'd learned at a young age that life didn't guarantee anyone tomorrow. A brain aneurysm stole his mother while she was in the downward dog position at her regular Tuesday yoga class. That was the other reason his surgical knife was trained in brain surgery. He saved more than he lost. But even he, with all his skill, couldn't hold off the Reaper each time.

So Asher made jokes. He smiled and laughed as much as possible. Frowns never crossed his face, even when he was dying inside. After all, it was better to laugh than cry.

"I hate not being able to help Dr. Miller." Nurse Sienna Garcia's words caught Asher's ears.

Anything to up his chances of getting in good with Dr. Miller, he'd try. A trade for a trade. She'd never made one before...but there was a first time for everything.

"What does she need help with?" Asher leaned against the nurses' station, offering his best smile. He watched the heat dance into Sienna's cheeks and offered a wink. "I can be very helpful."

"She's looking for a date to a wedding." Sienna returned his smile.

"And we're all aware of how helpful you can be, Dr. Parks," Angela, the head nurse stated as she nudged Sienna's hip with hers.

He and Angela had dated for six weeks, two years ago. Or was it three? They'd parted on well enough terms, but the experience had reminded him why he tried to keep his dating and professional life separate. A lesson his younger self had not realized until he'd earned a bit of a reputation as the hospital playboy.

He'd been single for over a year and hadn't dated anyone at the hospital since Angela, but reputations once earned...

Sienna walked off, and Asher turned his attention to Angela. "A wedding date? That seems simple enough." Rory was gorgeous; anyone attracted to women couldn't fail to notice her curly red hair, toned legs and freckles dotting her nose. She was also brilliant and at the top of her field. Maybe she didn't smile or laugh, but surely a wedding date would be easy enough for her. If she'd only relax a little, she'd be the definition of a complete package.

"That is what she said." Angela nodded, but he could see a look in her eye. Something unsaid...

"Come on, Ang. There has to be more to it than just a wedding date."

Angela crossed her arms, the giant engagement ring twinkling on the necklace she wore. He was happy for her. Marriage wasn't for him. He'd come close once. And lost his fiancée and best friend in the process. Kate and Michael had been divorced now longer than she and Asher had dated, but he'd learned his lesson.

He did six weeks of fun, something all his partners knew up front. Six weeks, enjoy the attraction and get out before anything deeper developed. Deep feelings lead to love, and love leads to heartbreak. And heartbreak was never on the table for Asher Parks.

However, he was genuinely happy when others found a life partner.

"I am sure there is, but all she asked was if we knew anybody who might be willing to escort her to her sister's wedding."

"Escort?"

"That was the word she used." Angela bit her lip as she looked toward the on-call suite. "I wish I had someone to set her up with. She asks for so little. Actually, Rory asks for nothing. She's the one doctor that never demands anything."

Asher held up his hands. "I know we are all imperfect sods."

"You said it," Angela chuckled.

"I bet I could be free to escort, Dr. Miller."

Angela's chuckle turned into a full-blown belly laugh. "Make me a promise. Let me be there when you ask. I'd love to see the Rock's reaction to the playboy's offer."

Asher kept the playful smile on his face while holding a hand over his chest in pretend wounded pride. "I'm a great date."

Angela nodded. "For a short time, you certainly are." Then she grabbed a tablet and walked into a patient's room.

Asher let the feelings Angela's statement raised wash through him then let them go. She'd wanted a family, marriage, the whole white-picket dream. And he hoped she got that with her fiancé. But that was not a life Asher ever saw for himself.

Rocking on his heels, he headed toward the consult room dedicated for on-call surgeons. He, Rory and Dr. Petre were the on-call surgical staff for tonight. With any luck Rory would be catching up on paperwork or just resting. Though he wasn't sure Rory ever really rested. The woman seemed to be always on the go.

Stepping into the consult area, he was glad to find no sign of Dr. Petre.

"Dr. Miller, how are you this evening?"

Rory's eyes met his, and she sighed as she leaned back in her chair. "I'm fine, Dr. Parks. Just getting a little paperwork done."

Her intonation was flat, no invitation for further conversation. But that was a minor roadblock. Offering his best smile, he started again. "Paperwork is my least favorite part of the job. Perhaps if tonight is quiet, I'll take your lead and get some of it done. We could push paper together."

"Everything is digital now—no pushing paper, Dr. Parks."

Another humor arrow falling yards short of the target. Surely Rory thought something was funny? "Besides, if Ang heard you make that statement, she'd tell you that you just cursed the surgical team." Then she turned back to her paperwork.

Conversation over for the Rock, except he wasn't ready to let it go.

"And you don't think I did?" Part of him had cringed when the words exited his mouth. He wasn't overly superstitious, yet such statements did seem to upset the universe. But he wanted to know if Rory was superstitious. They'd been colleagues for years, and he'd never figured that out.

Rory didn't look up from her papers. "You either did or didn't. Those are the only options, Dr. Parks."

"Interesting phrasing." *With no insight!* Asher took the seat across from her desk and hated the annoyed expression as she pushed her computer glasses up on her head and stared at him.

"Out with it, Dr. Parks."

"Asher." He grinned. Rory kept a professional distance from all her colleagues, but for this to work he needed to be Asher. After all, you didn't call your dancing partner by their title.

Rory folded her hands and kept her gaze trained on him.

"I heard you need a date to a wedding."

Rory pursed her lips and color flushed her pale cheeks. A genuine reaction! Though he wished the first time he'd managed something besides annoyance it was anything other than embarrassment. She closed her eyes, and when she reopened them, she shook her head.

"I do. But no, thank you."

"You haven't even heard my pitch yet." Asher started to lean toward the desk but pulled back. He wasn't trying to invade her space.

"I don't need to hear your pitch, Dr. Parks."

Her green eyes met his and there was a hint of something in them, or maybe that was just wishful thinking.

"Asher," he reminded her.

Rory looked at him. Really looked at him, and it took all Asher's willpower not to shift under her scrutiny. Dr. Rory Miller was the Rock of Mercy...but she was also devastatingly gorgeous.

Curly red hair, green eyes, freckles for days. She looked like she'd stepped out of a fashion magazine. But with a surgical cap containing the red hair, and her focus trained on the host of machines keeping a patient comfortably sedated during surgery, she was a force to be reckoned with. A force he loved having with him in the operating room, even if she was too quiet and serious.

"What do you want, *Asher*?" She nodded to the tablet in his lap. "You may as well ask."

He looked at the tablet and hated the resignation in her voice. Hated that she was right.

"I have a patient with a tumor in his spine."

Rory's head lifted as Asher pulled up the chart on his tablet and slid it across the desk. "Three other surgeons turned him away."

"But they aren't you."

He couldn't stop the smile spreading across his face. It was a compliment, and the Rock didn't do compliments lightly. "That is exactly what I told Dr. Levern."

She tapped a few things on the chart, and he saw her lips tighten. "I've worked with you for six years, Dr. Parks. You think you can tackle anything."

That was not a compliment. "I'm usually right." He winked but she didn't see it.

"There is a reason that god-complex stereotype exists with surgeons…particularly neurosurgeons." She flipped through a few more screens, shaking her head as each image passed. "This is a ten-hour surgery, Asher. At least."

"If it's neatly enclosed it's six…but it could be as long as ten."

"And the outcome is—"

"The outcome is that Jason gets to go home cancer free. Walking, full use of everything." Asher crossed his arms. He knew all the risks but focusing on them was a recipe for disaster. There were moments for caution and moments for full-on hope. He was choosing hope, even knowing the odds.

She handed him back the tablet. "Send me all the information. I will take a look and schedule an appointment with Jason. But—" Rory paused as she looked at him, clearly weighing her words.

Once again, Asher barely resisted the urge to shift as she looked at him. "But…?" he offered as the silence filled the room. The heaviness of unstated words hovering between them.

"But—" Rory tilted her head "—there is a reason three other surgeons told Jason no." She held up her hand. "I know how good you are. But that doesn't change the odds dramatically. Even with the best, which you are, the odds for full success here are still well under fifty percent."

"Well, I think with you running the anesthesia and me handling the scalpel, we can get it well above fifty percent." Asher stood. "And I will be a great date for the wedding."

Rory pulled her hand across her face as she turned back to her computer. "I didn't agree to the surgery, and I do not trade personal favors for patients."

"I know, but I don't mind going. I mean, if you don't want to go alone, I'm better than nobody." It was a ridiculous argument, and Asher wasn't sure why he was intent on making it. Rory had agreed to look over the patient file, which was what he'd sought her out for.

But Angela's words rang so clear in his mind. *Rory asks for nothing.* It was true. For her to ask, she must really not want to attend alone.

"Or you could just not go," Asher offered. "I mean, claim that you had an important surgery. We could even make that happen, depending on when the wedding is."

Rory kept her attention focused on the computer. "It's my sister's wedding, Asher. I'm a bridesmaid. Not going isn't much of an option." She bit her lip, and he suspected that she hadn't meant to tell him that. "Send me the patient file."

"I—" His pager went off as the mobile on her hip rang.

"Dr. Miller," Rory answered, "Dr. Parks is with me. What's the emergency?"

He mouthed, "Thank you," as she jotted on the notepad.

Thirty-eight-year-old female. Brain aneurysm. Being prepped now.

Brain aneurysm. Thirty-eight-year-old female. The words cooled all the jokes. Aneurysms were silent killers. If you were lucky enough to get to the hospital your odds went up, but twenty-five percent of patients still passed in the first twenty-four hours. *Like his mother.*

As a neurosurgeon he'd done this surgery many times, and it never got easier to perform.

"We are on our way."

Before Asher could ask any questions, Rory started, "It's unruptured. She came in complaining of the worst headache she'd ever had. An intern in ER rushed an MRI—guess he saw symptoms often overlooked in triage. You want her awake for the clipping?"

A little of the stress leaked from him. Unruptured, the odds of success went up dramatically!

Studies had found that patients who were awake for the part of the procedure where the doctor was clipping the affected blood vessels had significantly better outcomes. Patients were completely asleep for the first part of the procedure, where part of their skull was removed, then woken so the surgeon could ask questions and make sure they were doing as little damage as possible to the brain.

But in an emergency one didn't always have that luxury.

"Yes," Asher stated, his mind already focusing on the brain and the procedure. But he was not done trying to convince Rory to let him take her to the wedding.

Dr. Rory Miller watched the many monitors that were tracking Tabitha Osborn's breathing, heart rate and brain waves. This was an emergency surgery, but it still took time to make sure her patient was fully asleep, unable to feel the cuts the team would soon be making.

"She out?"

Rory could hear the urgency in Dr. Parks's voice. Brain aneurysms were incredibly dangerous, but she'd never met a surgeon who didn't like to operate. And neurosurgery was a highly competitive field, so the ones that made it through the ridiculous, burnout-inducing residency loved the role even more.

Rory kept her eyes on the monitors and held up a thumb. All her monitors read right, but there were rare cases when a patient appeared sedated, but their pain receptors were still active. Rory had never run across it, but she'd listened to a lecture once where a patient described feeling the reconstruction on their leg following a car crash. Despite a successful surgery the individual had struggled for years to overcome the fear the incident produced.

Because patients were given a paralytic to keep their muscles from reacting, they couldn't move if the worst happened. Only minor indications in breathing and heart rate changes would be noticeable. The odds of anesthesia awareness occurring were less than one in one thousand cases, but she always monitored for it—just in case.

"Yes. She's out." She kept her eyes on the monitors but mentally prepared herself for the rock music that Dr. Parks preferred.

She hated heavy rock. It wasn't Asher's fault, but it was the music that her ex-fiancé, Landon, had preferred when he operated. Her ex-fiancé…and her sister's current fiancé.

Landon hadn't walked down the aisle with her, but he seemed much more inclined to walk it with Dani. Dani, her dramatic pediatrician sister. He was marrying her sister even though he'd claimed Rory was too emotional. She'd had one bad day at the hospital when they were both interns, him in general surgery and her in anesthesia.

A bad day. That was the wrong descriptor for a day

when she'd lost a good friend and colleague, Heather. That hadn't kept him from calling her a cry baby. It was the final break in their already tense relationship.

And then he'd started dating Dani when he joined her father's surgical practice. Well, openly started dating her sister. They'd had an affair earlier. One they'd refused to acknowledge when Rory let them know she was aware of their secret.

And now she was supposed to be a bridesmaid. To act like none of it bothered her. Act like their betrayal was fine.

Acting like nothing bothered her was a skill she'd honed as a child. The only person who ever managed to get under her skin was the one currently holding the scalpel. She had to work hard to act unimpressed by his antics. Dr. Rory Miller did not break, but when Asher offered jokes or needled her, she wanted to. And for that reason she kept her distance from him as much as possible. It was easier to withstand his magnetism when she wasn't anywhere near him.

Dr. Asher Parks was the exact opposite of her father. She'd spent her childhood constantly seeking her father's approval, and the man did not care for emotions. Despised them in fact, considered them a weakness…

Dani had given up trying to please him by remaining even-keeled and emotionless. Instead she'd forced him and everyone else to accept her emotions. No matter what they were! Drama queen was an unkind label, but it was true.

She was the opposite of what Landon had claimed he wanted. But that hadn't mattered. And after a lifetime of competing and coming in second, Dani had won something of Rory's.

Rory didn't care about Landon. In fact, she thought Dani could do better, but it was her choice. Still, the fact that her family had decided it shouldn't matter that Rory had once worn his ring bothered her. Their general feelings that the past, and any tense feelings it brought, should be buried made her doubt herself.

She didn't love Landon. In hindsight, she doubted she ever really had. But the idea that he replaced her with her sister, who looked so much like her, was deeply unsettling. Their father still pitted his daughters against each other for affection. That Landon dumped her but still got to keep his close relationship with her father…it hurt.

But emotions and talking were not something the Millers did. Bury it, move on. Strive for the next the great achievement.

Maybe it was cowardly, but the idea of showing up to this wedding alone made her skin crawl. Particularly since she'd said she had a plus-one when Dani suggested she go with one of the doctors at her father's practice.

No, thank you.

"So, Ang, you know I am excellent on the dance floor, right?" Asher's voice was playful as he looked at Rory and winked. "Quite light on my feet, yes?"

Angela, one of the best surgical nurses she'd ever worked with, looked at Rory. She could see the sympathy in the woman's eyes. Asher was about to get silly…but Rory knew that. She could read the surgeon better than any of her other colleagues.

When his dark eyes met hers, her stomach flipped, and her skin felt heated after talking to him. He wasn't right for her, but that didn't mean she didn't know that he'd dated a sizable portion of the staff a few years ago. Recently, he'd dated outside the hospital. A fact she shouldn't know… and certainly shouldn't care about.

But she'd seen more than one woman exit his place early in the morning most days for a few weeks. Then one day they'd never show up again. The man never got close to anyone for long.

Like her, he was married to the job. Even if they were opposites in other ways.

"Ang?" Asher prompted without looking up from their patient's head.

"Yes. You are very light on your feet."

"And a good conversationalist too?" Asher scrunched his nose as he looked over the work he'd accomplished so far.

"Something wrong?" Rory looked from her monitors to Asher. He was usually upbeat and fun, but when he scrunched his nose, it meant something was going differently than he planned.

"No. Just trying to pull compliments from Ang to explain why I'd be a great wedding date." Asher looked up from the table. "I am in."

The playfulness in his voice died away as he took a deep breath. Life and death hung in the balance in neurosurgery more than they did in most of the other surgical specialties. Asher was fun, but he always put his patients' needs first. His ability to bounce from the serious to the playful was a skill Rory didn't understand.

And she was a little jealous. If she was honest.

Rory adjusted the medication for Tabitha, carefully pulling her into a sedated awareness. She wasn't truly awake, but she'd be able to respond and move her extremities.

"Is that music?" Tabitha's soft voice echoed over the table.

"It is." Asher smiled at the woman.

Rory had woken many patients for brain surgery during her time as an anesthesiologist. Their first words were always couched in wonder and uncertainty. Which was understandable.

"I prefer rock music while working. Though it annoys your anesthesiologist!" Asher grinned at the patient. His jokey tone was soothing as he gestured for Angela to have his instruments ready.

"I like it, but this is strange." Tabitha's voice was steady, a good sign, though Rory knew Asher would take far too much pleasure in her approval of the musical score.

"I'm sure being awake right now feels weird, but I am going to clip your aneurysm. Sienna, one of our fine nurses, is going to ask you a few questions. To make sure that I am only clipping what needs to be clipped."

That was a bit of lie. Sienna would ask questions to make sure that the placement Asher put in didn't cause any motor problems and didn't impact Tabitha's eyesight or ability to talk. But that was not the most comforting statement to tell a patient.

The actual clipping took very little time, and before too long, Asher was standing beside Tabitha again. "Dr. Miller is going to put you back to sleep while I finish everything up now."

"I'm going to be okay?"

"You did great," Asher assured his patient then nodded to Rory.

She upped the medication dosage again, careful to monitor Tabitha's heart rate and breaths per minute. All of it looked perfect, but so much could change in the blink of an eye.

"She's out again."

"All right." Asher grabbed the instrument Angela handed him. "As we were saying, I am an excellent candidate for the wedding date."

Rory nodded but didn't add anything to the conversation, not that she thought Asher was expecting more. The man was capable of carrying on without her. He'd done it for years.

Not that she minded. Not really.

Rory was the Rock of Mercy. She'd heard it whispered in the halls for a year before someone had said it to her face. The unflinching anesthesiologist, who never showed emotion.

It was meant as a compliment—now. All the surgeons wanted to work with her. She was exacting, unflinching… those were the words her colleagues used in a flattering way.

But she'd heard the other descriptors that had been applied too.

Cold. Unfeeling…

The truth was that she felt everything deeply. She wanted to laugh at some of the doctors' jokes, particularly Asher's. Wanted to cry in the break room when a surgery went wrong or even scream when administration turned the job of saving people's lives into statistics and line items. But she made sure never to show it. No display of weakness.

She was a woman in a primarily male medical specialty. She'd had to be twice as good just to get in the door. She never let anyone doubt her.

"So, Dr. Miller, what do you think?"

"Tabitha is doing well. All her vitals are stable."

Asher let out a soft chuckle, and she saw the lift in Angela's eyes that indicated the nurse was smiling.

"I meant about the wedding. Should I pack my dance shoes?"

"Why do you even want to come?" The question was out before Rory could think it through. She watched Angela and a few of the other staff blink. They hadn't expected to her to respond…and she shouldn't have.

But Asher didn't seem fazed as he finished the final sutures. "She's closed. Time for recovery."

He dropped the instruments onto the cart to be sanitized, and Rory let out a breath as she started transitioning the medications so Tabitha could be transferred from the OR to the ICU. Where she'd remain for at least a few days.

The surgery was over and no doubt by the time she left the OR, Asher would have forgotten her question. Or at least moved on to the next thing to hold his fancy.

She took a few extra minutes in the OR after the staff had transferred Tabitha, just needing to get herself in order. Push the emotions down that Asher's jokes had raised.

Because Rory wanted to say yes to his offer. He was right. He'd be a perfect date for a simple wedding weekend. Asher was gorgeous. Tall, confident, with dimples that made most of the staff weak in the knees.

He was successful. Hell, that was an understatement. The man had made the Thirty under Thirty national news pick in medicine…while he was still technically in residency. Dr. Asher Parks was one of the top neurosurgeons in the country and he'd only turned forty last year.

He was damn impressive. And she had no doubt he'd be fun for a few hours.

But she needed more than fun.

She needed someone who could make her family believe they were in love. Who'd play along that they'd been dating for a bit. A person willing to lie so she didn't have to deal with the questions, the looks, the pity…

"Rory?"

Asher's voice caught her off guard, but she locked herself down and spun to meet his gaze.

"What can I do for you, Dr. Parks?"

He tilted his head, his dark eyes looking at her. Really

looking. For the first time, in her memory he didn't look like he was thinking of his next joke.

It took far too much willpower to stand still. Most people glanced at her. Saw the cool surface and didn't think of anything else. But Rory saw the look of concern cross his features, and a look she couldn't quite decipher. Sadness wasn't the right descriptor, but for a moment he looked worn, tired…and sad.

"Asher," he repeated, his bright tone at odds with the look she'd seen. "If I am going to be dancing with you at a wedding, you should probably call me by my name."

Before she could say anything, he held up a hand. "I'm not going to push again. And if you don't want me as a date, fine. But I wanted to answer your question."

"Question?" She frowned, trying to remember, then her mouth fell open as she shook her head. "You don't have to—"

"You never ask for anything." Asher rocked on his heels.

"What?" Seriously, why was her tongue continuing this? She typically nodded and walked away from conversations. Heaven knew there was always paperwork to complete or patients to see. But that wasn't really true; when she was around Asher she wanted to talk. Something about him forced her chatty self to wake up. Another reason she kept her distance.

He took a step closer, and she crossed her arms. It wasn't much protection against the handsome surgeon, but in this moment, she felt like she needed it.

"You never ask for anything," Asher repeated. "It's a rarely discussed fact, but so much of medicine is transactional. Cover this shift for me and I'll do yours. Take this patient and I'll take the next one. Fill out this paperwork and I'll handle next month's. It's little, and sometimes not so little, favors."

She nodded. He wasn't wrong. It was an aspect of medicine she'd seen first in her father's office, then in med school, as an intern and resident. Then finally as a physician. She did her best not to participate in it.

"You never ask for favors. So this must be important."

It is. The words floated in her mind, but she didn't let them slip into the room. Didn't let the need that came with them escape.

She'd regretted asking Angela and Sienna as soon as the words left her mouth. No one knew that the Rock was so close to cracking...had already cracked. That the emotions she'd controlled for so long were harder to suppress now.

She couldn't stand the looks of pity that might bring, or worse, the sexist whispers that she was just another emotional woman. That wasn't a line she wanted to cross.

Asher waited another minute. Then he straightened. "All jokes aside. If you change your mind, I'd be happy to go with you."

Then he was gone.

Rory looked at the empty room and hugged herself tighter, keeping her feet rooted where they were. She needed a date for Dani's wedding, but it didn't need to be Asher.

It couldn't be him, because part of her wanted it to be.

And that was a recipe for disaster.

CHAPTER TWO

ASHER ROLLED HIS shoulders as he stepped out of the stairway in his condo and headed to his door. His phone buzzed. He glanced at the text from his father; he'd get back to him tomorrow. After an aneurysm surgery, the past was too close to the surface and the last thing he wanted to do was open the door to a potentially unpleasant conversation.

He was sweaty and more tired than he wanted to admit. He'd pushed himself at the condo's gym, desperate to push thoughts of the emergency surgery away.

And failing completely.

Aneurysms, particularly in young women, always got to him. The woman today was lucky, and he desperately wished his mother had had a similar story. Instead…well, instead the OR was the last place she'd taken a breath.

He'd stepped into the empty OR to collect himself. Maybe it was a weird place, but it brought him some peace knowing he'd fixed something that could have destroyed a family. But the room hadn't been empty.

Rory had been there. Alone. And she'd looked fragile. The Rock looking fragile was unsettling. And he couldn't shake the feeling that maybe she'd always looked that way, and he hadn't noticed.

Sure, he tried to make her smile or laugh. But that was a game, not something deep. The look of worry on her face was fleeting, and she'd put the calm facade back on quickly. But he'd seen it.

Hadn't he?

A food delivery person was standing at her door ringing the bell and looking at their watch.

"If she's already paid for it, I can wait with it," Asher said.

The delivery person looked at Asher then at her watch again. "My daughter's babysitter just called. My daughter has a fever…" She looked at the door. "But I am supposed to wait."

"I'm Asher Parks, I live in 16B. If there is a problem, you can feel free to give them my name. But I know Rory—she'll understand." And it offered him a distraction from his mind wandering back to his past too. A fun way to press past the uneasiness in his chest.

"Thank you." The woman passed the food to him, the scent of the Cuban dish making his mouth water.

He waited a minute then rang the bell again.

"Sorry!" Rory's voice echoed through the door a second before she flung it open. Her hair was wet, and she'd clearly thrown on clothes just to answer the door. But it was her red-rimmed eyes that made his heart stop.

"Sorry, I lost track of time…" Her voice halted as she met his gaze.

"Rory?" It took all his composure not to pull her to him. She looked like she needed a hug, comfort…but he'd just come from the gym, and wasn't sure how she'd respond.

"I…" She blinked as she looked from him to the food. "Is that my dinner?"

"The delivery person had an emergency. Kid got a fever. I told her that I'd wait. Are you okay?" Asher handed over the food, hating the question he'd asked. Of course she wasn't okay.

She'd been crying. And given what he knew of her, he suspected anyone seeing her this way was a nightmare for her. But a colleague seeing her this way was likely even worse. "Rory?"

"Thank you for helping the delivery person. That was kind." She held the food close to her. Her stomach rumbled and she gestured to it, clearly glad to have an excuse to retreat. "I'm going to eat. Thank you, Asher."

She closed the door before he could say anything. He raised his hand to knock then dropped it. He needed a shower, and Rory didn't want his company.

Asher grabbed a protein bar and paced his kitchen. He'd showered, changed and tried to make his brain focus on the football game. His usual distraction technique after a long day wasn't working. He looked at the door; Rory was less than five hundred feet away.

He started for his door then paused. Rory hadn't wanted his company thirty minutes ago. Asher didn't want to impose. Then the look he'd seen in the OR passed through his brain again.

Dr. Rory Miller was lonely. Loneliness was something he understood. The feeling of being alone, even in a room full of people. Accepting that the world could just overlook you. It was devastating.

After his mother passed, his father lost himself in grief. Asher had taken care of himself, but his world, already small, had shrunk even further.

Academics had come easy for him, but that didn't mean school had. Getting perfect marks had made his parents happy, but it had not been a recipe for close friends. Once his mother died, the few acquaintances he'd had drifted off too. No one understood his pain, and it had taken almost a year for his father to finally step out of his grief.

So Asher had adjusted. He'd become the funny guy. The class clown. Sure, his grades were still perfect, but people were less likely to poke fun at him when he was making them laugh. A happy face and snappy retort had become his saving grace.

But he'd never forgotten the despair of feeling alone... of having no one to talk to. Not even family.

He'd vowed never to feel that alone again. And if Rory was experiencing it...

He started for the door. She could always shut the door in his face or refuse to answer.

She answered before he finished knocking. Her hair was still wet and pulled up in a messy bun. But wet curls were breaking free. She was wearing yoga pants and a white T-shirt that clung to her in all the right places. She was so beautiful.

Asher mentally slapped at himself. He was here to check on her. Not check her out.

"Hi, Rory."

"I'm fine," she blurted out.

He nodded. "I didn't ask." Stuffing his hands in his pockets, he leaned back, never letting his gaze leave hers. "And I don't like to call people liars...but I think that might be a lie."

A quick chuckle flew from her lips, and Rory covered her mouth, her eyes widening.

She seemed nearly as shocked as him at the burst of laughter. The sound sent a thrill through him. That was a real reaction. A real one...and a happy one. It made his heart soar.

A kettle squealed behind her, and Rory looked over her shoulder then back at him. "I'm making tea."

"And the water is boiling." Asher wanted to smack himself. There were hundreds of things he could have said, and all of them would have been better than stating that fact. But his mind was trying to connect the light laugh, and the sensations shifting in him. Like he was finally standing in front of the real Rory Miller.

Her green eyes hovered on his face, then she turned and headed toward the sound of the kettle, leaving the door wide open. Asher hesitated for a second before he stepped inside and closed the door. If this was his chance, he was taking it. Besides, this was a much better distraction from the day!

He felt his mouth open but couldn't find any words as he took in Rory's condo. It was the exact opposite of what he'd always expected. The living room was painted bright blue, with abstract images in funky frames.

The kitchen was pink. Pink! With decorative teacups hanging on the wall. This was the Rock's sanctuary, and suddenly he needed to know more about Rory.

Now that he was here, he knew how ridiculous it was to assume her space would be all white, sterile…like an extension of her cool professional personality. But bright colors and over-the-top decorations were not what he'd imagined—yet it felt right. He couldn't stop the grin as he took in her sanctuary.

"Would you like a cup of tea?" Rory's eyes met his as he leaned against the counter. She didn't seem to mind his presence, but she seemed a little fidgety too. Like she was surprised he'd followed her.

Or surprised she hadn't sent him on his way.

"I'd love one." Tea wasn't his drink of choice, but he was not passing up this opportunity.

"What kind of tea do you want? I have just about anything. Green, black, herbal?" Her words tumbled forth as she held up a box with an overwhelming number of sachets. "And I have loose leaf too…if you'd prefer?"

Asher pulled at the back of his neck as he took in the variety. If he'd been asked, he'd could have named one kind of tea—iced! His mother had drunk it constantly, but she'd made it with cheap tea bags, claiming that once you added the sugar, the brand didn't matter.

He doubted Rory felt the same. "You pick. I know nothing about tea."

Rory's eyebrows drew together as she bit her lip. "I'm having *tencha*, a Japanese green tea. It's like matcha in flavoring but made differently."

"Sounds perfect." Asher watched her carefully measure out the leaves and put them in a blue teapot. She started a two-minute clock and sighed.

The room was quiet, but he saw her shoulders relax as she watched the pot. The process of making the tea seemed like a ritual for her, and he was grateful to simply be a silent observer in this practice.

When the timer beeped, she shut it off and expertly poured out two mugs. Rory handed him one, her fingertips brushing his. The connection lasted less than a second, but the heat traveling through his body had nothing to do with the warm mug. Her green gaze met his as she took a sip. Had she felt the same connection? Or was he imagining it?

Her mug caught his eye and he gestured to it, "Aurora? Like the princess? Are you a secret Disney fan?"

Disney, its princesses and characters dominated the city of Orlando. The pediatric wing of the hospital had had a sizable donation from the corporation, and now the rooms were all themed after characters. The kids loved it.

"Oh." She looked at the mug and shook her head. "No. It's my name."

"Aurora?" Asher let the name roll off his tongue. "Aurora." The soft sound of the name fit her. "I feel like I am learning so much right now. So is your nickname Princess?" He wanted to see her smile, wanted to hear another laugh.

Instead it was a frown that formed and tugged down her sweet lips. "The Miller family didn't do silly nicknames. My dad wanted boys. Calling either of us princess or darling would only remind him that he had girls. When Mom left, he found gender neutral nicknames for my sister and I. Aurora became Rory and Danielle, Dani."

Asher wasn't quite sure how to respond to that statement. He'd never met Dani, but how anyone could look at Rory and think *only a girl* baffled him. And the fact that Rory had said it without any inflection sent an ache through his chest. Names mattered.

"Do you prefer Rory or Aurora?" It was a simple question, but he saw her bite her lip, again. Had no one asked her that before? Surely she'd had a choice once she was old to voice her opinion.

"Everyone has always called me Rory."

"But you have a mug with Aurora on it."

She held up the mug and the tiniest smile hovered on her face. His breath caught in his chest as he watched it appear for a microsecond then vanish. It was the most beautiful thing he'd ever seen, and he wanted it to last.

"I do." She held the mug with both her hands, and he wondered if she was soaking in the heat of the drink or trying to keep herself from reacting to his question.

Either way, he now knew one way to make Rory smile, and that was to call her by her name. Aurora. From this moment on she'd be Aurora, even if only to him.

"So, Dani is your only sibling. The one getting married."

"Yup. In a few weeks, she'll walk down the aisle."

"And you're a bridesmaid."

Aurora nodded, but there was a look in her eyes that he swore was hurt, yet it faded so fast he couldn't be sure.

"So is the bridesmaid dress horrid?" He grinned, hoping to pull the smile back out of her. One of the surgeon's sisters had gotten married last year and the bridesmaid dresses were horrendous. The staff had joked and commiserated with her for weeks.

Aurora had been on the edges of those conversations, never commenting, but now he wondered if she'd wanted to be part of it and they just hadn't realized it.

Aurora's brows knit together again, and her nose scrunched. He took another sip of the tea she'd made, enjoying the expressiveness she displayed in her own sanctuary.

"It's not great, but what bridesmaid dress is?" She took another sip of tea and gestured for him to follow her.

Their condos were basically the same layout. She offered him a seat then sat on the couch and promptly crossed her legs. The room settled into silence, but it didn't feel uncomfortable. And for the first time in his memory, Asher didn't feel the need to fill the quiet with a joke or funny story.

After a few minutes, Aurora uncrossed then recrossed her legs. "I really am fine, Asher. Dani and her fiancé had a fight, and she called me upset." Aurora pulled on one of her loose curls, her eyes looking everywhere but at him.

It wasn't his place to push but he wanted to know more. After years of working together, living next to each other, trying to make her laugh, he wanted to know the woman sitting next him. "And that made you cry?" He nodded, though he didn't really understand.

He was an only child, and the dynamics in his family had shifted after his mother died. The easy conversations with his father had disappeared—all conversation had.

He'd hated seeing his dad lost, hated the loneliness his dad just seemed to accept after his wife died. Hated that he hadn't been enough in those moments.

It was a different kind of loss for his father. After all these years, his father still said there was an emptiness inside him that would never be filled. Asher was destroyed by his mom's death but he'd pulled himself together. Now he was determined never to know that level of loss.

Aurora looked at the teacup then back at him. "Dani's fiancé, Landon..." She hesitated then blew out a breath. "He and I were engaged."

Asher knew his mouth was hanging open. Knew that he'd made a sound that couldn't be described. There were hundreds of things running through his mind, none of them slowing long enough for him to form a coherent response.

Kate and Michael, his former best friend, had not invited him to their nuptials. And if they'd had the gall, he'd have thrown the invitation straight in the bin.

"He said something dumb, and Dani blamed me." She shook her head. "I shouldn't have let it get to me. But that is why I don't want to go to the wedding alone."

"Why are you going at all?" Asher covered his mouth. "That is none of my business, but seriously, Aurora, you are a better person than me. Because I would have told them to stuff it."

"Maybe I should have. But at this point it's too late to duck out." She let out another sigh. "And there's more to it."

Asher drank the last of his tea, waiting for her to decide if she wanted to explain.

It took another minute, but finally Aurora started, "A few weeks ago, my sister tried setting me up with a friend of Landon's for the wedding. A groomsman, I think."

"There are other men in the world, not connected to your jerk of an ex!" *Like me.* He barely kept that statement inside. Asher cleared his throat, "Sorry. That was uncalled-for."

Aurora laughed, this time a chuckle that started light then erupted into a belly laugh. Its deep tones echoed off the walls. It was the most beautiful sound Asher had ever heard.

"The Millers don't really talk about their feelings. It was just expected that when Landon and I broke up that I'd move on. He works in my father's practice. Dad likes him and supported the relationship with Dani. But that isn't the point."

Asher felt his blood start to boil. He knew that you never knew what went on behind the closed doors of a family home. Even he had hidden how terribly sad he was after his father stopped speaking following his mother's passing. Sharing that would only have hurt his dad more, and he'd been terrified it might result in child services visiting. But his father had lost the love of his life.

What was Aurora's family's excuse? Whatever it was, it wasn't good enough.

"Seriously, Aurora. I don't mind going. No strings attached—not even my surgery, I promise. Plus I am an excellent dancer."

"Unfortunately, it's me adding the strings." She uncrossed then recrossed her legs, again. He hoped his presence wasn't making her uncomfortable. "I'm not sure why I'm so chatty this evening."

Asher wasn't sure either. But he hoped she didn't stop talking.

Her green eyes looked at him, weighing him like she had in the on-call suite. This time though there wasn't judgment. Just uncertainty. "You can trust me, Aurora. Nothing said here goes any further. I'm a very good secret keeper."

"I suspect you are."

The vote of confidence from the Rock was a balm to his rough night.

"Guess there is no point in stopping now." She hugged the teacup to her chest, let out a sigh and started, "The issue is that I told them I was dating someone. So I don't just need a date to the wedding. I need someone willing to pretend we've been together for a little while. And attend an event at my father's practice the week after. When I said I was bringing a plus-one, Dad told me to bring them to his charity event too. Though that event is more about his practice and their success than the charity. I usually skip it, but I felt trapped. So it's not one date, but two…and a lie."

"So, what you really need is the premise from a made-for-TV movie." Asher chuckled. This was how so many of those fairy tales started.

Rory nodded, the tiny lift in her lips sending his grin even further.

"If this was December instead of March, I might be able to walk into a local bakery, find a secret prince and fall in love."

"Princess Aurora has a nice ring to it." Asher made sure the fake seriousness of his tone had a movie-quality sound.

Rory glared at him, but there was no intensity behind it. Instead there was a hint of mischief, one he wanted to see grow! He continued, "I think in order to find a secret prince in a bakery at Christmas you have to be in a snowy location. It doesn't get close to freezing here, even in December."

"True. Maybe I'll just say my beau was called out of town for the weekend." But she looked nervous.

Before he could respond, her cell buzzed. She looked at the number, her nose scrunching and her shoulders stiffening. "This is my father. I… I need to take it."

"Of course. Thanks for the tea." He stood and paused. "For what it's worth, I'm willing to play along, Aurora." And suddenly he really wanted her to choose him for this role. He wanted to be by her side, make her laugh. It was an uncomfortable feeling, one he couldn't quite explain. But he needed her to choose him.

I really do need rest! He didn't need anyone, but still, he held her gaze for a second more. *Choose me.*

She pressed the answer button on her phone. "Good evening."

The tone she used with her father was as far from the one he used with his as possible, and he once more hurt for Aurora. But now was not the time to press. He'd been given a glimpse into the Rock of Mercy's life, and even if it was all he ever got, he'd be grateful.

"Good night, Aurora." He knew she couldn't hear him, but it felt right to say it.

Rory sipped her morning tea and looked at the empty cup in her sink. Asher's cup…

Blowing across the hot liquid, she tried to remember everything she'd said. It had been…a lot. She closed her eyes as the memory returned of finding Asher at her door. Of letting him in.

But why did the first person she'd let in have to be the one man that always drew her eye? The one that made her smile, even if she never showed it behind her mask?

Her composure was why Dani had called. Sort of…

Her sister had two personalities. One was a bubbly pediatrician. She wore bright scrubs and talked in funny voices to her patients. She was excellent at it, and she had a silliness Rory had never developed. That personality hid the barbed tongue of her alter ego.

It was her bubbliness that had upset Landon. And he'd compared Dani to Rory.

Rory rolled her eyes to the ceiling. As the date crept closer, she grew more certain that this wedding was a mistake. A giant one.

She and Dani weren't close, but that didn't mean that her sister deserved to be stuck with Landon forever.

Landon loved the proximity to their father, Dr. George Miller—one of the top thoracic surgeons in the nation. Landon had shown interest in Rory only after learning who her father was—something she hadn't realized until after their relationship ended.

And something her sister refused to acknowledge.

Landon was doing his best to become their father's protégé. And that meant copying the cold and distant manner their father used with everyone.

The fight where Rory finally told him it was over was when he'd found her crying over a surgery that had failed. The surgery of a friend. It was devastating, a pain she still couldn't describe.

She never showed emotion at the hospital, or anywhere else. It was so ingrained in her that she wasn't sure she could even break in public.

But she hadn't been in public. By some miracle she'd made it home. And fallen apart as soon as the door closed. He'd found her sobbing on their bed, and Landon had told her it made him uncomfortable. They'd argued, and he'd said maybe he didn't want to marry someone so "over-the-top." She called his bluff and handed him the ring.

It was one of her proudest moments.

Her sister had gravitated to her ex-fiancé the first time they'd met. And privately Rory had worried, but she'd let Landon convince her that she was overreacting. Convince her that she was simply too emotional. The word he knew was Rory's kryptonite.

They'd had an affair. Something her sister had finally, though unintentionally, confirmed last night when she was complaining that Landon was upset that she was being so dramatic. She'd mentioned that when they'd first started dating *six* years ago that he'd thought it cute that she was bubbly, so different from...

Dani had caught herself then. Before she said, "...so different from Rory." And it seemed she remembered that Rory and Landon's engagement ended *five* years ago.

Rory hadn't reacted. Not on the phone at least. It was after when she'd hung up the phone, stood in the shower and all the things she should have said ran through her brain. All the angry words flooded her mind.

In her head she'd told her sister exactly what she thought of her hooking up with her then-fiancé. Sure, Landon was an asshole for cheating, but Dani should have turned him down and immediately told Rory what an ass her ex was. At least that was how sister relationships in the media portrayed betrayal.

But she'd learned long ago that her family wasn't anything like those on sitcoms. No surface-level fights that were easily resolved. No, the Miller's didn't acknowledge hurt, so no apologies were ever expected...or required. One was just supposed to get over things.

The worst part was realizing that if she backed out, everyone would say she was just being emotional. She'd earn the label *dramatic*, and she didn't want to deal with that. At the end of the day, they were her family. And that realization had made her furious.

So it was angry tears that Asher had seen the remnants of.

And then he'd come back to check on her. And she'd

wanted to hug him, to thank him for noticing. She'd walked into the kitchen to keep those emotions from breaking through. And he'd followed…and she'd been thrilled. Excited that someone was seeing her. Not the Rock, not the anesthesiologist, not the mask she wore.

Emotions were simply your body's way of alerting the mind to its need. And ensuring your needs were met was a sign of strength, not weakness. At least according to her therapist.

The timer she set each morning buzzed, and she rolled her shoulders. Time to head to the hospital. Mentally she stepped into the persona of the distant Dr. Miller that everyone wanted.

Everyone but me.

She pushed that niggle away. So what if part of her was tired of the role she played? It was what made her an excellent doctor. The one everyone wanted to work with. The one that helped her patients.

Making sure her hair was braided so it could quickly go into a surgical cap, Rory grabbed her backpack. The Rock was ready for the day.

Rory tapped her fingers against the desk as she looked over the case file Asher had left. The tumor was between the C5 and C6 vertebrae. There were few worse places for the astrocytoma cancer to have started growing. The cervical vertebrae, commonly labeled as C1 through C7, were the highest up on the spine. The higher up the injury to the spinal cord, the more of the nervous system was potentially affected.

The good news, if there was any, was that the cancer hadn't metastasized. It was only located in his spinal cavity. *Only!*

The tumor wasn't encapsulated. That was unusual for

astrocytoma, and likely why the other surgeons had turned Jason away. There was a good chance there were tiny tendrils of tumor stretching into the cavity below C6, and getting the tumor out completely was far from certain.

But if anyone could accomplish it, it was Asher. The man was a jokester who treated everything, even surgery, as a chance to have a good time. However, if she had to go under the knife, there was no one she'd rather have hold the scalpel.

That didn't mean this was a guaranteed success.

"Such a frown." Asher's voice boomed in the small, silent consult room. The man seemed to take up most of the room's air whenever he walked in. Though, if she was honest, that was a surgeon thing. One didn't go into those fields without a bit of a god complex.

She'd hoped to have an Asher-free day. Not that he'd done anything wrong. In fact he'd been the perfect gentleman last night. But her cheeks heated in his presence. He knew more about her now than any of her colleagues, and the fact that she didn't mind it as much as she thought she would was making her prickly.

She kept her distance, but Asher had walked right past her walls last night.

Because I invited in him. Because I wanted him there.

She hadn't wanted anyone in so long and she wasn't sure what to do with the feelings now.

Holding up the image of Jason's tumor, she watched Asher's brilliant smile die and hated its vanishing. "One can't smile when looking at this. And pointing out frowns is rude."

Asher slid into the chair across from her. She kept her gaze focused on the charts and images. They were in the hospital. She was not going to revert to the open book that had appeared last night.

She wasn't.

"Do you truly think this surgery can be successful?" she asked him.

"I do."

It was the answer she'd expected, but she kept pushing. "Define *successful*." Leaning back in her chair, she crossed her arms, waiting to see if he'd answer flippantly.

"There are three options I think constitute success." Asher leaned forward and pulled up the first image of the astrocytoma. "If we get the tumor out, all of it, but there is damage to C6, it's likely Jason never walks again and needs a full team of support for life. But he will have a life."

He flipped to the next slide and circled the base of the tumor. "Option two, we get in there and there is an area here where the tumor has spread into the thoracic cavity. We get almost all of it, except that piece. We've bought him probably five to six years of life. Not ideal, but more than he's being given now."

"And option three is you get all of it, do no damage and he walks out of here with no complications," Rory stated as Asher's eyes hovered on the area where he expected to find more cancer.

"I think that is the most likely option, but some call me an optimist." He shrugged and then tapped the images. "There are a hundred ways this could go. But Jason knows the odds. All of them are better than the one he's got if we don't operate. Better to try and fail than not to try at all."

Failure... That had not been an option in the Miller home. There were patients she couldn't save, but it still cut every time. To hear Asher's statement that it was better to try and to fail stunned her. Most surgeons didn't like to try if success wasn't guaranteed.

"You in for the surgery? I really do want the best. And you are the best, Aurora."

Feelings pulsed through her as she heard her name, her real name, slip from his lips. And he wasn't saying it to try to get his way. No, he'd realized she liked being called by her real name and that was enough for him. It made her want to throw caution to the wind and ask him to go to the wedding and the charity event with her.

"I'd still like to meet with Jason. But yes. You can tell Dr. Levern that I'll lead the anesthesia team." And this would be a team effort.

"Excellent." Asher clapped his hands. "Now on to the next issue."

"Next issue?" Rory raised a brow. "Is there another lengthy and dangerous surgery I should know about?"

"Not that I know of. But…" Asher held up his hands in a way that indicated that he wouldn't mind the challenge. *Surgeons.*

"No. I was talking about your sister's wedding."

Showing up to Dani and Landon's wedding on Asher's arm would make a statement. Her father knew him, or rather knew of him. Everyone did. He was successful… and attractive.

Hanging with the funny, cute surgeon would be the best way to spend the weekend and spice up the boring charity event where everyone wanted to talk about themselves. *So why did I say no?*

Because she wanted him to go too badly. It was a ridiculous answer, one rooted in the fear of want driving too many emotions. But she'd maintained her resolve last night—barely.

That made her oddly proud.

"I think we should go together. And I found the perfect way to make you comfortable with the idea." Asher grinned, so certain of himself.

What was it like to be so certain of yourself? Was that why she was drawn to him? The confidence?

No. That was a surgeon trait, and Rory wasn't drawn to the other surgeons. Just Asher.

Locking her desires away, she asked, "And that is?" Rory kept her arms crossed, surprised that she hadn't just said, *No, thanks.* It was what she'd meant to say, but the words hadn't materialized.

"A contract." Asher beamed, his face brightening and sending waves of desire washing through her. He really was hot. He was so certain this was something that made sense.

"A contract?" Rory shook her head, "I hate to ask, but what are you talking about?"

Another spot where you could have shut this down, Aurora!

"Exactly what it sounds like!" He winked. "A contract where you make the rules for our fake dating, and I sign it. You can make as many rules as you want…but I have three that must be included."

He raised an eyebrow, and she knew he was waiting for her to ask about the rules. But she was not going to ask. There was no need for her to know.

Even though her mind was racked with questions—

Asher's pager went off, and he pulled it from his hip. "ER consult." He stood. "Think about it, Aurora. Something tells me that anesthesiologists love making rules."

"And surgeons love breaking them," she muttered under her breath as he left.

CHAPTER THREE

ASHER RUBBED MUSCLE cream on his arms, even though he knew it wouldn't keep the soreness completely away tomorrow. With as much as he'd overdone it in the gym, they'd likely be sore for several days. A reminder that he'd tried to push the consult from today out his mind.

What had looked like a minor stroke turned major minutes after he'd arrived. Nothing could be done. He understood it. But the ER physician was new, and had taken it hard.

Which he sympathized with, but it had exhausted him helping the young doctor understand that it wasn't his fault, that calling for Asher sooner wouldn't have changed the outcome. And he hated telling him that he had to find a way to build a barrier between himself and his patients if he wanted to survive in this profession.

It was true, but the doctor had responded that he wasn't sure he'd ever be as jovial as Asher, but he'd find a way to manage. He'd have to.

Asher downed two pain pills and slammed the cup in the sink. He was jovial. It was how he dealt with things, the clown. The jester, the fool, the comedian. A coping strategy.

He had a mental wall. One constructed when his mom died and fortified by his ex-fiancée's affair. It kept him safe, and the jokes made his pain nearly invisible to the outside world.

A knock on his door caught him by surprise. Pulling at his face, he rolled his head back and forth trying to calm the aching muscles. Then he put on a smile.

The piece of armor he'd worn for so long.

"Aurora?" He blinked, not quite sure that he was seeing who he thought he was seeing at his door. "I don't have tea, but if you'd like to come in…" He moved to the side, raising his arm like he was a showman offering entrance to some grand illusion, rather than showing off his comfortable abode.

"Thanks." Aurora moved past him, a folder in her hands. "Are you okay? I smell menthol."

"Overdid it at the gym. Have to remember that I am not twenty-five anymore." He let out a chuckle that he didn't quite feel. He always overdid it when a patient went south, or when he was racing away from memories of the past.

Aurora's jade gaze held his, and for a moment he thought she might push the issue. Like she knew he was lying. Instead she held up the folder and a pen. "My sister texted. They finished the seating chart for the wedding and needed the name of my boyfriend. She realized that she didn't know it."

"Because he isn't real."

"Exactly." Aurora rolled her eyes. "I've officially run out of time. And I've dug myself a hole here. The right response is to come clean. I know that. But…"

Her lower lip trembled, and his heart ripped as she bit down on it, clearly trying to control the emotion.

He moved without thinking, pulling her into his arms. She needed comfort and he was more than willing to offer it. Her head barely reached his shoulder, and she was rigid for a moment before she sighed against his shoulder. He lay his head on hers, enjoying the moment more than he should. But Aurora Miller in his arms felt nice.

"But the right response means opening yourself up to your family's ridicule," he offered, keeping his tone light as she stepped out of his arms. He wanted to pull her back, the desire so strong it stunned him.

She blew out a breath. "It shouldn't bother me that Dani is marrying Landon."

"I want to be on record that I do not agree with that." He didn't have any siblings, but he disagreed vehemently. He suspected there were a few circumstances where a sister could fall for her sibling's ex-partner and it would be cause for celebration, but they were greatly outweighed by the number of situations where it was an outright betrayal.

And Aurora's sister had betrayed her. Whether she wanted to admit it or not. But Asher would not pretend on this.

Aurora smiled and tapped his shoulder, the connection lasting mere moments, but he liked the idea that perhaps she wanted to touch him as much as he wanted to touch her. "I appreciate that. I do. But I agreed to be a bridesmaid. Agreed to attend. And said I have a plus-one. I swear, past Aurora left some real messes for present Aurora."

He couldn't stop the grin on his face. He'd never heard her refer to herself in third person before, but hearing it now cemented his belief that she preferred her full name, rather than her nickname. And he planned to continue using it.

"I already told you I'd go. I will even promise not to start any family drama…though if you want me to, just say the word!" He hoped she understood it was a completely serious offer. He'd love to tell her sister, her ex and her father exactly what he thought. But he'd control himself for the wedding and the charity event.

"I wrote up that contract." Her cheeks turned bright red, and she looked everywhere but at him. "I made the list of rules and…and if you're willing to go along with it, I'll owe you. Not sure how I can repay this, but somehow…"

He was thrilled! She'd chosen him, and he planned to spend his time with Aurora making her smile and laugh. "Have a seat, please." He'd never demand repayment, but he wasn't concerned with that at the moment. Instead he wanted to know the rules. "What are the rules, Aurora?"

She moved to his couch, sat down and waited for him to join her before pulling out a sheet and handing it to him.

He raised a brow as he looked at it. "This is a real contract." It was dated, and even contained contract-like language.

"I doubt that it would hold up in court. But one of my college roommates works in marketing. Big firm out in Hollywood. She sent me the template they use for PR relationships."

"What?" He'd been serious about the contract, but he hadn't actually expected a real-looking one. More like a few rules written on notepaper that they agreed to.

"Oh, sometimes celebrities have a relationship just for the press associated with it. You know the paparazzi following them, getting candid shots…usually right before a big movie or television launch. They have specific contracts regarding how everything will go." Aurora brightened as she outlined the information.

"Do you secretly love celebrity gossip?" He almost laughed but kept it in as Aurora nodded, not wanting to make her feel bad.

"My guilty pleasure, I'm afraid." She shrugged and tapped the folder in his hand.

"Never understood that phrase." Asher tapped the pen against his leg as he read over the contract she'd developed. "If it's something you enjoy then it's just a pleasure. No need to feel bad about it."

"Sometimes I have a hard time believing you're a neurosurgeon." Aurora clapped her hands over her mouth, her eyes widening as she looked at him. "I didn't mean anything bad by that. It's just that you are so silly, happy, hot and down-to-earth. I mean, you are just…

"I am going to stop talking now." Aurora sighed and closed her eyes. "Sorry."

"No need to apologize. All of those were adjectives I love hearing. You find me hot?" Asher reached out and tapped her knee. He pulled back almost instantly, intently aware of the tingling in his hand. The desire to leave his hand on her knee, to offer comfort… But he wouldn't deny the desire hovering in his soul either.

"You have to know you're attractive." Aurora put a hand to her cheek. "If the floor opened up right now, I'd crawl into the hole and let the earth cover me for good."

He wished there was a way to draw the embarrassment from her, but for the first time in forever no jokes came forth to lighten the moment. So instead he went with the truth. "You're very attractive too."

He saw her swallow, and shift, almost as if she was locking away some thought. Then she pointed to the contract. "Are you okay with this?"

Asher blinked and tried to refocus. "Rule one—remember this is a fake relationship. No falling in love." Reading the words, he raised a brow. He wasn't likely to forget it, but he still wondered why she felt the need to include it.

As if she read his mind, Aurora shrugged. "That one was recommended by my friend. She said that feelings get hurt when one party forgets the rules. So no deep personal stuff."

"Ahh." No falling in love was a rule he always kept, but it was nice to know that Aurora was on the same page.

"Rule two—learn about each other's family and know at least one cute story to tell." That one was easy enough.

"Rule three—two slow dances at each event." Asher looked at her and grinned, "I did promise I was a skilled dancer." He continued reading the contract, "Rule four— mild PDA is expected." Mild PDA? He certainly wanted more information regarding that definition. "What do you mean by mild PDA?"

Aurora tapped her fingers against the folder again, and he saw her swallow. "I just… I mean, weddings are supposed to be magical, romantic, though this one might be a nightmare."

She cleared her throat and started again, "And charity events with dancing are fun, even when the topics are serious. I think people would expect us to hold hands. That you would put your arm around my waist, and that we might…"

Aurora's cheeks turned pink again.

"We might kiss," Asher guessed.

"A peck on the cheek. Sure. I mean, that would be expected. No graphic PDA. But…" She swallowed, straightening her shoulders. "If it's to look real…"

Her words died away.

Rather than extend her embarrassment, Asher nodded. Kissing Aurora certainly wouldn't be a hardship. "This all sounds good. As I said, I have some conditions of my own. They are that we go on a few dates ahead of the events, we have dinner with my father twice and this goes on no longer than six weeks." The last one was the rule he maintained in all his real relationships. This fling might not be real, but he suspected the time limit was more necessary here because of that. He was drawn to Aurora, wanted to know her…really know her. That was dangerous. The rule was as much a reminder for him as it was for her.

Aurora pulled her legs under her, even farther, and he wondered if that posture was a way to protect herself. "Dates…this isn't real."

"It isn't." He wasn't sure why agreeing made his chest tighten; clearly his day had been too long. "But if we want to fool people, having a few dates to work out the kinks will help."

Her front two teeth pressed into her bottom lip again, and Asher worried she'd pick the contract up, put it back in the folder and leave. He'd hate that, but his rules were nonnegotiable. It was true that he thought they stood a better chance of making this look real if they'd spent time together. But more importantly, he thought Aurora needed some fun.

Asher excelled at many things, and having fun was certainly one of them! Aurora was always so serious. He'd met her father…once. The man had sought him out after he'd been named in the Thirty under Thirty article.

Dr. Miller had wanted him to join his practice. But Asher had known three minutes into the dinner that he'd be a poor match for their practice. Not a single person had cracked a smile, let alone a joke. It was as serious as a funeral, and he'd made an excuse as soon as it was polite to leave. When the job offer had come, he'd turned it down, but Dr. Miller still reached out every so often.

It had been overwhelming for a two-hour event. Asher couldn't imagine actually growing up with him. Which was the reason for his second condition. He had dinner with his father at least once every other week. He tried to make it every week, but that wasn't always possible with his schedule.

Henry Parks cared for his son. Their relationship wasn't

perfect; there were uncomfortable silences and unspoken hurts. But Asher never doubted that his father loved him. His father had lost himself for a while when his mother passed away. And Asher had felt alone in his grief. But once his father waded out of the worst of his heartache, he'd started cheering his son on again. He'd never stopped rooting for him. Asher wanted Aurora to see what that looked like.

Perhaps they were silly requirements. But they felt important.

"Just dinner with your father? Not your mother too?"

The pain the mere mention of his mother always brought ripped through him. It had been over twenty years, and he and his father never talked about her. Or more accurately, Asher always changed the subject.

"We'd have to have a séance to chat with her." He didn't really feel the joke, but he cracked a smile anyway.

Rory titled her head, her gaze hovering on him for a moment. "You don't have to do that."

"Do what?" It was a reflexive response, but he'd used it effectively the few times anyone had called out his jokes as the mask they were. It always made people stumble, wonder if they'd been mistaken and shift the topic.

"You can just say a topic is off-limits or it hurts to discuss. No need to deflect with humor."

Asher blinked, and barely resisted the urge to shift under her examination. Why did Aurora always make him feel like she could see through his humorous shell to the painful wall? No one saw beneath it...not even his father.

The shell protected him.

"I like jokes. Even on the sad things, humor makes them more bearable sometimes." That was a lie, and he cleared his throat then shifted the topic back to the rules. "I'm good with your rules. You good with mine?"

Aurora twisted a piece of hair around her finger, her eyes shifting from the contract in his hand to the floor. "Your dad won't find it weird that you're bringing a fake girlfriend to dinner?"

His father would probably rejoice if Asher brought anyone to dinner. The man had never pressured him about settling down and providing him grandchildren, but he knew Asher's permanent ban on long-term relationships worried his father. His dad wanted him to find someone that completed him.

But if you let someone else complete you, then you fell apart if you lost them. He'd seen the aftermath of that devastation. Even after all these years, his father still commented on how part of his heart had simply departed this world with his wife.

That was a pain Asher never wanted to experience.

"I'd not planned to tell my father that we were pretending for your family. Just that you were a work friend."

"Friend?" Aurora blushed. "I guess after this that is the best definition for us. Though I know my stoicism annoys you."

"It doesn't." That was a bit of an overstatement. It *had* annoyed him, but not much. Yet when he'd seen her standing in the OR alone and then at her place, he'd realized she wore a mask. Just like he did. "I'll admit that I enjoyed making you laugh the other night. Laughter is a great form of medicine—that cliché is true. Your personality isn't annoying though." Asher figured honesty was the best policy now. He shifted, drawing a little closer to her. It felt nice being near her. "But my music bothers you."

He waited to see if she'd lie.

"It does." Aurora pulled a pen out her pocket and handed it to him. Her fingers brushed his and like last night, heat slid up his arm. No teacup present to blame. He was simply reacting to her.

"Always honest." Asher uncapped the pen and signed, uncomfortable with her acknowledging what he'd already known. It shouldn't matter.

"But only because it's what Landon preferred. It's nothing personal. But he always wanted hard rock in the operating theater, which we didn't share often. It was also the background music to most of our arguments.

"It was so dumb, but I could always tell when I'd upset him because I could hear the rock music blaring when I opened the apartment door. His giveaway. Even after all these years, my nerves still hear some songs, some of your favorites, like the third one on your playlist, and I want to run."

Taking the pen from his hand, she signed her own name to the contract. "There is a reason behavioral training is so effective."

It was straight-up emotional abuse. And it infuriated him. "Which songs?"

Aurora started to wave away the question, but Asher reached for her hand and squeezed it. "No. This is important. Make a list and I will remove them from the playlist."

"You don't have to do that." She looked at their clasped hands but didn't pull away.

"I know. But I will." Asher squeezed her hand again. He should let go, but he couldn't quite bring himself to do it. "Everyone deserves to feel safe in their workspace."

Her bottom lip started to tremble again, and he watched her teeth bite into it. He'd seen the remnants of tears the other night. But he doubted anyone had seen Aurora Miller cry in years.

All that energy bottled up…her protective shell.

"Thank you—" she blew out a breath "—for agreeing

to this." Standing, she straightened the light blue shirt, though it didn't need it.

Another nervous tic?

"And for the song list request. I might… I might just do that."

"If you don't, I will keep asking. I can be quite persistent."

She chuckled, and her hand covered her mouth. She'd done that the first night too. Mentally he added, *Make Aurora laugh happily without reservations* to his to-do list.

"I am aware of your persistence, Asher."

He walked her to the door, but before he opened it, he looked at her. "Kiss good night, to get into the practice of acting… Thoughts?" *Where had that question come from?* Sure, he wanted to kiss Aurora. She was gorgeous, smart, successful, but to just throw it out there? Now that the words were out, he wanted her to agree…desperately.

Aurora opened her mouth then shut it. Then opened it again, before slamming it shut again. It was actually adorable, and he wished he had it on video.

Shaking her shoulders, she lifted up on her tiptoes. Her lips grazed his cheek. The connection lasted the briefest of moments. His fingers itched to run a hand across the spot. To trap the feeling. He wasn't sure what the connection meant, and he had no plans to investigate.

"Good night, Asher."

"Good night, Aurora."

"I'm here to see Dr. Miller."

Rory heard her father's voice outside the on-call room and felt her stomach drop. She had no idea why he might be looking for her at the hospital. She sucked in a deep breath and closed out the last charting file on the terminal she was using.

As if the last twenty-four hours hadn't been enough.

She was still trying to deal with the feelings Asher's hug, his touch, their short kiss had elicited in her. Had he realized that she wanted his touch, that she'd lingered in the hug for a few seconds longer than necessary? He was like a magnet she was drawn to, and after years of maintaining her distance, the pull felt inescapable.

But she had other issues to face right now. Rolling her shoulders, she took the few moments she had to prepare.

"Rory." Her father's voice carried across the small room as he stepped in.

She didn't bother to put on a fake smile. According to her aunt, her mother had smiled all the time when she was little. Her aunt claimed that her father stole her mother's smile, piece by piece.

Perhaps she'd found it when she left him. But given that her mother had walked out on Rory and Dani too, she didn't know. She'd sent Christmas and birthday cards for the first few years, before drifting away. Last she heard, her mother was on the West Coast with her new husband. She understood why her mother needed to leave her father, but it hurt that she hadn't taken them with her.

At least her father never expected her to pretend to be happy to see him.

"What can I do for you?" Better to get to the reason for his visit and send him on his way before Asher made an appearance. She knew her father had offered Asher a position at his prestigious surgical clinic. Most of the top surgeons in the area belonged to it, but Asher had turned it down.

A slight her father had never quite overcome. And one she'd conveniently forgotten when she asked Asher to fake a relationship with her.

Or did I subconsciously want him to think I have something he couldn't?

It was a question she'd pondered since sending Dani the name of her date last night. Her sister hadn't responded right away. But when she had, the line had sent a chill down Rory's spine.

Dad will be impressed.

That shouldn't matter. But status mattered in the Miller family. In fact it was the only thing that did.

Her father's cold gaze held hers as she forced herself to keep from fidgeting. This was a power play—one she'd grown up learning. Dr. George Miller was brilliant with a scalpel. His patients overlooked his bedside manner because he often could accomplish what many other doctors couldn't. There was no doubt he was a great surgeon.

The jury was still out on whether he was a good person or not.

Or maybe it wasn't.

Pushing that thought from her mind, Rory spoke as her father just stood there, "I hate to rush you. But I need to start prepping for a surgery in twenty minutes. So what can I do for you?"

Her father blinked, probably stunned by her forwardness. In truth it shocked her too. But now that she'd forced him to say something, she couldn't back down.

"Dani says that you are bringing Dr. Asher Parks to her wedding."

So this was about Asher. Had her sister called her father as soon as she saw the text? Probably.

"Yes. Asher and I have been dating for…" Her tongue hovered on the lie. Finally she forced out, "For some time."

That wasn't great. She should end this now. She'd already told him she had a surgery she needed to prep for. She could just say that she wasn't seeing anyone, hadn't seen anyone since she'd learned of Landon and Dani's deception, and Asher was just being a good friend.

She opened her mouth to try to force those words out but the door to the on-call suite swung open.

"Honey! I'm home." Asher's brilliant smile settled the nerves threatening to swallow her and sent a wave of heat over her. Seriously, did her body always have to react to him? "Dr. Miller, I didn't realize you were here."

She didn't believe him. He was checking on her. It was sweet, the kind of gesture Asher gave without thinking. She'd spent years being annoyed by his antics. It shamed her to look back on them and think they were likely a way to make her feel comfortable.

Her father's lips twitched into a smile, one directed at her. Part of her wanted to wipe it from his face, and part of her wished she could trap it there. That she could believe that he was proud of her.

Except even if the relationship with Asher was real, it wasn't her that her father was proud of. No. She was a doctor, had trained in one of the most competitive fields, was considered one of the best by her colleagues, and it was her relationship with Asher—her fake relationship—that earned the smile.

"So you are dating?" her father enquired of Asher.

"It took far longer than I'd like to admit, but when I finally wore the Rock of Mercy down, there was no way I was letting her go." Asher winked at her, but the playfulness she typically heard in his voice was clearly absent.

"Rock of Mercy?" Her father raised an eyebrow.

She'd not shared the nickname with him. Hadn't shared much of anything with him.

Before she could explain, Asher filled in the answer. "Because she is solid as a rock, cool and calm. Never shows emotions, never breaks. You can always count on Dr. Miller."

And because she never smiles. Never laughs, never acts like a person. Her demeanor is more rock than person.

That was the real reason for the nickname. It had taken on the kinder meaning in the past few years or so. But the truth was that her father probably would have respected the original reason more than the one Asher gave.

"Calm…" Her father cleared his throat. "I've always found Rory and her sister to be drama queens."

Thanks, Dad.

She looked at her watch, ten minutes before she had to head to the prep area for Michelle Keager's gallbladder surgery. Why had she added a time limit? She should have just said she had a prep coming up, then she could have sneaked out at any minute.

With any luck maybe the maternity unit would page with an epidural.

Asher tilted his head as he looked at her. She almost felt the unasked question in his eye. His desire to correct her father. It was something a couple who'd been dating a while might be able to do, but they weren't technically dating. It was nice in a way she couldn't describe. A connection of simply knowing he was here for her, no matter what she wanted.

Still, when she barely shook her head no, she could see the resignation in his eyes…and the acceptance.

"Time is ticking." Rory tapped her wrist, which didn't have a watch, but it was the universal sign for time moving on. "What can I do for you, Dad?"

"I was wondering if you and Asher might have dinner with me at the club this evening." He beamed as he looked from Asher to her. It was his acquisition smile. He expected another shot at Asher joining his practice now that she'd said they were dating.

"Sorry. Aurora and I have a date this evening, and the

reservation can't be canceled." Asher put his hands in his pockets as he rocked back on his heels.

He wasn't sorry. Not at all—Rory was certain of it. But it was her name, her actual name on his lips, that brought a smile to her face.

"Aurora?" Her father's brow pinched together. It was his tell. His anger was just below the surface. Asher didn't know that, but Rory felt her insides twist. Which was ridiculous. "No one calls her that."

"I do." Asher looked at her, real affection hovering in his gaze.

She returned the look. There'd be another time for her to worry that she didn't have to fake the look of affection. That she wished this was a real interaction between someone who cared for her and her father. Someone seeing her for her.

Though Asher was enjoying this interaction too much. He'd followed her unspoken instructions not to directly argue with her father. But he was needling him. On purpose.

"Her mother chose their names, not that it matters now. We'll have to schedule another time, or if you're available sometime, Dr. Parks?"

It shouldn't hurt that her father was pushing her out of her own fake relationship. Or rather trying to, because Asher would never agree. But she was his daughter, a daughter who hadn't been invited to a family event outside of the holidays since she'd ended her relationship with Landon.

No dinners with dad for just Rory.

"We come as a team." Asher's voice was steely as he looked at the clock. "And we should be heading to prep. Have a nice day, Dr. Miller."

Then he opened the door and looked at Rory. "Shall we, Aurora?"

Once she was through the door, Asher closed it, leaving her father alone in the on-call room. No doubt wondering what had just happened.

"Thank you," Rory breathed as they started down the hallway. She started to lean toward him but caught herself. They were at work, and…and…and there were so many other reasons. She just couldn't think of them right now. "He's never really forgiven you for turning down his offer to join his practice. I'd forgotten that when I asked…"

Her voice trailed off as a nurse walked past them.

"I'm not a collectible."

Asher's blunt assessment brought a chuckle to her lips that she barely managed to contain. "He sees himself as an acquisition specialist. I can remember him talking about the prestige of having the best, across specialties, in one practice."

"And yet, he's missing the top prize."

This time Rory couldn't stop the chuckle from escaping. It felt good as she met his dark gaze. Her breath caught for an instant and this time she leaned in…just a little. "What is it about surgeons? Always thinking you're the best. Though I guess to be fair, in your case, it is true."

Asher threw a hand over his chest in mock humbleness as he leaned in too. His forehead nearly connected with hers. There was room between them, but the interaction, even with its levity, felt intimate. Like they were each giving a piece of themselves. "The Rock saying I'm the best and laughing. This may be the best day ever!"

There was no joking in his comment. He was serious, and his gaze made her wish they were anywhere else besides the hospital hallway.

"But—" He pulled back and she wondered if he felt the

same sparks that she did. "I wasn't talking about me, but you. And before you argue that you aren't a surgeon, you are the best anesthesiologist in the state. One of the best in the nation. We can't do surgery without you. You're the trophy he's missing. Even if he can't see it."

Rory blinked, at a complete loss for words. But Asher didn't seem to expect a response.

"Have a good surgery. And I wasn't lying about that date. I have reservations at seven. I'll pick you up at six—wear something you don't mind getting dirty." Then he took a silly bow and walked away.

CHAPTER FOUR

ASHER WAS QUICKLY losing the battle to contain his excitement for this date. In theory he understood this was a fake relationship. But he was drawn to Aurora. Drawn to the quiet woman…who he was beginning to believe might not be that quiet.

In the hallway today, he'd wanted to kiss her, wanted to spirit her away from the hospital and explore whatever seemed to ignite when they were close to each other. How had he never noticed that?

She intrigued him. And he wanted to hear her laugh and see more smiles come to her lips. *Her lips.*

He shook his head as the sight of her full lips appeared in his mind. Her full…pink…kissable lips. Kissable lips. That was what Aurora Miller had. And Asher had spent far too much time thinking of how she kissed.

He hadn't been this excited for a date in forever. Even if this was a fake date, tonight's experience was real. He'd designed it perfectly. All to make Aurora happy.

Happy. Hopefully that was something that was still possible after her father's unexpected hospital visit.

He'd meant what he said this afternoon. She was the trophy her father overlooked. Though he doubted she'd enjoy his practice. Most of the surgeons there, maybe even her ex-fiancé, joined the practice because of the sizable paychecks and prestige associated with it. Not because it had a reputation as a great workplace environment.

He knew two surgeons who'd worked in Dr. Miller's clinic before starting their own practices out of state. One claimed it was due to his husband's job and the other said she wanted to be closer to her parents as they entered their golden years. But the truth was the environment was overbearing, competitive in the extreme and toxic.

All traits that were the exact opposite of the woman he was picking up tonight. How her father had managed to raise such an amazing woman was something he couldn't understand. But he was glad she was who she was.

Knocking on her door, Asher didn't try to keep the smile from his face. He was here, picking Aurora up for a date. *A fake date.*

That reminder turned in his stomach. But Asher didn't want to question why. Tonight was about fun. He forced himself to not think of the fact there was part of him that wished it was a real first date.

"Hi, Asher." Aurora opened the door, dressed in short denim shorts that displayed her gorgeous, tanned legs, and a white tank top, highlighting well-toned arms. Her brilliant red hair was piled on top of her head, and she had on a green headband.

She looked relaxed, but the white shirt might be a problem. Pushing a hand through his hair, Asher decided to make sure she understood they were going to get messy. He'd had this idea from the moment he'd offered to be her fake date.

"Are you okay if that white tank top isn't white after tonight?"

Aurora reached for his hand and squeezed it. Then she slipped her fingers between his. "Figure we should practice."

"Sure." Asher agreed, enjoying the feel of her small

hand in his. It felt…right. He mentally shook the thought away. Holding hands was just holding hands. It was.

Focus!

"But the shirt…"

"Is just a plain tank top. It has no personal value, promise. Though I admit that your focus on getting dirty has me intrigued. What are we doing?"

Pushing the button for the elevator, Asher wrapped his arm around her waist. *Practicing…*

That was all this was. If he enjoyed it, well, that was a good thing. His six weeks with Aurora would be the best. Six weeks… For the first time it felt too short. But that was why he kept the strict time limit in place.

"It's a surprise." He leaned his head against hers, finally able to complete the connection he'd wanted this morning at the hospital. He sighed as his heart settled. This was nice.

"A dirty surprise?" Aurora's cheeks colored as she covered her mouth. "Oh, that sounded like a double entendre."

"No." Asher kissed the top of her head, not bothering to hold in his laughter. "That *was* a double entendre. And you look adorable when you turn tomato red."

Aurora raised a hand to her pink cheek but didn't say anything. Though he could swear she wanted to.

It was the same feeling he'd had this morning. She'd looked at him and almost imperceptibly shaken her head. He'd realized she knew he wanted to tell her father off, but he'd recognized that she didn't want him to.

It was a connection he remembered his parents having. They'd always seemed to be able to read each other's minds. He and Kate never managed it, though that was probably because she'd been hiding so much. Now he never dated anyone long enough to get to that second nature.

Long enough to have a good time. Never long enough to be a true couple.

Maybe because he and Aurora had worked together for so many years, they'd developed the ability without realizing it. That had to be it.

He pushed the thought from his mind. This was a nice thing, a helpful tool in the operating theater even. But it didn't mean anything.

"So we are eating before we get dirty, I hope?"

The door to the elevator opened, and Rory stepped out of his arm. He barely resisted the urge to pull her back to him, to push the wayward curl falling from her bun to her cheek and drop his lips to hers. If this were real, he wouldn't have hesitated.

Sliding his hands into his pockets to give them something to do besides reaching for her, Asher lifted his face, enjoying the early-evening sun.

"I figured we'd go to A La Carte. The street food vendors have a collection of food."

"And craft beer!" Aurora clapped her hands. "Oh, and the doughnut place. Beer, doughnut and BBQ. Check!" She made a pretend check motion with her hand.

"I figured this might be a new place. A surprise. Though the excitement you have is great. You're basically giddy." They were the wrong words. He knew it as soon as they left his mouth.

Her shoulders straightened just slightly. If he wasn't watching her so closely, he would have missed it. "Aurora…"

"I've been there a few times. It's one of my favorite places." She smiled, but it didn't quite reach her eyes.

The Rock was here now, Rory…not Aurora. And he hated that realization.

He'd learned to compartmentalize his life after his

mother died. Learned to put his feelings away, but he'd covered them in humor. He hadn't shut down…not really.

Aurora was shutting down. Because he'd mentioned she was excited? It wasn't criticism, just a statement. Did she even realize she was doing it?

"Have you ever had the lemonade doughnut with Nutella? It might be the best thing ever invented." Her voice was calm now, no hint of the excitement from before. Just an even tone…even as she described the thing she liked best.

"I haven't. But I think I should change that tonight." He slid into his car, started the engine and immediately reached for her hand.

Her palm was warm in his, the connection calming a piece of him. Tonight, Aurora was going to have fun. And her smile, her real smile, was going to return.

"I am stuffed!" Asher pulled the car into the shopping center parking lot and rubbed his belly.

"Perhaps the second doughnut wasn't the best idea." Rory pursed her lips as she looked at him.

Asher had never eaten at A La Carte, and she'd warned him that about the generous serving sizes. A warning he'd ignored.

"Sizable doesn't begin to describe their portions." He grinned. "But everything looked so good! Was so good. Who knows if we'll make it back?"

She both hated and loved her reaction to that statement. The reminder that his third rule, rule number seven, was a time limit. A reminder that even if they had fun, if they enjoyed themselves, it ended the week of the charity event.

This wasn't real, a fact she shouldn't have to remind herself of so often. But it was easy to slip into a fun pattern with Asher, to let the world slide away and just be Aurora.

Not the Rock, not the exceptional daughter of a surgeon. Just a woman having a good time with a handsome man.

The last question though stung. She knew he dated a lot. There was no shame in that, but did he not go back to places? Did he avoid locations where he'd had fun with a woman he'd dated?

And was that a touch of jealousy in her belly?

"Enough about my overindulgence though. Now we are here to paint!"

"Paint?" She felt her mouth fall open as she looked at the stunning man beside her. He was grinning from ear to ear, and she felt her own lips tip up. He really was intoxicating to be around.

"Yup. I booked the extreme experience."

He was so proud, but Rory felt her eyebrow rise on the extreme statement. What could that possibly mean for an art studio?

"Extreme? Asher, is that a real thing, or did the studio peg you as a surgeon and think, well, he'll go for anything?" She patted his knee, trying to ignore the desire pulsing through her, the need. The urge to lean forward and find out how Asher Parks kissed.

Was he gentle? Or did he give in with wild abandon?

They needed to look like a couple dating…a couple in love, when they got to her sister's wedding. But she'd expected to have to act. Expected it to be difficult. It should be…shouldn't it?

Maybe they just both needed some fun. A few weeks to pretend.

"I think it's only those in the medical profession that realize that surgeons have a bit of reputation for being daredevils." He tapped her nose with his finger, his eyes dancing with laughter.

"This will be fun. Trust me." With that he hopped out of the car.

Rory pulled on the door handle and climbed out. She trusted him. It was as simple, and as complicated, as that.

Pulling on the coveralls covered in paint, Rory nudged her hip against Asher. Why couldn't she stop herself from touching him? "Guess you didn't need to be so worried about my white tank top."

He laughed as he pulled up his own coveralls too. "I guess not."

"All right, the paint and the canvases are set up in the room. You have the room for the next two hours. If you need more paint, just hit the switch on the wall." The painting attendant looked at Rory's flip-flops and shook her head. "You might do better barefoot, ma'am."

Rory looked at her feet. The thong sandals weren't anything special. Something like them was sold at nearly every store in Florida, or at least it seemed that way. But as she watched Asher slip the disposable slippers over his shoes, Rory knew they wouldn't stay on her feet.

Asher's dark eyes met hers and he paused, pulled the covers off his shoes and then removed his shoes and socks. "We can be the barefoot brigade, Aurora."

She slid her flip-flops off and put them next to his in the locker. The image of her purse, his wallet and their shoes in the little cubby made her heart leap. It seemed so…so perfect.

Wow. She really did have a crush on the surgeon! That had developed fast…or maybe it had been there for forever? Better not to think too hard about that.

"Now to get messy!"

"Sure." Rory nodded, still not quite sure what they were doing.

"Oh, my!" The exclamation left her lips before her brain even registered that she'd spoken. The room was covered in paint splatters. All the colors of the rainbow mingled together on the wall and the floor.

There were even footprints, indicating they were far from the first ones to enter this space barefoot. Buckets, actual buckets of paint, lined the left wall. Two canvases and a plethora of brushes, with canisters of regular-sized paint, were set in the middle of the room.

Asher grabbed the paint palettes, handing her one. She held the small board awkwardly. "What exactly are we supposed to do?"

"Anything." He grinned as he dropped a dollop of bright blue paint on the palette. Picking up a brush, he dipped it in the paint and swiped a line across the canvas.

"See." Then he drew a similar blue line on his coveralls. "Anything!"

She looked at her canvas, still unsure. She'd attended a few paint parties with some of her girlfriends, but they'd followed the instructions given…usually while sipping wine.

One time the canvas had even had the image lightly drawn in pencil and she'd basically just painted by numbers. She'd had fun but had always followed instructions.

"Have you ever heard of a rage room?" Asher's voice was soft as he flung a bit of black on the canvas. More paint splattered across his coveralls than on his canvas.

"The places where you go in and break stuff?" She knew a few of the nurses had gone to one a few months back. They'd laughed about smashing bottles and busting televisions with bats. They'd tried to recruit her.

It had sounded…well, dangerous. Though they'd sworn it was safe. But still, Rory had demurred, thanking them for the invitation and promising that maybe next time she'd go.

"Exactly." He swiped some pink paint across the canvas, not bothering to look at where the paint landed. "This is exactly the same thing. Want to throw paint on the walls? The buckets are there for you to go for it."

"No instructions."

"None." Asher swirled paint on his palette, the resulting color a mess of green that belonged in a baby food jar. Though he didn't seem to care.

Looking at the paint, she reached for the pink—her favorite color—then set it back down. The blank canvas had all sorts of potential. What was she supposed to do with it?

She'd never been an artist. Never felt called to create. She liked structure, rules, instructions. None of which were here.

"Take a deep breath." Asher set his palette down. "This is supposed to be fun, no thinking."

"How do you just turn your brain off?" She heard the tension in her voice and inwardly flinched. "I mean, I... I like instruction. Rules to follow, so it isn't just a mess."

"All right." Asher grabbed her blank palette and picked up the paint she'd reached for first. He dropped some of it on the board, grabbed a brush and stepped behind her. "Trust me?"

She nodded, not trusting her voice as his body heat poured through her. He'd checked on her when he'd seen she was upset. He's agreed to attend her sister's wedding as her boyfriend so she didn't have to admit to her family that she'd lied.

There was every reason to trust Asher Parks.

"Close your eyes."

She did as he asked, his breath so warm against her ear. His left hand wrapped around her waist, grounding her in the darkness. Her body ignited at his touch. Shivers darted down her spine as his breath brushed her sensitive skin. It was overwhelming, then he put the paintbrush in her hand.

"Now, paint."

"I can't see."

"I know." Asher's head rested on her shoulder, his body seeping comfort and desire through her. She'd never known those two emotions could be present at the same time. "These canvases are meant to be fun. Just do a stroke."

She moved the brush but her mind was focused on the man behind her. The weight of his hand, the heat of his body, the way she curled right into him. It was like she fit—like she was finally where she was supposed to be. It was absurd, but that didn't change her thoughts.

"There is no agenda here, Aurora. Whatever you do in this room, whatever you paint, it's between the two of us. Promise." His voice was soft, but it made her tingle all over. The urge to turn in his arms, to lift her lips to his and see what might happen, was pushing through her soul.

"Do I need more paint?" That was safer than kissing him, even if it wasn't as satisfying.

"You tell me." The hand on her waist lifted as he stepped away.

She wanted to call him back, beg him to hold her. The world seemed to slow when she was in his arms, seemed to right itself somehow.

Opening her eyes, she looked at the canvas. Six strokes in hot pink, ranging in size, were mixed along the canvas.

"Now it's not blank." Asher stood straight, and there was a look in his eyes that Rory was certain was desire. Had he enjoyed holding her as much as she'd liked it?

She hoped so.

Pulling at the back of her neck, she turned to look at the painting. He was right, now that there was paint on it;

it didn't feel quite so overwhelming. She let out a sigh and grabbed some yellow.

She brushed the color on, slowly at first. Then reached for the blue that Asher had used first. Without giving it any thought, she put a glob on her finger then ran it across the canvas. It was ridiculous.

And fun. A weight she hadn't realized she was carrying lifted from her shoulders.

She laughed. Hearing the noise, she let out another laugh, though it was really more of a giggle as she reached for more colors. Aurora picked up a few brushes, put a different color on each then pulled it across the canvas.

"Fun, right?"

Asher was close to her. She drank in his dark gaze. Pleasure was dancing all around them and she acted without thinking. Lifting her hand, she pulled the paintbrushes across his chest, leaving streaks of pink, purple and green.

He looked at his chest and shook his head. "So that is how it's going to be?"

Then he grabbed a brush and drew a line along her stomach, right where his hand had been.

She put her hand to her face then immediately pulled it away. "How much paint did I get on me?"

"A bit." Asher reached for her hands and put them on his cheeks. The rest of the paint on her hands transferred to his cheeks.

Pink, green and blue blended together in a tapestry of perfection.

Abandoning all her inhibitions, she lifted on her toes, giving in to the magnetic pull. Her lips connected with his and the brushes in his hand dropped to the floor.

His arms wrapped around her waist, pulling her close, his grip firm, grounding her as the world shifted. His mouth opened, an invitation she took. He tasted of sugar, desire and heat. Her heart raced as she let the pleasure possess her, submitting to all the emotions that lifted from their dormant place in her soul when she was near him.

Pulling back, she wished she had more experience, the ability to act sultry after kissing a handsome man who drove her to do things she'd never considered before. Instead she bent and grabbed the brushes, knowing the heat coating her cheeks was visible. "Want to paint on the walls?"

Asher grabbed the biggest brush off the table, "Do we paint…or do we throw the paint?"

The mischievous look in his eyes was infectious.

"I guess we go with the moment and see where it leads us."

He grinned and she wondered if he was really thinking of paint…or something more?

"Oh, your car." Rory held up her hands as she looked at his car. The coveralls had kept her clothes clean, but they both had paint in their hair and on their faces.

"The paint should be dry, and it's water based." And if it wasn't, well, it was worth the price to see Aurora have so much fun. "It's fine, Aurora."

And kissing her…

Asher could still feel the ghost of her lips on his. When he'd stepped behind her, his goal was to help her relax. But as soon as he wrapped his arms around her waist, held her tightly, his body had reacted immediately.

Desire, longing and the need to protect claimed him as he guided her to make a few strokes of paint. He'd stepped away because the connection left him feeling raw. A feeling he hadn't experienced in forever.

He made jokes and kept everything surface level. Somehow Aurora had sneaked past the defense system he'd thought impenetrable. A piece of his well-constructed wall had crumbled as she'd leaned against him.

He wasn't sure what to do with that. This might be the longest six weeks he'd ever had…and maybe the best too.

"Tonight was fun." He kept the words even. But it seemed like such an understatement when the kiss was hanging over them. The undiscussed firecracker just waiting for a match.

"It was a blast. Sorry if I got too excited." She sat up straight.

"You didn't get too excited. But what is too excited?"

She waved a hand, her motions so expressive when she wasn't shut down. "You know, emotional. Over-the-top. It makes people uncomfortable. The painting was just so fun and I lost control. Painting on the walls, um, and…"

"And kissing me?" he prompted as he pulled her hand into his. Better to have this out now. He didn't regret kissing Aurora, but he wanted her to feel comfortable with him.

"And kissing you." She squeezed his hand. "I…" She shifted in her seat but seemed unable to get fully comfortable before taking a deep breath. "I am different with you."

He opened his mouth, but no words came out. No jokes, no flippant statements to ease the tension. How could five words render him speechless?

"You don't have to say anything. But I am sorry if I made you uncomfortable."

"You didn't." This time the words came fast. He squeezed her hand then dropped it as he pulled into his parking spot at the condo. Switching the car off, he turned in his seat and looked at her.

Her cheeks were bright red, her hair was falling out of the messy bun and streaks of paint covered the strands. She was gorgeous, full stop.

Lifting a hand, he ran his finger along her cheek, "When I wrapped my hand around your waist…" He paused, decades of keeping to himself, of never fully opening up to partners, pulsed through him. But Aurora had opened herself up to him; he could honor that.

And he wanted to. That was new. So many new things in the past few days. All tied to the beauty next to him.

"When I wrapped my hand around your waist, I wanted to kiss you too. We have a connection."

"I think of it like magnets. We're drawn to each other."

It was as good a description as any. He ran his finger along her arm. *Why couldn't he stop the urge to touch her?* "Which I guess is good since we are trying to convince your family we've been together for a while." The mention of the real reason they were here cut through the haze.

It was true. This wasn't supposed to be real. *Wasn't real.*

But it felt like maybe it could be. If they tried. Like it could go the distance… But no, he wasn't going to travel that path.

"So what do we do now?" Her green eyes held his.

"Whatever you want." He dropped a light kiss on her cheek.

"What I need right now is a shower." She held up a piece of hair covered in paint. "It will take at least two shampoos to get this out."

"I'd apologize for the trouble, but it wouldn't be honest. Tonight was a blast, Aurora."

"I don't need or want an apology." She kept her hand on his knee and looked at him. "Want to join me?"

Yes! His mind screamed as Aurora's gaze held his. He wanted her—desperately. Wanted to hold her. To claim her.

But he'd sworn off dating colleagues years ago. What happened after he attended the wedding and the charity event? When the charade was over?

"I know this isn't permanent, Asher. You don't have to worry about me clinging." She patted his knee.

Clinging.

That was the last word he'd use to describe her. The last word he'd use to describe any of the women he dated. He set clear boundaries early on and parted on decent terms with everyone.

It should be easy to do the same with Aurora. He'd even built his deadline into their rules. So why did his mind refuse to say the words out loud?

She kissed his cheek. "Thanks for tonight." Then she opened the door, grabbed her canvas from the back seat and stepped out.

He'd missed his shot. Thought too long instead of leaning over the console and kissing her, like his body was begging him to.

Opening the car door, he followed her to the elevator bay. "Aurora," he said and reached for her free hand, desperate to find a way to roll back the seconds.

She held up her canvas, "I think I may have to find a place to hang this." Her voice was even, but he could hear the hint of uncomfortableness lying underneath it.

Aurora had put herself out there, and he'd said nothing. The elevator door opened, and she stepped inside. The trip to their floor took less time than he'd ever remembered.

"Good night, Asher." Rory slipped the key into her lock.

"Aurora, wait…"

She opened the door, set the canvas inside then turned. "Please, you don't have to say anything. Really—"

"I want you. More than I've wanted anyone in forever." It was direct. More direct than he'd ever been. But he wanted her to know, needed her to know.

Leaning toward her, he dropped his lips against hers,

and she wrapped her arms around his neck. He kicked the door closed as her lips possessed his. Demanding…

His fingers ran under her tank top as her hands raked through his hair.

"Asher…"

His name on her lips nearly sent him over the edge. God…he felt like a teenager in his first blush of lust. Her fingers slid under his shirt, her nails sweeping across his abs, little strokes that sent heat rocketing through him.

He'd never felt hunger like this. Lifting Rory in his arms, he walked to her bedroom. Maybe each of the condos was a cookie cutter example of the one next to it, but that made it easy for him to know exactly where to go.

Setting her down next to the bed, he lifted the shirt over her head, his body sighing at the sight of her perky breasts. Rory pulled his face to hers, kissing him deeply before pulling his shirt off.

"It's only fair." She whispered in his ear as she skimmed her nails across his back. The light raking demanded groans from him.

"Fair?" He breathed against her neck as he drew a line of kisses on her shoulder, before unhooking her bra and dropping it to the floor. "Now it's fair."

Her smile lit up the room as he slid his thumb across one breast and then the other. Her breath picked up as need glittered in her eyes.

"You like that?" He drew a circle around her nipple, watching her face, enjoying the passion he saw building there.

"Yes."

"And this?" He dipped his head, suckling one nipple, his own need blazing.

"Yes." Her breath was steamy against the back of his

neck as she pulled his head back up. "But I want more," she stated as she unbuttoned his pants.

"Demanding." Before she could worry about that, he added, "I love it." He saw her grin and felt like he'd won the world. And he did mean it. He loved a demanding Aurora. Loved watching her seek her own pleasure.

She slid his boxers to the ground with his pants. But before she could reach for him, Asher grabbed her wrists. Pulling each hand to his mouth, he kissed her fingers before reaching for her shorts. "Fair, remember?"

Her shorts and panties slid over her hips and he dropped to his knees. Kissing his way across her belly, he moved his mouth lower. Blowing on her skin then trailing his mouth along the line of goose pimples he'd raised. Listening to every catch in her breath, every moan, memorizing where she liked to be touched.

Lower and lower, he drove down her body. He forced himself to take his time, when his body ached to claim her. Slowly, he guided her back until she lay on the bed, her body open to him.

"You are so beautiful." Asher stroked the inside of her thigh, diving ever closer to her center, but not quite there.

"Asher…" Her hips gyrated as he skimmed her thigh. "Touch me, Asher." Then she grabbed his hand, guiding it to exactly where she wanted him.

He pressed his thumb against her pleasure bud, and she groaned.

"Yes."

Following the cry, he dropped his head to where his thumb was. She tasted of honey and fire, and his body hummed as she rocked her hips against his mouth. Licking her, he slipped a finger inside, never ceasing his pressure.

"Asher, yes…" Aurora's hips surged against his hand as pleasure swallowed her.

"Sweetheart…" The endearment slipped between them as he kissed his way back up her body. "I need you, Aurora."

Sitting up, she reached in the top drawer of her nightstand. Kissing him as she ripped the package open, she slid the condom down his length.

Then she fitted their bodies together, wrapping her legs around his back as she rode them both into oblivion.

Rory leaned her head against Asher's shoulder, not quite certain how today had gone from a fun painting date to them naked in her bed. But she couldn't regret it. For the first time in forever, she felt sated.

"Shower time?" Asher kissed her neck, the feel of his lips sending shivers down her spine.

She reacted to every touch.

"Shower time," she agreed as she slid off him, hating breaking the connection. He followed her to the bathroom, taking care of his needs as she started the shower.

Stepping inside, Aurora let the hot water run over her long hair. The attendant at the paint shop had assured her that the paint was water based. Steam heated the shower door, and the blast of cool air entered as Asher stepped in with her.

"Hogging all the hot water, princess?"

"Princess?" Rory raised an eyebrow as Asher stepped next to her, his big hands running over her abdomen as he kissed the back of her neck. "That feels like a silly nickname."

"Not silly." His voice sounded dreamy in the steam.

"Mm-hmm." Rory leaned her head back, kissing him. "I need to get this paint out of my hair."

"Let me help." Asher grabbed the shampoo. "It's easier

for me to see which strands have paint." His hands started massaging the shampoo through her scalp.

Rory let out a sigh. If this was princess treatment, she could get used to it. At least for a short time.

"Rinse time." Asher kissed her cheek.

Turning, she leaned her head back, letting the water clear the shampoo from her hair. "Did you get it all?"

"I think so." Asher grabbed her loofah and dropped some gel onto it before lathering it in his hands. He stroked it across her skin as she conditioned her hair.

It was… Her mind blanked on words. *Comfortable?* That didn't seem possible. But it was the closest she could come to a description of what this felt like.

She'd directly asked him to come to bed with her. Told him she didn't expect forever…and she didn't. But she was surprised that she didn't feel any discomfort in this moment. Rather it was like they were a longtime couple.

Pulling the loofah from his hands, she ran it over his sculpted body. Dr. Asher Parks was the definition of hot. The man belonged on magazine covers and he was naked in her shower!

"You're smiling." Asher's baritone sent a thrill through her.

"Just admiring the view." Her boldness should shock her, but it felt right in this moment.

"I could say the same thing." Asher pulled her to him.

Water fell over them as he captured her mouth. But this kiss wasn't the demanding one that had driven their earlier coupling.

It was soft, slow…almost purposeful as their bodies melted together in the steam.

Time slowed as they just enjoyed each other.

The blast of cold water caught Aurora off guard. "Ach!"

With a speed and care she didn't anticipate, Asher spun

them so his back was against the icy water as he turned the shower off. "Guess we lost track of time and used all the hot water." The bravado of his words dimmed as his shoulder shook with the chill.

Hopping out of the shower, Rory grabbed two towels. She threw one to him as she wrapped herself in the other. As he stepped from the shower, Rory couldn't stop the giggles building in her chest.

"Is cold water so funny, princess?" Asher's tone was low but playful as he toweled himself off.

Ignoring the nickname, she turned to look in the mirror. Her red hair was once more just red, no hints of pink or blue paint. It was a little silly but she missed it.

"I think I got it all." Asher wrapped an arm around her waist and she leaned into him.

This was nice…so nice.

"You did." She closed her eyes, enjoying the moment. "I was just thinking it was a little fun having pink and blue streaks. If I showed up to the hospital with it, that would make tongues wag. They'd think the Rock was losing her mind."

"Tongues might wag… After all, a hospital is a gossip market too. But no one would think you were losing your mind." Asher kissed her cheeks and stroked her arms, almost like he was having trouble keeping his hands to himself. "But if you want pink or blue streaks in your hair, you should do it. It's your hair."

She laughed, "Asher, I will be forty-one next month—"

His finger lay over her lip as he stopped her. "If you are about to say you are too old for such things, I feel I have to interrupt."

He captured her mouth, and she gave in to the kiss, letting all her worries float away.

When he pulled back, he ran a finger over her cheek.

"You are the best anesthesiologist at the hospital. No one doubts that. If you want to do something that makes you happy, whether it's colored hair or fancy doughnuts or bright, obnoxious scrubs, do it. Life is too short not to reach for things that make you happy."

There was a flash of something behind his eyes. She turned and rested her hand against his chest. "Asher…"

The look passed and he squeezed her tightly. "Besides, if you don't want to dye your hair, there is hair chalk that's temporary."

She wanted to ask him what he was thinking a moment ago. He was a surgeon. They'd both seen the unfairness that life sometimes delivered. But it felt like he was talking about something different.

Something deeply personal.

So much had happened in the past few hours, but Rory suspected if she pushed now, he might pull away. So instead she chose the light question…the safer option.

"And how do you know about hair chalk?" She nudged her hip against his.

He kissed the top of her head and started back toward the bedroom. She followed, toweling off her hair. "I dated—" he hesitated for a moment "—a pediatrician who used it after one of her patients gave it to her. I guess they stock it in the hospital gift shop."

The hesitation caught her off guard. They each had a past, had dated others, weren't even really dating now. They'd had fun, been attracted to each other. They were adults with needs. There was no shame in that.

Though a bead of jealousy tugged at her. That was one emotion she would not give in to!

"The hospital gift shop stocks hair chalk?" She chuckled, "And I bet the pediatrician put it in her hair lovingly. That specialty does have some of the best."

His shoulders relaxed a little as he pulled on his pants. She pushed away the disappointment as it pressed against her. She hadn't asked him to spend the night, and it was probably best that he didn't.

Better not to set a precedent of any kind.

So why does it bother me?

"I'll see you at the hospital tomorrow?" Asher pushed his hands through his wet hair. Clearly he was a little uncomfortable with how this was supposed to end too.

She nodded. "Good night, Asher."

"Night, princess."

She rolled her eyes, "No silly nicknames!" Still, the chuckle he let out as he left her room sent a thrill down her spine.

CHAPTER FIVE

AURORA SETTLED HERSELF as she leaned against her car and looked at the hospital. A little more than twelve hours ago she'd clung to Asher. Twelve hours since she'd told him she was different with him…

Why was that the part causing worry and not the idea that they'd slept together? She didn't believe hookups were shameful, but she'd never sought one out either. Never asked a man so directly. But her directness didn't bother her.

Maybe it should. That would be the easy way to explain this morning's anxiety. Easier to accept than the truth. She'd opened herself up more with the truth that she was different with him than she had with the offer of her body.

She'd lost control.

One of the things she prided herself on was her control. There were exactly three times where she'd completely lost it. The first was when she'd discovered her high school boyfriend was cheating on her. Her father had scolded her for crying over something so frivolous. He was right: teen love was frivolous. That's what made it beautiful. With hindsight she knew that boy wasn't worth her tears, but in that moment she'd needed comfort. Instead her father had sneered that this was why he'd wanted boys. Too many emotions.

For years she'd controlled herself. Trying to earn his approval. It hadn't worked, but she'd gotten other people's approval. She'd soaked in the compliments from all her teachers and professors, then the residents and doctors, on her composure. But then Heather was in a car accident. That was the second time she'd lost control.

Heather, the other anesthesiology resident. Her friend in the cutthroat specialty dominated by men. She'd held her friend's hand after the doctor called time of death.

But last night was the first time she'd lost her control for something fun. For something frivolous…and sensual.

For months, years even, she'd felt the cracks around her persona. The Rock pushing against the internal woman she was at home. The bright, sunny person she wished she could easily be late at night when she was lying in bed…alone.

The woman that had seemed to rise to the surface last night, covered in paint…with Asher.

"You okay, Dr. Miller?" Angela called as she raced to her car.

"Just enjoying the last bit of fresh air before stepping into a twelve-hour shift," Rory stated. It wasn't completely untrue.

But Angela didn't seem concerned with Rory lollygagging by her car. In fact her head was down and she was pulling stuff to the side in the back seat of her car. "What's wrong?"

"Izzy Martinez…" Angela drew in a breath.

"My appendectomy patient?" Izzy was five and had presented with symptoms of appendicitis last night. She was Rory's first patient this morning, according the scheduling text she'd gotten very early this morning.

"Yes." Angela huffed. "Mom is on her first business trip in years, and Dad panicked when he brought her in and left her favorite pink bow at home. I guess she wears it everywhere and is already upset. I thought I might have some ribbon in my craft stash out here, but no luck."

Rory understood. A pediatric patient was already more likely to be stressed. One missing her mom and a comfort item would stress even more. And stress could impact the surgery. From rising blood pressure to increased respirations and heart rate.

And some studies indicated anesthesia impacted the stress hormones too. Calming Izzy needed to be a priority.

"And the gift shop has no bows. So much random stuff and no bows."

Gift shop.

"I have an idea." Rory motioned for Angela to follow her.

Rory could hear the girl's soft cry as soon as she opened the door. She looked at her watch. She could give Izzy an extra sedative to calm her, and might need to, but if she could get her calm enough to start the regular meds to prep her for surgery, that would be best.

Izzy's dark eyes met hers. Her father was holding his daughter, soothing her, while a voice spoke out of a phone.

"But pink is lucky," she cried as her dad looked at Rory.

"Another doctor is here. I'll call you back—love you." Izzy's father patted his daughter's hair and kissed the top of her head.

"So pink is lucky?" Rory bent and made sure she made eye contact with the little girl. She heard the door open, but didn't look to see which nurse or physician had come in.

Izzy nodded. "My bow is at home and this—" she pointed at the hospital gown, which was blue and covered in white bears "—has no pink."

It was said with the indignation that only a small child

could manage, but Rory made sure to keep her features solemn as she listened to Izzy, even as she heard the nurse behind her cough out a laugh.

"Well, if it's okay with your dad, I think I might have a solution." She pulled out the package of hot-pink hair chalk.

Izzy looked at the package suspiciously, so Rory opened it and pulled the chalk across a bit of her own hair. Hot pink coated her hair and she grinned as Izzy's eyes lit up. "I am one of your doctors, and I'll have pink in my hair."

"And me too?"

"Is it okay?" Rory looked at Izzy's father. When he nodded, she pulled a bit of the girl's dark hair through the chalk. It wasn't as bright as Rory's but it was definitely pink.

She pulled the chalk through four more pieces of her own hair and watched as Izzy calmed, then handed the chalk to her dad so he could do the same for Izzy. "How about you get in bed, and I'll get you ready for surgery?"

The little girl bit her lip but didn't complain as her father laid her on the hospital bed while Rory washed her hands.

"I like your pink hair," Izzy muttered as the initial sedative Rory put in her IV started to work.

"Me too."

"I assure you, Mrs. Fields, your husband will be in the best hands. But you need to stay in the waiting room. I'd hate to have to call security." Asher's voice preceded him as he rounded the corner.

Rory paused as she was getting ready to go into the OR to wash and prep their next patient. Mr. Ronald Fields was her father's, and most of the best surgeons in the area, malpractice lawyer. He was a high-powered associate who charged thousands on retainer. And his wife, Annette Fields, was one of the best lawyers in the state for securing malpractice money. A powerhouse couple on both sides of the aisle.

Mr. Fields had had a motorcycle accident. The paramedics had called the ER, and the ER had the OR prepped.

Which was good, since they needed it, though it bothered Rory that those without connections often waited hours before diagnosis.

"Dr. Miller." Mrs. Fields's voice carried in the usually busy hallway. The woman had a way of clearing almost any space she walked into. "What is going on with your hair?"

Rory opened her mouth, unsure how to respond. Of all the questions she could have asked, this one was not on the list of possibilities.

Before she could think of a response, Mrs. Fields continued, "It's pink!"

Only a few strips, right around the front of her face, were bright pink. She hadn't had a chance to wash it out since Izzy's surgery. Well actually, she hadn't bothered. She liked the pink in her hair; it was fun, even if it was under a surgery cap most of the day.

She knew patients' loved ones often focused on random things when they were concerned. It gave them a sense of control in an uncontrollable situation. Still, she didn't like the twist in Mrs. Field's mouth as she glared at her.

"I had a pediatric patient this morning. She loved pink. But now I need to ensure your husband is stable and comfortable for his procedure."

She entered the OR wash area, but the door didn't close quick enough.

"Pink! Pink hair! On someone taking care of my husband. Completely unprofessional for a physician!"

It was loud enough that she saw a few heads turn in the

OR. She didn't respond. Even as she watched the eyes of her colleagues widen as the tirade continued.

Family worried when loved ones were critical. Spouses lost their cool at doctors, at nurses, at staff. She knew that.

It didn't matter. It couldn't. There was work to be done.

"So, you have pink hair?" Oliver, the nurse anesthesiologist, commented. His eyes indicated he was smiling as he double-checked their patient's blood pressure.

"The Rock with pink hair." The resident's whisper carried in the room, even with the beep of machines and rustling feet.

"The patient's under." Rory kept her voice level as she looked to Asher. Yes, she had a few strips of pink hair. She didn't regret doing it at the start of her shift, but it was unfortunate that Mrs. Fields had seen it.

It shouldn't be a big deal—people dyed their hair all the time. But Mrs. Fields had a way of making people uncomfortable…because she'd sued most of the doctor's insurance companies in the hospital. And that made hospital admin treat her with kid gloves.

The word *unprofessional* rang in her ears. How often had she heard her father talk about the unprofessional antics of a doctor or nurse who got too close to their patients? It was a routine statement given to first-year residents: don't get close.

Swiping hot-pink chalk through her hair wouldn't even raise an eyebrow if she was in pediatrics. Heck, Dani routinely had colored extensions in her bleach-blond locks. But Rory wasn't in pediatrics.

She'd clawed her way to the top her profession by never being called unprofessional, by becoming the Rock, by never losing her cool.

"You should have seen her spring into action." Angie's

voice echoed over the first beats of the rock music that Asher picked…three songs until the song she truly hated came on.

She hadn't given him a list…though she thought it was sweet that he'd offered. If he preferred rock music in the OR, who was she to change that for him? Still, the offer had touched her.

She mentally took a deep breath and watched the rise and fall of Mr. Fields's respiration and heart rate. Watched the steady beep and oxygen level while her colleagues talked.

"It was adorable…"

The word was meant as a compliment. She knew that. But she'd been warned by her mentor, Jess. *Never let them see you break, no emotion. Things that are strengths for men are weaknesses in us.*

"Everything all right, Dr. Miller?" Asher asked.

It was a question about her, not about the patient, though their colleagues probably wouldn't recognize that he always asked if everything was all right with their patient. Three tiny missing words.

"Mr. Fields is holding well." She kept the words low, not raising her voice, but she subtly nodded too. She was fine.

"Pink hair chalk… Who even knew that was a thing?" Oliver shook his head. "May have to get some for my teenager!"

"Anyone planning to watch the basketball game this evening? I think the Heat are going to lose."

A chorus of noes went around the room, and she looked at Asher and mouthed, "Thank you." She knew he couldn't see it behind her mask, but the sentiment was necessary.

"Whoa, song change, Dr. Parks!"

Rory felt her cheeks heat as the pop song she'd mentioned while they were flinging paint hummed through the speakers.

"Figured a bit of a change is always a good thing," Asher stated, but she saw his nose scrunch. Something was wrong.

"Dr. Parks?"

"He's seizing."

The beep of her machines turned frantic as Mr. Fields started to crash. The jovial tone of the OR switching to organized chaos as Asher stabilized Mr. Fields and Rory managed the anesthesia.

The seconds turned to minutes as the team administered the paddles. When the beep echoed in the room she felt the collective sigh.

"Heart rate back."

"Too rapid."

The words flew around the room as the professionals in charge handled the care area they'd trained for.

"Spinal bleed under control."

"His breathing is normalizing." Rory watched the monitors; Mr. Fields was back. She looked at the clock; it had been less than five minutes…but that was still long enough that some damage may have occurred.

Though given the extensive spinal damage and brain bleed from the motorcycle crash, it would be difficult to determine if the last few minutes would drastically change Mr. Fields's outcome.

"He's stable," Angie called as she handed Asher another surgical instrument.

"Let's get him closed before that changes." Asher looked at Rory, "How are his vitals—is he still handling the anesthesia well?"

"Blood pressure one-ten over seventy-four. Heart rate still a little fast at one hundred beats per minute, but noth-

ing that raises my concerns." Rory looked around the room.
The faces of all the medical professionals looked lost.

By all the measurements they could make, Mr. Fields
was doing as fine as one could expect after a motorcycle
crash and clinically dying on the operating table. A decade
or so ago, he wouldn't have made it to the table. But she
knew they were all thinking the same thing.

Mrs. Fields.

They'd done everything they could for her husband,
but…

Rory bit the inside of her lips as she studied the monitors. She didn't want to travel down that mental path. The
woman was typically out for blood when fighting for her
clients, for her own husband…

And Rory couldn't really blame her.

Asher tapped his fingers against the readouts on the tablet in front of him. Ronald Fields, the malpractice lawyer
for more than a quarter of the physicians at Mercy, was in
an induced coma while his brain healed from the bleed.
His face was growing more bruised by the moment. Asher
knew that was due to the motorcycle accident, and Annette, his wife, should know that.

Mrs. Fields…

The woman had been unhinged as she followed her
husband into the ER. They'd been riding motorcycles and
a sudden rainstorm had caused Ronald to lose control.
He'd stood up on the side of the road and then collapsed.

He understood that patients' families worried. It was
natural, but most people trusted their physicians. With
good reason—they were highly trained after all.

Even with all that training though, mistakes happened.
Most people didn't think about it, but Annette made a

healthy living on the malpractice suits she brought. But nothing about Ronald's surgery had gone wrong.

Other than the code. Which happened. But they'd revived him. It was textbook.

If he had to rewind the situation and replay it, he'd do everything exactly the same. But worry clawed at him. If Annette demanded an inquiry…

"His vitals are holding steady." Aurora's voice was soft as she stepped beside him.

His body relaxed as she stood next to him. That was something he'd never experienced, even when he'd dated a colleague. It wasn't unwelcome, though it was a little unsettling.

"Are his eyes responsive?"

She slid a little closer, her shoulder touching his—barely. If someone walked in, there'd be no issues. The connection meant a lot as he looked at Ronald Fields. He'd only been gone for a few minutes, and he was breathing on his own. Asher had checked his pupils as soon as he was in recovery.

"Yes." All signs indicated that Ronald would make a full recovery. But that could change. Life wasn't fair. He knew that. Still, he felt confident that this situation was under control.

"But you haven't spoken to Mrs. Fields?"

He let out a breath as he shook his head. "Annette is a bulldog." He crossed his arms. "She's going to ask questions." Asher rocked back on his heels.

"If she wants an investigation, the hospital admin will grant it."

"True." He knew Aurora was just telling the truth. That didn't mean that hearing it settled his mind.

"And it will show that every protocol was followed," she continued.

"I know." And he did. Every protocol *was* followed. They'd revived the patient; this wasn't a cover-up situation.

"But…" Aurora pulled the tablet from his hands. Her fingers brushed his, lingering for just a moment and comforting the threads of anxiety racing through him.

"But if there is an investigation, it means everything gets looked at. It might delay Jason's surgery. Or the hospital might decide it's not worth the risk. That surgery—"

"Isn't for another few weeks."

Jason had balked when Asher offered to do the surgery as soon as he got clearance from the hospital. If he'd gotten his way, it would have happened this morning. But Jason had asked for a few weeks.

He wanted to attend his sister's graduation and take one more family vacation. His reasoning was that there was a chance it was his last. Asher didn't believe that, but he understood the desire.

"And Mrs. Fields is here now." Aurora tapped her hips with his. A gentle pressure, meant to get him moving. She was right. "Do you want me to come with you to talk to her?"

"Yes." The word was out before he could even think it fully through. He'd meant to say no. There was no reason for her to go with him. He'd never asked anyone to go with him for a family notification. Sometimes other doctors came because of joint care. But that was the patient's care team, not because he wanted Aurora there.

Sure, the hospital recommended people not talk to Annette or any malpractice attorney alone. Even if she wasn't here in a professional capacity, it was still probably smart to have someone with him.

But he needed that person to be Aurora.

And that unsettled him. Asher had fun in relationships, for exactly six weeks. He never needed anyone.

Look at Annette. She was the most feared malpractice attorney in the state. A call from her office was enough for many doctors to reach out with a settlement offer, even if everything was done right. She was fierce.

And her husband's accident had broken the woman's cool. If she'd been thinking clearly, the strips of pink in Aurora's hair wouldn't have even warranted a comment. When you got attached to someone, the fear of their loss made you irrational.

But he wasn't attached. Not like that. They'd shared a cup of tea, painted crazy pictures barefoot and spent a blissful evening together. He wanted her to go with him because it was the smart move. The professional choice.

He almost believed the mental hoops he was jumping through.

"Lead the way." Aurora opened the door and waited for him.

He looked at her, her green eyes calm, her shoulders set. Like they were heading into battle. And maybe they were. Together.

Annette wasn't easy to deal with when it was a client, and this was her partner of several decades.

This had to go well. He had to make Annette understand that this was textbook. Convince her not to demand an inquiry that could take weeks to clear.

"You want to handle the discussion or you want to tag-team it?" Aurora's voice was relaxed. Being the Rock had its advantages at times like this.

"Tag team?" Asher let out a breath, releasing some of the tension in his shoulders. "Never really considered a tag team. I like the sound of it, but how?"

"No idea. Just trying to loosen your body language." She offered him a genuine smile and his heart rate calmed a little more. He reacted to Aurora so easily, and so quickly.

He wasn't sure what to make of that, but he wanted her with him.

"It worked." Asher rolled his head from one side to the other.

"You've got this, Asher. I'm right beside you."

"Okay, together then." Then he opened the door and stepped into the waiting room.

"You all right?" Asher's question hovered in the elevator as she ached to lean against the wall, or better yet, against him.

She was used to long days. Used to stress, to making sure she didn't crack under it. But today had gotten to her.

And it shouldn't have.

All of the surgeries were successful. Mr. Fields had crashed but they'd revived him. Today should feel good.

Instead, all she could think of was Mrs. Fields's statement that she was unprofessional for having pink hair. A statement she'd reiterated when Rory had stood beside Asher. She'd gone to show him support and somehow become the target.

Granted Annette told her she was unprofessional, then cracked and started sobbing about how she had forced them to go riding. That her husband hadn't wanted to and now he was here. She was projecting her anger at herself on Rory. Realistically Rory understood.

However, words had consequences. People heard things and made judgments. Jess had instilled that in her. Hospitals, like Asher pointed out, were gossip mills.

A stray rumor or random statement could have ripple effects for months or years. Even if there was no basis in truth.

Pink hair wasn't a big deal on its own. But she'd seen the looks on the faces of her colleagues. Heard the comments. They were jokes, but Jess had always warned her that she was in a man's world.

Over the past few years more women were entering the field. However, studies still showed that women had to work harder to be promoted and the pay gap was significant. One study showed female anesthesiologists were paid, on average, thirty percent less than their male colleagues.

"Fine." The word was one she'd said a hundred times, and everyone let it go. Some days she could even convince herself she meant it.

She needed to get into her refuge. Get to her own space. Then she could lose it. Let it all go.

Before she could say anything else, Asher wrapped his arms around her. His heat slowing seeped into her. If she could pause time, she'd stand here for hours.

Even after a long shift. Even when her feet were sore and she desperately wanted a shower and food, this connection, this togetherness brought her such solace.

"My father hated when my mother said that." Asher kissed the top of her head. "Said it was always a warning signal."

"It's not a warning signal." Rory felt her bottom lip start to protrude and immediately yanked it back in, glad that there was no way for him to see it since she was against his shoulder.

"Thank you for going with me to see Annette. I appreciate it more than I can say." His lips brushed her cheek. "She isn't really upset with you."

"I know." She leaned her head back and kissed him. This wasn't the fake relationship they'd agreed to…though maybe sharing six weeks with Asher was just what her soul needed.

Six weeks…so little time.

"Well," he began as he kissed her head again, a soft brush that brought a sigh to her lips. "What if we shower, order dinner and spend the night watching the game?"

Seconds ago she'd craved alone time. Craved the ability to fall apart in her own space. This sounded like another date, or rather a night in that a couple might do. Maybe it was a step too far in what was supposed to be a short-term arrangement, but it sounded perfect.

The cracks that were opening in her soul released screams for connection. She could hold herself together for a while longer if it meant spending time with Asher. That was a small price to pay.

"If you don't want to order in, I have one of those meal prep kits in the fridge. It's a walnut chicken and Greek salad. Takes about twenty minutes." She wasn't much of a cook, but the meal prep kits let her pretend and kept her from ordering in more than a few times a week.

"Sounds perfect." He wrapped an arm around her and followed her to her condo.

It was easy, and nice. And for tonight, she wasn't going to think too hard about it. "While I preheat the oven, you go start the shower."

"That sounds like a plan." He dropped a kiss against her lips, then headed toward the shower.

Rolling her shoulders, Rory pulled the chicken from the freezer and preheated the oven. She was overreacting today. She knew that…and it drove her crazy.

After years of controlling herself, she should be able to control the reaction to something like this. It was juvenile and unprofessional.

Exactly the type of behavior her father had conditioned her and Dani to avoid. Rory had always been better at it. Her sister had stopped trying, instead leaning into the bubbly personality that had attracted Landon. But it annoyed their father, and she'd prided herself that in at least this aspect Rory had made her father and then her mentor, Jess, proud.

A knock at the door took her by surprise. She looked at her phone. She wasn't expecting anyone. She had a few girlfriends she met up with regularly, but people didn't just stop by.

The shower was running with a hot…and naked Asher in it. She looked at the door and considered ignoring it. When the second knock came, she resigned herself to a lonely shower while Asher made dinner.

"Dani?" Rory couldn't stop the tone of surprise as she opened the door. In the all the years she'd lived here, Dani had never stopped by.

"You do have pink hair!"

Rory blinked. "Seriously, it's hair chalk and how the hell—" She took a deep breath. Mrs. Fields and her father had a professional relationship spanning decades, so clearly the woman had spent her time texting in the waiting room.

Anything to avoid focusing on her husband's surgery. It was a stupid fixation, but it happened when people were scared. But why did it have to be Rory she hyperfixated on?

"It's hair chalk. Well, that's good. I was stopping by to tell you that it needed to be gone by the wedding."

Rory didn't challenge that, but she knew Dani could have texted that mandate. "It will be. Do you need anything else?"

"Are you really dating Asher Parks?"

Here was the real question. The real reason she was here. *Asher.*

Landon was a prize, but Asher, with the accolades he'd earned and a reputation that even her father coveted, was the gold standard. It was a status she'd craved, one of the reasons she'd stayed with Landon far longer than she should have. But Asher wasn't a prize to be displayed in the Miller trophy case.

Even if their relationship had been real.

"I mean come on, Rory. Asher Parks? The man is too good for you."

It was their father's bitterness. His lies coming through at this moment. They'd grown up together, but close was the farthest description from their relationship. By design, they'd competed for everything. But it was exhausting.

And for the first time in her memory, she didn't want to lean into the game. Didn't want to try to prove herself. Didn't want to beat her sister.

"Asher is kind and sweet, and not part of our family issues. I mean…" She let out a breath; this was too much. "You're marrying Landon in three weeks, Dani."

Her sister's bottom lip wavered, and uncertainty ripped through Rory. She'd acted happy about the relationship since the moment they'd publicly acknowledged it. But what if…?

"You don't have to marry him." The words were barely more than a whisper, but she saw her sister's eyes widen.

"I love Landon. And he loves me, more than he loved you."

"He didn't love me." The words were freeing once they were out. She'd known it for years, but she'd never said it to anyone. "He loved the idea of me. The successful daughter of a man he respected. Not Aurora Miller."

"Well, he *does* love me." Dani raised her head. "And Dad is excited about walking me down the aisle, and I don't believe you're dating Asher Parks."

Before she could offer a response, Asher walked out of the bedroom—in just a towel. His six pack and tanned skin was hot, but it was the protective action that made her knees week.

"Aurora? I shut the shower off. Did you get lost in the kitchen?" He crossed his arms. "Didn't realize we had company."

It was a lie. Her condo was a nice size, but Dani's voice definitely carried. He was looking out for her…again.

I could get used to this.

At least for six weeks.

"Aurora?" Dani blinked. "No one calls you that."

"Not true. I do." Asher gestured to his towel, "Not really dressed for introductions, but I'm Asher." He looked to Rory, and she saw his teeth clench before he added to Dani, "Guess it's nice to meet you."

Then he offered Rory a brilliant smile. "Should I shower alone?"

She shook her head, "No. I think we're done."

Dani glared at her then looked at Asher before reaching for the door. "Dad knows about the pink hair. He's disappointed." With that, she opened the door and walked out.

It's hair! And I am a damn adult!

The screams in her head begged for release. But decades of control, of bottling up her emotions, kept them in place. Her sister wanted a reaction. Wanted her to chase her into the hall and make a scene.

It was the path Dani took. If she couldn't control her emotions, she released them, never holding back. In fact Rory suspected she was in the hall waiting…hoping Rory would lose her cool.

But it wasn't going to happen.

"For what it is worth, I like the pink hair." Asher motioned for her to follow him to the bathroom.

"Enjoy it now, because it's never coming back." It wasn't a grumble. Not really. Just the truth. "Can't be unprofessional."

"Annette was worried about Ronald. Lashing out."

"It's a common grief response. I know." Her tone was even, and she saw him raise an eyebrow as he restarted the shower. "But I can't let anyone suspect that it's more than just a worried wife overreacting. One of the residents commented. The Rock—"

"Is allowed to be human."

"Really?" Rory crossed her arms. It wasn't fair to take her emotions out on him. Her father and Landon had never allowed that, but the words refused to stay buried. Her years of control simply broke in Asher's presence.

"Have you been called emotional when you lose a patient, or a diagnosis goes wrong? Have people ever accused you of weaponizing feelings?"

"No." Asher shook his head then stepped toward her. There was no anger in his voice. No disappointment.

"I'm sorry. I know it's not you." She let out a sob and covered her mouth. "I'm overreacting."

"Overreacting isn't a crime. At least not in my book." Picking up a washcloth, he wet it in the sink then slowly pulled a strip of pink hair through cloth, wiping away the color. Then he carefully repeated the process. His hands were gentle as they brushed her cheek.

"I will never understand what it is like to be a woman in the medical field. Never understand the frustration and pain that comes with questions that should never be asked."

He turned and started the shower. Then lifted her arms and took off her shirt. Asher carefully undressed her. It was sensual, but not sexual.

It felt…it felt like nothing she'd ever experienced.

He led her to the shower, stepped in and pulled her with him. "I do, however, know a bad day. A taxing day that makes you question everything."

"It's hard to believe you ever question anything." She

sighed as he ran the loofah along her back. "You're so certain all the time. So funny and happy."

She felt his hands pause, the gentle massage on her body slowing. "I question many things. The humor..." He paused, a haunted look in his eyes.

"Asher—"

"I am human," he interrupted, "and there are days, like today, where I worry that my actions will result in consequences I can't see yet. Annette isn't a physician, but she wields a lot of power."

She turned, wrapping her arms around his neck, and she kissed him. A light kiss, not demanding, just enough to stop the worries from dripping out.

"You did everything right. If—and it's an if—there is an inquiry, it will find that the team was perfect. You were perfect."

"It's easy to feel perfect when I'm with you. Careful, my surgeon brain might start really believing it."

"Perfection isn't necessary. But you are pretty special." She pulled the loofah from his hands and started to wash him. There was something almost ritualistic about the motions. Cleansing the day, the worries, from each other.

"Dinner and relaxation time." Rory kissed the tip of his nose as she turned the shower off.

"Sounds perfect."

CHAPTER SIX

"I LIKE SEEING you smile." His father looked so happy in the video chat, his light blue eyes bright in the sun. No matter when he called his dad, the man was always on his porch. Soaking in the Florida sun or enjoying the cool night air. It was a practice he'd started after his mother passed, said he felt closer to her when he was outside.

"I smile all the time," Asher chuckled. He was always grinning. It was one of the things his patients liked to comment on. *Easy to trust a smiling surgeon.*

"No." His father shook his head. "You have a grin you wear constantly, but it's not a real smile." The words were said without any malice or judgment. Just the truth of a father knowing his son far better than Asher realized.

So he decided to let the discussion of whether his smile was real most of the time or not die away. His relationship with his dad was easy—most of the time. But there were things, hurts and angers, that he never addressed. His dad had lost enough already; he didn't need to know how angry Asher had been at him too. How hurt... Light conversations, jokes, that was what he did best. "I'm bringing a friend with me to dinner this weekend. Hope that's okay."

"It's always okay. Who is the friend, and do they have any dietary restrictions? I had planned to make chicken-and-feta-stuffed ravioli, but if they are a vegetarian or celiac or just hate pasta, happy to adjust. I have a stack of recipes still to try."

"A stack of recipes?" Asher raised his eyebrow. He loved his father, and the man cooked more than he did, but that bar was exceptionally easy to get over. His dad had three "fancy" meals he made for their dinners. Chicken-and-feta-stuffed ravioli, tacos with seasoned shells and a vegetable curry that Asher always thought needed more kick.

"I signed up for a cooking class last week. The seniors' center is offering a six-week course. The tagline was *Explore your palate before you're dead*."

Asher felt his mouth fall open. His father was very relaxed with the idea of passing now that Asher was an adult. He was fit, and tried new experiences, but he always said that being reunited with his wife was the thing he was looking forward to most.

Now he was just trying to rack up experiences. Many people feared death. Even Asher, who saw it more than most, was uncomfortable with his father's easy acceptance of his mortality.

"That is an interesting marketing metric."

"I thought so, though Alfred said it was a bit much." His father hit a couple buttons on the video call, turning the camera to show Asher his blooming flowers before turning it back around. "That man plans to live to a hundred."

"Is that such a bad thing?" Asher did his best not to sigh into the phone. He knew his father missed his mother, but life was exciting too. And a long life was an admirable goal. Surely enjoying time with his son was a thing not to be rushed? But he kept those thoughts to himself.

His father was silent a moment, and Asher watched the crease in the center of his forehead deepen. "Living a long time is a fine goal. But no one lives forever. We make the best of the life we have. But I will always argue that it is better to cling to those we love instead of life itself. After all, love is what makes life worth living."

Asher didn't argue. It wasn't worth it; neither of them was going to change his mind. His father hated that Asher had resigned himself to short relationships after Kate. He didn't understand that it was because Asher knew he was too much like the man that raised him.

Love had brought his father to his knees. It had sent him spiraling into an abyss, one that Asher couldn't draw him out of—no jokes, no screams, no pleas.

Just time, therapy and a resignation that life wasn't fair.

To hear his father talk, love was the greatest thing one could experience. But losing it destroyed you.

He'd somehow found himself again after Kate's betrayal. He wouldn't risk his heart again.

"So, tell me about your friend. I didn't forget." His father tapped his noggin. In his late sixties, his father's hair was sliding from speckled brown and gray to full gray, but his memory was as sharp as ever.

"I don't think Aurora has any special dietary issues." He pursed his lips, weighing whether to tell his dad the real reason he wanted to bring her by.

"You're thinking hard. I promise to be nice to your friend." His dad's face shifted slightly, and Asher felt the tug of worry on his end.

He'd never brought a woman home after his engagement ended, never wanted to get his father's hopes up. So that made the decision for him.

"Aurora is just a friend." The word *friend* tasted horrible. He'd lost himself in her arms, looked forward to seeing her every day and found himself looking for her. Their six-week timeline was racing toward the end and for the first time he'd considered asking for an extension. But that desire was the reason he couldn't do that.

She wasn't a friend with benefits. That was a phrase he'd never be able to apply to her. That made their current situation more difficult to accurately describe.

There were rules for their fake relationship, rules meant to protect them. A fake relationship that had slipped into a physical passion so fast. He swallowed, pushing past the uncomfortableness in his belly.

"But…" He took a deep breath, "Her father, Dr. Miller, is a piece of work. The man treats his daughter terribly, and she is so perfect. She's brilliant, funny, kind, gorgeous."

He saw his father raise an eyebrow but he didn't interrupt. "Anyways, Aurora's sister is marrying her ex-fiancé next week."

His father's mouth fell open on the video screen. "I'm sorry, what?"

He rolled his eyes, "That was exactly my thought, but Aurora feels like she has to go. She is even a bridesmaid, so we are attending together as boyfriend and girlfriend… a fake relationship."

"Fake… Why are you telling me this?"

"Because we've been practicing, so it looks realistic at the wedding."

"Too much information, son."

He felt the heat flood his cheeks. "I meant hand-holding and kisses on the cheek." He saw the look his father gave, the one that said he didn't quite believe him, but wasn't going to argue.

"Her family is a nightmare, but she seems to think it's normal, or at least normal enough. That is where you come in. One of the rules I set was that she had to have dinner with us twice. I'm hoping if she can see what a loving family looks like, maybe then she'll stand up to hers."

He exhaled, and pulled his hand across his face. He'd not meant to go into this much detail, but now that he had, more words seemed to tumble forth. "I just want you to be your normal, nice dad self. But I also don't want you to get your hopes up if you see us hold hands."

Because Asher wasn't certain that he could keep his hands to himself for that long if Aurora was next to him at the table. Holding her hand, leaning into her shoulder, kissing her. It all just came so naturally.

So easily.

That was the thing he didn't understand. He'd dated… a lot, if you asked some of his previous partners. Most of the relationships were fun, and the few that weren't he'd ended even quicker than his six-week rule. A few weeks of fun, which benefited both parties without getting hopes up of forever. Still, none of those relationships had felt this easy.

The laughter came quick, the desire even quicker.

"Because one of the other rules was six weeks, right?"

Sometimes having a close relationship with your parents was a detriment. And he hated the reminder of the timeline he'd set.

Before he could say anything, his father started, "I understand." His father's words were the ones he wanted to hear, but there was a look in his eye that made Asher want to shift under his attention. His father said he understood, but he could see the hope glimmering in his eyes.

Hope that maybe, just maybe his son might have found a match.

Aurora wasn't his match. He didn't have one. But if he did, he'd want it to be her, and that truth frightened him as he waved goodbye to the man he was so much like. He couldn't risk spending his life lost to love. That was not the life he wanted.

* * *

"Mr. Parks, it is so nice to meet you. Asher speaks highly of you. I'm Rory." Rory reached her hand out to Asher's father. Her belly squirmed with nerves. Technically she was meeting him because it was one of Asher's rules, but it felt deeper. Even though she knew it shouldn't.

He shook it quickly and smiled. "We usually hug on greeting in this house. Would you like a hug?"

She blinked and felt herself nod. Her family rarely touched. Gestures of affection, even simple touches, were not things the Millers did. But Asher was always touching her.

And not just in passionate ways. Little touches, brushing a stray hair out her eye, running his hand along her back, hugging her. It was… Her mind failed to find the word. But her body seemed to instinctually understand.

It was amazing how fast she'd gotten used to being touched this way. How much she seemed to crave it.

Asher's father hugged her then stepped back. "Welcome. Please call me Henry. Do you prefer Rory or Aurora?"

She looked at Asher. Obviously when he'd talked to his father, he'd used her real name.

"Aurora." The name…her name slipped into the air and she watched Asher smile. "It's just a name, Asher."

"It's your name." He squeezed her hand. "And hearing you say it just cements my certainty. Your family can call you Rory, but mine will call you what you want. Aurora."

My family.

It was just a throwaway statement. She knew it, but it warmed her heart to hear him say it. For at least a few more weeks she could bask in whatever this was.

"You just look so certain of yourself…gloating almost."

She grinned and nudged her hip against his. Then she kissed his cheek, forgetting they had an audience.

"Oh." She looked at Henry, unsure of how to explain why Asher's friend had just kissed his cheek. "I, um…"

Who was she when she was with Asher? Feelings, emotions, things she'd controlled all her life bubbled to the surface. And rather than hating them, she was embracing them.

"Dad understands what is going on." Asher wrapped an arm around her waist. "Friends…who are playing pretend for a short while." He dropped a kiss on the top of her head.

Playing pretend. It was true, but it still hurt to hear. Though "mild public displays of affection" was her one of her rules.

"Yup. I understand perfectly." Henry's eyes twinkled as he motioned for them to follow him.

Pictures of Asher covered the living room. There were pictures of his high school and university graduations, with the corresponding announcements framed next to them. It was clear that his father was proud of him.

Her father hadn't even attended her high school graduation. He'd said that it was expected she graduate from high school. One did not celebrate an expectation.

Neither her quiet acceptance of her father's position or her sister's outburst and tears had made the man change his mind.

But it wasn't just pictures of celebrations on the mantel. There were pictures of him as a baby, a small child and awkward teen. There was even a picture of him covered in mud and smearing it on his mother's face.

"What were you doing?" Aurora pointed to the picture. The woman in the image looked brilliantly happy even as her son covered her in mud. It was perfection, even if it was a mess.

"That is one of my favorites." Henry grabbed the picture off the mantel. "You can't tell, but there is a soccer uniform under all that mud. There was a huge puddle in the middle of the field and Asher and his friends spent most of the game putting the ball in the mud so they could go after it themselves."

"The pitch was soaking!" Asher shook his head. "There was no nonmuddy place to drop the ball."

"I don't think you had to come off the field covered in mud from head to foot." His father looked at his son, and Aurora could see such love in his eyes.

Had her father ever looked at her that way? No. It was a simple and harsh answer. If her mother had, she'd been too young to remember.

"Your mother laughed the whole way home." Henry's eyes shifted from Asher to his photo, lingering on the image of the young woman frozen in time.

Asher shifted on his feet, and she caught the look in his eye.

She wasn't exactly sure what had happened to his mother, but it didn't take a lot of guesswork to understand the hole her loss caused. The way Henry looked at the image and Asher looked away. Henry's look carried a touch of sadness, but it was the hurt she saw radiating from the man who looked so much like his father that broke her heart.

She reached for Asher's hand, wrapping it around his waist. Henry knew what was going on, but in the moment, it felt like Asher needed the connection. "She looks like she was a fun lady." Aurora meant the words. She couldn't imagine her parents laughing at mud. There would have been consequences…harsh ones.

Henry ran a finger over the image. "I miss her every

day. But she gave me the greatest gifts. Her love and a son who is my whole world."

It was the kind of line one saw in movies. In those movies, Aurora had always wanted to roll her eyes, cringing at the cheesiness of the moment. But Henry's words weren't cringy.

They filled the room with truth and love, and she was thrilled to just be part of it. And a bit sad that this wouldn't be a long friendship. Though maybe Asher wouldn't mind if she came around for dinner every once in a while after this was over.

Sadness ached in her chest as the thought settled within her. And she knew she'd never ask. Not because Asher or Henry wouldn't want her around. She suspected both men would welcome her.

But after the wedding, when she and Asher went back to just colleagues and hopefully friends, this would be too much. Asher tightened the grip on her waist and she leaned her head against his. He was practicing for their events, but was she?

Grief hovered in her heart. It was ridiculous; there was no reason to mourn something that wasn't over… that wasn't real. But looking from Henry to his son, her heart ached. This felt like home, felt like family. And she wanted it.

Desperately.

"So!" Asher clapped his hands, clearly ready to move on from this conversation.

Henry looked at the picture once more and then placed it back on the mantel, clearly ceding to his son's desire. Did they ever discuss their loss? Their grief? There was an underlying tension…or maybe she was just looking for it, since that was how her family operated?

"What's for dinner, Dad?"

"I made a new dish. It smells good…but you two have to tell the truth."

And the atmosphere shifted. She looked to both men. Surely they felt it, but neither acknowledged it, just danced around something important to more superficial topics, like dinner.

"Is this from your 'learn new dishes before you die' class?" Asher chuckled as he slid his hand into hers. "Don't look so horrified, Aurora. The tagline for the class at the seniors' center was literally, expand your palate before you croak."

"It was only slightly more delicately worded." Henry winked at her, a motion that made him look so much like his son it stilled her heart. "But that is the general theme. This week we are working on Mediterranean food. I think because it is supposed to be healthier.

"Anyways…it's an eggplant stew. It was pretty easy and I learned how to pick a ripe one." His excitement was infectious.

"I'm sure it will be lovely." Aurora smiled.

"Your father is a wonderful man." Aurora gripped Asher's hand as he pulled into the parking garage of their condo complex.

"He is." *Mostly.* Asher hated that unkind mental add-on. His father wasn't perfect, but no one was. He'd been a man lost to grief, something so evident when he held up his mother's picture, it had cut through him until Aurora stepped to his side.

Aurora. He'd enjoyed having her there…maybe too much. Today had felt so fun and normal. There hadn't been a single awkward pause. No uncomfortable moments where he'd had to fill the silence that sometimes fell between his dad and him when they broached uncomfortable topics.

"Though you didn't have to encourage him with the eggplant dish." Asher parked in his assigned spot then leaned over and kissed her cheek.

Today was perfect. His father had done exactly what he'd expected him to. He'd made Aurora feel seen and heard. She'd seen a laid-back family dinner. No fancy clubs or hidden agendas, just a man enjoying time with his son and his son's...friend.

God, he hated that term when it was applied to Aurora.

Aurora fit his small family perfectly. Almost like a piece of a puzzle he hadn't realized was missing until it was put in place.

A puzzle piece, Asher? Really?

He mentally rolled his eyes. Aurora wasn't a puzzle piece. He'd invited her to dinner to help her, but he felt... well, different when he was with her. And today had highlighted that. The wedding was next week, the charity event the week after. Maybe he was close to her but not too close.

"I liked the eggplant dish. It's not your father's fault that we discovered today that you don't like eggplant. Made it to forty without ever trying it... Who is to blame for that?" Aurora lightly slapped his knee. "He's trying new things. You've encouraged me to do the same, so I will encourage your dad."

Her cheeks turned red as she bit her bottom lip, "Assuming I get to see him again."

"We still have a couple of weeks." The timer in his head echoed loudly as he looked at her. "Though you'd be welcome anytime of course." His chest felt tight as he made the offer.

As far as Henry Parks was concerned, Aurora Miller would forever be welcome in his house. But when the six weeks were up, the excuses he had for touching her, for kissing her…for wanting to be near her…would vanish.

And it hurt to even think of it.

A look passed through Aurora's eyes, and he wondered if she was thinking the same thing.

"I liked seeing the pictures of your mother. You were lucky to have her. I can't even imagine my mother's reaction if Dani or I had smeared her with mud. The woman always looked her best."

"My mom was amazing." It didn't hurt as much to speak about her now. Though he'd never gotten used to talking about her in the past tense. "Where is your mother?" He'd heard a ton about her father, mostly from others, but no one ever mentioned the former Mrs. Miller.

"Miami. Maybe. That is where I knew she was the last time I looked but it's been years. She and my father had an explosive union. She was all sunny like my sister."

And you. He barely managed to keep that thought inside. She didn't realize it, but the Rock, the persona she wore to survive her upbringing and then medical school and a cutthroat residency, was a mask. The woman behind it was bright and bubbly. Even if she wasn't ready to acknowledge that to herself.

"And my father… Well, you know he isn't much for the emotions. Opposites may attract, but in my parents' case they eventually imploded." Aurora kissed his cheek as she opened the car door. "I bet your mother would be so proud of you. And I bet she would have liked the dish your dad made." Her smile was brilliant but there was small twist in his belly as he stepped out of the car.

"Mom always enjoyed cooking." The words left his mouth, and he felt the air catch in his lungs. It felt ridiculous that after all this time, it still made him uncomfortable to discuss her. To acknowledge how life had shifted without her.

"Maybe she is smiling down watching him learn then."

He was older now than she'd ever gotten to be. It shouldn't hurt to think of her enjoying his father's cooking experience. But this conversation was too long…and he wanted out of it. That wasn't fair to Aurora, but his insides were shivering with memories. Ones he'd packed away when she'd passed.

To survive.

"So, you don't really know where your mother is?" The question popped out before he could think of something else. That wasn't a funny joke or a silly comment. He'd spent the better part of more than two decades deflecting with humor, and in this one moment he'd chosen the exact wrong words.

"No." Aurora looked at him, and once more he saw her eyes look through him. If it was possible for one to see into another's soul, Aurora was looking at his and he shifted against the elevator's wall as they rode up together.

She crossed her arms and leaned her head against the wall of the elevator, an imaginary wall seeming to form between them. One he desperately wanted to tear down.

But if I do…does everything change?

Yes. It was an easy answer, and unsettling. Aurora was the first woman he'd gotten close to since Kate. Hell, many of the women he'd dated after his failed engagement hadn't known he'd lost his mother.

But here, now, in this moment, he wanted to rip each mental brick out. Throw all of them away and unburden the load he'd maintained on his own for so long. Let someone else into his heart…to carry part of his soul.

No, not just someone—he wanted to let Aurora in. But he saw the damage that getting so close did.

Yes, his father was trying new things. Yes, his dad was having fun, laughing, all things that had disappeared from their lives for so many years after his mother passed. But his smile was never the same. He didn't laugh as long or loud. Part of the glimmer in his father's soul had died with his mother.

And their relationship had never been the same. They were still close, but there was a separation, caused by the years of silence now. They never acknowledged it, but it was an invisible barrier in their otherwise lovely father-son connection.

"If you don't want to discuss your mom, Asher, all you have to do is say so."

"So the truth is better than awkward and nosy questions that lead nowhere?" He said the words in a jovial tone, hoping they'd land better than the last round. And immediately realizing they'd fallen flat. Again.

Why was he so unable to make inconsequential jokes around her? It was a skill he'd spent so long perfecting.

Stepping out of the elevator, Aurora reached for her keys. "And you don't have to use humor with me, Asher. You can just say, 'I don't want to discuss it.'"

"Most people don't like directness." The words were harsher than he intended, and he hated the resignation he saw in Aurora's face. "Sorry, maybe I just need a few minutes."

He pushed his hair back as she opened her door.

"Take all the time you need." She squeezed his hand. "Have a good night."

He bent his head, dropping a light chaste kiss against her lips, then pulled back. Years of self-protection guided his actions.

Stepping into his own condo, Asher wanted to scream

at himself. He'd managed to take a perfect day and end it uncomfortably.

There were only so many days until their timeline ran out. A few more weeks where he could hold her, kiss her. And he'd let a wayward question steal a night.

Talk about making a mountain out of a molehill!

Except it didn't have to be this way. He rolled his head to the left and right as if trying to work out some pretend knot in his neck. The knot was in his soul…and the thing that calmed it was Aurora.

His feet moved without thinking. At the very least he owed her an apology. And a real good-night kiss.

He raced across the hall, knocking rapidly. He needed to see her. If she sent him away after he apologized, fine, but he needed to see her.

"In the kitchen, Asher."

He didn't bother to question the fact that she'd called out his name. Didn't worry that she'd expected him. He rounded the doorway of the kitchen to find her holding out a mug of tea.

"It's mint-chamomile—a very calming blend."

"You made me a cup. What would have happened if I hadn't come back?"

Aurora kissed his cheek then sipped the tea from her mug. "You had two more minutes." She nodded to the time on her kitchen counter. "Then I was bringing the cup to you. If you'd turned me away…well—" she shrugged "—guess I would have figured out how to make you let me in then."

Picking up the timer, she turned it off as its high-pitched ding echoed.

"I still don't want to discuss my mother." He sipped the tea, enjoying the rich flavor and the serenity the hot drink filled him with.

"Of course," Aurora said and nodded, "I would like to talk about eggplants though. Do you hate all purple plants, or do you reserve the disdain for eggplants alone?"

Her grin brought a smile to his face, and it felt different. Maybe it was that his father had pointed out that he wore a fake smile far too often, or maybe he was just paying more attention. But he knew the one on his lips right now was real.

"Aurora Miller, making jokes? How lovely." He set his cup down and reached for hers, setting it next to his before pulling her into his arms. The world righted as she laid her head against his shoulder. He ran a hand along her back, soaking in her soft smell, the feel of her in his arms. He was trying to memorize this.

Find a way to mold this into his brain so when their time was over, he could bring it forward. Remind himself of this connection, which for a brief period had made him feel whole.

They were living on borrowed time.

And he could fall for Aurora Miller. Probably already had.

A little.

He should back out, but he'd promised to take her to her sister's wedding and the charity a week after. So he might as well get every drop of enjoyment out of this as possible.

Then her lips captured his. Running her hands through his hair, she pulled him as close as possible, devouring him. He let his final worries float away for the moment. If stopping time was possible, this moment, this one slice of perfection, was where he'd spend the rest of his life.

CHAPTER SEVEN

"So THAT IS the bridesmaid dress?" Asher sat on her bed, his nose scrunched as a fake smile spread across his lips.

"Is it really that bad?" Aurora knew the answer, but she was hoping it was just her uncomfortableness with the whole situation that was making her judgmental.

She'd loved the hot pink she'd threaded through her red hair, but she avoided pale pink. It washed out her already pale, freckled skin. The dress's ruffles were over-the-top, hitting her short frame in all the wrong places.

"It's not an ideal dress." She knew Asher was choosing his words carefully. It was kind. And unnecessary. It wasn't the dress that was bothering her...not really. It was the coded message behind it.

Aurora had heard of brides choosing an ugly bridesmaid dress that wouldn't upstage the bride. She didn't understand why you'd dress someone you supposedly cared enough to ask to stand up at your wedding in something that made them look horrid...except she did understand.

For most families, weddings were just celebrations. But the Millers competed for everything. And Aurora usually won...as much as was possible in their family anyway. This dress was a reminder that she'd lost this. At least in Dani's mind.

She'd chosen a dress that would look beautiful on the

other women standing beside her. All of whom had dark hair, fewer freckles and were several inches taller. Only Aurora would stand out in a bad way.

And she hated how she understood. How a small part of her wished it was her.

Not marrying Landon. She'd never want that. But the pride of being first. Of looking better. Of making their father proud. All things that she rationally knew didn't matter.

And worst of all, she knew the best way to upset her sister was to act like the ugly dress didn't bother her. Like nothing bothered her.

Dani wanted a reaction, and Rory wasn't going to break.

"I look like a pink exploded marshmallow." She lifted her red hair, piling it on top of her head. Maybe an updo hairstyle might make it less horrid.

It wouldn't.

"You don't have to go." Asher pulled her hand into his and squeezed it tightly. "Send her money for the plates of food we won't eat, if it will make you feel better. Hell, I'll send it. But you don't have to do this."

"I know."

"Do you?" Asher pulled her into his lap.

She snuggled into him, not sure how over the past few weeks it had become normal for him to be here. He never spent the night, but he was often here until bedtime.

They enjoyed each other's company, but still made sure they maintained separate spaces. No toothbrushes on counters, or clothes in drawers. Nothing that made it seem like they were going to extend the relationship past his six-week deadline.

That was enough reason for her go to the wedding. Spend the evening dancing with him, enjoying a few hours in his arms.

But there was pride too. She didn't want to admit how

her sister was hurting her. How her family was hurting her. Didn't want them to see the real Aurora…the one she knew her father wouldn't like.

"If we don't go then this ends. Because my father won't want me at the charity event if I make a scene at Dani's wedding."

"His practice is a sponsor of the event, but the charity is raising money for childhood cancer research. It doesn't matter if he wants you there."

Asher was so sure of himself. His father always wanted him around. He didn't know what it was like to live in a cold shadow. How silence could be so loud.

Rather than address that, she went with the other truth. "Maybe I want the full six weeks, Asher." She dropped a kiss on his nose and slid out of his grip, wanting to make the moment sassy and fun instead of desperate. "Can't wrinkle the dress."

"The dress should be burned." Asher stood and started toward the door. "I'm feeling like pizza tonight. If that sounds good, I can order it."

"Sounds fine. I like veggie delight." She hoped that her response sounded unconcerned. Like there was no issue with her pointing out that this was over soon and him shifting the conversation to pizza. Like that didn't bother her at all.

It did. And God, she wished it bothered him too. Wished he'd say something like they could keep this going or ask what if it was real? She wanted to hear him say he wished it was something more than whatever it was.

"I'll get two then. A real pizza with lots of meat…and your veggie delight." He winked and then walked out.

Aurora took one more look in the mirror, stuck her tongue out at the horrid abomination she was wearing, then took it off. Once the wedding was over, this thing was going in the dumpster!

* * *

Asher watched Aurora chatting with one of the nurses. The calendar hanging next to her head made him want to scream. They were leaving for the hotel where the wedding was as soon as their shifts were over. He'd driven them to work this morning, their bags packed next to each other in his small trunk.

He was excited about spending the night with Aurora… but dreading it too. It marked the start of the last week of their time together. And the first time he'd spend the night with Aurora in his arms.

He'd held her close so many times, and wished she'd asked him to stay. He'd almost offered too, but always pulled back at the last moment. They'd both acknowledged the time limit on this. Maybe he wanted to extend it.

It wasn't a maybe. He wanted her…too much. He could love her…maybe already did—a bit.

"You all right?" Angela's words were soft as the nurse stepped next to him.

"Fine." He grinned, but even he could feel the fakeness in it. Aurora made him smile, really smile. It was weird to realize that he'd spent so long faking a smile. The mask he'd slid on when his mother died had felt like a second skin.

The smile was a comfort that protected him. The ability to smile was just part of that. And he hadn't minded… not really. But now that he'd experienced something real, it felt wrong.

Still, it was a habit he couldn't break. He was the happy surgeon. The clown, the joker…the one that never took things too seriously. It was as much a role as the Rock.

Who was he if he discarded it?

"I'm fine. Fine." Maybe if he said it enough it would turn to truth.

Angie raised an eyebrow, "That word typically means the opposite of its stated meaning." She blew out a breath. "You're happy with her. For real."

"This isn't real, Ang." The words were wrong. He'd spoken wrong words before, a lifetime of them. A joke when his soul was breaking, an off-the-cuff statement when the world was uncomfortable. None of those instances made him want to yank the words back in.

"You lying to me or to yourself?" She held his gaze a moment then walked away before he could find a funny response to lighten the mood.

Both.

"We've got a woman coming up. Brain aneurysm bleed. Seizing in the ER! Emergency surgery!" The call rang out on the speaker by the nurse's station.

Asher saw Aurora take off. He ran after her, his long legs catching up with hers. "Do you know if the ER administered propofol?"

If the ER had given the patient the sedation drug, it would shorten the time it took for Aurora to get her fully under for brain surgery. If not, it added minutes...minutes their patient might not have.

"It's standard, but I'll know for sure when we get into the OR." She started washing immediately as Asher pulled up the pictures of the aneurysm on the screen. It was in the worst possible place.

Bleeding, but not fully ruptured...yet. He looked at the bulging vein; the woman must have had the worst headache of her life. If she survived, and the odds were fifty-fifty at this point, she'd face months of rehabilitation therapy.

"I'll make sure a central line is put in, and ensure she's fully under. No more than seven minutes." Aurora gloved up and entered the operating theater.

Seven minutes. Asher looked at the image on the screen

while he scrubbed in. That aneurysm could burst any moment, but catastrophes happened when you rushed.

"Asher?" Aurora could see the worry dripping from him. Bella Opio was breathing, with assistance. The surgery was as close to success as one could hope for in this situation. Asher had snipped the bleed, but Bella still faced a long road to recovery.

Assuming she made it through the night. Twenty-five percent of patients with a rupture or near rupture died in the first twenty-four hours. Another twenty-five percent passed in the first year. However, fifty percent recovered, many with few long-term effects. There was nothing left for the professionals to do but hope.

It wasn't an easy situation, but her vitals were strong. That was as good a sign as they were going to get right now.

"Do you want to stay?" She wanted him with her at the wedding, but she knew sometimes there was a patient you hated to leave. If he needed to be here, she understood.

"No." He shook his head, but she could see the scrunch in his nose.

"No, but also yes?" Aurora tapped her hip with his, a little reminder that she was here with him. That he wasn't alone.

"No. I want to go. I just…" He crossed his arms. "She has two kids, both under ten. A nurse told me that they've been sleeping against her husband in the waiting room for the last two hours."

He squeezed himself and closed his eyes. He rocked back before opening his eyes. The haunted look sent a shiver down her spine.

"A family is hoping and praying and waiting. And I don't have all the answers…won't have them for days.

Maybe weeks. Right now, I have to tell him that his wife is stable, but the next twenty-four hours are critical. And I can't guarantee she will make it."

He blew out a breath, and she ran a hand along his arm. As an anesthesiologist she cared for her patients but was somewhat removed from them. Asher was one of the best, but even the best couldn't fix everything.

Life wasn't fair. It was a lesson medical professionals learned early—one he'd learned as a child. But knowing it, even accepting it, wasn't the same as liking it. No one wanted to tell a family their loved one was gone, or forever changed.

"Come with me to talk to the husband?" He patted her hand.

"Of course." She was stunned he'd asked her to come with him. Stunned at the vulnerability radiating from his features. This was the real Asher Parks, the real man behind the levity.

And he was hurting. She'd be beside him for whatever he needed...for as long as he'd let her.

"Then we get out of here. Spend the weekend roasting marshmallows over the firepit and forget about this place for a while." He sighed and shook his shoulders. He didn't force a smile, but she could see him step back into the role he played.

Was that how she looked when assuming the Rock persona?

The walk to the waiting room didn't take long, but with each step, Asher stood a little straighter. His shoulders were a bit more rigid. Anticipation of what was to come slowed his quick steps.

They stepped through the door, and the father looked up. His dark eyes were bloodshot, and two children, a girl and a boy, slept against his shoulders. He looked to each one, bit his lip and carefully readjusted them.

The little ones shifted then curled into their chairs, their breaths coming in slow steady motions. At least they were asleep for this news.

"Bella… Bella is okay. Right?" Tears coated his eyes and he didn't bother to raise his hands to wipe them as they stole down his cheeks.

"She is stable—"

"Stable…no." He shook his head. "Stable isn't okay. She loves those medical dramas. Makes me watch them with her—we sit on the couch. She has popcorn and I have chips. She always steals my chips even though she says she wants the popcorn. That is okay. Stable just means…"

He put his hands to his face and let out a choked sob.

"Stable means that your wife came through surgery. She is in recovery. I stopped the bleed—"

"And she is going to be okay?"

Aurora knew that Bella's husband didn't mean to keep interrupting. Or maybe he did, fearful of what he might hear.

Asher took a deep breath and patted the man on the shoulder. "The fact that she came through surgery is a big win. But the next twenty-four hours are critical. If she makes it through—"

"If…" Bella's husband collapsed onto the floor, and Aurora moved to the small phone on the wall to dial a hospital counselor.

She said a few words while Bella's husband rocked back and forth on the floor. There was no right way to hear this information, but she wanted to make sure that he had support in the next few hours.

Asher bent and waited for him to look at him. "I know this is a lot. And I wish I could tell you everything will be all right. I hope it is. Right now she is stable, but her aneurysm was very serious."

"If she goes… I can't go on without her."

"You have to." Asher's voice was stone, and Aurora blinked at his tone.

The harsh tone grabbed Bella's husband's attention.

"Listen to me and understand. You have two beautiful children. If the worst happens, you must go on. And you need to understand that *now*. No matter what happens, you have two little people that need you. Need you to help them understand why Mommy isn't home right now. Why she has to stay here to get better. And, God forbid, understand why she isn't coming home if that happens. You are their father, their protector."

Bella's husband looked at Asher then back at his children. "Their protector."

"Exactly." Asher stood and offered his hand. "My colleague contacted one of our counselors. Is there anyone else we can reach out to for you?"

"My pastor is on his way. And Bella's sister already has a flight booked. She lands tomorrow morning." He wiped the tears from his cheeks, "I don't want to do this."

"Of course you don't." Asher gripped his hand as he pulled him up. "This isn't an easy path to walk, but you have a support system. And your wife is going to need that system, too."

The hospital counselor stepped into the hospital waiting area. Aurora nodded to her, and she stepped next to Asher and introduced herself.

"Can I see her? Can I please see my wife?"

"Will you stay with the kids?" Asher directed the question to the counselor, who quickly agreed and moved to sit next to them, so that if they woke while their father was gone they'd see her first.

"Why don't you follow us?" Asher looked to Aurora and then to Bella's husband.

She followed the quiet procession, aching to reach for Asher too. She didn't know exactly what had happened when his mother passed, but this patient was touching a raw space in his soul.

CHAPTER EIGHT

The ceiling fan in the hotel room spun as he lay on the bed. Aurora stepped out of the bathroom, letting her hair down from the high ponytail she'd worn at the rehearsal dinner. He'd attended the dinner, made small talk, but he didn't have any memories of the night.

He should be relaxed. Should be enjoying every moment with the amazing woman with him.

His body left the hospital, but his mind…

His mind was still trapped in that waiting room. Replaying Bella's husband's reaction. The look in his face, the worry…the statement that he couldn't go on without her.

His father had muttered the same thing over and over again in those first few dark weeks. It was the only thing he'd said.

"Asher?" Aurora opened the window, which looked out on the dark night sky at the lake resort where Dani and Landon were getting married. She turned out the light in the room then lay on the bed, curling into him. She rested her hand on his chest, and comfort flowed into him. "We can go back to the hospital. If you need to be there. I can drive back up here early tomorrow."

He appreciated the offer, but he didn't want to give this up either. If only there was a way to be in two places at once. "I can't do anything else for Bella." That was a fact. One he hated.

She had to fight. Modern medicine was a miracle, but the patient had more control than people realized. The human will was a fantastic thing—one science wasn't able to quantify. A physician could do everything right and the outcome might still be bleak.

On the other hand, a patient that shouldn't make it, one who was facing so many uphill battles it seemed impossible, might rally. Bella might go either way, but her husband needed to be there for his children, no matter what.

Aurora pointed to the window. "I've always enjoyed looking at stars." The lights of the resort dimmed out all but the brightest stars. "Not that you can see many of them here. But it's enough to know they're there. To know that some things go on, even when everything seems lost."

"Stars?" Asher followed her gaze. "I've never given them much thought." Rationally he knew the balls of light were brilliant stars, but they were simply an unshifting thing in a world that moved too fast. Nothing to focus on.

Her hand ran over his chest. Its smooth motions eased some of the tension from his body. "It always amazes me how the whole world can go on when bad things happen. It feels like time should stop. Like the stars should dim to acknowledge the pain."

His breath caught as Aurora's words sunk in. "Did you want the stars to dim when Landon ended your relationship?" If given the option, he'd have dimmed them after his mother's death and again after walking in on Kate and Michael in their bed. To lose a fiancée and best friend in one day...

He hated the question, the intimacy of it. But he wanted to know too. Wanted to know if she'd wished the world paused in that moment…wanted to know if she'd want it to pause when they stopped this.

"I ended our relationship." Aurora sighed as silence settled around them.

That surprised him, but also brought a smile to his lips. So even years ago, she'd been willing to step outside her father's expectations. Maybe one day she'd shed them completely. It would make her so much happier.

"But yes. That day I wanted the world to stop. Not because of Landon, but because of Heather. I wanted the whole world to weep."

"Heather?" He reached back through his memory, trying to remember her mentioning a Heather. Nothing came forward. And he'd listened to her…memorizing nearly every word. Writing them on his soul.

"That was why Landon and I broke up, or rather what made me realize that he didn't love me." She rolled onto her back and he pulled her into his arms, burying his head in her hair. He hated that anything bad had ever happened to her. Aurora deserved the world. *If only he could offer it.*

"Heather was the other female anesthesiology resident in my program. We were close. She was in a car accident. The doctors did their best, but…"

Asher didn't need her to finish the sentence.

"Landon came home to find me mourning my friend. He accused me of being emotional. Said no one would take me seriously if they saw me. Told me I was making him uncomfortable."

"After you lost a friend?" Asher had heard a lot of nonsense in his life, but that was the top line.

"After losing my friend, and in my own home." Aurora nodded. "It was a ridiculous argument. We rarely argued. He liked to argue with others, but not me. He was used to me not getting worked up, cool, calm and collected Rory. I believe that was the first time he saw me cry."

"After losing a friend." Asher couldn't wrap his mind around the reaction. Aurora's reaction to losing Heather was the normal one. Even his father's reaction to losing his mother was normal...for a period.

It was the months of ignoring everything, of feeling nothing, that Asher resented. Even if he understood.

"Remember, he was sleeping with my sister already by then, so maybe he just wanted an excuse. Either way, I told him to pack his stuff. I even started tossing it in piles for him. It was right out of a melodramatic television script."

"Wow." Asher sighed as he stared at the sky, looking for the stars he knew were hidden by the resort's light pollution. But they were there, and it was oddly comforting to think of it that way.

"You're still mad at your father." Aurora's voice was quiet. It was a statement not a question.

Shifting on the bed, he started to pull away, but she followed his motions. "I love my father."

"Of course." She wrapped her arms around him, trapping him, but also comforting him. He wasn't alone, and he craved that reminder. "That doesn't mean that you aren't mad at him. Those emotions can live together."

He opened his mouth but no words came out.

"I saw your reaction to Bella's husband—"

"Do you think I was wrong?" He rushed the words out. He'd rethought that interaction over and over. Each time he worried that he'd been too rough, not delicate enough in the situation. But he was also hoping that he was honest, that if the worst happened, Bella's husband knew he had to pick up the pieces around him.

It wasn't an option to just stop. No matter how much he might want to.

"No. But have you ever told your father how you feel? How what happened impacted you?"

Where were his funny quips now? His entire persona was making jokes to get out of painful situations. It was the skill he was proudest of.

God, what does that say about me?

All of the humor was gone. Another brick fell out of the mental wall he'd erected when his mother passed. And with it, the last of the wall came crumbling down.

"My dad stopped talking for five months, two weeks and three days after my mother's funeral. One hundred and sixty-nine days." Aurora's hand slipped into his. The connection to this world…to her…mending a piece of his heart.

How long had it been since he felt like he didn't have to worry or put on the happy face? A lifetime. Even Kate had never known that. That he'd counted each silent day.

"The first thing he did when he finally came to was laugh at one of my silly jokes." Asher let out a breath and with it another weight lifted from his soul.

"And the clown was born." Aurora brought his hand to her lips, the soft touch just a reminder that she was there.

"No, the clown was already there. It was the persona I developed at school, a way to turn the pity frowns into smiles. Better to be laughed at than pitied." He ran his fingers down her arms, his need to touch her, to hold her, overcoming him.

Aurora kissed the top of his head before burrowing into him. "I can't imagine how difficult that was."

"Really?" Asher wrapped his arms around her shoulders, squeezing as he laid his head against hers. "I assumed your father stopped talking to you often."

"That's different. That was a disappointment issue, and I always knew how to work my way back into his good graces. In fact I excelled at it. Why do you think Dani gets so angry with me?"

It was different, but it still sucked. She'd spent her life trying to make herself acceptable to a man whose standards would always shift. Chasing parental love he doubted her father was capable of delivering.

"I know he loved her. Still loves her." He breathed Aurora in. "I know that witnessing that love should be a blessing…"

He'd never uttered aloud his frustration that the love they'd had, the irrevocable bond that remained intact even decades after his mother's passing, had left him feeling like an orphan.

Left him adrift in his grief.

"But…" Aurora's voice was quiet, barely audible over the sound of the fan.

He suspected that was on purpose. Suspected that if he pretended not to have heard it, she wouldn't push. Wouldn't make him answer. She was leaving it up to him.

"But I was alone. And there is part of me that still burns with fury that I was left alone to deal with that hurt." He couldn't reel the words back in, but he held his breath, waiting to hear how wrong it was to say the truth.

Aurora laid her hand over his heart. "I think that is completely understandable."

"It doesn't sound hateful?" He let out a chuckle, not a funny one, but his body releasing frustration, anger and hurt that it had held on to for so long.

"No." Aurora's fingers stroked his chest, just over his heart. It wasn't sensual; it was a comfort that one partner offered to another. It felt deeply intimate…so much more intimate than anything he'd ever allowed.

"It sounds truthful. And I doubt your father or mother would begrudge you those feelings. And…" She paused as she lifted onto her elbow, making sure her eyes were level with his in the dark room. "And I think it was something Bella's husband needed to hear. Something I suspect she'd want to make sure he heard in case the worst happens. I've never felt called to be a mother, but I think most moms, the good ones anyways, want to make sure their children are taken care of."

"And my mom was one of the good ones." Asher smiled as the memory of her face floated in his memory. Her laughter, and the brightness in her eyes.

"She was," Aurora said with such certainty it was hard for him to remember that she'd never gotten to meet his mother. "For what it is worth, I think your father wouldn't mind hearing it either."

"Maybe. But he's already been through so much." Asher looked around Aurora.

"It's getting late," Aurora said, voicing his thoughts. It felt like they were on the same page, their thoughts nearly one.

"Ready to be done with our deep, dangerous conversations already, princess." Asher lowered his voice, sounding like a cartoon villain.

Aurora giggled then kissed his cheek. "I'll listen anytime you want to talk about your mom, or your dad. Or anything weighing on you."

His heart seized. The world, time, all the paths he'd taken, felt like they'd led to this moment, here, now with her. His lips connected with her, and the world and its problems seemed to evaporate.

Aurora shivered as Asher's lips glided across her neck. Tonight they'd opened up to each other…and his touches felt different.

Or maybe it was her that was different.

They'd kissed for a while, not passionately, just two people seeking and receiving comfort. But now they'd lost all their clothes and he still hadn't joined their bodies.

She wanted him. Desperately. But as his fingers skimmed across her skin, she couldn't help the emotions running through her. Pulling his face to hers, she captured his mouth. Tasting him, memorizing how his body molded to hers.

"Aurora." Her name was a plea in the night.

She smiled against his mouth, enjoying the need floating through her. "I want you." She shuddered as his kisses slowed.

It was not the reaction she'd expected. Part of her ached for him to join their bodies. To rock them both into oblivion. Another part of her wanted to stretch this moment out for forever. Perhaps, if they spent the night loving each other, daylight might stay away.

He slid his hand across her hip, his eyes drinking her in. "I want to spend tonight worshipping every inch of you." His lips followed the path his fingers had just traveled.

"You are my own personal siren, Aurora. You call to me." He trailed his lips along her stomach, before sucking her breasts.

Running her hands through his hair, Aurora sighed. "A siren? No one has ever called me that."

"Perhaps you haven't sung for anyone else." His words were warm against her body, the silky feel of his skin against hers making her arch her back.

She was nearly desperate for him.

"Asher…"

His mouth caught hers, his tongue dancing with hers, and his hand moved between her legs. His thumb pressed against her as his finger slipped inside. Her body took over as her nerves exploded with pleasure.

He lifted her leg over his, and they lay spooning. Skin against skin as his fingers delighted her and his mouth brought her as close to heaven as earth allowed.

"Aurora… Aurora…my Aurora."

My Aurora.

The simple statement sent her over the edge. Passion cresting through her. "Asher," she moaned and gripped his hips, desperate for him. "Asher, please…" The words sounded nearly feral, but she needed their bodies together. Now.

He reached behind her, grabbed the condom, sheathed himself and pressed into her.

He held himself very still as they lay spooning, joined as one. Raising a finger, he ran it along her cheek. "You are perfection, Aurora."

Perfection.

Kissing her, he finally started to move. Unhurried, in a maddening pace that ignited her entire body. Together they crested across into oblivion. Then lay together, their breath syncing in the night until Asher's soft snores took over.

Lying in his arms, looking out the window at the setting moon, Rory sighed. Perfection… This was perfection. And she never wanted it to end.

"I'm falling for you." She let the whispered words hover in the silence. If he was awake, she'd never have the courage to utter them. But she wanted them spoken, needed the power of the spoken word in the universe.

She was falling for Asher Parks. No. She'd fallen for Asher Parks. Their fake relationship hadn't been fake since that first date.

But it was temporary.

She hated that knowledge. They enjoyed each other and Asher had opened up to her in ways she doubted he ever had for another. Tonight had felt different, but he'd never mentioned anything after their six weeks together.

"Only a week left." She turned in his arms, kissed his cheek, careful not to wake him. Laying her head against his forehead, she breathed in his scent and whispered the full truth.

"I love you."

CHAPTER NINE

THE MORNING SUN'S rays danced across their bedroom as Aurora shifted in Asher's arms. The wedding was here, but she wasn't dreading it like she had up until now. No matter what happened today, he'd be here. There was so much comfort in that.

Her phone buzzed and Asher groaned.

"We aren't on call." He kissed her cheek as he slid out of the bed.

"You aren't. But as a bridesmaid, I certainly am." She lifted the phone, her heart dropping as she read her sister's text.

Rules for the Wedding:
1. You will not talk to Landon without me.

As if she wanted to!

2. Asher and you will sit at the family table with Dad.

Asher wouldn't like that, but he'd deal. For her.

3. Smile. This is my wedding. I don't care if you are jealous.

Not jealous, sis. Worried. But not jealous.

4. Need to be at the wedding venue in an hour. Hair and makeup will be done at the venue. I've already chosen everyone's style.

In other words, she'd made sure no one would look better than her.

5. Smile. Repeating this for you!

Aurora looked at her watch. She'd smile. Act the way her family expected, then she'd start putting distance between them.

Her family was never going to be like Asher and his father. That was disheartening, but it didn't mean she had to keep subjecting herself to the dysfunction her father forced on his girls.

I can see you read the texts, Rory. Do you understand the rules?

Nope. Need to give them to me in better detail! She actually typed out the words, glaring at the snarky response. Then she deleted it.

Understood.

The twinge of headache beat against her eyes. Today was going to be a long day, but she'd get through it.

"By the look on your face, I think now is a good time for your gift."

"My sister just wants to make sure that I am following her rules." She rolled her eyes. "Like I am not an expert rule follower."

"True, you've kept all the rules you laid out for us," he joked as he held up a small pink bag.

Except she hadn't. She'd broken rule one. The most important one. She was in love with the man standing in front of her, ridiculously proud of the bag in his hand.

Reaching for the gift, she grinned at him. "You didn't have to do this." Her eyes widened at she pulled the box of hair dye. Hot-pink hair dye.

"I saw it at the store. I thought…hey, if Aurora ever decides she wants to give it a go, I want her prepared!"

"Asher… I am never…"

He kissed the never away as he pulled the box away. Holding it up, he pointed to the barcode on the back.

"I checked. It won't expire for three years. Lots of time to think on it."

She grabbed the box and read the instructions on the back. Just so she knew what they were…not because she planned to the use it. Though it was the perfect shade of pink. "This was a very sweet gift."

"I know!" He laughed as she playfully backhanded him.

"So sure of yourself."

"I usually am."

"Usually?" Before he could answer her question, her phone buzzed again. "My family is going to be very difficult today."

He took the box of dye from her hands again and pulled her to him. She clung to him, enjoying the soft scent of his soap, the fresh mint of toothpaste and the subtle scent of simply Asher. This was her happy place and she wished she could linger.

"You don't have to take any of their anger or drama today. You get to decide how to handle them," he said before he captured her mouth as she opened it to argue.

His tongue danced with hers, taking her away from the day's upcoming hassles.

"You are worthy, Aurora Miller. Nothing they do changes that."

The phone buzzed again, and Asher pulled back. "Go. I'll see you at the wedding. I'll be in the back row in case you want to make a run for it."

"Rory!" Her father tossed her a bouquet of flowers.

She barely managed to catch the bundle. The white flowers Dani had chosen looked a little brown, it was difficult not to think that was the universe's way of saying this marriage was a mistake. Dani had made her the errand runner. Her sister probably thought that was a punishment, but Aurora was perfectly fine spending as little time in the bridal suite as possible.

Holding up the bouquet, she looked at her father. The man's frown was not what one usually saw on the father of the groom, but it was the look he wore most often. "Why are you throwing a bouquet?"

"Because your sister tossed it at me and told me to get out when I asked if she was planning to be so emotional when she walked down the aisle."

Emotions. Really! Aurora wanted to shake him. His daughter was getting married, there was stress and happiness and probably some uncertainty all mixed in. Add in a grimacing father of the bride, and it was a recipe for anyone to lose their cool.

"It *is* her wedding day." Aurora looked at the roses and wondered if there was any way to pull the brown-speckled petals off. The white flowers shocked her. Dani was loud. Over-the-top, dramatic. The muted colors weren't her.

Was she changing for Landon, or her father?

It wasn't Aurora's concern but she hoped not.

Her father grunted. "Please. This is too much. Even for Dani. I mentioned how cool and collected you always are. I bet if you loved someone you wouldn't make a huge deal out of it. Just a simple statement. Yet she—"

"Enough." Aurora held up her hand, "For God's sake, enough."

"Rory."

"Nope." She shook her head and straightened her shoulders. A wedding was not the right place for this interaction, but she was done listening to her father extoll the benefits of being an emotionless drone. On his daughter's wedding day!

Asher was right. She was enough as she was, and she was not going to listen to a diatribe on her sister's wedding day.

"I have no idea what you said to Dani, but I am sure that it warranted throwing you out of the bridal suite."

Her father's cheeks brightened, and she saw his palms clench. But she was not backing down.

"If I am ever lucky enough to have a wedding, I expect that I will be a blubbering mess." She looked at the roses and wanted to scream. "Emotions aren't weaknesses."

"We'll have to agree to disagree."

"Yes. We will." Aurora held her head high. She wished Asher was here to witness this interaction. He probably would have cheered her on, maybe even whooped a little.

"I'm disappointed in you, Rory."

"And for the first time, I don't care." It was the truth. Asher had told her she was enough, and he was right. She was.

Her father's mouth fell open. "What?"

She didn't bother staying to answer that question. The only way she ever pleased him was by being an emotionless drone, and even then he'd never told her he was proud of her. Or used the word *love*.

Well, she loved herself. And that was enough.

Pushing open the door to the bridal suite, she slipped in and held up the bouquet. "You threw this?"

Dani grabbed the bouquet from her hand. "He told me I was being too emotional."

"Most brides and grooms are emotional on their wedding day."

Dani scoffed, "Yeah. Well, the groom spent last night with his ex-girlfriend. I was pissed at him, and Dad is mad that I'm angry."

"With an ex-girlfriend?" Aurora didn't mean to repeat the statement, but she couldn't believe her ears. Her father thought Dani was overreacting. She thought her sister wasn't furious enough!

"Some chick he dated right before you and him. Sowing wild oats or something." Her sister's cheeks were red, her brows tight, but her eyes were dry. What was happening?

"You shouldn't marry him." Aurora looked to the two other bridesmaids, hoping for their support. Neither of them looked at her.

"I am not going to disappoint Dad." Dani crossed her arms, her stance so reminiscent of their childhood fights, Aurora would have laughed if it wasn't so sad. "And he already said he's sorry."

"Danielle, this is your life. Landon is a cad." She was worth more than a man their father approved of. How could she not see that?

"But a rich one," her friend piped up and winked as the other bridesmaid nodded in agreement.

"None of this is healthy." Aurora bit her lip and made a choice. Time to speak the truth—all of it. "You and I are not close. I know Landon cheated on me with you."

Her sister didn't bother to disagree.

"But you do not have to marry him. You and I can walk out to my car right now and drive away." It would create a scene. That would anger their father, but life was too short to agree to such a union.

"I will even walk into the chapel, tell them that the wedding is off. You don't have to do it. I can tell them as little or as much of what happened as you want. Throw him under the bus or don't. But Dani…"

"And I'm supposed to be the dramatic one." Dani huffed as she looked at her ring. "I do think I will make him buy me a new ring for the trouble."

"Oh, certainly," one of the other bridesmaids agreed.

She felt like was stuck in a bad movie. This was out of control. Weddings were supposed be celebrations; marriages were unions. Dani would regret this, but if she wasn't willing to walk out now there was nothing Aurora could do.

Shaking her head, she backed toward the door. "I… I…am not standing at the altar and smiling for this." She would not watch her sister make this mistake.

"Fine. Don't." Dani turned to the other two bridesmaids and started plotting new jewelry. This wasn't love…and she wanted no part of it.

"If you ever need my help…"

"I won't," her sister snapped without looking back.

As she stepped into the hallway, Aurora's hands shook. This was the right choice, the right decision, but that didn't mean it didn't hurt. Sucking in a deep breath, she started for the chapel, hoping Asher really was sitting in the last row.

He was.

She smiled, even though her body was still shaking

as she caught his attention. At least she hadn't had to do this alone.

"What's up?" Asher asked as he wrapped an arm around her.

Aurora bit her lip. "I kind of removed myself from the bridal party."

"Oh." There was no judgment in his handsome face—a little surprise, but no judgment.

That calmed her nerves a little.

"Apparently disapproving of the groom's affair the night before the wedding is looked down on."

Asher's mouth opened and he moved his head from side to side, but there were no words. He blew out a breath as the bridal procession music started. "I bet there is some epic drama at the reception. Sure you want to miss that?"

She appreciated the question. This was a huge step. She could stay in the back of the venue, watch the wedding and go to the reception. But what would that accomplish?

"I was actually thinking we could grab some BBQ and doughnuts…and maybe stop at the painting rage room. This dress needs more color!" She laughed. "Thoughts?"

Asher squeezed her. "An excellent plan! I want a doughnut badly and we can definitely go mess up that dress!"

"Good. 'Cause I need you to keep my spirits up if they sink!"

A look crossed his face, one she couldn't quite understand, but it sent a shiver down her back. She raised her hand to his cheek. "Asher?"

"At your service, my lady." He wrapped an arm around her waist, the playful tone doing little to shake the shiver of concern slinking through her soul.

CHAPTER TEN

ASHER STARED AT the wall in his kitchen, wishing he was in Aurora's colorful condo. But that wasn't the best idea. No matter how much he wanted it. After grabbing lunch on the day of the wedding, they'd spent the afternoon destroying the bridesmaid dress. It was colorful and over-the-top now. It had been a lovely afternoon, despite the day weighing on Aurora.

But the ride home from the painting place had been quiet. How he wished there was a way to blame it on exhaustion, Aurora's emotions about standing up to her family or something other than the truth. Each of them seemed to know the fantasy was coming to an end.

And it hurt.

They'd spent all day yesterday watching movies and relaxing. The last Sunday in their six-week adventure. The fundraiser was next Saturday afternoon. A fancy brunch affair. He wasn't sure how it would go, but he'd be there for Aurora, even though his body felt like it was being pulled in two.

Half of him wanted to throw his own rule book out, see how this might go. The other half was screaming at him to get out now, before he caught any more feelings.

He leaned his head against the counter, lifted his coffee to his lips and wondered what tea Aurora was fixing this morning. What fancy bag was she pulling out of her cabinet? Or was it loose leaf? Was she ready for Jason's surgery? How had she slept?

A million other questions raced through his brain. All easily answered if he walked over to her condo. It wasn't yet five, but he knew she was up. Prepping to go in for Jason's surgery.

He mentally wandered through the procedure, brought up the X-rays and scans in his mind. Things he'd run through hundreds of times already. This surgery was going to be perfect.

It was just the thing he needed to take his mind off Aurora Miller.

The knock at the door brought an involuntary smile to his lips. "Come in."

"Bella is awake and answering questions." Aurora's smile lit up the room as she did a little dance. "She still has a long road ahead of her, but she is awake."

Setting his cup on the counter, Asher reached for her. "That is wonderful."

"It is." Aurora leaned against his chest. "It is."

Wrapping his arms around her, Asher breathed in her scent. The light scent of strawberry shampoo and toothpaste.

"Asher."

"Mmm?" He closed his eyes, enjoying her presence. Needing just a moment with her.

"The charity event is Saturday." Her voice wobbled then he felt her suck in a deep breath.

"I haven't forgotten." The date was tattooed on his heart.

"Want to go on a date, Sunday? Add on an extra day… just to complete the weekend."

The question reverberated through his soul. His heart

screamed for him to yell yes. His mind argued that a clean break—or as clean a one as possible—was best.

They cared for each other. That was an understatement. He was falling in love with her. He hadn't meant to. Hadn't tried to. But love was forming; he felt like he needed her.

Needed her beside him. Needed to make her smile. Needed her when the days were long and hard. His father had needed his mother too. Still needed her, even after all these years.

His reaction to needing Aurora sent chills through his soul…and fireworks through his heart. It was a strange dichotomy. And it terrified him.

In movies this was the point the main character threw out their lifetime of expectations and accepted their fate. Willingly. And he wanted to…mostly.

Need.

Such a powerful motivator…and destroyer.

"It's fine, Asher. Forget I asked." She pulled back and he let her go.

"I didn't say no." The words sounded pathetic, even to his ears.

She looked at him. The eyes of the Rock appraising him. He couldn't stand still, couldn't handle being weighed and found wanting.

"It's just… I don't do long-term. I'm not made for forever. I just—"

Aurora held up a hand, and he snapped his mouth shut. He was rambling, making no sense, even to himself.

"A simple no works." She let out a breath and looked at her watch. "We should get going. Jason's surgery is going to take most of the day. I need to grab a to-go mug of tea and my lunch. I'll see you there."

She headed for the door, gripping the handle then turning. He braced himself for her anger, or hurt, or any range of emotion she wanted to give. He'd earned it.

"You're going to do great today, Asher. See you at the hospital."

He was prepared for an argument, for hurt, for some kind of emotion. Instead, the Rock arrived. And he hated it.

But before he could find any words, she was gone.

"Retractors." Asher held out a hand, and someone, whose face Aurora couldn't see behind all of her equipment, handed the instrument to him.

For years she'd hidden behind the equipment she managed during surgery. Always an active participant in patient care, but never participating in the general discussion many patients didn't realize occurred during long surgeries. Once she and Asher had started dating, she'd participated more.

Can I call it dating if we never planned on it lasting? If it was just for a designated time? If he doesn't even want to consider extending whatever we have by a single day?

She'd kept her composure this morning. Grateful for a lifetime of hiding hurt and pain. He didn't want to continue what they had. It hurt…but better to know it now instead of deluding herself.

"Heart rate stable, O2 levels holding." She made sure her voice carried over the curtain, sound of machines, discussions and the playlist Asher had selected.

"Thank you, Auro— Dr. Miller."

He caught himself, but the team knew they'd gotten closer. And they'd soon realize that closeness was gone.

"Tumor located. At least three branches detected."

The general hum of the operating room quieted. The scans had shown the tumor and three branches. Three branches, with shadows indicating the possibility of more that were too small for imagery to clearly detect.

If it was just the three, this surgery had a good chance of success. If it was more… Well, this was what they were here for. These next few hours were going to decide Jason's fate.

"Fourth identified."

The room took a collective deep breath.

"Fifth and sixth."

Rory closed her eyes. This was the nightmare situation. The reason the other neurosurgeons had turned this case away.

"All right, let's do this." Asher's voice was steady, but she could hear the uncertainty hiding in the tone.

The next several hours were spent with Asher meticulously removing tinier and tinier pieces of tumor. In total he'd located nine branches and the surgery originally slated for six hours was heading into its ninth. The entire team was focused, but exhausted.

"I think I got it all," Asher sighed.

Think… Everyone in the operating theater heard that word. There were no rounds of congratulations. No celebrations. An uncertain Asher was a thing no one was used to. But she respected his decision not to state that it was a complete success.

"Time to close and move him to recovery."

The rest of the procedure proceeded smoothly. The team worked quickly, and Aurora started to adjust the anesthesia. Hopefully his recovery went smoothly.

"Aurora?" She looked up from the charting she was finishing and offered Asher a tired smile. "Yes?"

He hung in the door of the small office his face tired but resolute.

"You free next Sunday?"

She blinked as the question's meaning registered. "Um, Asher, we don't have to."

"I know we don't, but maybe I'm not quite ready for goodbye either."

Not quite ready.

A tingle hugged the back of her brain. This wasn't forever. She hadn't considered forever since she'd worn Landon's ring. At forty she knew many unions didn't last; it wasn't a fairy tale she was looking for, but it seemed off that he'd worded it that way.

Still, her heart wanted more time. Even if it was only a day. "I'm free."

"The charge nurse called. Jason is awake. Groggy but awake. Want to stop by with me before we head out?"

"Wouldn't miss it." She slid around the desk, her heart aching more than she wanted to admit.

"Good evening, Jason." Asher kept his tone low, even though his body was vibrating with excitement. He'd been conservative when he'd closed Jason up. Said he thought he got it all…but it wasn't true. He *knew* he'd gotten it all.

Yes, that was an arrogant thought given the fact that the tumor wasn't enclosed. Maybe others wouldn't be so certain, but Asher was great at what he did. One of the best…and he'd gotten it all!

Nine branches of the tumor, each smaller than the last. More than he'd expected but all dispatched by his scalpel. He'd wanted to cheer, wanted to shout with excitement, but operating room decorum had tempered his exhilaration.

"Dr. Parks." Jason raised a hand, the simple wave proving that he was able to move his arm.

"How are you feeling?" He stepped closer, pulling up the tablet chart. His vitals had stayed within the normal

range for the past several hours, not a small accomplish-
ment given the length and complexity of his surgery.

"Pretty good." Jason pulled his arm behind his head,
resting it.

"But?" Aurora stepped to Jason's side.

Asher raised an eyebrow as he looked at Jason. She'd
seen or heard it first, but now that he really looked the
young man didn't radiate joy. His eyes were down, his posture rigid, his face frozen with concern. "I got the cancer,
Jason. The tumor and its tendrils are gone. I am certain."
He saw Aurora's eyes flash to him; he was certain.

He also understood that after surgery, many patients
didn't feel the immediate relief they thought they would.
One expected to finish surgery and walk out feeling great.
Instead they woke up groggy and sore. And the pain usually increased as the anesthesia and pain pills wore off.

It was a process, but acceptance and joy usually came
with time. Jason looked at the ceiling, closing his eyes, and
Asher saw tears under his lashes. "Jason?"

Worry slipped across his spine as he watched Aurora
look at the notes in her tablet chart and step a bit closer to
Jason. Something wasn't right—something he hadn't told
his nurses about or they'd have told them.

"I can't move my legs." He bit his lip, a tear rolling
down his cheek. "I know I should be happy that you got
the cancer. That I can move my arms, that I am still here.
I know, but…"

"Take a deep breath for me," Aurora instructed as Asher
reached for a pen and moved to Jason's feet.

He hadn't cut away anything but the tumor. Yes, the
surgery was dangerous, but leaving the tumor in was a
death sentence too. Paralysis was a complication they'd
discussed, acknowledged, but Asher would know if that

happened. Would have ensured he was present when his patient woke so he could discuss the new reality.

He'd been perfect. Jason should be tired, and his body sore, but he should be able to move his legs without any problem. Asher had done everything right.

He had.

"Jason," Aurora said, keeping his attention while Asher ran his pen along Jason's foot. "I had to give you a nerve block while Dr. Parks operated on your back. It is possible that it hasn't worn off yet. Sometimes it takes up to forty-eight hours to fully leave your system."

"And that would make me unable to move them? Unable to even wiggle my toes?"

"It would," Aurora responded. "The nerve block disables the feeling in the nerves, but it also means the nerve doesn't respond to commands either."

Asher ran the pen along Jason's foot, and he didn't react. He knew Aurora was trying to reassure both of them. And she had used a nerve block. That was one explanation.

It had also been a nearly ten-hour surgery. There was swelling in his spinal cavity, from the trauma. Trauma that could not be avoided. Still, as Asher moved the pen up Jason's leg without him reacting, his heart sunk.

"I know you're touching me, Doc. I just can't feel it." Jason wiped the tear from his cheek before looking at Asher. "But the cancer is gone?"

"Yes," Asher stated. "I can't guarantee it won't come back, but that tumor is gone. And Dr. Miller is right, this might be temporary. You've been in recovery for less than six hours. That isn't very long, given the surgery. There is swelling and this might just be a temporary setback."

"Maybe." Jason's quiet reply reverberated in the room.

"Get some rest. Tomorrow, if your legs are still numb and unmoving, we'll reassess." Asher's words felt hollow.

They were the right things to say, but he'd come in here expecting a celebration. Something to take his mind off his tumbling thoughts about Aurora.

Was that foolhardy? Yes. Still it didn't change what he'd anticipated.

His brain focused on the surgery, replaying the time in the OR. What if he'd failed? He'd been so certain he'd managed this surgery perfectly. All the other surgeons had turned it away...but Dr. Asher Parks could do this.

"Dr. Parks?"

Asher pushed his own feeling of failure away as looked at his patient. At the end of the day, the cancer was gone. They should be celebrating that...so much easier said than done.

"Thanks for getting the cancer." Jason blew out a breath. "Even if I don't—"

"Let's wait a full twenty-four hours past surgery before we start talking about don'ts," Asher interrupted.

"All right." Jason nodded, but he could see the worry waffling across his features.

"You need to get some rest." Aurora patted his hand. "It's the thing your body needs most right now."

Jason closed his eyes, and Aurora motioned for Asher to follow her.

He wanted to stay here. Wanted to spend the next several hours waiting to see if the nerve block or swelling or something more permanent was the issue. It was easier to focus on the issues with Jason, even if they weren't things he could fix at the moment.

Instead, he followed her.

"Jason isn't the only one that needs rest." Aurora's voice was light, but the words were direct and he could hear the authority behind them.

"The on-call room—"

"You need to rest in a real bed." She crossed her arms as her green eyes met his. "You can't do anything here, Asher. Come home and relax."

"I don't want to." He knew he sounded petulant, but he it was how he felt.

"Which is why you need to."

She was right; he knew that. "Is there a tea that can fix this?"

The joke was weak, but he saw the twitch of her lips. "Some believe there is a tea for everything, but you don't know that this needs fixing yet."

He pushed a hand through his hair, looked at Jason's closed door and wondered if there was something he'd missed. If he'd failed...

CHAPTER ELEVEN

"WHAT?" ASHER FORCED himself to look at Aurora. The mug of tea had cooled and he couldn't remember taking more than a sip or two. "Sorry, Aurora. What did you say?"

Aurora looked at him, her gaze holding his as he watched her weigh her words. How quickly he'd come to understand her looks. The bud of worry that was routinely crossing his mind pressed against him again.

He'd accepted her offer of a date, extending their union by one day. A single day... It wasn't an impulsive move, but he'd rethought it a few times too. So, what happened next?

He could get hurt here. Maybe not hurt like his father losing his mother—but what if it was that bad?

"I said—" Aurora laid her hand over his and all the worries, the concerns, floated away "—do you want me to warm up your tea? It's meant to be drunk hot. A soothing blend to help you rest. But cool it tastes a little bitter."

"Soothing blend?" Asher kissed the top her head before handing her the cup she was reaching for. "Are you trying to tell me something, princess?"

She didn't roll her eyes at the princess nickname anymore. In fact he thought she secretly liked it. Though he doubted she'd ever admit to that.

"Yes." Her mouth pursed as she set the tea in the microwave. Leaning against the counter, she tilted her head as the machine reheated his drink. "You aren't here."

Raising his arms, he turned in a slow circle. "I feel like I am right here." He playfully touched his nose and grinned. "See."

Aurora's face didn't change. Not even the tiniest movement of her lips. "Asher."

"I'm fine."

"I didn't ask." She crossed her arms. "But how did you word it…?" Laying a finger on her chin, she parroted his words back to him. "And I don't like to call people liars… but I think that might be a lie."

"You have an excellent memory." Mirroring her gesture, Asher crossed his arms, uncomfortable with the direction this was going.

"And you're avoiding the conversation. You're upset over a surgery that went fantastically."

"He can't feel his legs, Aurora!" The words echoed in the kitchen, and he was grateful that the condo on the other side of the wall was his.

"And there are multiple reasons why that might be." Aurora kept her tone even, but her voice was raised too. "And even if he can't, you removed the tumor—"

"I did it perfectly."

"Is this about Jason, or you?" Color rose in her cheeks and her eyes flashed.

"What the hell is that supposed to mean?" He felt his nose scrunch, the feeling of failure making him itchy. He wanted to run from this conversation. Wanted to run to her, and just let her hold him. Like he'd watched his parents do when they had troubled days.

And that amplified his fear. He never ran to other people. Not even Kate once upon a time.

"You know what it means. Is this about Jason, or about

you not doing a nearly impossible surgery perfectly? You are not a god."

"That isn't fair." He knew she was right. "I took the surgery when no one else did."

"To help the patient…or to prove to yourself that you are the best? To have an achievement that almost no other surgeon could boast?"

"I'm not your father."

"Not that different in some ways either."

"How dare you!" Asher spun out of the kitchen. "I am nothing like your father."

"You seek perfection…maybe only in yourself. But you are angry that six hours after a massive surgery on his spine, your patient isn't reacting the way you thought he would. You were expecting it to be not only perfect but miraculous, despite knowing the odds. Your entire focus is there, pushing everything else out."

Not quite everything, no matter how much he tried.

She took a deep breath and squared her shoulders, "Even if Jason doesn't regain the use of his legs, the surgery was a success."

"No! I was perfect." The microwave dinged, and he shook his head. "I don't need your anger, Rory."

The color drained from her face. She took a few steps back and shook her head.

"That came out wrong." Asher set his teacup down. "I just…" No words came.

"I think you should leave."

He wanted to kick himself at the relief spreading through him. He should stay, should try to find an explanation for why this bothered him so much. Except he was pretty sure that might mean opening himself up to how much he needed her.

Instead he took the coward's way out. "If that is what

you want." At least leaving demonstrated that he didn't need her. He hesitated for only a moment before heading for the door.

Aurora pulled the mug of tea from the microwave and wiped a tear away. She hadn't meant to push Asher…no. She'd meant to make him see that his brooding was unnecessary.

"Instead you started our first fight." She said the words into the empty kitchen, catching the sob at the back of her throat. *Maybe our only one.*

He'd sat on her couch not saying anything, not moving for almost twenty minutes before she'd broken the silence. She wasn't a surgeon, but she'd witnessed enough surgeries go south to know what success looked like.

When taking the surgery, he knew the possible outcomes. One hundred percent success was a great goal, but unrealistic. Yet it was still within his grasp. She thought there was a good chance that with a combination of the nerve block, the surgical swelling and the need for the body do some recovery, Jason might still have the miracle outcome.

It was Asher's response that was making her worry. He was a great surgeon. If he wasn't the best in Florida, he was certainly in the top three. Yet one would think he'd had to tell Jason's family the worst news.

And he'd snapped when she'd pushed him.

I don't need your anger, Rory.

Rory. Squeezing her eyes shut, she tried to remember the last time he'd called her Rory. From the moment he'd seen the cup, she'd become Aurora…or princess.

But the second she displayed anything more than happiness or excitement, she was suddenly Rory again.

And she hated it.

Unlike her father, Asher didn't mind all her emotions. No, laughter, smiles, joy. All of those were acceptable. But what about the harder things, sadness, frustration…anger? He'd never had those directed at him, until tonight. If you weren't free to show everything, were you really free?

"It's too late for this discussion, Aurora." She choked up as she poured his tea down the drain. Then pinched her nose. The twinge behind her eyes was threatening a full-blown migraine. She'd felt it at the wedding, but a relaxing day and a preemptive pain pill kept it away. She grabbed the pain reliever and hoped she'd caught it in time.

Her phone dinged, and Aurora grabbed for it. Her spirits dropped even further as the notification showed one of her friends instead of Asher.

Asher didn't bother to wipe away the sweat dripping down his forehead as he upped the speed of the treadmill for the fifth time. He wanted to go faster, needed to move as fast as his body would allow. Needed to push his body as much as possible. Regain some kind of control over himself.

His world was shifting. No, it had already tilted. The years of control he'd garnered keeping partners at a distance had slipped away. After a lifetime of never getting close, it was easy to pull back, to mentally retreat behind his internal walls.

Except Aurora had pushed away his retreat mechanism. The alarm bells that had sounded for years were silent against her smiles, her laughter, her words and her touch.

And last night he'd hurt her. The Rock finally let him in, completely. Yet the first time she showed frustration, he'd snapped. She'd pointed out obvious things, things his rational, medical side knew. It was the personal side, the overachiever so sure he could do what no one else could, pouting last night. And it had let him focus on Jason instead of his ever-escalating feelings for her.

But that wasn't Aurora's fault. Hurting her was the one thing he never wanted to do.

He'd slept fitfully, reaching for her soft, warm body over and over again in the night. One night of sleeping together and he found himself needing her just to rest.

Needing…there was that word. The emotion again.

His lifetime of retreating behind his mental wall wasn't an option now. Because Aurora had obliterated it. She hadn't even been trying either. That was the strangest thing. He'd dated a few women who'd made it their mission to pull away the bricks covering his heart. He'd successfully kept them away. But Aurora…

Aurora.

His heart pounded in his ears as he thought of her. How he wished there was an easy way to blame the experience on his elevated heart rate. He needed her, and he wasn't sure how to stop.

Turning up the music, he tried to focus on the heavy beat of the bass, matching his footsteps to the rhythm. Even with all the noise, he could still hear Aurora's voice.

"Asher!" She stepped in front of the treadmill, as if his thoughts had conjured her being.

He slowed the treadmill then pulled his earbuds out. "Aurora…"

"Jason can feel his legs." She held up a hand before he could say anything. "He's not moving more than his toes yet, but it appears to be a swelling issue."

"How?" He wiped his face and held on to the side of the treadmill as his breath came out in pants. "How do you know?"

She looked and him and then held up her phone. "You

see there is thing called a phone. You can use it to call the charge nurse."

"Snarky, Aurora?" He rolled his shoulders and pulled one arm across his chest, then the other as he stepped off the treadmill. He'd called the charge nurse last night three times and finally been told they'd let him know if there were any changes. Clearly, they just hadn't had a chance yet, and Aurora hadn't worn out her welcome with the nurses. "That is a side of you I haven't seen, princess."

Pinching the bridge of her nose, she tightly closed her eyes and took a deep breath. "Snark isn't a personality trait I like giving in to often. But it was a silly question."

"It was indeed." He tilted his head, the stretch in his neck feeling delicious, but it was concern over the woman in front of him driving the motion. She sucked in air between her teeth before starting for the gym's door.

Reaching for her, he pulled and hated the flinch crossing her brows and the sharp intake of air. "Aurora, about last night—"

"Can we leave before we have this conversation?" The wrinkle in her brows deepened as she took another deep breath and released the air through her teeth.

"What's wrong?" Panic raced across his spine. He understood her being frustrated with him. He deserved that... but there was no one else in the condo's gym this morning. Heck, he was usually the only one here; most of the residents ran outside or were members of the fancy location across the street offering significantly more machines and exercise classes.

No, something was wrong with Aurora.

"It's just a headache, but the lights in here are making me nauseous." Aurora closed her eyes, her body tilting to the side. She felt awful, and she'd still searched him out. And she'd called the charge nurse to check on his patient.

Even after he'd been a jerk. God, he didn't deserve her. But that was an issue for another time. Right now he needed to take care of her.

"Nausea and light sensitivity are not *just* a headache." Asher led her toward the door, his years of studying the brain racing through symptoms, focusing heavily on the worst-case scenarios. Because while rare, there were times when headaches snatched away your loved ones.

Stepping into the hall, Aurora started to shake her head, then immediately stopped. "It's a migraine. A terrible one, but I didn't sleep last night. Haven't had one in years but stress—and just life—triggered it. At least that is my guess."

"Do you have neck stiffness?" People put off an aneurysm diagnosis because they suspected a migraine. If his mother had gone to the hospital when she'd first felt the headache, his father might not have spent the last few decades sleeping alone.

"Didn't sleep well last night, Asher. So yes." Aurora wrapped her arms around herself, tilting to the left.

Was that an intentional tilt or was something else going on?

"I just wanted you to know about Jason, so I checked, and you didn't answer your phone. I took a chance you were burning off stress down here."

"I kept checking it, so it's in my gym bag. I have my smart watch set up to notify me if someone calls more than once."

She nodded and flinched again. "Okay. Well, I'm heading back to my condo. I already let my partners know that I can't work today."

"You did?" Asher knew his mouth was hanging open, but he couldn't remember Aurora calling out sick a single time in their career. "You never call out."

"Yes, well, there is a first time for everything." There was an underlying statement in her voice suggesting the statement was not just about her calling out, but he'd worry about that once he was certain she was all right.

"It wasn't a comment on you not attending surgeries, but this can't be the first headache you've had over the course of your career."

"Of course not." She rolled her eyes to the ceiling and immediately tilted again before catching herself.

"I know you're frustrated with me," he said as he held up his hands. "It's earned but I am talking about how bad the headache is, Rory."

"You only call me that when you're mad at me."

He wasn't sure that was an inaccurate statement, but he didn't want to investigate it now. "Did you take anything for the headache? And if so, when?"

Pushing the elevator button, Aurora sighed. "I've taken some over-the-counter meds. If they don't work in the next hour or so, I will call my primary care…" Her voice trailed off as her body shifted unnaturally.

In an instant, his world flashed before his eyes as Aurora slipped to the floor. It was blank…dark without her. A roar echoed in the hall that he knew came from him, but time slowed as he reached for her. "Aurora!" Her body was limp as his arms wrapped around her waist, barely catching her as she crumpled to the floor.

Pulling his phone from his pocket, he hit the emergency alert button. Blood pounded in his ears as he waited for the emergency operator to pick up. His fingers found her pulse, thready but steady. She was breathing…

"Aurora?" He'd never understood the television portrayals of this moment. People bent over their loved ones, shaking their shoulders. But it was all he wanted to do in this instance. Only years of medical training stilled his hands. "Aurora, baby. Open your eyes."

"911. What is your emergency?"

"I need an ambulance to 45 West Cove Road. By the elevator bank on Level 2."

"What is your emergency?"

The repeated question made him want to scream. Hadn't the operator listened to him? Had he told her? His mind was racing as he waited for Aurora to wake.

"My...my...my girlfriend complained of a headache and then collapsed. Please, send an ambulance. 45 West Cove Road." *Girlfriend* wasn't the right term. It was too much for what he and Aurora actually were...and somehow not enough either.

"Is she breathing?"

"Yes!" The yell echoed around them, as he felt for Aurora's pulse again.

"I need as much information as possible for the paramedics, sir."

"I know..." His voice cracked. Rationally he knew all of that, and when a patient was arriving at his hospital he needed all that information too.

"I've dispatched an ambulance. They should be arriving at your location shortly. Do they need anything to access the floor you're on?"

"The doorman can let them up. What is today?"

"Tuesday, sir." The operator was trying to keep him calm. In high-pressure situations people needed grounding, and operators often answered questions that had nothing to do with the crisis to help control the situation for the first responders.

"Tony is on duty. Tell them to let him know Dr. Parks is on Level 2 by the gym with Dr. Miller, who has collapsed following a headache. He'll waste no time getting them up here. What is their ETA?"

"About two minutes."

Two minutes…a blink of an eye and forever all at once. "Asher…"

His name was so soft, he thought he might have imagined it. "Aurora?"

"My head hurts." Aurora closed her eyes, her breath slow but steady.

"I know, princess. I know. We are going to get it checked out." If this was more than a migraine, there was no way he could operate, but his partner Meredith was on call today. If it couldn't be him, he'd want Meredith.

"The migraine was causing an aura." Aurora's hand pushed against his cheek. "Aura and no pain behind my eyes."

Listing the common differences between aneurysms and migraines wasn't going to stop him from making sure she had a full screen at the hospital. But he knew she was trying to reassure him. However, nothing was going to do that until he was sure she was fine.

"Dr. Parks!" The voice came through the elevator before the doors had fully opened. Paisley Lots and her new fiancé, Dean Ontr, stepped from the elevator.

Aurora started to sit up but Asher put a hand on her shoulder. "Stay down, princess. Let Paisley and Dean take a look at you."

He saw Paisley look at Dean following his endearment and he could see the silent conversation happening between them. He didn't care what they thought of his nickname for Aurora. All that mattered was that she was okay.

"She complained of a headache, light sensitivity, neck stiffness—"

"From sleeping weird." Aurora's interjection lightened his soul a bit. If she was arguing, that was a good sign.

"And the collapse? Was that just swooning over my good looks?" Asher patted her hand. The joke felt good, but it also let Paisley and Dean know she'd collapsed too.

"How long was she unconscious?" Paisley knelt next to Aurora's head as Dean started taking her vitals.

"Not long." Aurora started to cross her arms, but Dean straightened them out as he secured the blood pressure cuff.

"Were you timing yourself while your eyes were closed, princess?" Asher's response was light, but he was determined she be seen at the hospital. He'd throw her over his shoulder and carry her there himself if necessary.

Paisley chuckled, but he knew it was a forced laugh to defuse the situation rather than a funny sound. "Doctors really are the worst patients, aren't they, Dean?"

"I don't know. Paramedics might be top…followed closely by doctors."

His fiancée ignored that statement as she focused on Aurora, though he saw her cheek twitch. Clearly there was some inside story between the two of them.

"Her blood pressure is eighty-nine over fifty-nine."

Hypotension. The technical term for low blood pressure, it was discussed rarely compared to its opposite, hypertension. Low blood pressure could cause syncope, fainting spells, and migraines occasionally caused it.

"We are going to transport you to Mercy, Dr. Miller." Paisley nodded to her fiancé and partner as he lowered the transport bed.

"I suppose it is for the best." Aurora closed her eyes.

"If you don't go with us, I suspect Dr. Parks will make you go with him." Dean looked at Asher, and he saw an expression in his face, a sympathy Asher didn't quite understand.

"I will." He wasn't as fearful now that she was awake. Her cheeks weren't as pale, and her breath was even, though she still flinched at light. The sooty imprints under her eyes indicative of sleepless night—a reminder that he'd walked out last night. She'd suggested he leave, but he hadn't argued, hadn't even considered it.

If he'd stayed, argued with her then made up, would she be in this situation today? Stress triggered migraines...but it also could trigger an undiagnosed aneurysm.

"I'll meet you at the hospital." Asher kissed the top of her head before Dean and Paisley rolled the transport bed to the elevator bank. "I'm right behind you. Promise."

"We'll take good care of her," Dean declared as he watched Paisley pull Aurora into the elevator. "I know what it's like when your heart lives outside your body." Then he stepped in with his fiancée and partner.

Heart outside your body...

Asher slid down the wall and sucked in a few deep breaths. He'd hurt Aurora last night, argued with her, caused the lack of sleep and now she was headed to the hospital. Correlation did not equal causation. It didn't...

He was accomplishing nothing sitting here. Standing, Asher headed for the elevators. He'd check on Aurora. Apologize for his behavior last night, then he'd pull back. He wasn't worth sleepless nights, migraines or anything else.

CHAPTER TWELVE

AURORA SLIPPED ON her shoes as Asher studied the MRI and CT scans for at least the tenth time. The CT scan showed no abnormalities, but Asher had pushed for the MRI with contrast to rule out an infection. An ask only granted because it was Asher making the demand.

"I have a normal brain, Asher." She stood, grateful for the dihydroergotamine and metoclopramide the emergency room doctor had ordered. The IV drug combination reduced the symptoms of the migraine. Now all she wanted to do was crawl into bed and sleep for the next ten hours.

"Nothing about you is normal, Aurora." Asher turned off the scans the ER doctor had projected onto the room's screen. "However, your brain is healthy. Just me causing a migraine."

Exhaustion must be clogging her ears. "Asher, you didn't." A person didn't cause a migraine. Triggers made them worse for some people, but the simple answer was usually the right one.

She was a ball of stress, even if she covered it well. Aurora's therapist once told her that she wasn't sure she knew what unstressed felt like. And stress was one of the major triggers for migraines.

Maybe the situation following Jason's surgery exacerbated it, but she was overworked and concerned about the charity event where she knew her dad was attending. She could avoid him, but… And she was hurt that the man she cared about was upset. Hurt that he'd kept her out last night.

Refused to talk to her about the surgery, other than demanding that it was perfect. Something else was going on; she was nearly certain. But if he wouldn't talk to her… well, that hurt.

Combine that with not sleeping and you had a recipe for a bad day. Which was all today was.

"Well, it won't happen again."

Why did his words sound ominous? It was a migraine, and arguments happened. That was human nature.

"Asher…" A yawn overtook her.

"Let's get you home," Asher wrapped an arm around her waist.

She was too drained to argue, but tomorrow… Leaning her head against his shoulder, she let his warmth comfort her.

"Want to take a nap with me?"

Yes.

He wanted nothing more than to snuggle up next to Aurora. Hold her tight and cling to the fantasy of happiness for a few more hours. However, he'd made a decision. He was too close to Aurora.

He could still pull back, still protect them. It might hurt a little but it would hurt less now than it would if he waited any longer. There were only a few days before the charity event and then their final date. He'd schedule a trip to the painting store, enjoy one more perfect day…then cut the connection between them. But to do that successfully he needed to detach some now.

Otherwise he wasn't sure he'd manage it.

"I need to get some things done. And I want to go back to the hospital to check in on Jason." They were the right words, but it hurt to utter them.

Aurora leaned against her door. "I need a nap. My head feels better but I'm still a little fuzzy." She lifted up on her toes and kissed his cheek. "But how about dinner? We can go over my plan for when we see my father at the charity event…and if he talks to us."

"If anyone caused my migraine it was me, worrying about all the things." The smile flicking across her face wasn't real. She was trying to make him feel better.

She really was perfect.

He should say no, but he heard the "yes" slip from his lips.

"I'll see you at seven-thirty?"

He nodded. "Seven-thirty."

"Look! I moved my leg." Jason's happy tone carried in the room. "Just a few inches, but still!"

"Dr. Miller was right. It looks like the swelling and nerve block was what caused the issue." Asher pulled out his phone, intending to text Aurora to let her know.

No.

She was hopefully still napping. And he was stepping back. That meant not reaching for her, or out to her, every time he wanted to.

"My legs still feel heavy. Is that the nerve block?"

Sliding his phone back into his pocket, Asher stood. He wasn't on call right now, so treating Jason wasn't an option. But he could at least relieve a bit of his fear.

"You were immobile for almost forty-eight hours. I know that doesn't sound like a terribly long time, but to your muscles it's forever. The human body is never fully immobile. We even move in our sleep." Asher leaned back, stretching his muscles.

"It is an unwritten rule that for every day you are in a hospital bed, it's three days of recovery. Give it time."

"Patience is a virtue." Jason hit his fists against the rails of the bed. "That was what my mom always said. I know everything went better than I should expect. Yet…"

"Yet you want more." Asher understood the need. The desire to want more. To constantly keep achieving. Climb every mountain. Especially the ones people said were hard. It kept uncomfortable thoughts away too.

The room's door opened and Dr. Levern stuck his head in. "Dr. Parks, can you take a look at a case for me?"

The timer on his watch went off at almost the same time. He needed to head home if he wanted to make dinner with Aurora.

"I think it may be an impossible case."

"Impossible?" That was his catnip. The thing he chased…the type of surgery he could contemplate instead of the threads of thoughts about Aurora. A way to focus on something other than the deep need in his soul.

Asher grabbed his phone and sent a quick text to let Aurora know he'd be a little late. "Nothing is impossible."

The clock ticked to nine-thirty, and Aurora shook her head as she boxed up the final bits of the dinner she'd saved for Asher. Two hours past their date time was too long to wait for "a little late."

It wasn't like she'd made anything fancy. Hell, she was wearing yoga pants with a top knot that had slipped well past the messy-bun stage. This wasn't a big deal…

So why did it hurt so much?

At eight she'd texted to ask if he was headed back yet or if she should just put the food away.

On my way!

The response would be funny if she wasn't feeling pathetic for believing it. Something had shifted after Dani's wedding. And her migraine had exacerbated whatever the issue was.

Sure, the fainting was scary. It was terrifying to wake up on the ground with no memory of how you got there. But Asher seemed different.

The carefree nature he'd mastered hid a much deeper soul. It felt like she'd gotten a peak into the real Asher. Then Jason's surgery had thrown their easy relationship into something that felt real.

A real relationship wasn't easy. It wasn't the stuff of fairy tales. It was honesty. It was pushing your partner when something was wrong. It was more than jokes and fun. It was the good times *and* the bad.

Except he'd hated her pushing him. Happy Aurora was fun, an emotional being he wanted to bring out. What if she released all the emotions bubbling up from her soul? A person wasn't only happy, joyful or serene.

Life was difficult. They worked demanding jobs, and her family was prone to more drama than she enjoyed. That meant anger, frustration and sadness would invade their lives. That was life and she wouldn't throw those things away.

She stepped into the hallway just as a note slid under her door. She didn't bother to pick it up before opening the door, anger filling her belly.

"You weren't even going to knock?"

Asher was almost to his door and flipped around. His nose scrunched, and she hated that she knew him well enough to know that was an annoyed response. Hated that she was standing in the hallway facing the man she loved, who'd slipped a note under her door rather than knock when he was late.

It felt desperate. And Dr. Aurora Miller was a lot of things. But she was *not* desperate.

"I thought you might be asleep. I didn't want to wake you." He shifted, his hands digging into the pockets of his jeans. Dark circles highlighted the exhaustion she knew he felt.

They'd come back from the wedding only four days ago. Four days and everything was different. After Jason's surgery...

After I got angry.

No. She was not going to take on the blame for this. "You said a little late, Asher. I just put dinner away...you could have at least called me."

"Are you trying to start a fight, Rory?"

Rory. Third time was the charm. The only time he referred to her by her father's chosen nickname was when he was angry with her. But what had she done to deserve it?

"A fight?" She crossed her arms, mentally retreating behind the walls she'd erected so long ago. They'd felt safe for so long, but now controlling herself felt confining. But she was not going to have a blowout fight over dinner in the hallway of their condo.

"You haven't even apologized for standing me up."

"It is in the note." Asher pushed his hand through his hair. "I mean, I am sorry. I am so sorry, Rory."

"Don't apologize if you don't mean it." She felt her bottom lip twitch. She was going to lose the loose grip she had on her control.

He moved toward her, "That's not fair!" His feet halted as the exclamation radiated down the hall. "There was a case Dr. Levern needed help on. A case he called impossible."

"And you couldn't resist." He wasn't her father, but in

some ways they were very alike. Pride controlled more than it should. Her father wanted outside praise…she wasn't sure exactly what Asher was chasing. But it couldn't be found in the OR. Of that she was certain.

Asher pulled on the back of his neck. "It's an anaplastic ependymoma, recurrent and in the frontal lobe. It's starting to cause personality changes."

Aurora wasn't unsympathetic to the patient's plight anaplastic ependymoma was a tumor that formed in the central nervous system, often in the brain or brain stem. It typically multiplied rapidly and could be very difficult to treat.

She understood all of that, better than most partners would, and if he'd called or texted or just been honest and said he didn't know when he'd be back… This didn't have to be that difficult.

"Rory—"

That broke her. She'd spent her life listening to others call her Rory. A lifetime of accepting a nickname her father chose because she was a girl. But Asher's use of her real name had helped her feel whole. Him retreating back to her nickname felt like betrayal.

She held up a hand. "I am going to bed. I will see you tomorrow. Maybe by then you will be calm enough to call me Aurora again."

She didn't wait for a response. Didn't trust herself not to rage cry at his use of her nickname. That shouldn't be what was affecting her so much…but it was.

CHAPTER THIRTEEN

Looking to schedule surgery for patient we talked about yesterday. Availability?

ASHER RUBBED HIS EYES, the motion doing little to fix the sandpapery feel from sleepless nights. The surgery he'd stayed to discuss with Dr. Levern yesterday. The reason he'd missed dinner with Aurora.

Just get it scheduled. I'll make it work.

He shot the text back as he poured his second cup of coffee. If there was a way to hook up the machine to inject the caffeine directly into his veins this morning he'd take the option. He needed to talk to Aurora.

Needed to offer a real apology. Try to find a way to explain why he'd acted like such as ass. The worst part was that he'd called her Rory…repeatedly.

It wasn't intentional.

No. If he was honest it was, but not because he was angry with her. It was easier to think of Aurora as Rory knowing that they were going to go back to being friends and colleagues. He needed to retreat. Protect both of them from the pain of love ending. Because that was a truth he couldn't escape.

"Lying to yourself doesn't do you any good. You love her and this is going to hurt." He downed the mug of coffee and poured the last of the coffee into his cup as the words he'd spoken to himself evaporated in the kitchen.

It wasn't the bone-deep love his parents had. No, their attraction was still surface level. They could still fall back into their old roles. They could.

He had to. Seeing her fall, fearing losing her…he couldn't do that. He was too much like his father; he'd lose himself if he wasn't careful.

Setting the empty mug on the counter, Asher threw a bit of cold water on his face, hoping that might clear the final cobwebs from his brain. Then he forced himself to walk to Rory's… Aurora's.

Why does my brain keep doing that?

She answered on the third knock. The dark circles under her eyes were deeper today, but she looked like she felt better.

"I should have called last night."

"You should have." Aurora crossed her arms, her green eyes poring over him. In the past few weeks she'd gone from showing no emotion with him to being an open book.

And he hated the anger he'd brought out. Hated that he deserved it.

"I am sorry. Dr. Levern called it impossible and I…"

"That is your catnip for whatever reason." Aurora's body softened as she pushed back from her door. "Do you want a cup of coffee? I needed something stronger than tea."

"Already had three cups."

Aurora raised a brow but she didn't say anything as she poured herself a mug.

"Impossible cases are not my catnip." Asher leaned against her counter.

Aurora's eyes pierced him over the rim of her pink mug. "Please. In that way you are very like my father. Chasing the impossible, adding another success to an already impressive set of accolades."

"I am not your father."

"I didn't say you were." She rolled her shoulders. "But you got angry when I made you examine Jason's case as a success, even if it wasn't a complete success."

"Frustrated. I was frustrated." It was a small distinction but one he felt inclined to point out.

She made a noncommittal noise. "The point is that you can't control everything. Sometimes life happens. Things happen…feelings… Things you don't count on."

Silence stretched between them, and they were no longer discussing the hospital or patients. His heart raced as he looked at her. This was a turning point…if he only took it. His heart screamed for him to try, but fear stilled his words.

"Doesn't mean I can't try!" The jokey voice he used sounded hollow this morning.

"Asher."

"Aurora." He grinned and leaned over to kiss her cheek. "I don't want to spend any of our time fighting."

They were speeding toward a deadline. Even if they'd pushed their limit by twenty-four hours. This…this wonderful, blissful time would end.

"I see." She blew out a breath.

There was a hint of something in the words. A tingle slid down his back. He'd lost something here, something precious. "Aurora—"

When he didn't say anything, she looked at him. "Yes?"

"I don't know. Lost my train of thought." It was a lie. His chest ached for him to tell her the truth. To tell her he loved her.

To throw a lifetime of control and safety aside. The image of his father sitting silent at the kitchen table flashed in front of him. The hurt still palpable after all these years.

He opened his mouth, but once more the words refused to come.

"I need to get a few things done before my shift." Aurora kissed his cheek, but he felt her slip away.

"I'll see you at the hospital."

She smiled, but it was the Rock standing here now. She'd slid back behind her walls. And that was why he couldn't get attached.

Aurora could slip behind her walls, protect herself from the fallout of their relationship. Asher knew himself. He was his father's son. He felt everything. Love brought his father to his knees, and it nearly destroyed Asher, once. He wouldn't do that again.

No matter how much he cared for Aurora.

"Dr. Miller, are those teacups on your scrubs?" Diego Arnold, the newest anesthesiologist to join their team, pointed.

Aurora grinned as she looked at the pink scrubs with teacups all over them. There were specific scrubs the hospital provided for the operating theater, but for general rounds, physicians could choose their own.

She'd bought these on a whim, years ago, and promptly pushed them to the back of her closet, never choosing them over her plain blue ones. But this morning, she'd grabbed the top and slid it on.

She loved it. She was stepping into herself. Better late than never. Asher had helped her see that. Now if only he'd open himself up to her.

"I like it." Diego pointed to the small embroidery above

the pocket of his scrubs. "It's small but the *i* in my name that my wife embroidered is a little coffee mug."

"Perfect."

"It is." He paused. "Speaking of my lovely bride, any chance you can cover a surgery for me on Saturday morning? The twins' soccer game was rained out last week, and my wife reminded me that I have yet to see the girls play this season. Who even schedules a surgery for six in the morning on a Saturday? Geez."

Aurora looked up from the tablet chart in her hand and shook her head. She felt bad for him. She knew Diego was doing his best to be an active father. Not the easiest thing in their profession.

Aurora had never felt called to motherhood. Though it had annoyed her when she'd been questioned about her family plans upon entering the specialty. She loved her job; it completed her. She often took shifts for others when their family obligations conflicted with surgeries.

However, that wasn't an option this weekend.

"I've already agreed to attend a charity event this weekend benefiting cancer research. It's a brunch and I've got two seats for the practice…"

"I understand. That is important too." Diego leaned his head back and then dropped it forward. "Leona is going to kill me for missing another game day. But it's not my fault that Dr. Parks scheduled a surgery with little warning."

He shook his head as he pulled out his cell. "I know emergencies come up, but he wasn't even on the schedule." He turned his back as he said into the phone, "Sweetheart…"

Aurora's skin flamed then cold washed through her. Asher had scheduled a surgery for Saturday. Saturday…

She wanted to curl into a ball and weep, wanted to scream, wanted to do so many things. None of which she was going to give in to. Theirs had always been a temporary arrangement.

A little more than a friends-with-benefits situation.

She let out a sad chuckle, and waved her hand when Diego turned to look at her.

She and Asher weren't friends. She loved him. She wouldn't deny that truth, but it was over. It some ways it had ended the night she got frustrated.

He'd changed. Maybe he didn't realize it but she'd noticed. The moment her emotions went from the fun, playful Aurora to the more serious one, Asher had started pulling away.

And now he'd scheduled a surgery on the day of the charity event. Sure it wasn't the wedding, but her father was going to be there. Probably ignoring her, but she'd wanted a friendly face. No. She'd wanted Asher.

There weren't words to describe the hurt rolling through her.

Asher strolled through the door, and Diego turned as Aurora did to look at him.

"I'll call you back." Diego slid his phone into his back pocket then crossed his arms.

Aurora knew her face was stone; at least her father's many betrayals had prepared her for this moment. Asher's eyes slid from her to Diego and back again.

"Two upset anesthesiologists." Asher held up his hands. "What if I walk out the door and then walk back in wearing a silly face?"

Neither she nor Diego moved.

"Tough crowd." Asher grinned, but it wasn't real. How quickly she'd come to see behind the mask he wore for everyone else.

She was the Rock, but Asher's funny-man persona was an illusion too.

"I just had to call my wife and explain that I was going to miss our twins' soccer game this weekend."

Asher tilted his head. "I am sorry about that."

"You scheduled a surgery…" Aurora's voice cracked. She saw Diego's head shift toward her, but she didn't look away from Asher. "For Saturday morning?"

He opened his mouth then closed it. "Aurora, I'll be done before the brunch. The surgery starts at six. It'll last three hours. Out by nine-thirty and at the venue by ten-thirty. No problem."

Diego shifted and headed for the door. "My wife is frustrated, but I'm gonna step out on this one. We'll talk about the patient later."

Asher nodded to Diego as he left.

"Aurora…"

"Don't worry about it." The words slipped from her mouth before she'd even thought them through. "I'll go on my own."

"The surgery will be over—"

"Why do *you* have to do this?" *Tell me what is going on?* She barely kept that final plea inside.

"I just do."

Such a nonanswer. It nearly broke her. "And what if something goes wrong? What if the patient doesn't recover as quickly as you like?

"Will you even be in the mood to have any fun with me?"

"I'll be fine. We'll get through it fine."

That wasn't an answer to the question she'd asked, but it was revealing. *And it hurt.*

"The patient needs the tumor removed." Asher took a step toward her, and she could see the frustration on his face.

"And no other doctor can do it?" Aurora asked, knowing there were other options. Asher was the best, but that didn't mean that the others in his practice weren't nearly as accomplished.

"Dr. Loep or Dr. Kuil? What about Dr. Reges? They're all excellent surgeons, aren't they?" She was impressed by the quiet of her voice when all she wanted to do was scream. "And the tumor must come out on Saturday?"

"It was the first open operating time." Asher's nose scrunched, but she didn't care that he was annoyed.

"The first open operating time." Aurora shook her head. "We both know for surgeries deemed emergency the OR is ready to go. Monday, Tuesday, Wednesday…all days that were options." Blowing out a breath, she let the energy inside go, at least for now.

"Don't worry about the event, Asher. I'll go on my own."

"Rory—"

The thread of control she'd maintained snapped, "I am only Aurora when you are happy with me. Not when I am not kicking up a fuss or pushing you, or forcing you to look past the happy-go-lucky mask you wear. Otherwise I am Rory."

Water swam in her eyes, but she was not going to lose any more control, not here. "At least my father is honest about me failing to meet his standards."

His mouth hung open.

No jokes to be found now.

She inwardly cringed at the unkind thought. "Goodbye, Asher."

Shifting her shoulders, she took a deep breath. Then Aurora grabbed the tablet chart and headed out for her rounds. The Rock was fully in control. There'd be time to mourn this loss, but not here. Not now.

CHAPTER FOURTEEN

Asher passed Aurora in the hall, but she didn't make eye contact with him. In the past two days, he'd forced himself to keep his distance. Forced himself to act as though nothing was bothering him.

Because the Rock was unfazed. She wore her cute new scrubs, and her hair wasn't always pulled into a tight bun. Aurora had finally relaxed. That should thrill him, but instead he was stunned that she'd moved past what they had so fast. Sure, they'd said it wasn't real…and he'd set the timeline.

But it still stung that she was all right.

"The surgery tomorrow," Diego began as he handed him a tablet chart. "Your patient checked in with a fever of one hundred and one point three degrees."

"A fever?" Asher forced his eyes away from the room Aurora had entered. The lab results were still pending but it didn't matter. There was no way for him to operate on a sick patient.

The surgery he'd impulsively scheduled to keep his mind off the feelings he was developing for Aurora wasn't happening. He'd known it was a mistake the moment he'd agreed to it.

She was right. There were others that could do it. Or it

could have waited, but he'd wanted the distraction. Anything to focus on besides the feelings rocketing off inside.

Can't get hurt if you leave a relationship first.

So why do I feel so terrible?

The end of their fake fling hurt more than discovering his best man in bed with Kate. The weight of that discovery resulted in weeks in soul-crushing heartbreak.

But this… This felt like the world was darker. Like the colors had dimmed and the sounds weren't clear. The happiness and joy had been sucked out of it. He'd coped when his mother passed and when Kate cheated by losing himself in jokes and achievements.

But none of that was keeping the weight of losing Aurora at bay…and he wasn't sure anything ever would again.

"I will be on call, but I don't plan on being at the hospital. If you need me, have the page sent. But, man, if it isn't an emergency I will make you deal with my wife's fury." Diego pulled his phone out of his pocket and sent a quick text before holding up the phone.

"See! I told her…you don't want to deal with a furious Leona!"

"Do you ever wish you weren't married? You wouldn't have other responsibilities? Wouldn't matter if you upset anyone?" Asher's head snapped back as he held up his hands. "Diego, I am so sorry. I don't know where that came from."

"I think you do." Diego slipped his hands into his pockets.

Asher looked at his feet, unable to think of anything silly or funny to deflect this conversation. All his jokes had disappeared with Aurora too.

"No, Asher. I never wish I wasn't married. Leona is the best thing that ever happened to me. And she'll tell you that if you ask her." He let out a chuckle, clearly thinking of something about the woman he loved.

"Dr. Levern is on call tomorrow. I was only coming in for the surgery, so there is no way for your Leona to get mad at me." Asher winked. "Hope the kids score lots of goals."

"They're four. No one scores…it's basically just a ton of kids clustered around the ball. The coach calls it bumblebee soccer at this age since it looks like a hive moving from one end of the field to the other." Diego raised his hand. "Have a good evening, Dr. Parks."

"You too, Dr. Arnold."

"Excuse me, Dr. Parks." Aurora pointed to the door behind him. "I need to chart before I head home."

"The surgery tomorrow is canceled."

Aurora made a noise he couldn't quite decipher as she slipped behind one of the desks in the on-call suite and pulled up her charts. Her eyes never left the screen. He should leave, but he didn't want to.

"The patient has a fever."

The click of keys as she charted out her notes was the only sound in the room.

"I could still come tomorrow. If you didn't want to go alone." Asher swallowed, hoping Aurora would at least consider the offer. Maybe it was selfish but he wasn't quite ready to say goodbye.

And maybe that was okay.

"I don't think that is a good idea." The click of the keys created an unsettling hum in the room.

He should leave, shouldn't push but… "Why?"

"What happens after tomorrow, Asher? After Sunday?" Aurora clicked through a few more screens.

Was there a hint of uncertainty in her tone? He wanted to say no. Wanted to believe that there was some kind of undertone, but the truth was all he heard was the Rock's clear tone.

She'd slipped so easily back into her old self...why couldn't he?

"After?" He knew his nose was scrunched...knew he was clinging to a few more precious seconds with the woman before him.

"Six weeks is what you give your girlfriends, isn't it? Six weeks of fun, then you part while everything is still fun, right? No hurt feelings."

It felt like a trap, but he waded in anyway. "Yes."

"And we are almost there." She clicked a few more buttons then turned, her gaze holding his.

"We are."

"I broke rule number one." Aurora crossed her arms. Her lips pursed then she took a deep breath. "I broke it and there is no going back."

"Rule number one is don't fall in love." That couldn't be right. She couldn't have broken that rule. She'd looked fine since they'd parted while he was barely holding it together!

Plus this wasn't exactly what a declaration of love was supposed to look like. Though he'd only done it once. Kate had made a big deal of it, then... Well, then it had crashed and burned.

"I know what the rule is, Asher. I made it." Turning back to the computer, she closed out her account. "I don't want another few days. I want it all."

"Maybe, uh, we could try long-term?" Four words. Four words he knew he might regret for the rest of his life. He'd lost himself after Kate's betrayal. He had his father's heart. He knew that. For her, he could try.

Aurora closed her eyes, her body wobbling for just a moment. But when she opened her eyes, her face was set. No emotion. "I'm not asking for long-term."

The words felt like a hammer as they dropped. The air in the room evaporated and he felt like he was falling through the universe. He'd offered a potential relationship, more than he'd offered anyone since his ex-fiancée's betrayal, and Aurora turned it down.

Maybe he hadn't acted as excited as he could, but just the offer had nearly choked him on its way out. The worry that he was setting himself up for more pain. To be a walking ghost…

And she wasn't asking him to extend his deadline. Wasn't asking him to try. His heart felt like it was splitting in two.

He wanted more time, but a lifetime of protecting the gentle heart he knew rested in his soul pressed against him.

She stepped around the desk, her features never moving, no anger, no disappointment, nothing. She was fine… or she would be.

And him…? He was fine too. He was. Maybe if he said it enough it might be true.

CHAPTER FIFTEEN

Aurora stood in her bathroom, staring at the strips of pink she'd dyed in her hair. What had she done? It was rash and unpredictable. The exact opposite of everything she'd done the rest of her life.

Her eyes slid to the box of hair dye Asher bought. He'd joked on their way home that she must want it if she wasn't stuffing it into the trash can immediately.

And he'd been right. Like so many other things, he just seemed to know about her.

Following their breakup... Could she really call it that? They'd argued after he'd scheduled the surgery. Then had a tense conversation when it was cancelled. Maybe it wasn't a traditional breakup, but she felt broken.

And she needed to do something. After spending two days in his presence at the hospital, barely keeping it together she was ready to shatter. She'd never understood why people cut their hair immediately after a relationship ended. But after this afternoon...could she even call it a breakup?

Did something with a known end date ending mean anything?

Boy, was that a messed-up series of words her mind put together. Whatever she'd had with Asher was over. That was all that mattered.

She'd told him she'd broken rule one. Told him she loved him and he hadn't said it back. Instead he'd said maybe they could try long-term.

Maybe. A world he'd forced out. A word like a knife to her soul. But her eyes were finally dry. Only through sheer force of will had she managed to turn down Asher's offer.

She'd wanted to scream yes. Wanted to cling to a few more weeks, with the hopes that he might open up to her like she'd opened up to him. Finally letting each other see all the light and the dark they had to offer.

It was the *maybe* that stopped her.

Such a simple two-syllable word with so much wiggle room. She didn't want wiggle room. Aurora loved Asher. She wanted more than *maybe*. She wanted it all.

Happiness and love were easy, but she wanted the hard things too. The anger, the frustration, the bad days that made you treasure the good ones. All the emotions, not just the fun ones.

Asher had helped her realize her father wasn't avoiding all emotions. Not really. He was competitive, demanded the best out of his daughters, but it was loss he always ran from.

She didn't know why. Perhaps her mother's abandonment had hit him harder than he wanted to admit. Maybe it was something from his childhood. But his burden wasn't hers to carry. Not anymore.

She was living her own life now. The woman she wanted to be, the woman she was, had strips of pink hair. Drank tea out of silly bright mugs. Wore colorful scrubs. She laughed and made jokes with her colleagues. She was real.

None of that meant she wouldn't be professional. It just meant the Rock had cracked and the woman hiding under the stone wanted to be seen. And she'd wanted to share all that with Asher.

Except each time they'd treaded close to those emotions, Asher pulled away. With him especially, she wanted to be her authentic self. And that was worth more than a few extra weeks. Clinging to the illusion wasn't good for either of them.

When he'd approached her today, she'd pulled back into herself. Hidden behind the mask she'd used for so long. And it felt false. She knew it always had, but she hadn't been willing to be authentic. She'd still been living with the restrictions her father placed on her and her sister. Restrictions she'd placed on herself in hopes of winning the competition her father forced her and Dani to play.

But she was done restricting herself.

Asher pulled into his father's driveway and leaned his head against the steering wheel. It was early, and his father wasn't expecting him, but he hadn't been able to go home with Aurora a doorway away.

So close and so far.

His father tapped on the car's window. "You want something to eat?"

Asher opened the door, and before he could think it through asked, "If you knew all the pain losing Mom would cause, would you have married her? Or even gone out with her? If you could save yourself decades of pain, would you?"

His father didn't answer; he just wrapped his arms around his son's shoulders and held him. For the first time since Aurora found out about the surgery he'd scheduled, he lost it. In the Florida heat, he gave in to the grief of letting her walk away.

Asher didn't know how much time passed as his father simply held him.

"You want some eggs?"

"Yeah. And coffee," Asher added as he wiped his eyes. His soul was still bereft, but it felt a tiny bit lighter too.

"Of course." His father walked up the steps to the small home Asher had grown up in. The entire home would fit in his luxury condo with a little room left over, but it was where his mother had brought him home from the hospital. Where his parents danced in the kitchen. It was simply a home.

His father didn't say anything as he plated the food and passed the coffee. Asher tapped his foot on the floor in rhythm with his finger. Had his dad forgotten his questions, or did he just not want to answer them?

The food sat on the plates before them and his father raised his mug, took a healthy swig and then offered, "Yes to your first two questions. And no to your third."

His father's wrinkled hand wrapped around Asher's wrist. "If I had known how limited my time was with your mother, I would have loved her the same. Maybe with more force."

"Not sure that was possible." Asher lifted his coffee and wished it was some fancy tea he couldn't pronounce.

"I could have tried." His father smiled as he looked at the picture of his bride on their wedding day so many decades ago. "And I wouldn't have spared myself the pain to avoid loving her. But I would have spared you my reaction, if I could."

"I was so mad at you." The words slipped out and Asher shook his head. "I didn't mean that."

"I think you did. And I am happy to hear it." His father shrugged. "I won't pretend that I handled grief well. Everything stopped."

"You didn't talk for one hundred and sixty-nine days." Asher took a long sip of his coffee. "One hundred and sixty-nine days of silence. Then you laughed at one of my jokes. Part of me is still mad."

He hung his head, not wanting his father to see the shame that word brought.

"I think that is fair. I suspect part of you will always be mad. And that is okay." His father squeezed his hand. "I love you. I can handle your pain and anger too."

"Really?" Asher nearly knocked the silverware off the table.

"Of course." His father held up a hand. "You are her legacy, and I know she is so proud of you. I was so lost those first few months, I lost myself and I lost you."

"You didn't lose me." Asher shook his head, not quite understanding. They had a great relationship. He knew what a poor parental relationship looked like and it did not look like the one before him right now.

"I did. I lost your smile…your humor for humor's sake. You dived into academics as your way to hide from the pain. You use success and jokes to hide from hard things."

"I…" Asher opened his mouth but no more words came out. School had come easy, so he'd tried advanced classes. Pushed himself so he didn't have to feel anything. Dived into one the most complex specialties.

"Aurora said that too." The surgery. He'd watched Aurora suffer a terrible migraine, worried about losing her and immediately gravitated toward a difficult surgery. She'd even tried to force him to face his desire to work on such difficult cases.

And he'd dismissed her.

"I loved your mom like you love Aurora."

"We haven't been together long enough and it wasn't even supposed to be real. I love her but it's not the same… not as deep." The words were broken as he tried to work through all the information he was taking in.

"Now you're lying to yourself. I saw it with my own eyes when she was here. I loved your mother from our second date. I didn't tell her for months, worried she wouldn't feel the same. That I would change." His father let out a sigh.

"Aurora loves me." He bit his lip. "She told me yesterday that she'd broken her first rule."

"And you didn't tell her you loved her? Asher…"

He pushed back from the table. "It felt…normal. We were at the hospital. We had argued…love is supposed to be big grand gestures."

"No." His father shook his head. "Big gestures are for the movies. Love is every day, if you do it right. It's making breakfast for your partner. It's going to boring work events and taking care of them when they are ill. It is terribly everyday and that is why it is so perfect."

"I don't want to hurt like I did when Kate…" He wrapped his arms around himself. Like he wasn't already more devastated than he'd been all those years ago. "Or like you did with Mom." And there was the real fear, finally spoken aloud.

"Kate's betrayal is not Aurora's fault. It has nothing to do with her." His father's voice was soft, but he heard the truth in it. "And don't lose Aurora's love because you're terrified of walking this planet without her." His dad gripped his hand.

He looked at his watch: a little after nine. He needed to see Aurora. Now!

"Go."

"Thanks!"

Thump. Thump.

Aurora set aside the book she hadn't really been reading and looked at her watch. Almost nine. She'd need to leave in an hour. She didn't want to get her hopes up. It wasn't Asher. He'd left first thing this morning.

And she hated how she knew that. How accustomed she'd gotten to hearing his footsteps outside her door. Or the gentle hum of the television on the other side of her wall. Never loud enough for her to make out what he was watching, though it was probably sports. Just enough to know he was there.

"Aurora. Please. I need to see you."

Asher's voice stalled her feet. He was really here. Her heart raced as she covered the last few feet and pulled open the door, not realizing she had no idea what she was going to say.

For most of the night she'd replayed their interaction. She hadn't even used the word *love*. She'd just told him that she broke a rule. Then she'd told him she wasn't asking him to do long-term because he'd used the word *maybe*. What would have happened if she'd used at least some real emotion to tell Asher the truth?

That she loved him, and she was fairly sure it was the irrevocable, love-you-forever-no-matter-what kind of love. Would he still have been unsure?

Now he was here. She could right the wrong…if she summoned the courage.

"I love you. I broke rule one and I want to break rule seven. I don't want six weeks and a day with you—I want it all." Asher's hands were plastered on the side of her door. His fingers were gripping the sides.

"I know I've messed up. God, so badly. I was running from this, from the feelings. Using a surgery to drive my focus away. To distract me. Because I'm terrified of losing you. But I want to be terrified, Aurora. I want to be wonderfully happy and terribly sad and all the emotions in between with you. If you'll give me another chance."

The words rushed out of him, and Asher looked at her, his eyes desperate.

"Wow." Aurora's whispered words carried her forward, closing the bit of distance between them.

Her lips met his. Her heart felt like it might explode as his arms wrapped around her waist. This was where she wanted to be…forever.

"Wow indeed." Asher cupped her cheek.

Before he could say anything else, Aurora laid a finger on his lips. "I love you. I should have said that today. I shouldn't have couched it in the rules. I should have…"

His mouth captured hers, stealing away all her should-haves and what-ifs. He pushed the door closed with his foot then leaned against it as he held her. "I vote we start over today. No worries about the past or the rules or anything. Deal?"

"Deal." Aurora laughed as he ran her fingers on his cheeks. He was here and he was hers.

"Love the pink hair, by the way. It's very you." Asher kissed the top of her head, his hands wrapping around her waist as they started for her bedroom.

"It is." She lifted her lips to his. Aurora Miller was finally exactly who she wanted to be.

EPILOGUE

ASHER DOUBLE-CHECKED HIS pocket for the fifth time as the craft worker pointed out all the paintbrushes and paints in the painting rage room. His mother's engagement ring was still there.

Where else would it be?

Nerves were not a thing that he was accustomed too. But today he'd started fidgeting from the moment he'd woken.

"Thank you." Aurora smiled at the young woman. "We've actually done this before. A few times." She laughed, the sound he loved most.

"Does that sound bad? Regular attendees at the painting rage room?"

He shook his head, not trusting his voice at this point. There was a plan…one he was going to follow. He was going to wait until the woman left, then let Aurora start throwing paint all over the walls before he painted, Marry Me?

"Are you okay?" Aurora stepped to his side, a strip of pink in her hair glittering in the light.

"Absolutely." He kissed her cheek, the desire to ask her to marry him bubbling up.

No.

Aurora deserved the plan. She deserved the memory. Just a few more minutes.

Her green eyes studied him, then she reached for one of the paintbrushes. Dipping it in paint, she held it up, indigo paint dripping down her fingers. "You are sure you're okay?"

"I am here with the woman I love." Asher tapped his pocket one more time. They'd started wearing the same old clothes to this outing, and her shirt was speckled with all the colors of the rainbow.

"Good." Raising the brush, she drew a heart on his chest.

Her smile melted his heart.

"Marry me."

Aurora dropped the brush, and his mind snapped.

"Shoot! I didn't even get down on one knee." He started but she grabbed him.

"Yes. Yes. A hundred times, yes." Her hands were warm as she placed them on both sides of his cheeks.

"I had a whole speech, Aurora. And I was going to paint my proposal on the wall, something to make this memorable." He grazed her lips as he pulled the ring from his pocket.

"It's perfect." Aurora slipped the ring on and then pulled him to her. "Perfect."

* * * * *

SINGLE MUM'S
NEW YEAR WISH

SUE MacKAY

MILLS & BOON

This is for my girl. Love you.

PROLOGUE

SANTA SMILED AT the boy climbing onto his knee. 'Hello, young man. What's your name?'

'Jarrod, and I want a bike for Christmas. It's got to have lights and a bell and bags for carrying my stuff.'

Nicolas Reid stifled a groan. Another kid with high expectations of Father Christmas. It was normal, but wasn't there any kid out there who wanted a toy train or a doll that didn't come with every bell and whistle that had been invented? If he had children he'd want them to be happy, but not expecting to be given anything and everything they asked for. He'd be a bit of a softie, but they wouldn't win every demand they made. Surveying the room, chock-full of excited children, longing flared. A family of his own. Wouldn't that be the best Christmas present he could have? Wasn't happening.

'Santa?'

'What colour bike would you like, Jarrod?' Why had he let Evelyn, his best mate's wife, talk him into getting decked out in stinking-hot clothes in summer—not even thinking about the fake beard making his chin itch—to sit here being tripped over, elbowed, and hearing 'I want, I want' a gazillion times?

'Black's a cool colour.'

'You reckon?'

The kid looked at him and grinned. 'Yep. Can I have a black helmet to match?'

'I'll put it on the list, but I can't promise you'll get what you've asked for. I haven't got lots of bikes in my shed.'

The boy leaned closer and said quietly, 'Mum can hear me telling you what I want and she'll get it.'

Cheeky little blighter. Nicolas found himself smiling at a memory of saying much the same thing to Santa when he was little. He glanced across at the man and woman standing to the side of the plastic fence surrounding Santa's seat. They were smiling and taking photos of their son sitting on the decorated stool beside him, no doubt to be framed and put on the wall. 'Okay, Jarrod, time to give someone else a turn. Merry Christmas and ho-ho-ho. Here's a candy stick.'

'Merry Christmas, Santa.' The boy slid off the stool and ran across to his parents. 'Santa's cool.'

Nicolas looked to the line of youngsters waiting their turn to tell him what they expected to find at the end of the bed on the twenty-fifth. These little guys were having the time of their life at the preschool Christmas party and talking to Santa was the highlight of their day, while all he could think was how many more kids were in the line. Was he jaded, or what? What about getting over his distrust of women brought on by his ex, and find someone to settle down and have a family with? He'd love a brood of his own kids. Unfortunately he'd learned it was safer going with a light and fun lifestyle. No power punches to the heart.

'Hello, Santa.' A shy voice brought him back to what was important today—making the little kids happy.

'Hello, young lady. Do you want to talk to me from there or are you going to climb up on the stool beside me?' Not every child was keen to do that, and he respected their choices.

'Can I sit on the stool?' the cute little girl dressed all in pink asked.

'Of course you can. Use those steps to get up. What's your name?' Nicolas asked as she shuffled onto the narrow seat.

'I'm Mia.'

'Mia, what would you like for Christmas?'

She looked beyond the fence, and Nicolas's gaze tracked in the same direction to land on a brunette beauty watching the child, presumably her daughter, her face full of love. Love that struck him hard. It was beautiful, uncomplicated, with no expectations whatsoever. What was it like to be on the receiving end of that? Did she have any to spare? To have a woman look at *him* with all that love would set him up for life, add to his motivation to be the best he could, to share himself. The look in that woman's eyes for this little tot was so special, so deep, it stole his breath away, and made him hungry for love in a way he hadn't known since his failed marriage.

Then Mia leaned close and said, 'I want a cuddle from my daddy.'

Nicolas blinked. Pain knifed his heart. This girl wanted a hug from her father. Not a shiny new bike or a fancy doll's house, but a hug from the most important man in her life. Every child unreservedly deserved to be loved by their parents. The one thing he suspected she was not going to get any day of the week, let alone Christmas Day. He should've been careful of what he'd wished for only seconds ago. His arm inadvertently pressed into Mia's. It wasn't a present he could pretend to consider delivering. What the hell did he tell her? Again he glanced at the mother. Shock had widened her eyes. She was obviously used to hearing her daughter's quiet voice in noisy places. She looked at him, gave a desperate shake of her head. Which didn't help his predicament. The one thing he wasn't going to do was promise to deliver a hug from a father who obviously wasn't in the picture. But he didn't know how to answer the child without adding to her pain.

'Santa?' Mia was staring at him with big brown eyes, hope dying right before him. 'Can't you get me what I want?'

His heart squeezed tight. Of all the requests he'd had in the last thirty minutes, this was the one he really wanted to make happen, and the one he couldn't deliver a promise on. 'Let me see what can be done, Mia. It's not an easy present to find.' He mightn't know how, but hell, he wanted to make her smile with happiness.

'Mia, tell Santa about the doll's kitchen you want.' The mother now stood a metre away, her gaze fixed on her daughter, worry staining that love.

The little girl exhaled a slow sigh, making him want to hug her to remove the sadness.

'A doll's kitchen, eh?' Nicolas said, relieved to have a prompt. 'Are you going to cook for your dolls?'

'Don't be silly, Santa.' She gave him a little smile, while the sadness still lingered in her eyes. 'It's a pretend kitchen so I will pretend to make breakfast for my favourite dolls. There will be pots and plates and spoons too.' She was off and running, excitement beginning to light up her eyes. 'I can't wait.'

'Have you got a favourite colour?'

Mia tapped her chin with one finger. 'I think pink.'

Nicolas glanced over to the mother. The love in her expression as she watched her daughter made his heart pound with a mix of envy and sadness. This woman adored her girl. His parents used to look at him like that when he was a child, but it had faded some as he grew up and didn't follow their dreams for him. They didn't stop loving him, just not as openly, and never as freely as they used to. 'So a kitchen?' he said loudly to get confirmation in case he'd read the situation all wrong and the mother had only been trying to divert Mia from wanting her father.

The woman nodded once, firmly. Her dark brown curls were cut in a bob that finished below her ears, where a set of opal earrings swayed against her cheeks when her head moved. Captivating.

'Santa's going to get your present arranged for Christmas.' Fingers crossed her mother managed to get one at this time of year. The shops were crazy busy already. He didn't want to end this but there was a line of impatient kids waiting and he had no reason to continue talking to a little girl who wanted her father's love, and whose mother had him wanting to know more about *her*. 'Here's a candy stick. Merry Christmas, ho-ho-ho.'

'Thank you, Santa. Please put the kitchen at the end of my bed.' The child slid off the stool and ran to her mother.

Nicolas watched Mia wrap her arms around her mother's legs and gaze up at her. 'I'm getting a kitchen for my dolls, Mummy. Santa said so.'

'Did he? That's awesome.' The woman glanced over at him, her love for her daughter back in place. 'Thank you,' she mouthed.

'No problem.' He looked away. Falling deeper into the gaze that was meant for her girl, not him, would be pointless. He wasn't in the market for a relationship, even if it turned out to be the best thing to happen in a while. His ex had taught him never to give his heart away again, unless he was prepared to risk having it thrown back in his face.

Nicolas beckoned the next child forward, hoping there weren't any more shocks in store. Being a parent must be a lot of hard work, with emotions obviously all over the place at times, but Mia's mother seemed to have her daughter's request under control. Where was the father? Why wasn't he around to hand out hugs? Nicolas disliked the man already. Being there for *his* child would be a priority for him. Always. No matter what else was going on in his life. Unless the man wasn't alive. Could be the reason behind the child's sadness. If only he had a magic wand to make that emotion disappear for ever and replace it with happiness. Likewise for the mother. Her shock had affected him to the point he was thinking about her and his past all at once.

Having children had been on his radar when he was married but his wife was on another page without saying so. They'd been trying for Valerie to get pregnant for months with no luck. He'd suggested they start down the path of fertility tests. That was when Valerie told him she'd been offered a job in another city, and she was taking it. It had been a shock, but he'd listened to her enthusiasm and figured he could forget what she'd done. Her career in interior design was just starting out but already she'd been doing well. They were married. That meant supporting each other, so when he said he'd start looking for work in the same city she was heading to, Valerie shocked him further. She told him she'd begun an affair with a guy working at the company she was going to and she didn't want Nicolas in her life any more. The other man was her new love. That was when he'd also learned she hadn't stopped taking the pill, had only said so to stop him talking about them trying for a family. So much for believing in love and being on side with his wife. Turned out he'd had no idea who this woman really was. He'd trusted her too easily.

'Hello, Santa. Can I have a trampoline?' A young boy stared up at him with wide eyes and a small smile.

Nicolas did the quick glance-at-the-parents thing, and

received a sharp head-shake from Dad. 'Come up here and tell me your name first, eh?'

'Can I stay down here?'

'Sure you can.'

The kid relaxed a little. 'I'm Archie. I don't really want a trampoline. I want one of those building sets to make a jet plane.'

'A big plane that swoops down?'

'That's it.'

Nicolas saw head-nodding going on from the parents, and got on with the job of making this boy happy. How many more were there? He could do with a coffee and chilling out with some of the parents he knew from working at the same medical centre. Hopefully that would push away the vision of Mia's mother's face. Lovely when she wasn't looking stunned. Somehow he doubted that image would disappear any time soon. It was so real he had a desire to help her. It was as though there was a connection with her, which was blatantly untrue. Did she feel she'd failed her daughter in some way? He must've failed Valerie somehow if she had to go searching for love elsewhere.

Where was Mia's mother now? A quick survey of the room showed her talking to Joachim, the GP who'd started in the Urgent Care medical centre a fortnight before Nicolas had taken a month's leave to work on his vineyard. Was she a doctor too? Or a nurse? Where did she work? Most of the parents of the children attending this preschool worked at the hospital in one capacity or another. She might be a lab tech or a secretary.

She was laughing at something Joachim said, her eyes wide, and he felt a pang of longing. Which was so unlike him, his brain had to be fried under the hot hat and beard.

'Hello, Santa. What are *you* getting for Christmas?' A

lad dressed in an elf's costume stood in front of him, hands on hips with a wide grin from ear to ear.

Nicolas grinned back. It was fun with these kids. Mostly. 'A late morning sleep-in while you're opening your presents.'

CHAPTER ONE

As she drove towards their new accommodation, Claire McAlpine bit down hard on the end of her finger. The tears that had threatened on hearing Mia say to Santa, 'I want a cuddle from my daddy,' were finally leaking down her cheeks. There was no holding onto them any longer now she was alone.

Mia was with Claire's colleague, Joachim and his wife, whose daughter she loved playing with. Far easier to go through the checklist of furniture with the house movers without a little voice interrupting every five minutes. Also a chance for Mia to make another friend. Something she was pretty darned good at, Claire admitted. Didn't get that from her mother. Definitely a paternal characteristic.

I want a cuddle from my daddy. Those words had resonated in her head again and again during the rest of the drawn-out time spent at the children's party. After seeing the shock in Santa's eyes when Mia spoke to him, she'd avoided him once he'd stepped away from his chair, and hadn't relaxed until he'd walked out of the building not long afterwards. For a while she'd worried he'd come back as a normal guy to talk to some of the parents he might know, but as far as she knew he hadn't. He might've confronted her about Mia's request, or tried to be too friendly and kind, which would've made her edgy. It was a private matter. She didn't hide the fact she was single, but it was nobody's business that Mia's father was nowhere to be seen. She knew how bewildering and awful it was to grow up without a father, and had never wanted the same for her child. Hearing Mia ask for her daddy's hug had been a punch in the gut.

It was the first time she'd openly said such a thing, and then to a complete stranger. Santa, Claire reminded herself. Santa was the magical man who could bring all sorts of wishes to fruition in a child's mind. His reaction struck her as touching. He'd been stunned but he hadn't passed that onto Mia, instead he'd glanced her way and immediately understood Mia needed diverting. The empathy that had passed from him to her and her girl said a lot about the man behind the fake beard.

'Why haven't I got a daddy like other girls?' Mia sometimes asked, but never before with such longing. So far she'd managed to divert Mia, saying she didn't know where her dad had gone—which was true—but that she was loved so much she was safe. She couldn't bring herself to tell her girl that the man she'd accidentally fallen pregnant with had wanted nothing to do with his child. Not a thing. He hadn't wanted to know when she was due, or her sex, what her name might be, certainly not her whereabouts once born. Nothing. Today hurt because she'd tried so hard to convince Hank to at least let her send him updates of their child's progress once it was born. His blunt 'No' had said it all.

While pregnant she'd wondered if she was selfish bringing a child into the world with little chance of knowing her father. The sense of loss caused by her own father not being there to watch her ride a bike for the first time, take her to school the day she turned five, to stand and clap when she received her doctor's degree never left her, so how could she put that onto her child? But because of her upbringing she knew she'd be twice the parent her mother had been in her father's absence. Her mother was distant towards her as though afraid of losing her too.

For Mia not to know her father, to never have met him and not likely ever to, was beyond cruel. As harsh as Claire's father walking out on *her*. Hank had knocked the ground out from under her when he'd held up his hands in a stop sign way when she'd told him she was pregnant, and said, 'Whoa, stop there. I want nothing to do with this. We had a fling, nothing more. Any consequences are yours to deal with. Get an abortion, keep it, whatever. Your choice.'

He'd turned around and walked away, covering his ears with his hands as she'd begged him to stay in touch for his child's sake, not hers. Apparently he'd left Dunedin that same day. She hadn't loved him, or wanted anything from him other than to love their child. She'd known she would keep it, raise and love him or her to bits. She tried to believe she didn't care if *she* never saw Hank again, but the fling had gone on long enough for her to feel safe with him. Something she hadn't felt since the breakup of her long-term relationship with a doctor while she was training. Anthony's dismissal of her had made her feel more unloved than ever, something Hank had added to.

Mia deserved better. Especially unconditional love from the man who'd given her his genes. Hank's words had never left her, though more often than not they were filed away somewhere in the recesses of her mind under the label *Bastard*. On the other hand, Mia had been the surprise of her life, and so worth all the sleepless nights and long days. She loved her daughter to the end of earth and back. She'd do anything for her, including never get so close to a man that Mia became vulnerable. Or her. At the same time, she did have a deep hankering for a loving partner and maybe have another baby. When Mia was a lot older, and *she* was ready to trust again.

If she learned to trust a man not to walk away, breaking her heart, and Mia's, as he went, she might eventually take a chance and cope with whatever came her way without looking over her shoulder for trouble. With her track record it seemed unlikely. Men preferred to walk out of her life.

She had tried to find Hank. Seemed he'd disappeared off the face of said earth. All she knew was he'd come from Britain to New Zealand via any number of countries about six months before she'd met him, and that he was an outdoors man who loved nothing more than mountain-climbing and skiing. He'd explained once, briefly, that he followed his dreams all over the world, never stopping long anywhere, and she'd been enthralled by his sense of adventure. Money hadn't appeared to be a problem, but then they hadn't got into any discussions about anything that didn't involve eating, drinking and sex. Yet the fling had gone on longer than usual for her and she had begun to wonder if he was thinking of settling down.

Once her pregnancy was confirmed Claire had continued working all hours, cramming for exams. She'd become a mother twenty-four hours after she'd finished her final paper. Mia was the best reward imaginable, even better than her qualification. Something she'd never have believed until then. Being a doctor had always been important, so much so that she'd focused on getting through high school with more than high enough grades to get into the pre-med school year at university. Yet one tiny pink, wrinkled little girl had changed everything. For the better. She had someone to love and who loved her back unconditionally. She did not want her child knowing coldness from a father who didn't love her. She knew what that was like all too well. Her father had left when she was four, never to be heard from again. Still she'd tried to track down Hank because his daughter deserved to know him.

Turning onto a side road running between vineyards, she glanced in both directions at the spectacular sight that still amazed her. This was a wonderful district to have come to. They were going to love their new home. Fingers crossed. A small, modern two-bedroom unit she'd signed up to rent, sight unseen, three weeks ago was on the outskirts of Blenheim, close to the hospital. They'd been staying in a motel until the previous tenants moved out.

Excitement stirred in her. Her mother's decision to move to Perth, Australia to live with, and care for, her sister who had cancer, had freed Claire to make a fresh start away from memories of a lonely life growing up with her mother's bitterness and her own pain over her father leaving thirty years ago. Hard to imagine her mother wanting to be with Auntie Jocelyn when they'd only corresponded once a year at Christmas and never talked on the phone, but apparently old age had softened the two women into believing they should be together for this difficult time.

A new start in a location she was unfamiliar with excited Claire. A complete change she'd never experienced and was so looking forward to. She'd chosen sunny, warm Blenheim because it was smaller than Dunedin and seemed very friendly to outsiders and, more importantly, the job on offer was ideal.

Further ahead, a police car with lights flashing was parked across the road. Leaning forward, Claire peered ahead. 'What's going on?' A cop waved her to stop. Beyond her there were two cars concertinaed into each other so hard it looked impossible to tell where one started and the other finished. Next to them a forklift was slewed on its side across the ditch. Winding down her window, she said, 'Hello, Officer. That looks serious. I'm a doctor. I can help if required.'

'Thank goodness. There're three people with major injuries. Both ambulances are on their way, but in the meantime I'm sure your help will be appreciated,' the policewoman said as she lifted her radio from her belt. 'I'll let the others know you're coming.'

Claire was already out of the car and opening the boot to get her medical kit. 'Both ambulances?'

'That's all we have in Blenheim. If we need another it has to come from Picton or Havelock.'

'At least half an hour away?'

'Yes.'

Claire was met with a scene of carnage as she reached the vehicles, and the sound of screams filled her ears. 'I'm a doctor,' she told the policeman approaching her. 'Your colleague said I might be useful.'

The man grimaced. 'Definitely. We've got two teenage boys in a bad way in the blue car. They're the ones making all the noise. Neither was wearing a seat belt so they were both thrown around the interior of the car and appear to have some serious injuries. In the sedan there's a woman who seems unconscious and losing a lot of blood from a deep gash in her head. I don't know where you start.'

'Usually we check the silent one first, as that's an indicator of severe head injuries. I'll take her while you see what you can do for the boys. Call me if you're stuck. The sooner those ambulances arrive the better,' Claire said as she stepped across to the sedan.

Peering through what had once been the driver's side window, she saw the woman, lying in a contorted position with her head jammed into the steering wheel. A wide gash was apparent on the side of her face and across her scalp. 'Hello? Can you hear me?' Claire asked, while trying to open the door. It didn't move. Impact had squashed this side of the car back into itself. Glancing around, she found it impossible to tell where one car started and the other ended.

Leaving the door, she squeezed her upper body through the gap. 'Hello? Can you hear me?'

Nothing.

Holding the back of her hand under the woman's nose, then against her open mouth, Claire felt pops of warm air and saw her chest rising and falling unevenly. Thankfully the woman was breathing, if not perfectly. A good start. Placing a finger on the woman's neck, she found an erratic pulse. The woman didn't stir at Claire's touch. A dark contusion on her forehead suggested she'd slammed into the steering wheel and been knocked unconscious. Claire's fingers found soft areas on the skull near a bleeding wound.

The sound of a siren split the air. Claire remained focused on her patient. The other two victims would have more attention in a moment, and this woman was in a serious condition. Her vitals might be passable, but there was no knowing what other injuries she'd sustained that might've affected the heart or lungs or other internal organs. Internal bleeding was a real possibility, but first to slow the bleeding from the head. Reaching into her kit for a wide crepe bandage and padding, Claire blindly found what she wanted while watching the woman. 'Hello? I'm a doctor. You've been in an accident. Can you hear me?' she tried again.

No response.

Claire sighed. She hadn't been expecting any sort of answer, but she could always hope.

'Hi, I'm a nurse. Nicolas. Do you need a hand here?' A male voice from behind caused her to jerk upward and bang her shoulder against the window frame.

'I've got it.' She pulled out and turned to face the man, and felt a tug in her chest. Tall and broad, he was dressed in jeans that accentuated his muscular frame and a dark blue open-necked tee-shirt that matched the colour of his eyes. 'You might be required to help with the other victims.' Something niggled. Did she know this guy from somewhere? Another quick look. No recollection came to mind and she wasn't blind. Those blue, blue eyes sent a shiver down her spine. That was new.

'The paramedics who just arrived are looking at the boys and said to see what you might need.' He was looking at her with surprise. Why? Feeling the same sense of recognition? But she didn't recognise him, just had a vague sense of déjà vu, and didn't have time to think if she'd met him anywhere. 'One of them will talk to you as soon as the second ambulance gets here.'

'Good. This woman requires evacuating from the car urgently.' She wouldn't have to leave her for a moment. 'She's got a major head trauma. The way she's twisted in the seat makes it difficult to check for internal injuries.' She added, 'I'm a doctor, by the way. Claire.'

'So I was told.' He moved next to the mangled car.

Claire returned her focus to her patient, ignoring the new tingling along her spine. Placing her hands carefully on the woman's head to check for injuries, she said, 'Need a neck brace.'

'Here, I grabbed one from the ambulance in case.' He'd stepped closer, bringing an earthy masculine scent with him. An outdoor kind of smell that brought sunshine and fresh air with it. 'Let's get it in place before trying to get the lady out of the car.'

Claire gently moved their patient's head away from the wheel while the man put the brace in place without hesitation.

Experienced, she knew. But still, he had a way about him that said confident and competent. As every good nurse was.

Nicolas elbowed glass fragments from the windscreen, careful not to let any drop on their patient, and tried to ignore the beautiful doctor beside him. Claire, the mother of the little girl who'd asked Santa to deliver cuddles. Guess he had his answer as to her career. She had to be new in town or he'd have come across her somewhere in the small, close-knit medical world of Blenheim. There were shadows under those mesmerising eyes. Working long hours? With a child in tow?

Leaning in, he took the woman's shoulders firmly in his hands. 'I've got her if you want to start moving her upper body.'

'Thanks. There's a trauma injury above her temple that needs a pressure bandage.' Obviously she knew her stuff in emergency situations. 'I need to check her over first. There's more blood under her lower body.'

'I'll hold her steady.' He pushed further through the front and between them, without a word, they moved the woman back against the seat.

'Oh, no. Bigger problem.' Her hands were firm while gentle as she felt around the woman's groin. 'Femoral artery's bleeding. There're bandages in that kit.' She nodded to a bag lying on the ground.

'Onto it.' Nicolas grabbed packets of sterile bandages and opened one to pass to the doctor.

Immediately she pressed hard on the wound to stem the bleeding.

'Want me to do that while you continue checking for further injuries?' he asked.

'Yes.' She didn't waste time on talking, just waited for him to take over with more large swabs.

Reaching in closer, rose scent wafted past his nose as he placed his hand where hers had been. Glancing around, all he saw was a field of grapevines, not a rose in sight, though often bushes were at the end of the rows to alert growers of disease in the vines. Another, deeper, indrawn breath. Roses and the doc. Again that instinctive sense of connection. Something he did not need. She might intrigue him but he wasn't looking for trouble with a woman. Swallowing hard, he pressed even deeper in an attempt to stop the bleeding altogether until the paramedics arrived. 'Her foot's caught between the accelerator and brake pedals,' he noted.

'We can't shift it without help. Any movement will cause more bleeding.' She wriggled her slim frame to get closer to the woman, and glanced at him briefly. 'Her right arm's broken too.' Something resembling surprise flickered across her face before she continued assessing their patient's injuries.

Did she recognise him? When his face had been covered in a fake beard and his red outfit had been at least three sizes too big? He doubted it.

'Hello, there. I'm Jeffrey, advanced paramedic,' came a voice from behind them.

Claire said over her shoulder, 'We need to get this woman out of here to really see what we're dealing with. Nicolas has the bleeding in check but she needs oxygen.' Then she added, 'I tried prying the door open but it didn't budge.'

Right then a fireman turned up, a crowbar in his hand. 'This any help?'

'You're onto it, Mark.' Nicolas nodded at the guy he'd known since he'd started working at the Urgent Care medical centre and had to treat him for a burn.

Jeffery said, 'Right, Mark, get the door open so we can

leverage the woman out. Then Doc, can you finish your assessment while I get the oxygen attached and we can start sorting out her problems?'

'Of course. This one is urgent.' The doctor backed out and straightened up, a grim expression on her face.

'I'd like you and Nicolas to work with me here.'

As soon as the door was wrenched open, the doctor pushed in next to the unconscious woman and reached for the jammed feet, removed the shoes without difficulty or more damage. Her movements were efficient and professional as she checked toes and feet, then moved up the ankles. The kind of doctor anyone would want on their side in this situation. 'Both ankles broken,' she called over her shoulder.

'We haven't done the GCS yet,' Nicolas told Jeffrey. The Glasgow Coma Score would give an indication of how serious the patient's brain condition was. It wouldn't be good considering the woman's head had hit the steering wheel. 'I haven't seen any movement or eye recognition. I'm presuming the score will be low.'

'We'll sort it once she's out and on the stretcher. Right.' Jeffrey surveyed the situation. 'Nicolas, can you keep the pressure on that haemorrhage while we shift her?'

'Someone will have to take over once you've got her off the seat.' He would lie across the mangled front of the sedan where it was scrunched into the other car.

'I'll do that,' Claire answered.

Minutes later she was putting her hand over his, taking up the pressure as he quickly slid away from the wound. No further bleeding appeared. Like they'd practised the move often. He scrambled off the car and took his place beside the fireman as they all lifted the woman onto the stretcher.

'Want me back there?' he asked Claire. 'Or shall I do the GCS?'

'You do it and then we'll swap.'

Nicolas began lifting the patient's eyelids. No response. 'Hello. Can you hear me?' Her mouth moved. When he poked her shoulder she winced slightly. 'GCS of six.'

'Worryingly bad,' Claire said, accepting what he said, not coming across as a doctor who liked to be seen to be in charge.

He liked that. It meant she was more about helping a patient than making sure she was seen to be perfect. He'd worked with his share of opinionated medics, though not so much since he'd started at the Urgent Care medical centre, where everyone seemed grounded and keen to get on with doing what they did best, which was always aimed at helping patients.

Again they changed positions without a glitch. In fact, she barely took more than a glance at him. Which irked a little, he admitted with a grin as the paramedic tightly wound a crepe bandage round the injury he was preventing further bleeding from. Patient first, his ego second.

Claire straightened from examining the woman and glanced at the nurse with his stubbled chin. Did he say his name was Nicolas? She wasn't sure, being more concerned with the woman needing help. Sudden, unusual longing for excitement she hadn't looked for since Mia was born filled her. That deep gravelly voice tightened her skin some. Another unusual reaction. Add in that outdoorsy scent, and he added up to quite a package. Seemed she was human after all if she could get wound up around a good-looking guy. *Except*, she reminded herself, *my New Year plans don't involve getting too close to a man.*

'What have you found?' he asked.

Who *did* that voice remind her of? Surely she'd remember someone who sounded so nerve-tapping? Pushing the errant thoughts aside, Claire focused on what was important. 'There's an internal rupture near the ribcage. I suspect the liver. She was probably thrown sideways before her head hit the steering wheel.'

'Anything else?' Jeffrey asked.

'Massive bruising on the left outer thigh. Impact with gear shift?' It wasn't uncommon in car accidents.

'As soon as we've got everything in place we're heading for the hospital.'

'That's good.' Claire felt a weight lift from her shoulders. She was good at helping injured people in tricky situations. She'd made it her go-to place, somewhere she could believe in herself and know she was good enough to be a doctor. But in cases like this the best option was always to have the patient taken ASAP to the emergency department with all the high-end equipment in case something suddenly went very wrong. A real possibility with this lady.

As soon as the patient was loaded, she asked the paramedic, 'Do you want me to look at anyone else?'

'The other crew's got the boys covered, but no one's had time to examine the girl who was driving the forklift, more than ask a couple of pertinent questions. She's in shock, but no apparent serious trauma.'

'Onto it.' Then she'd get back to her car and go onto the house and the movers, who'd be wondering where she'd got to by now. Claire took a quick look at Nicolas and felt another tug in her chest. Why? She didn't usually take a second look at any man. But no denying the unfamiliar sensations ramping throughout her body.

He was checking his watch, and winced. 'If I'm not needed I'm heading away. I'm late for an appointment.'

At five o'clock on a Friday afternoon? Drinks with his mates? A hot date with a beautiful woman?

Claire McAlpine, get a grip. You're behaving like a be-sotted teenager.

Her shoulders slumped a little. Must be the Marlborough air, warmer and more seductive. Looking across to the girl slumped against the forklift with a policeman talking to her, she said, 'You go. I've got this one.'

'You sure?'

'Yes.' She watched him stride away, those long legs eating up the ground as if he were in a race. Interesting. She hadn't noticed a man quite so blatantly sexy in a long time. Moving here was a much-needed change, would hopefully bring some fun to her life. She hadn't planned on factoring men into her day-to-day activities. A new start with no one to remind her of the past. Eventually she might relax enough to start dating and having a warm, loving relationship that breathed permanency, but she wasn't rushing.

There was plenty to do over the coming weekend. The movers might have unpacked most of her belongings into the unit, but there'd be all the kitchenware, clothes, toys and bathroom bits and pieces for her to put away in cupboards and drawers. Tomorrow night was the Urgent Care medical centre's Christmas barbecue.

Evelyn, another doctor working at the centre she'd started at last month, had insisted she and her husband, Bodie, would pick her up. Her reason being that no one should go to a party alone. It was a nice gesture, though unnecessary. Evelyn was fast becoming a good friend, offering advice and help about Blenheim, where to live and shop, and the best coffee in town, so she'd accepted graciously. All part of settling into her new life.

'Mummy, can I wear my pink dress? I want to look pretty for Michelle.' Mia stood beside Claire, holding her favourite outfit against her chest.

Mia looked pretty in green baggy PJs, but still, Claire got it. Even at four years old her daughter was very feminine—a trait she might've got from her mother, Claire smiled to herself.

'Since it's a special night you can.' Evelyn's daughter was looking after Mia while Claire went to the centre's Christmas function at a winery on the outskirts of Blenheim. Another plus to this area was all the vineyards and their restaurants. Choosing where to move to had been a bit like throwing a dart at the board. She'd applied for three positions around the country, and accepted the one here because it seemed likely to fit in with being a solo mum, plus interesting and different from positions she'd had before. It had come up just as she'd been about to accept another offer. Apparently the doctor who'd taken the position had had a change of heart and pulled out, leaving the centre with an urgent need to find someone else.

She'd still prefer going alone to the party and be able to leave early, not have to put on her pleased-to-be-with-you face and stay for more hours than she could imagine being fun. Her social life mainly consisted of preschool events, or Mia's friends' birthday parties. For a change, tonight she was going to be an adult, no childish talking allowed. Hopefully she'd be up to speed.

Had she become somewhat withdrawn from reality like her mother had done when her father left? Quite likely. It had been an example of how to move on from a broken relationship. Yet when Anthony left she'd bounced back enough to have a couple of flings, but when Hank did his number on her and their unborn child she'd crawled into a hole and hidden her heart away. Probably way past time to get out there and make more of what was on offer. Being like her mother, crushed for ever by bitterness, looking at the world as though it owed her something, wasn't the sanest option.

'Look at me, Mummy. Aren't I pretty?'

'Yes, darling, you are.' Seeing Mia's happy smile, a thrill touched her. If her daughter was excited to be babysat then she should take something from that, look to enjoying herself, not think about how soon she could return home. She could end up having a fantastic night out, and not want to come home. Sure thing, Claire.

The doorbell blared. Michelle had arrived. 'Hi, Claire. Hey, look at you, Mia. That's a cool dress.'

'Thanks for doing this, Michelle,' Claire managed between her daughter's excited shrieks as she pirouetted for her babysitter.

'No problem.'

Her phone rang. The night had got busy all of a sudden. 'Hi, Evelyn. What's up?'

'Just calling to say we're running late. Bodie's got problems with the irrigation plant.'

'I'll drive and meet you there.'

'No need. I've called Nicolas and told him to pick you up. He's a nurse at the centre, been on leave for a month. He's also a close friend of ours. I'm sure the two of you will get on like a house on fire. He's already left, so should be on your doorstep any minute. See you soon.' She was gone.

Nicolas. A nurse. Guess who that was? The air stuck in her throat. The sexy nurse who'd set her hormones dancing. Had to be. This turn of events meant she wasn't slowly moving forward. If she reacted to him as she had yesterday she was racing into a new life.

Her fingers spun the ring on her little finger as she absorbed how her evening had changed before it had begun. It could still be a straightforward night out with colleagues, so she should relax and have fun, but even now there was a new level of heat under her skin. Did Nicolas know who she was? Evelyn would have filled him in enough to know who he was picking up, but would he have realised they'd met twice yesterday?

Gorgeous. Claire breathed deep as she looked at the man she'd opened her front door to. There was that tugging in her chest again. Definitely gorgeous. Still sexy. 'Hello, Nicolas.'

There was something like an ah-ha moment in the deep blue eyes fixed on her. 'Hi, Claire. I figured you might be the doctor at the accident yesterday.'

The strong jawline and soft laughter lines at the corners of his eyes were as real as her imagination had teased her with. She refrained from thinking about a body that suggested he worked out a lot. Then it hit her. Those eyes above the white fluffy beard. *I want a cuddle from my daddy.* Her stomach clenched. 'You were Santa.' How could fate do this to her?

'I was, yes.' His smile was soft—and genuine. 'Are you still comfortable coming with me?'

Knock her down. The guy did understanding as well as sexy. She swallowed. Right now she needed the understanding more. 'I'm not denying my surprise. But I did sense something about you at the accident that made me think I might've already met you somewhere. I just never put it all together.' Another breath. They couldn't spend the evening standing on her doorstep chatting about work. 'I'll say goodnight to Mia and grab my bag. Come in.'

Nicolas glanced inside, then back to her. He spoke in a low voice. 'It was a tricky moment but we got through it. Was Mia all right last night?'

'It was as though she'd forgotten all about it. I don't know what to say, except thank you for diverting her onto the doll's kitchen.' *We got through it.* Claire liked him for that, which was odd because anything to do with Mia was hers to deal with. Would he stop at that? Or want to know what brought on her girl's request? In a bid to keep the conversation on the straight and very narrow, she said, 'Mia was happy, talking about Santa's present nonstop.' Hard to believe how quickly she'd moved on. Swallowing a sudden reluctance to share her space even for a few minutes and having Nicolas see Mia again, she said, 'Come in. She's with the babysitter.'

'Michelle.' Nicolas nodded as he followed her inside. 'Evelyn's my closest friend's wife.'

'She's been so helpful and friendly since I arrived here.'

'That's Evelyn. Hello, Michelle. How was your day?'

'Cool, thanks. Did you know I'm working at the chocolate factory over summer?'

'I heard. There wasn't any peanut brittle in my letterbox when I looked earlier.'

'Give me a chance.'

Nicolas's deep laugh turned Claire's stomach to mush. Nothing like a vibrant, deep tone laugh to lift her spirits. Despite who he'd turned out to be, Nicolas seemed to be an okay guy who mightn't torture her with questions about Mia's father. Fingers crossed, in case she was wrong.

'Mia, darling, this is Nicolas. He's giving me a ride to dinner.'

'Hello, Nicolas. You be good to Mummy, all right?'

Again that deep laugh. 'You bet I will. That's a promise.'

More cramps in her stomach.

Then Mia threw her arms around her. 'Goodnight, Mummy. Have a good time.'

So Michelle had won her way into Mia's heart already. There weren't going to be any tears or arguments. A weight lifted as Claire picked up her evening bag. 'Love you, Mia.' She headed for the door, not giving Mia time to change her mind about being happy for her mother to go out.

Nicolas followed, obviously aware of the need to leave quickly. Claire wasn't surprised. Santa had been fast to check with her about Mia's present. The nurse had been on the ball with the woman in that mangled car. What else was he quick on the uptake about?

Hopefully not her sudden awareness of him in a way she hadn't noticed any man in a long while. That could be beyond awkward, make her feel like an idiot. They'd be working together and, going by her previous, one and only, real relationship with a doctor on the same ward she was training in years ago, workplace romances could get messy. Anthony had been quick to move on with a nurse she'd worked alongside, rubbing it in that she wasn't special.

I'm not looking for another relationship, she reminded herself as she walked down the path beside Nicolas. Mia came first. No other man was going to let her down. Once was enough for any child to live with. Nor was *she* prepared to be let down. Lifting her chin, she headed for the large four-wheel drive parked in her drive and pretended Nicolas wasn't at all sexy or interesting. Or knew that her daughter had father issues.

CHAPTER TWO

NICOLAS HAULED IN AIR. He was feeling as if—what? As if the ground had disappeared from under him. This woman, Claire—Mia's mother, the doctor he'd be working with, the woman who'd snuck into his dreams last night—was beautiful. Opening the door to his four-wheel drive for her to get in, he struggled to breathe.

And when he did manage to, the scent of roses drifted past him. He dragged in another lungful. A scent taking him back to his childhood teased his sensory glands. Summer and his mother's garden. Nicolas looked around. No rose garden in sight. Back to Claire. Her perfume had teased him yesterday, and now it brought on nostalgia for a straightforward love and acceptance from those who mattered. A love he hadn't known for so long he'd wondered if it was all in his imagination. Had to be.

After Valerie had packed her bags he'd gone bush for five days, hiking in the ranges, trying to come to terms with what had happened. It wasn't the first time he'd been hurt. Maddy, his first love, had left him for another man who was always hanging around while he was working on the fishing trawlers. Between Valerie and Maddy, he was left thinking he lacked whatever it took to make them happy. By the time he'd returned home from the bush he was determined to remain single and have the occasional fling when he became too lonely. It had worked up until now. Would continue to, despite the wearer of that scent twisting his gut and making him sit up and take notice of everything about her.

He knew little about Claire, apart from what he'd seen at the accident yesterday, and her devotion to Mia. Yet here she was, stirring him in ways he couldn't explain— or understand. What about a fling? Problem with that was when it was over they'd still work together. Plus there was her daughter to think about. After yesterday he knew Mia was vulnerable and he wouldn't hurt her to have some fun of his own.

Naturally he liked women. There was red blood in his veins. Enjoying sex was normal. Getting close to the woman afterwards didn't happen. It took too much trust on his part to get past the wariness about being vulnerable, something he wasn't prepared to put the effort in for. Could be he hadn't met the woman to make him believe it would be worthwhile. Make him believe *he* was worthwhile.

Claire swung a leg up to get in the vehicle. At least she tried, but her skirt was tight—and emphasised the shapely thighs beneath the light fabric. 'Great,' she muttered.

Taking her elbow, Nicolas helped her up. 'Here you go.' He hadn't considered his vehicle would be awkward for a well-dressed lady to get into.

'Thanks. I'm in.' Her polite smile made him feel awkward.

Why was Claire twisting his gut like this? All he was doing was giving her a lift to the restaurant and he couldn't keep his eyes off her. Or his brain quiet. Keep this up and he wouldn't be able to swallow a mouthful of dinner. Closing the door, he walked around the front of his four-wheel drive, trying to ignore the turbulence his date was already causing. A date with a woman who looked like the friendly girl-next-door when she relaxed—something he hadn't seen too often so far.

'You buckled in?' he asked as he settled into his seat. It was the best he could come up with since his mind had gone stupidly blank except for Claire. The moment he'd slid inside his vehicle the rose garden again filled his nostrils, raising hope for what, he wasn't quite sure. More like, he didn't want to admit to what was causing the tightness in his chest. Physically Claire was his type. Average height, curvy in all the right places, and right now a shy smile that tipped him off-balance in an instant. What was behind that smile? Why shy? Not used to dating lately? If not, they were a right crazy pair.

'All ready to go,' Claire answered. Nothing shy about the steadfast look she was giving him, as if to say, *What else would I be?*

'You been to Grapelands Restaurant before?'

Her light laughter swept over him like a warm breeze. 'I've only been in Blenheim a few weeks. I haven't done any getting out and about so far.'

Just like that, she had him in the palm of her slim hand, wanting to touch her, feel her heat against his skin. *Back off, fast. Aim for friendly, not intense.* 'That won't last now you know Evelyn. Before you know it, she'll have you at every dinner party or event going.' As he well knew. Evelyn, his long-time best friend's wife, was determined to see him settled with a woman who'd make him so happy that he could override his hang-ups from the past, mainly his marriage. She and Bodie had never liked Valerie, and he suspected they weren't unhappy to see her go. Though after putting up with him on many evenings when he was tired of his own company, they might've changed their minds about convincing him to move here in the first place.

'How long have you worked at the centre?' she asked, changing the subject.

Where was the relief when he needed it? A neutral subject should be quietening his stimulated senses. Instead his hands were gripping the steering wheel. 'About four years. I was working at a hospital in Nelson before that, then decided I'd like a change. No more night shifts for one. What about you? You're not from around here, are you?' That was why he hadn't seen those toffee-brown eyes that had filled with love, professionalism and that random shyness before.

'Can't say I've ever missed those either,' Claire said. 'Before moving north I worked at a general practice, which suited me well, what with Mia to look after. The position here is similar, though I do like working with families and getting to know them, so I'll probably go back to family practice at some point.'

'They're always crying out for GPs in Blenheim.'

'Much the same throughout the country. I wouldn't mind setting up my own practice.' Claire was twisting a silver ring on her little finger. Round and round.

Nervous of him? That was a new one. Worried she shouldn't have mentioned going out on her own when they worked for the same company? *Relax, Claire.* He wouldn't say a word to anyone.

'You'd be busy before you knew it.'

'That'd be good.' She was still on edge.

Who had given her that ring? Mia's father? It didn't look like a typical wedding band, but what would he know?

'I think everyone who's not working tonight will be at the restaurant. And even those on shift will turn up after the centre closes. Hopefully not long after eight for their sakes.'

'They're a great bunch. I'm enjoying working with everyone.'

'You haven't worked with me yet. Apart from attending yesterday's accident scene. You might change your mind,' he joked, glad to see her ring finally left alone. A quick glance left and his heart sped up. A lovely vision filled his head. A real woman, not a figment of his imagination. Though he was imagining holding that sexy body against him, running his fingers through those soft curls.

'I've been warned you're a handful.' The shy smile touched her full lips.

Sensual lips that tightened his muscles way too easily. Yes, all of them. 'Thanks.' He drove in silence for a few minutes. Finding out more about Claire seemed important, as if this was his chance to tighten that connection he felt with her. 'Where did you move from?'

'Dunedin. I went from high school to university to med school to a GP practice.' She looked out at the passing vineyards. 'And now I'm here.'

Nicolas couldn't decide if she was happy with that or not. 'Seems to me, you might've been in need of a change of scenery.'

'It was way overdue.'

'I'm a bit the other way, having left home in Auckland at seventeen and never returned. I mostly lived in Nelson, where I went fishing, then enrolled for nursing school.' He flicked the indicator. 'Here's the restaurant.' It had appeared far too soon. Sitting in this cocoon with Claire was charging his batteries. Making him feel good in a manly way. Pushing buttons long out of use.

He pulled into the car park and sighed. 'Let's go and

have fun.' The short drive had been fun. Now they had to go mix and mingle with people. The bubble had popped.

Claire didn't move. Her breasts rose and fell on a long breath.

'Claire? I won't hog all your time if that's what's bothering you.' He would make sure she had a good time though.

She turned to him, a wry smile replacing the shy one. 'It's not that. I'm out of practice when it comes to socialising.'

She had to be kidding. But Claire did appear reserved when she wasn't sticking up for her daughter, or helping a woman jammed inside a smashed car, so maybe this was daunting. 'You'll be fine. You know almost everyone and, from what I heard from Evelyn, they all like you. I'll give you five minutes and I bet by then you'll be talking and laughing like the best of them.'

If you're not, I'll be right at your side, encouraging you to relax.

'I can't believe I'm nervous. It's silly.' She shoved the door open. 'Thank you for picking me up.'

His mouth dried. She knew how to get to him without trying. Hurrying around to her side, he took her elbow. 'Any time.'

Claire hesitated again, those big eyes burning into him. 'And thank you for how you handled Mia's request to Santa. I imagine it came as a shock.'

Quit the thank yous. He was only being himself, with a load of intrigue now added in the mix. 'No more than what I saw on your face. It's okay. We got past it.' His arms were fighting to stay at his sides and not wrap around Claire to hold her close and relieve her of the despair creeping over her face. 'That kitchen's going to be well received.' Though probably not as well as the cuddle Mia wanted.

Obviously Claire thought the same because she said, 'It's

a diversion, not an answer. But again, thanks. You were great. For the record, obviously I'm single, but there's no ex on the horizon being a pest. It's just me and Mia.' Then a slow blush reddened her skin. 'Sorry, way too much info.'

'It's safe with me.' Happiness flooded through Nicolas, which shouldn't be happening when he wasn't looking for anything more than a bit of fun. And standing this close to hot and sexy Claire was ramping up the fun factor. He'd happily spend time with her, if she wanted the same. But he would continue to play the friendly colleague role and forget what was going on under his skin. Laughter reached them from the restaurant garden. Saved. 'Sounds like the party's started without us.'

'Better than being first to arrive.' Had Claire realised she'd moved closer to him?

'Hey, Nicolas, good to see you.' Joachim walked in behind them. 'You too, Claire. Jess is inside, Claire. She was hoping you'd be coming.'

The elbow in Nicolas's hand relaxed entirely. Would've been more exciting if he'd taken her hand instead. But he wasn't her date. No one was, he reminded himself. And grimaced with frustration.

'This looks good.' Claire looked around the room they'd entered and smiled at a few people.

'Would you like a drink?' he asked her.

She blinked. 'A drink?' Then she turned on one of those blinding smiles he'd seen when she'd said goodnight to Mia. 'Of course. I'm out and don't have to worry about driving Mia home.'

She really was out of practice. 'What shall I get you?'

The smile widened. 'We're at a vineyard. It'd be rude not to sample their wine, wouldn't it? I wonder if they do a Pinot Gris.' Now her smile was cheeky. How many other smiles did she have? It could be fun finding out.

Excuse me? He wasn't here for that. 'I'll go see. Joachim?'

'Mine's on the table. Claire, come and see Jess.'

Nicolas leaned against the bar, waiting for his order and watching Claire as she chattered easily with Jess. Out in the car park she'd been nervous, yet he'd swear she was already completely at ease now. So her social life had been a bit of a drought. When she was beautiful and kind? Had to be a history there to make her that way. Welcome to his world.

'Here you go.' The barman pushed two glasses across the counter.

'Thanks.' Unable to take his eyes off Claire, he sipped his wine slowly, it would have to last the whole evening since he was driving. Something about her kept snagging his attention. Not something. Many things. Her looks stirred him, sure, but she appeared beautiful on the inside too. Genuine, didn't try to be overly confident when she felt awkward. Though yesterday, helping that woman, she'd been nothing but confident. Seemed to be many sides to Claire McAlpine. He'd barely started getting to know her. The fact he wanted to keep going was disturbing, but he wasn't heading for the door. It had started yesterday when Mia requested that hug for Christmas. Claire's shock and pain had reached inside him, tugged at his heartstrings. It had made him sit up straighter, while wondering who she was and what made her tick. Claire McAlpine was lovely with a capital L.

'You going to stand there all night?' Bodie, his closest friend, laughed, also looking over at Claire.

'No, the wine will get warm.' He'd been so engrossed in Claire he hadn't noticed Evelyn had joined her and Jess. 'Thought you were running late due to problems with the irrigation pump.'

'Got it sorted about the time Evelyn rang you.'

Had Evelyn done it on purpose to set him up with Claire? He wouldn't put it past her. 'That's a relief.' This time of the year the vines soaked up water by the litre. Stepping away, he headed over to hand Claire her glass. 'Pinot Gris as ordered. It's very good, by the way.'

He watched her sip it and saw her eyes widen. 'That's exceptional.'

'You like your wines?'

'I do. I sometimes used to go to Otago with friends for a wine-tasting tour. I have a small collection in my cupboard.'

'No fun drinking alone.'

She said, 'You're welcome to come over and try some.'

The surprise he felt was nothing to the shock widening her eyes. 'I might take you up on that,' he said fast, not willing to give her a way out of her sudden invitation. Visiting with her away from work might fix his curiosity and quieten the noise in his head and chest. *Yeah, sure. Got lots of spare time, have you?*

The grapes in his vineyard were on schedule, and he'd got the bird netting in place during his break so the major projects were under control, but there was always plenty to do. Adding in some social visits would stretch the time budget. Time away from either of his occupations, to relax and enjoy another person's company, could be good for him.

Not that he was lonely. He saw Bodie and Evelyn most days, but having that special woman to laugh and talk with, to share the daily gripes and fun with, would be a bonus. But it wasn't happening. After Valerie, he'd steered clear of involvement, but there were the lonely nights and empty future without a special love to cope with. However, he wasn't filling those nights for the sake of it.

Claire was staring at him. 'We were talking about wine.'

'Yes, I'll see that you do, in the next week or two.' Damn, but she could distract him. There were women he'd had fun and sex with, but none of them had sparked the deep longing and tightening sensation Claire managed without a blink. Frightening. His heart could be broken all over again if he gave into this need clawing throughout him. *So don't.*

She leaned closer, looking amused. 'Are you always this quiet?'

If only it was appropriate to wind his arms around her and hold her close, to breathe in roses, to tuck his chin amongst those soft curls. 'Make the most of it.'

Her eyes sparkled. 'You think?'

His heart clenched, his breath stuck in the back of his throat. This was getting out of hand. 'How's your wine going?'

Her laugh was deep, and sexy. 'I've hardly started.'

On the wine? Or him? He was in deep trouble if she was referring to him. But she wouldn't be. Until now she'd been quiet, almost shy. It couldn't be him bringing her out of her shell. More likely she felt comfortable surrounded by people she knew. 'Then let's get you going.' Blah. That was bland. Like he was tongue-tied.

The woman Claire had been talking with looked up at him. 'We haven't met, have we? I'm Joachim's wife, Jess.' She put her hand out.

'Hello, Jess. I'm Nicolas, a part-time nurse at the centre.'

'Part-time?' Claire asked. 'The way everyone talks about you, I thought you must be there twenty-four-seven.' She was laughing at him.

He laughed back. 'Sorry, only three days a week.' Often that equated to thirty-six hours. 'The rest of the time I work on my vineyard.'

'You're a wine-grower as well?' Her eyes had widened

slightly and were full of intrigue. 'And I just suggested you try some from my cupboard.' She shook her head.

He had her attention and—admit it—he was enjoying it. His smile faded. Was he setting himself up for a fall? The usual restraints on his emotions were slipping sideways, which was unusual in itself. But one look into those beguiling eyes and he carried on. 'When I moved here I was going to buy a house in town but couldn't get away from how much I enjoyed being out on Bodie and Evelyn's property. It was quiet and the open spaces drew me in, so I bought some land next to them that had been on the market for a while.'

'Was it already established in grapes?'

'Not a vine in sight. But Bodie wasn't letting me languish on the land and I was soon planting vines and putting up wires and posts.'

Claire smiled directly at him. 'Doesn't look like you're sorry.'

'No, it was the best thing I could've done. I enjoy working the land, getting my hands dirty and fighting the elements. But I also love nursing, so it's been a compromise. I sell my harvest to Bodie to add to his, which he then turns into great wine. I'm never without a drop, by the way.' Nicolas felt his chest expanding with pride. For a guy who'd spent the first years of his working life avoiding his parents' demands to get serious and study medicine he'd done more than okay in an unexpected enterprise.

Sure, there were times he regretted walking away from school too soon because the pressure to follow his brother as head boy, then as a top medical student and finally as one of the most sought-after plastic surgeons in the country had ground him down. He'd wanted to be himself, achieve *his* dreams, which were similar to his father's, but he'd needed to do it without the added pressure of being as good as his brother. In the end he'd given up and gone in a different direction.

Which had been successful. First he'd spent years on fishing boats out of Nelson, making and banking a small fortune that he'd used to buy his first house and pay for his years studying to become a nurse. The disappointment on his parents' faces on the day he qualified still haunted him. A nurse didn't compare to a surgeon. Even when they'd given up trying to turn him back onto what they believed was the right track and accepted he was following his own ideas, he sensed their disappointment. If only they'd realised he'd have done what they'd wanted if they hadn't spent his whole childhood comparing him to his brother, because it *had* been his dream to be a surgeon. Not in plastic surgery, but general surgery, which still would've made them proud. Now he was okay with his choices, preferred his lifestyle to that of an overworked, harried surgeon.

'Seems you've got the best of both worlds.' Claire appeared to understand what that meant to him. Because she'd dealt with problems taking her own route through life? Raising Mia alone without doubt would've added to the pressures of working as a doctor.

'I have.' There were still a few worlds out there he hoped to conquer. The most important being to have a family with a woman he loved to bits. Who loved him back. Children he'd never compare with one another, nor set his goals for them to make their lives around. Where was Mia's father? If he'd died, wouldn't Claire have worded it differently when she'd mentioned no man lurking in the background? So there had to be a father somewhere who apparently didn't show his daughter any affection. But how could a man not hug his little girl? He must've got it wrong. That was beyond comprehension.

'Hello, you two. Enjoying yourselves?' Evelyn asked

with a mischievous smile on her face. She couldn't be trusted not to interfere if she thought he needed a kick in the pants to make a move, either about his career or his single status.

'We're doing fine, thank you.'

Claire glanced at him with one eyebrow slightly raised, matching the way the corner of her mouth turned upward. 'We are indeed.'

Evelyn was still grinning. 'I thought it wouldn't hurt for you both to meet before you got here and had no time to talk.'

Soft laughter spilled from Claire. 'You were way behind the ball, Evelyn. We'd already met. Twice.'

'Twice? Where? When?'

'For us to know and you to keep wondering.' Claire sipped her wine. 'You should try some of this. It's excellent.'

Nicolas kept his laughter tucked inside, but the look on Evelyn's face was hilarious. Right now she had no idea what was going on, and he wasn't about to let her off the hook. It was fun seeing her confusion. Point to Claire. He could get to like Claire even more.

'I'll get you a Sauvignon Blanc, shall I, Evelyn?'

'I've got that.' Bodie held a glass out to his wife.

Claire was still smiling. 'Mia thinks Michelle's wonderful. She put her favourite dress on for her.'

'There you go. Hope Mia likes chocolate because Michelle took some with her. The staff are given samples every day.'

'Think I'll get a job there,' Nicolas said. 'They make the best chocolate imaginable.'

'I haven't tried it,' Claire told them. 'I've been buying lots of cherries instead. They're my favourite fruit.'

He watched her sip her wine and his stomach lurched.

Her lips were full and gave him tingles just imagining them on his skin.

'I'll be back.' He needed to step away, get under control before Claire saw the need in his eyes. He headed outside into the garden, where the chefs had the barbecues cranked up.

'Here, get that into you.' Bodie handed him a replenished glass. 'You look like you've taken a hit.'

'I haven't finished my first drink.' He took the proffered glass anyway. Now he looked desperate, holding two drinks.

'It's iced water, known to fix dry mouths,' Bodie said. 'I checked your grapes today. They're bang on target for harvest.'

Two months away. Bodie was giving him a chance to catch his breath and get back on an even keel. 'I figured they're coming along as they should.' Harvest was a crazy time with little sleep and a lot of work. 'I've already arranged to hire casual labour for the week it'll take to collect the grapes.' It would be up to him to oversee everything, meaning another break from the medical centre, but he had plenty of leave up his sleeve.

'As long as the summer doesn't turn wet, we'll both have bumper crops.'

'Pinot Gris and Chardonnay to fill the cellar.' They always kept some back to enjoy throughout the year. Claire liked Pinot Gris. Something they had in common.

Bodie was sniffing the air like a spaniel. 'Think the steak's almost done.'

'Let's bring the women out to one of those tables under the trees.' It was a beautiful setting and the night was warm.

'I'll claim one,' Bodie agreed with a cheeky look. 'You round up the women.'

Thanks, mate. Could've given me some breathing space.

But Bodie was on the same page as his wife. The two of them couldn't leave him to sort out his single status. They knew how little he was trying to change his lifestyle. They also knew how one day he'd like to fall in love again, and have some kids to raise and cherish. And that he wasn't just taking it slow, but instead was actively protecting his heart. Someone had to, and who better than him?

Draining the glass of water, Nicolas headed inside. 'Claire, Evelyn, want to join us outside? Bodie's nabbed a table. Jess, Joachim, why don't you come out there too?' Claire looked so relaxed with these people he wanted to keep it that way so she didn't wander off to join another group.

She walked beside him as they headed out to the table. 'This is fun, having adult time and not having to worry about Mia.'

'Do you really not get out without her?' It was hard to believe when she was so vibrant at the moment.

'My friends in Dunedin had a daughter the same age and we took turns babysitting for each other. I'd go to book group and a couple of other groups like that.'

He held back saying she should be getting out with people who knew how to have light-hearted fun. Instead he said, 'You can do the same here.'

'I haven't had time, what with moving into the house, getting to know the job and settling Mia, though, to be fair, she's been cruisy about the move. Not worried about meeting new friends or having a new bedroom.' Claire's smile was all for her daughter. Lucky kid.

What would it take to get her to smile at him like that? He needed to calm down. 'Throw in the fact it's December and most groups close until February and your timing sucks. But there are plenty of other things to do around Marlborough in summer. Boating, fishing, swimming, picnics.'

She was staring at him as if he were crazy. 'Boating? Fishing?'

'You know? Floating on the sea, a line hanging over the side of the boat, a gentle tug on the hook and winding it in like fury to get the blue cod on board for dinner.'

'I've never fished.'

'You like eating fish?'

'That's what fish shops are for.'

'Then you haven't tasted fish so fresh it falls apart while it's cooking.' A plan was forming as he talked, but he kept it to himself. Too early in the evening to be suggesting they spend a day together on the briny. Or anywhere. She mightn't like him enough, might think he was downright uninteresting and start looking around for somewhere else to sit.

'Can't say I have.' This time her smile was teasing. 'But there are a lot of things I haven't tried.'

'If you think you and Mia would like wandering around the vineyard let me know and we can arrange a time to suit. Kent, Evelyn and Bodie's boy, could join us. Has Mia met him?'

'They go to the same preschool and get on well.'

That made things easier. 'I can take Mia for a ride on a tractor, if you think she'd like that.'

'You'd be making a friend for life. Anything with four wheels intrigues her. I believe she wants to learn to drive my car before she's got the hang of her bicycle without trainer wheels.'

Did that friend for life come with her mother? He always knew when he was onto something or someone who intrigued him. He and Bodie had met at a rugby game and become instant friends. They'd never let each other down in a big way since. The day he'd gone to knock on the door of a fishing company at Nelson Port to make enquiries about work on a trawler, he'd known from the moment he'd been taken on board to look around it was the right job for him to get ahead. When he was first introduced to Valerie, his ex-wife, he'd been hesitant at first. She seemed kind and fun, yet there'd been something about her he couldn't put his finger on. Whatever it was, he'd put it down to the insecurities his family handed him and moved on to fall in love with her, only to have it all backfire a few years later. Something to hold onto so he didn't make a mess of his life again.

'I'd better hide my four-wheel bike. Can't have Mia thinking she can ride that yet.' Four-wheel bikes were involved in far too many accidents on farms.

Claire shivered. 'I've seen the stats, and dealt with a couple of farmers who've come a cropper when out in the paddocks on their bikes. It wasn't pretty in either case.'

'They're one of the best inventions for getting around the land, as long as whoever's on board wears a helmet and doesn't try to overdo speed or steepness on an incline. My land's fairly flat, but I'm still cautious. Haven't got the need to break a leg or worse.' At the table, Nicolas pulled out a chair for Claire.

'Can I get you a refill of wine?'

'Please. More of the same. It's so good being able to relax and not worry about Mia or getting home.'

'Be right back.'

'That's good.' Claire put down her glass and relaxed some more. It was so easy to do around Nicolas. For a moment there she'd wondered if she should get up and go talk to other people instead of hogging Nicolas to herself. But he was easy to be with. If she didn't focus on the tightening of her skin every time his eyes met hers. Or how her toes seemed to be dancing inside her sassy shoes.

The guy was something else. Toned muscles filled his shirt and shaped his trousers. His hands looked strong and gentle, capable of teasing her awake in a blaze of heat. While his face appeared open she'd seen his muted concern for that woman in the accident yesterday. As for his lips—they could turn her into a blithering idiot with one touch. It wasn't as though she hadn't dated a good-looking man ever before, but it was rare for her to get so wound up so fast. Nicolas was sexy beyond her experience. *We're not on a date.* Shame about that. She might've let her hair down if they were. A short fling wouldn't hurt. And was long overdue.

Another sideways look and her heart hammered. The moment she'd opened her door to Nicolas she'd felt a connection. The cause was probably the Santa incident and working together at the accident scene. She was certainly more aware of him than usual with men she didn't know.

Nicolas leaned closer. 'Word of warning. Now you're friends with Evelyn be prepared to get elbowed in a multitude of situations.'

Claire laughed. 'Think I worked that out already.' Plus he'd already hinted at it. Then that manly scent reached her and she sat back, holding her breath. It was too good. Heated her in places she didn't need right now.

Nicolas was watching her as though reading her mind. He'd better not be. She'd curl up in a ball of embarrassment. Then what he'd said about Evelyn hit home. 'Asking you to pick me up tonight doesn't come into that category—' his eyes widened '—does it?'

Surprise flicked across his face, before he shrugged. 'Honestly, until you said that I didn't think so, but now? Who knows?'

'Great.' Just what she didn't need, someone trying to set her up with a guy. While she'd moved here to break out of the dreary life she had in Dunedin, and to hopefully find happiness with someone eventually, she was not ready. Certainly had no intention of rushing into a relationship until she knew how life here was going to be.

Nicolas was still watching her closely, as though he wanted to find out more about her.

Again she hoped his mindreading skills were poor. Time to put some space between them and let the heat that look instigated cool off. She picked up her glass in preparation to head over to talk to someone else.

Nicolas reached over with his to tap the glass she held. 'Here's to a fun night.'

The air puffed out of her lungs. She didn't really want to go be with another group, with anyone else. She liked sitting here with Nicolas. She was liking him more with each passing minute. Whatever that might mean. A few hours chatting and enjoying dinner. Or more. Taking Mia out to his property as he'd suggested, or a short fling. With all the heat cruising throughout her body, anything could happen. One thing—*no hurting each other, please.* She couldn't take another broken heart.

'Come on, you two. They've put the steaks on the service table,' Bodie called.

Nicolas blinked as though he'd forgotten where they were. 'Coming.' He stood up and made to pull her chair out when she rose. 'Ready for dinner?'

'Absolutely.' The urge to slip her hand in his as they crossed to the tables laden with salads, fish and vegetable dishes was so strong she had to clench her fingers into a ball. When had she ever done that? She couldn't remember. Had to be eons ago. Reaching out to Nicolas was wrong. The man had given her a ride, not invited her on a hot date. All very well to be excited being with him, and thinking about things she hadn't in a long time, but she needed to know more about him if she was following that path. Truthfully, she wasn't. She didn't want to be let down again. Two men had done that already. They were the reason she was OTT hesitant about getting into a relationship. Too easy to give her heart away, a damned sight harder to put it back together. Anyway, she had to be super-careful for Mia's sake. No man she brought into their lives was going to hurt her girl.

When she was training to become a doctor she'd met Anthony, another trainee, and they'd soon got together as a couple. He'd been kind and generous to a fault, and she'd loved him for it. Then one day when they'd been together almost three years, he'd said he didn't love her enough to spend the rest of their lives together. She'd been devastated, and from then on more afraid than ever to let any man too close. But behind that fear lay a longing to fall in love with a wonderful man and have children. She still wanted those things, but not at the cost of her daughter's trust and love, let alone hers.

Nicolas handed her a plate. 'Here you are. There's an amazing array of food to choose from.'

'My stomach's rumbling already.'

He leaned closer. 'I can't hear it.'

A whiff of his scent teased her again. Nothing like a good male smell to set her hormones dancing. *Down girl.*

'Be glad you can't.'

'What are you going to have?'

'A bit of everything?' She grinned.

Doing a lot of smiling, Claire.

Why not? Nicolas made her happy and brought on the smiles. There was nothing much she could do to stop them. 'I'll start with the steak.'

'Nothing like a good steak cooked to perfection and these certainly look like they are.' Nicolas handed her the servers. 'Here you go.'

The food was excellent, the company even better. Claire sighed happily as they left the restaurant after ten. She couldn't remember the last time she'd enjoyed herself so much. The crowd had thinned out and when Evelyn and Bodie said they were heading home Claire decided it was time for her too. Much as she was enjoying herself—and Nicolas—she was tired. Or was that an excuse to cut the night short before she had to make any serious decisions about where she went from here? Did she invite him in for coffee? A kiss? It wasn't a date, but that wouldn't matter if they wanted to get intense.

Intense. She couldn't risk it. Too much to lose. Her heart sank when it should be standing strong. His easy nature and caring way attracted her, but didn't explain the heat in her veins, nor the tightness in her legs. That was down to sex, nothing else. Even that wasn't happening. Not tonight anyway. And Nicolas mightn't be interested anyway. Though he had spent most of the evening with her, but hadn't cramped her style—not that she had a lot of that. She smiled to herself. She was so out of practice socialising it wasn't even funny any more.

'Did you enjoy yourself?' Nicolas asked as they drove away from the restaurant.

'I did. I feel as though I belong even more now. Being social with colleagues makes the day-to-day grind easier somehow.' Everyone had made her welcome and treated her as though she'd always worked with them. This move was turning out to be better with each passing week. Glancing sideways to the man she'd spent most of the evening with, she shook herself mentally. He was so different to Anthony with his openness and not trying to win her over with platitudes. Hard to imagine him denying her pregnancy either. That excited her. *Careful.* She was reading too much into his straightforward ways. One dinner together—amidst a crowd—didn't make a future. But it had started her dreaming of possibilities.

Put the lid back on the box, Claire. You're not ready for a full-on relationship. You've only just begun this new adventure in Blenheim. Tread softly and slowly or you're going to get hurt.

'I've never thought of it like that, but it makes sense,' said Nicolas.

'You can tell I've hardly changed jobs any more than I've moved towns,' she said with a tight laugh.

'You're glad you've made the move?'

'So far it's one of the best things I've done in a long time. Mia's happy too. Not that she wasn't before, but I did worry she'd find it hard making new friends, but I should've known better.' Her girl was a little toughie, most of the time. Didn't do so well whenever she hurt herself physically. Then she needed hugs and kisses to stop the tears. Nothing wrong in that. Claire loved handing them out any time, not only when they were needed. Only to her daughter, that was.

Men usually let her down. If she was even thinking there might be more to come with Nicolas she had to take it ultra-slowly. Not only for her own safety when it came to her heart, but Mia as well. More so Mia. Her girl longed for a father to love her, cuddle her. She understood how hard it was not to have that, so the absolute last thing she would do was let a man into their lives who wasn't going to stay—for ever. So no hugs or kisses going on tonight. They would've been exciting though.

CHAPTER THREE

NICOLAS'S HEART WAS pounding as he drove away from Claire's after seeing her to the front door. What a roller coaster of a night. They'd got along ridiculously well, while all the time alarm bells had been ringing. Claire was wonderful. He wasn't ready to get close. Claire was wary. He was enthralled. Not to mention cautious.

If only they were in the sack right this minute, making out like he'd been denying he wanted from the moment she'd opened her door to him. When was the last time he'd been so intrigued, felt so much fizzing in his blood? There'd been a connection. He was certain of it. His more wary side was relieved Claire had firmly stepped away from him at the door with a quiet smile. He wanted to leap into whatever was brewing between them. He wanted to head out of town and not stop until the sun came up, bringing some clarity with it.

Guess if Claire was at all interested in some fun then she was being careful. Knowing nothing about her past, he had to accept her move. Even if there was nothing to make her wary of getting close, he understood she mightn't be feeling it for him. Some of her glances his way had suggested otherwise—eyes flashing brief glimpses of hope and longing. If he knew nothing else, he knew she wasn't about to rush blindly into a relationship that could backfire and hurt her and Mia badly. He felt she was worth waiting for. If he was ready to go further—and really there was nothing to say he was—he had to be patient and careful. Even if only for a brief fling.

Could be that he should be grateful to her. Rushing into getting close was not a good idea. He'd taken his time with Valerie and it had still gone belly up. He hadn't been good enough for her. Another man had given her what she wanted apparently, though he'd seemed to disappear from her life shortly after their breakup.

Toot, toot. A car came up behind him as he slowed for his entrance. From the logo on the front he knew it was Bodie and Evelyn. No doubt they'd be laughing their heads off about the fact he was already heading home.

His phone beeped as a message came in. He braked to a stop and glanced at the screen, then cursed his friend.

Lost your touch, mate????

Evelyn had to be driving since that was Bodie's number. And his wit. He turned up their drive. They owed him a drink for their cheek. He'd walk the couple of hundred metres across the paddock to home afterwards.

'Got a thirst going?' Bodie asked as he clambered out of his state-of-the-art four-wheel drive, a grin on his annoying face.

A larger thirst than a glass of wine would fix, but he'd keep that to himself. 'It's still early. I'm not ready for bed.'

'I bet.' That grin expanded.

Should've driven straight home. Sipping the wine Bodie poured a few minutes later, Nicolas looked around at the family photos on the walls of the lounge, and paused. Evelyn had Michelle ten years before she met Bodie. Her marriage had fallen apart two years earlier and she'd raised her daughter singlehanded until Bodie came along and won her over.

'Do you know how long Claire's been on her own?' he asked Evelyn. He was open to the idea of raising a partner's children, and adding more to the mix. Being a dad was right up there with being happily married. But first he had to find the right woman and, since he hadn't been looking, Claire had blindsided him.

'From the little she's said, I think she was single when she had Mia, and I don't think there's been anyone in her life since then. But you'd have to ask her. It's not for me to gossip.'

'Fair enough. She said very little, but it is early days.'

'So there'll be some days?' Evelyn wasn't teasing. She was watching him closely, as if this was important.

Which it was, if he was to get together with Claire. These two were his closest friends, they knew his past, and how he had to be careful because he didn't think he could face heartbreak again. But others did and were happy. Like Evelyn.

'I hope so.'

If Claire's keen.

She *had* leaned in closer to talk to him a couple of times, cutting others out of their conversation.

They needed to shift the conversation away from Claire. She wasn't here to stick up for herself, or to refute any suggestions they might come up with about who she was. His fault for raising the question.

Evelyn must've had the same thought, because she said, 'You both seemed to get on well, for which I'm glad. So, what's on the work menu for tomorrow? Servicing the harvesters?'

'I've got some spraying to do,' Nicolas answered. Hopefully that would keep him busy all day and his mind off a particularly attractive and alluring woman.

It worked for most of the day, but first he'd had a sleepless night, tossing and turning while his mind kept flipping up images of Claire. Claire smiling. Claire looking shy. Though somehow he suspected it wasn't shyness, more reticence about letting go too much. Then there was the wave of heat she caused in him time and again when he sat near her. Getting down and greasy on the harvesters had been good for him. Checking oil levels, tyre pressures, motor status, had kept Claire at bay. Until he tossed the rags in the bin and headed inside for a well-earned beer and dinner.

Come Monday and work, and Nicolas was keen to pull on his nurse's persona and get to the Urgent Care medical centre. Working in two entirely different jobs gave him a lot of energy and enjoyment. One very physical, and the other more about caring for other people.

'Morning, Nicolas,' Claire called as he stepped into the office, where another doctor and three nurses stood around with mugs of coffee in hand. She looked bright and cheerful, and was smiling widely. Was work her happy place?

'Hello. You had a good weekend?'

'Yes. Finally finished unpacking the last boxes. Took Mia to Pollard Park. Nothing major but all good. What about you?'

If only he could've been a part of her weekend. Though unpacking cartons of her household gear wouldn't have been exciting, the company would've been. Interesting.

Pouring a coffee, he replied, 'Sprayed the vines, mowed between the rows, and had a soak in the hot tub at the end of the day.' With a beer and dreams of a holiday on an island with a sexy lady named Claire. Unbelievable how much of his time she took up just by being in his head.

How unusual it was. Scary. As if he'd started on the long, slippery slope to opening up his heart and there was no stopping him. There had to be. He wasn't ready. Might never be.

'That sounds like a lot of work. You're here for a break then.' So she could tease him. Good.

'No break happening,' Tina, the receptionist, chuckled. 'We've already got a queue waiting outside the door.'

'We'd better get started then. I'm triage today.' Nicolas headed to the office to place his coffee on the desk before going to unlock the front doors and start the day rolling. 'Morning, everyone.'

He was greeted with the usual calls of hello and concern.

'Take your turn at Reception. We'll be seeing you in order of priority, so don't feel you have to push ahead of anyone.' It happened all the time, people wanting to get in first. Getting to work on time didn't come before chest pains or suspected fractures. But it was also true that the first patients registered usually were seen immediately as two doctors were waiting to start their day. People with serious injuries or conditions would've gone next door to the hospital emergency department. This centre was for those with less urgent problems or those who didn't have a regular GP to visit.

Back in his office, he hummed to himself as he watched the computer screen and waited for the first patient's name to appear. He'd get that one assessed pronto, then they'd go straight through to Claire or Ryan.

'Thank you again for Friday night,' Claire said from behind him. 'I really enjoyed myself.'

Surprised, he spun around on his office chair. 'So did I. It turned out to be fun.' Standing up, he met her wary gaze full-on. 'I truly enjoyed spending time with you. We should go out together some time.' Sooner rather than later.

She blinked, and her smile returned. 'I'd like that. A lot,' she added in a rush.

'Good. What—?'

'Claire, can you take the first patient?' Ryan appeared in the doorway. 'I've got to go across to ED to sign off some paperwork on a patient I sent them yesterday.'

'No problem.'

Nicolas sat back down and looked at the screen. 'Thirty-one-year-old male, query fractured wrist. You want to take him straight through to your room? I don't need to triage him.'

'Sure.' She came closer and leaned over to read the sparse notes. 'Joey Sanders. Got it.'

Nicolas breathed deep, inhaled roses. The scent was becoming addictive. 'There's the next case coming up.' Go away and take that scent with you. 'Hope Ryan doesn't take too long.'

'Me too.' Finally the roses floated out of the room.

Five minutes and he was already screwed. It was going to be a long day. Shoving off his chair, he headed out to the waiting room. 'Trish White? Come through.'

The thirty-six-year-old hobbled after him and sat on the seat he pointed to.

'I'm Nicolas, the triage nurse. You've hurt your ankle. What happened?'

'I tripped over the cat on the way to the bathroom and went down in a heap on my ankle. I hope I've only sprained it, but it is very painful when I put weight on it.'

'Place your foot on my chair so I can have a look.' Moderate swelling made it difficult to feel anything. 'Did you knock your head or feel faint before you tripped up?'

'No, nothing like that.'

'I'll check your blood pressure in case there's a medical reason for your fall. How did you get here?'

'My neighbour dropped me off at the emergency department on her way to work. I was told to come over here as this isn't considered urgent.' Trish sounded peeved. 'Walking over was painful.'

An orderly should've brought her across in a wheelchair.

'They prefer to keep the department free for serious injuries, and you'd have had to wait longer to be seen there.' BP normal. 'So there's no one with you?'

'No.'

Darn. Always better to have another person to hear what the medical staff had to say. 'Stay here while I get a wheelchair.' Along with a nurse to take her to Ryan's room, since he could hear the other doctor out in the hall. 'Jude, can you grab a wheelchair? I've got a patient for Ryan.'

'Here we go.' Jude rolled a chair in.

Nicolas held the wheelchair while Jude helped Trish stand and swivel around to sit again.

The woman winced. 'It can't be broken if I can limp along on it. I haven't got time for a broken ankle. I'm getting married in two weeks and I don't want to be on crutches for that.'

That explained her agitation. 'Let's not get ahead of things. The doctor will examine your ankle and if he thinks there's a concern he'll send you for an X-ray.'

The next patient was a six-year-old boy with bruises on his face. 'What have you been up to, young man?'

'I fell off my stool at the table and crashed into my brother's highchair. He laughed. It wasn't funny.'

'Not really.' The bruises were large and red, indicating they were very recent, but Nicolas looked closer and noted patches of green and dark blue around the edges of the new bruises. Older bruises. Something not right here.

'You'll be all right, Noah,' his mother said. 'You shouldn't have been bouncing around on the stool when you were meant to eat your breakfast and get ready for school.'

'But Dad said—'

'Dad said to hurry up or you'd have to walk.' The woman's face was tight, and her mouth grim.

Nicolas asked Noah, 'Did you hurt yourself anywhere else? Your arms or back?'

The boy looked to his mother, then down at the floor. 'No.'

'I'm going to touch your head in places and I want you to tell me if it hurts, okay?'

He nodded, still looking down.

Checking the boy's skull elicited not a sound from him. Nicolas then lifted the boy's tee-shirt and gently felt his ribs and shoulders, down his spine. A couple of old bruises but no pain. So he might be reading more into this than was real. Then a small shudder as Nicolas touched his left side. Something was not right. 'There you go. I want you to sit in the waiting room with your mother for a few minutes. The doctor will come and get you very soon.'

'He's always been accident-prone,' the mother said as she helped Noah off his chair and took him by the shoulder to head out of the room.

Heard that before, Nicolas thought as he went to see if either Claire or Ryan were free to talk to. Claire was at her desk scrolling down the in-patient screen.

'Got a minute?' he asked.

Her head rocked back a bit as he closed the door behind him. 'Have you got a medical problem?'

'Not at all.' Seeing her for medical advice wasn't on. They worked together, and some things were best kept separate. 'I'm concerned about the next patient. Six-year-old Noah has major bruising to his face. There appear to be older bruises beneath today's, and he got uncomfortable talking about them at first, saying he'd fallen off the stool into his brother's highchair. As though he'd been told to shut up about anything else. I could be completely wrong, but my antenna's up and pinging. He flinched when I touched his left side.'

'You're concerned about abuse?'

'See what you think. He tensed up when his mother mentioned Dad.' Nicolas headed for the door. 'I'm probably overreacting, but I've seen this before and would hate to miss the signs. Of course, what happens next if I'm right lands on you, and might add up to zilch if the mother isn't prepared to talk. She appears to be a tough nut to crack, but I've seen them fold before once the questions get too close for comfort.'

'I'm glad you mentioned your concerns. It's hard enough dealing with abuse without having to tread carefully around the parent.' She stood and looked directly at him. For a brief moment he forgot why he was here. 'I'll be on the lookout now.'

It was all he'd asked for. 'Good.' Stepping out of the room, he went back to his room and looked up the next patient.

'Nicolas,' Claire called.

He turned.

'I'd like you to join me with Noah and his mother. They've already spent time with you so we'll do a thorough exam together.' Her shoulder lifted subtly. 'A second opinion is always important in these cases.'

'I'll bring him in now.' His feet were all but dancing as he headed to the waiting room. They were on the same page. Great.

* * *

Claire breathed deep in an attempt to loosen the knots in her belly. Nicolas hadn't turned into a frog over the weekend. He was still good-looking in that outdoorsy way, his skin no doubt tanned from working in his vineyard, his stride firm and confident and his head held high. Her kind of man—if she had a type. So far she hadn't done well in that area.

Nicolas appeared to know what he wanted from his life and was going for it. He'd treated her well on Friday night, and made her feel special by being genuine. Not the sort of man who'd take what he wanted and walk away from the consequences. Then there was the kind way he'd treated the kids when he was Santa, suggesting he cared about children and their feelings. Add in his suspicions about the boy she was about to see, and he was winning more points by the day.

He's winning me over too easily.

Something that never happened—because she refused to allow it, was on guard about her feelings all the time. She had to protect herself and Mia. Except Nicolas seemed to be overriding all her barriers in one fell swoop. How come that didn't send her running from the building? Thinking back to Friday night, a tingle of anticipation repeated itself. Excitement was possible if she opened up a little, relaxed and went with the new sensations Nicolas caused.

A loud metallic crash came from the sluice room, and some low mutterings.

'You all right in there, Liz?' Claire asked the nurse picking up a metal bowl from the floor.

'Having a brain fade moment,' Liz replied. 'Teach me

to be daydreaming about the weekend and not focusing on what I'm meant to be doing.'

Eek. Better get ready to see Noah before my daydreams cause me to do something silly.

Within moments her room was crowded, her young patient looking bewildered and scared. His mother appeared defiant, but the fact she was here with her son said lots in her favour. 'Hello, I'm Claire, one of the doctors. Are you Mrs Robertson?' she asked the woman firmly gripping the lad's shoulder as Nicolas showed them in.

'That's me. Noah was playing around on the kitchen stool when he fell off and hit his face on the highchair. He says it's very sore and one eye has closed up.'

'Take a seat.' Claire closed the door and moved to her desk. 'I'm going to touch your face, Noah, to find out if there are any broken bones under those bruises. Is that all right?'

'Yeah.'

'Sit up and speak nicely,' Mrs Robertson growled.

The boy shuffled his bottom on the chair.

'Look up at me, Noah.' Nicolas was right about older bruises under the red and purple swellings. She suspected he'd also got it right about the abuse. 'Tell me if I hurt you,' she added softly.

'He's tough,' the mother said.

When Claire felt along the cheekbone Noah winced and jerked sideways. 'That hurts there?' she asked.

'Lots.'

Sitting down, Claire typed some notes into Noah's file. It wasn't the first time he'd been to the Urgent Care medical centre with a fracture, which might make the conversation she was about to have more difficult.

'Mrs Robertson, I see Noah has other, older bruises on his face. Did he have another fall a few days ago?'

'Yes. He's clumsy like that.' The woman looked everywhere but at her.

'Did you take him to get medical help then?'

'No. He said it wasn't hurting too bad.'

Claire's finger was tapping her thigh as she asked, 'Are you sure he fell?' If anyone hit Mia she'd be after them like a crazed woman. 'It seems odd to have bruising in the same place, that's all.' That wasn't the half of it, but softly, softly was the only approach.

'I brought him here to get fixed, not to be questioned like I've done anything wrong. Come on, Noah. We're going home.'

'Wait, Mrs Robertson. Noah needs to have a facial X-ray because I believe there are broken bones in his cheeks. It's really important to find out so we can fix them without him suffering more pain. We don't want that, do we?'

'No, I suppose not. But what if they were broken the first time he was hurt?'

'Let's wait until we know if there are any fractures. If there are then I'll be referring Noah across to the hospital to see a paediatric orthopaedic surgeon. A child's bone doctor,' she explained as Mrs Robertson started to look confused.

Relief replaced the confusion. 'That's good.' She probably thought the questions about how Noah had sustained his injuries would go away when they saw a specialist. She was wrong, but Claire wasn't about to tell her so.

'First I would like to give Noah a thorough check-up.'

Nicolas immediately helped the boy onto the bed. 'Lie on your back, Noah. I'll lift your shirt so the doctor can see your chest. Okay?'

Noah stared at Nicolas as if debating whether to trust him. 'Yeah.'

'Got to make sure you're all good everywhere else,' Nicolas told him.

No internal swelling around his organs, Claire noted.

Nicolas helped Noah roll over onto his stomach, and his mouth tightened.

Three old bruises covered the boy's shoulders. Claire touched them lightly. 'Any pain here, Noah?'

The boy moved his head back and forth on the pillow. *Bet you hurt when those were inflicted.*

'Can I look at your legs?'

Nicolas was already preparing him for further examination. She hadn't had to say anything but she did want Noah to hear her talking so as not to get too spooked. He already had enough to deal with and his mother wasn't saying a word.

Minutes later she sat down at her desk and filled in some notes. 'Mrs Robertson, Noah needs to go to radiology urgently.' It wasn't an urgent case but any time spent sitting in the waiting room would be risky. He might be taken away without any treatment at all.

The woman sat there, gripping her hands in her lap, keeping silent.

'You want him to be taken care of, don't you?' Reminding her of why she'd brought Noah here in the first place might ease the tension.

Her head dipped slowly. 'Yes,' she whispered.

'Noah, I'm getting you a wheelchair and taking you for a ride. What do you think?' Nicolas asked.

'Okay.'

Nicolas looked to Claire, sorrow in his eyes. 'Give me a moment to find Liz. She'll take over triage while I help Noah. I'll stay with him.' He understood what she was worried about.

'Thanks.' Empathy came to mind. Most men were em-pathetic around children. She knew that, but sometimes had to remind herself that it was true. Her father had never hurt her physically, but he'd broken her heart when he'd walked out of her life. Mia's had done the same, though she was only now starting to understand what she was missing out on.

I want a cuddle from my daddy. Those words hadn't left her. Worse, there was nothing she could do about them. It was as though Hank had never existed. Except whenever she looked at Mia she saw his wide open smile and enjoyment of most things that came her way.

Nicolas returned quickly, pushing a child's wheelchair. 'Let's go, buddy. Mum's coming too.'

'I'll see you soon, Noah,' Claire said. *You'll be under constant care so you can't be removed from the hospital until this is sorted.*

Claire's heart felt heavy. 'That poor little boy. Why doesn't his mother stand up for him?' she asked Nicolas when he returned half an hour later to say Noah had been admitted with fractured ribs and cheekbones.

'She's probably another victim. I saw a bruise on her upper arm when the sleeve of her tee-shirt shifted. She was quick to pull it down,' Nicolas said angrily. 'Some men don't deserve children.'

'Or wives,' Claire agreed, then instantly regretted saying that.

He glanced her way, as if to check her out.

'No, I've never been physically abused by anyone,' she added quickly.

'Glad to hear that.' Nicolas wasn't looking away though. Almost as if he could see right inside her and knew she had more to tell.

Which she had no intention of doing. Not now, more than likely not ever. It was a sad, pathetic story that she'd come to terms with as an adult, accepting her mother couldn't change and that deep down she'd loved her daughter. That alone had kept Claire at home looking out for her until she'd suddenly packed up and headed to Perth. Her mother had loved deeply and never got over what she'd lost, even when inadvertently inflicting pain on her daughter.

No wonder I am afraid of loving too much, Claire thought. Not true. She loved Mia more than she'd once have believed possible. Did that mean she might one day love a man as much? On a positive day she'd say anything was possible. She'd loved Anthony with all she had. Look where that got her.

Nicolas refocused her with, 'There's another priority one patient for you. Twenty-four-year-old male, heart palpitations, high BP, light-headed. Fell at work. I've put him in a bed and attached the monitors.'

'Name?' She turned for the room where four beds were ready for patients who needed monitoring.

'Jason Maynard.' Nicolas stepped away, stopped and turned around. 'You agreed with me re that boy?'

'Yes, one hundred percent. I'll call the child therapist once I've seen Maynard.'

'Good.' His smile went straight to her belly, and made her feel warmer than she already was.

There was a bounce in her step as she went to her next patient. Anything was possible on a good day, and seeing Nicolas at work, being on the same wavelength when it came to a patient, went some way to making this one of the best. Almost as if she hadn't a care in the world.

At five-fifteen Claire walked into the childcare centre to the sound of tired children grizzling. Mia was pushing a plastic truck around the sandpit with Kent. 'Hi, you two. Have you had a good day?'

'Kent ate my sandwich, but I had his chocolate cookie because he didn't want it.'

'He's conning you already.' Nicolas spoke from the other side of the room. 'He loves those biscuits.'

So he was picking Kent up again. Made perfect sense since Evelyn hadn't come into the centre today. He had the makings of a good dad. The lad seemed to adore him, and they had a great rapport. How had he fooled Kent when he was Santa? His voice would've been familiar, surely?

'Kent's not saying anything,' Claire observed, unable to deny feeling happy to see Nicolas, despite having spent all day in the same building, bumping into each other, discussing patients, sharing a coffee break.

Nicolas laughed. 'All part of the plan, suck 'em in and make them think he's the best boy in the play centre.'

'Who did he learn that from? His father, or his father's mate?'

Was that what Nicolas had been doing to her at the barbecue? Sucking her in so she thought he was the best thing out? She might be a fool, but so far she hadn't seen any ill intent in his actions. So far she couldn't fault him. Her eyes were wide open, so when he wanted to be kind and supportive and made sure her glass and plate were full, there'd been no argument from her. She was ready for a little fun.

Air stuck in her throat. That was her usual relationship—a little fun before pulling the plug, no feelings involved or hurt. That mightn't be enough with this man. Not that she understood why. Or did she? At least she was being cautious. She'd sent him away on Friday night when he'd dropped her off. No coffee or a nightcap, nor a kiss, let alone sex. She'd suddenly gone coy on him. Which said more than just about anything else could. When she wanted sex with her date, she got on with it, nothing like she'd been around Nicolas. Not that they'd been on a date. Not officially, anyway.

'Who? Me?' He was still laughing.

'I thought so.' Claire was laughing right along with him—and feeling more comfortable with each passing second. Even after a day of working together and having no hiccups along the way. 'Right-o, Mia, time we headed home and put dinner on.'

'Nicolas, are we going now too?'

'We sure are, kiddo. Where's your bag?'

'On the peg.'

'Then get it, or you won't have a lunch box to fill for tomorrow.'

'You're not running around after him?' Claire watched the two kids race to the wall where their bags hung.

'What? Make him soft? No way. Evelyn would have something to say if I did that.'

'She's got you wound round her little finger.' They were all obviously close. The way Evelyn had befriended her made her think it wouldn't be too long before she was also part of that closeness.

'Only because I let her.' Nicolas took the bag Kent held out to him. 'She's been so good for Bodie, turned his life around when he was in a very bad place. I'd do anything to thank her for that.'

Claire's heart turned over. Most people had a history that had either made them strong or squashed them. Having understanding friends went a long way to helping. Nicolas was obviously one of those. The sort of man who'd be good to have on her side.

'I'm sure they've supported you too.'

'They believe in me, and I can't ask for anything more than that.' He turned away. 'Come on, kiddo. I've got water pipes to shift.'

He didn't think others believed in him? Who had hurt Nicolas for him to feel like that? He was so open and sincere. He worked hard for his patients, and the fact he also ran and operated a vineyard on his land said a lot about his determination and grit. He was very believable.

'See you tomorrow, Nicolas,' she called after him before rounding up Mia, who'd sat down with another girl who was dressing a doll in a wetsuit.

Nicolas waved over his shoulder. 'Sure will.'

Working together meant they'd see a lot of each other, but still a thrill of anticipation ran through Claire. Her job had become a whole lot more interesting and exciting. All because of a man who flipped her switches with a simple smile or a serious comment. For the first time since she could remember tomorrow and work couldn't come fast enough.

I let Claire see my vulnerability? When I'm taking things slowly. Nicolas kicked the tarmac with the tip of his sneaker as he waited for Kent to climb into the back of his four-wheel drive. He'd have sworn but certain little ears would pick up on the words faster than a lightning strike.

'I like Mia's mum,' Kent said as he clicked his seat belt in place.

'You like Mia,' he replied with a cheeky smile. 'You gave her your chocolate cookie.'

'Her lunch was nicer than my peanut butter sandwich. She had a cheese muffin and grapes.'

'Tell your mother, not me. I'm only here to give you a ride home,' he said with a laugh. Evelyn had enough to do without coming up with creative lunches for her son, who usually swapped them out with some other kid. But never his cookies. Just like *he* never said anything about needing to be believed in to anybody. Certainly not to a woman he'd only met a few days ago and was keen to get to know a whole lot better. Showed how much Claire was doing his head in.

Working with her hadn't helped. She was a competent, calm and skilled doctor. Not one patient he'd seen had left her office looking frazzled or upset, even when in pain or on their way to the emergency department next door. Apart from that young boy they'd believed had been abused. Turned out they were right. The boy was now having counselling, and, better still, the mother had admitted she needed help too. It had happened fast, partly because Claire had insisted. She'd been kind and discreet, and fiercely determined, and the woman had buckled fast. She'd even thanked Claire in a roundabout fashion. That family had a long way to go, but they'd taken the first step. He felt some pride in his small part. The medical staff were a team, a team he loved being involved in. More than that, he liked that Claire had joined the centre.

He liked Claire, full stop.

'Can I have an ice cream, Nicolas?'

'No, mate, you can't. It's nearly your dinnertime.'

Your mother would have my head on a tray if I stopped at the shop.

'Knew you'd say that.'

'Of course you did.' No harm in trying though. So, was he going to try to get know Claire better? It could mean risking his head and heart if he found more to like. Then there was her little girl to consider. Because they were a package. He already knew nothing would ever come between those two. As it should be. Any man Claire let into her life had to be sincere and serious, otherwise she'd be afraid of Mia being hurt. He got it. In bucketloads. And believed in it the same.

CHAPTER FOUR

'NICOLAS, THERE YOU ARE.' Mia rushed across to stop right in front of him and tipped her head far back to stare up at him. 'Mummy's here too.'

'I can see that,' he replied, tossing Claire a grin before looking around. 'Where's Kent?'

'Gone wees.'

'Then I'll have to wait for him, won't I? What have you been up to today, Missy?'

'Reading and learning to count some more numbers. You want to see what I did?'

'Of course I do.' He glanced over at Claire again.

She was laughing. 'You know better than to ask.'

He could spend hours listening to that sound. It made him spongy inside. Soft and happy. Glad they were getting along so well. 'I like hearing about their days. It's kind of cathartic after our busy ones.' He bent down to look at the paper sheet Mia held out to him, covered in colourful numbers on a ladder. 'You did that?'

'Yes. See—one, two three, four.' She poked at each number up to ten.

'Well done. You're very clever. You know that?'

'Yes.' Mia bounced away on her toes, arms wide as though trying to fly.

Unexpected softness wound through Nicolas as he

turned to her mother, whose eyes were also filled with a similar softness that could only be love. A sudden need to envelop Claire in a hug, to feel her against him, filled him. This woman was undoing his resolve to go slowly. But he had to. For both their sakes. He felt she wouldn't take fast and loving before slow and caring. Could be she wasn't used to being loved so easily.

Was she like him in that she hadn't measured up to the standards of someone important and was now careful to look out for herself and Mia, to save them heartbreak? If that was so, then he'd be extra alert because he fully understood. But hey, because of that he had a career as a nurse which he loved, and was doing just fine with his vineyard. Sure, nothing like a top-notch surgeon, but there were times after visiting with his brother when he wondered how happy David truly was.

Claire rubbed her arm, her gaze still on her daughter, as she asked, 'What are you up to this weekend?'

Who? Me? 'More of the same. Checking the vines, mowing between the rows.' *Wondering what you're doing?* Ah, to hell with going slow. There was such a thing as a dawdle. 'Would you like to come out to my place tomorrow? Bring Mia to see Kent too.' For all he knew, Mia might've spent the first years of her life on a farm, and she wouldn't be interested.

'That's a lovely offer, but won't we be holding you up from those jobs?' There was a hesitancy about Claire that touched him. She didn't dive right in without checking where he stood.

'They'll keep. I deserve some down time. Have you organised—' he paused, looked to see how far away Mia was and relaxed '—the Christmas present?'

'All sorted. Got the last one in the shop. Guess what I'll

be doing after a certain someone goes to bed on Christmas Eve? Hopefully I can work it out in time. More often than I like admitting, I mess up these things.'

'You have to put it together?' Unless… 'Here's an idea. How about I take the package home and do that for you, then deliver it to your house later on Christmas Eve?' He held his breath as he waited for Claire's answer.

'Why would you want an extra job when you're so busy?'

'Why not? I have hours to spare once the sun goes down.'

'The pieces of plastic are tiny.' She was mulling over the offer.

'What harm can it do? If I get stuck you can help me when I bring it around.'

'You're right. I'm being silly. Thank you. And if your offer to visit tomorrow still stands then I'd love to come out to your place.'

His lungs returned to normal. 'Done. I'll text the address. Come later in the afternoon and we can have dinner on the deck afterwards. Early enough for Mia,' he added. 'Kent will turn up at some stage. He's never far away. If he gets a hint that Mia's around I'm betting he'll be there with a bag of cookies.'

'Young love, eh? They're only four and look at them.'

The two kids were running around the play mat, laughing and shrieking. Maybe not young love, but they were happy. He felt much the same. Claire was coming to visit. What more could he want? Not answering that because there might be plenty. Every day he was opening up to the idea of engaging with her further. Even to the point of letting go some of his reluctance over getting involved. Only a little, but that was a lot more than he'd managed in five years.

* * *

'When are we going, Mummy?' Mia was dancing from foot to foot, impatience plain on her face.

'Soon. Now quieten down, will you? I've got to finish making this brownie cake or we won't be going anywhere.' She'd decided to bake it for dessert since Nicolas was cooking dinner.

'I want to go now.'

'Go to your room and read a book or we won't go at all.'

Please do as you're told because I really want to see Nicolas.

Seeing his vineyard might show more about him, how he thought about the land and what was important to bring in a perfect harvest of grapes.

'But—'

'Now.'

Stamp, stamp, stamp went two little feet all the way down the hall.

Claire sighed, and then smiled. Being a single parent was not always easy, but the rewards were worth the hard moments. So she kept telling herself on the bad days. Mia was four. She didn't dare think about the teenage years. Hopefully she wouldn't be on her own by then. It'd be great to have a man at her side and covering her back when the going got tough.

That man had to be someone she could trust with their hearts. Nothing like her father. Afraid to take the risk for so long, she was finally admitting she'd love to have that special person in her life. Whether Nicolas had started this, or the new life she'd begun here was the cause, she didn't know. Could be that she'd reached the point where there was only one way to go—forward, chasing those long-buried dreams to find happiness.

Her phone vibrated on the bench. Nicolas. He'd better

not be cancelling. Disappointment hovered as she picked up. 'Hi.'

'Hey, Claire. Just checking that Mia eats barbecued chicken.'

Oh, wow. He was a softie. 'Chicken cooked any way is her favourite food. But you didn't have to go out of your way. She has to learn to accept whatever she's given. Except eggplant. She hates it and I accept that.'

'Not an eggplant in sight. Come out whenever you're ready. I've finished working for the day.'

'Is that Nicolas? We're coming now,' Mia yelled from the hall.

He laughed. 'Are you doing what you're told, Claire?'

'We're about an hour away from leaving here. I've got something in the oven.'

'That's okay. I've been mowing so I'll grab a shower before you get here.'

She wouldn't think about the picture those words conjured up. 'Okay.'

'I'd also better clear up the mess I've made in the kitchen. See you soon.' Nicolas was gone.

Her arms squeezed into her sides as she smiled to herself. As easily as that, Nicolas made her feel good about her parenting skills. He hadn't seen her in action around Mia often, yet knew how to make her feel proud. The few men she'd dated over the last four years hadn't been interested in Mia, other than to find a babysitter for her. That had hurt Claire and made her cagey. No wonder she thought Nicolas was something else. Special even. He'd certainly accepted she came as a package. He didn't ignore Mia.

'Mummy? When are we going?'

'Soon.' Right now would be great. Why hadn't she thought to make the brownie when she'd crawled out of bed that morning instead of doing the vacuuming? According to the timer, twenty-three minutes before she could take the cake out of the oven. Then it had to cool enough to be put on a plate and covered with a paper towel without steaming it into a gluey mess. Guess the added minutes would ramp up her anticipation and make for an even more enjoyable afternoon spent with Nicolas.

'I'm going to get ready. Are you wearing that top? Or do you want to put on the green one I bought last week?'

'I'm wearing this pink one. It's my favourite.'

Last week the pink and blue one was her favourite. Claire shook her head. She couldn't keep up. Where did her daughter get the fussiness from? *Probably me*, she decided after she'd tried on two pairs of jeans and two pairs of knee-length shorts and three tops. What did it matter what she wore? They all fitted nicely, suited her and highlighted her brown hair and tanned skin. Staring at the image in the mirror, she had to admit the sky-blue shirt with gold lines went perfectly with the navy shorts. Decision made. Now for sandals. That was a lot easier. Navy with gold edging, low heels that wouldn't get stuck in the ground if they went for a walk around the vineyard.

Brushing her hair away from her face, she sighed again. It had been a long time since she'd got in a tizz over what to wear on a date, and this was a visit to a vineyard, not a high-end restaurant, and she was enjoying every moment.

'Mummy, the timer's pinging. Can we go now?'

If only. 'Not so fast.' Placing the brownie on a wire rack, she stared at it, as if to cool it down quicker, and laughed at herself. This was crazy. 'Have you got a jersey and a pair of trousers to put on later if it gets cold?'

Mia's shoulders rose and fell. 'Yes, Mummy. You told me that before. They're in my bag at the front door. I put two books in the bag too.' She was way ahead of her mother.

'Good girl. I'll get a jersey for me.' Plus a bottle of wine. Yes, taking a bottle of wine to a vineyard owner's house might seem odd but she wouldn't go empty-handed. Apart from the brownie, that was. Which wasn't cooling down anywhere fast enough.

'It might need uncovering,' Claire said to Nicolas in his kitchen thirty minutes later. 'Mia was getting impatient.'

Not me. Oh, no.

She glanced at Nicolas and started laughing at the look in his warm eyes. 'All right, I admit it. I was ready to get on the road and didn't want to wait any longer.'

He laughed with her. 'It'll be yummy. Thank you, but you really didn't need to make anything. I've got it covered.'

'I'm sure you have, but it's how I am.' Her mother had instilled in her to always go to other people's home with some form of gift, be it baking, wine or a present. Not sure why she'd been so insistent, but Claire had taken it on board and never went empty-handed.

'Freshly baked brownie is a favourite.'

Polite or genuine, it didn't matter. Her feet itched to dance while the blood was racing round her body. She felt special.

'I'll remember that.'

He might become tired of brownie if she got to visit as often as she wanted to at the moment. Never mind, she made a mean carrot cake too. She looked around and stepped across to the bay window overlooking neat rows of grapevines. They went for ever, all facing north and south, and looked beautiful in the sunlight.

'Are those rows planted for optimum sun?'

'Yes.' Nicolas had come to stand beside her. 'If you've ever flown into Blenheim Airport you'll have noted the numerous vineyards going for miles and miles with the rows in the same direction.'

'I've only ever driven here, but I've heard people talking about how impressive the view is from above.'

'It's endless. And expanding every season.'

'You don't worry there'll be too many vineyards and the prices for wine will start falling?'

'If I did that, I shouldn't be in the industry. It's a growing market at the moment, and that's what I focus on. I like your choice of Chardonnay, by the way. It's a good brand.'

That was a relief. 'I didn't know if you'd like it, but I do and that's my benchmark. I'm no expert.' How many people were? Surely it was about what you enjoyed?

'Experts are overrated in my book. It gets back to personal taste. Let's go outside and take a wander around.'

Good answers all round.

'Let's.' This was so ordinary it was fun. She didn't feel she had to be on her best behaviour, or act as if she was more than she wanted to be. 'How many acres have you got?'

'Forty, thirty of which are in vines, and I'm working on planting another five acres. It's been an interesting experience.' His voice resonated with pride and satisfaction.

'You enjoy it.'

'A lot.'

Nicolas checked to see that Mia was with them. 'We'll walk around the sheds to the vines growing on that slope.' His arm brushed Claire's, sending sparks throughout her.

For a moment she thought he might take her hand, but instead he put some space between them. Why? It'd be wonderful strolling along holding hands. Could she reach for him? Take his hand? But this was a visit to see his place, not a hot date.

It is a date though. Isn't it?

Could she? Should she? The uncertainty was undoing her happiness.

'Watch out,' he said sharply, taking her hand to tug her sideways. 'There're a few sods of grass and soil between the house yard and the shed. I should've told you to wear boots or sneakers.' His hand was firmly wrapped around hers.

Happiness restored. She wasn't pulling away from the warmth and firmness of his hold. The buzz of adrenalin was heating her inside and out. He was too good to let go.

'I'll be more watchful.' *While making the most of this contact.*

His fingers started to let go. She tightened her grip. So did Nicolas.

They kept walking towards the sheds. A spontaneous smile broke out. Who'd have believed she could derive so much happiness from holding hands? Went to show how much she'd been missing out on. The move to Blenheim was opening her eyes to a future that held even more promise than work and being a mother. Opportunities to accept a man into her life.

It would be hard after her previous experiences to completely open up, but she was willing to give it a go. All because Nicolas tightened her belly and set her heart racing? Those counted for a lot. She couldn't imagine falling for a man who didn't make her heart sing and her body swoon. But there was so much more to Nicolas, like his kindness and genuineness, which were huge pluses in her book. So much more to find out about him before she'd be brave enough to trust her instincts.

Mia was skipping alongside Nicolas. When she tripped he reached for her but Mia pulled away. 'I don't need anyone to hold my hand.'

'That's good.' He looked slightly bemused.

Claire couldn't help herself. She laughed. 'She can be quite independent.'

He turned those stunning eyes on her and gave a half laugh. 'So I see. I'm not complaining. You all right?'

Her head dipped, then lifted. 'Absolutely.' He was a kind man. She was liking him even more. Well, that was what she wanted, wasn't it? Possibly. Probably. Try yes. 'Did you always want to be a nurse, or did that come about later when you'd been working somewhere else?'

His silence had her wishing she could retract her question. She didn't want to upset him. Though how she was to get to know him better if she didn't ask what seemed straightforward was beyond her.

His honed shoulders rose, dropped back in place. 'I wanted to be a surgeon.' Another shrug followed. 'Instead I quit school at sixteen and left home to go to Nelson, where I got work on a fishing trawler.'

She held onto the next question. He'd tell her if he wanted, and if he didn't she'd respect that, while itching to know the answer.

'No reason not to tell you. I was under a lot of pressure from my parents to go to med school and do as well, if not better, than my older brother.' Bitterness tainted his words. 'I'm as intelligent as David, as capable of qualifying as a medical specialist, and I would've done so if I wasn't continuously being compared to him.'

'That's hard. Plus unfair.'

'In the end it became too much, and I started to wonder who I was trying to please—my family or myself. Believe me, they weren't too happy about me being a fisherman. The funny thing is I loved it. I got a thrill being out on the water for weeks on end, beyond sight of land, and dealing with weather I had never experienced. I grew up fast.'

'Why did you stop?'

'Despite what I was doing on the water I still had a hankering to be involved in the medical world. By then I couldn't envisage spending the next ten or so years studying and being stuck inside endlessly, so nursing was the best option.'

'You balance that with this.' She waved her free hand around at the land surrounding them. It made perfect sense. He moved like an outdoors man, strong and confident, yet in the medical centre he was quieter, calm and gentle.

Nicolas swallowed hard, looked away, around at his property. 'You got it.' His fingers squeezed hers before he let go. 'Mia, want to feed the chooks?'

'Yes, please, Nicolas.'

There was more to his story. But the fact was, he'd shown her a vulnerable side and she respected that. Hell, she knew all about vulnerability. Her biggest being her gorgeous little girl chatting away to Nicolas as if he was her new best friend.

Her heart swelled for her child, and even for the man showing Mia some weaned lambs. But watch out anyone who hurt Mia. They wouldn't stand a chance. She'd do anything to protect Mia from the hurt she'd grown up with. Anything.

Give up the chance of romance and love?

The crux of all her reasoning. If she ever settled down with a man, she'd be adding joy to Mia's life along with hers. A chill crossed her skin. Would she know she'd got it right or wrong before it was too late? She shivered. Getting involved was risky. For her. And her girl.

Watching Nicolas leading Mia to the chook pen with hungry hens chasing them, longing filled her, nearly dropped her on the ground. This was what she wanted—more than anything. Family. Love. Understanding and kindness. It might be here, hers for the taking if she was brave enough. But... Again her skin pricked. So many scary 'but's. Nicolas probably wasn't the slightest bit interested in a few innocuous dates. What did he really think of her? Another question she wouldn't be asking.

'Mummy, look. The chooks are going to be shut in for the night.'

Rubbing her arms, she joined them. 'Aren't they funny, the way they run?'

'I want one.'

'We haven't got a shed or lots of yard for one.' She refused to look at the laughter breaking out across Nicolas's face. It twisted her stomach and made her want to lean in and kiss him. Truly? Kiss Nicolas? Why not? Those lips were to die for.

Not in front of Mia.

Of course not. That was partly an excuse. So was the fact they didn't know each other well enough yet. Huh? She'd had flings where the kissing had started pretty damned fast, followed by what flings were made of. The fast follow-on wouldn't be enough with Nicolas, she suspected. Despite the multitude of doubts cramming her head, deep down her brain was telling her he was more than a fling. If she took the time to get closer and more intimate in ways other than physical, there might be a good chance of it turning into something special and lasting.

'Your mum's right. Chooks need somewhere to dig up worms.'

'Mummy eats chickens. I don't like that now.' Mia ate chicken like there was a famine about to happen, but now wasn't the time to point that out.

Nicolas raised an eyebrow. 'Dinner should be interesting,' he said in an aside.

* * *

Nicolas couldn't believe how much fun he was having letting Mia feed the chooks, with Claire at his side, chatting away about anything and everything as if she didn't have a worry in the world. Not once so far had there been any sign of reticence about being with him. He'd taken her hand without thinking too much about it, and when she didn't pull away it was as though he was floating over the ground.

Who'd have thought giving Claire a lift last week could've led to this? He would've met her at the function, but they might not necessarily have spent any time together. He'd probably still have been attracted to her, but it would've been harder to ask her out here.

'What can I do?' his daydream asked, looking very real and sexy in her fitted clothes and with those curls falling around her shoulders.

'Nothing. Everything's prepared. I just have to barbecue the chicken and we'll be ready.' They were eating early because of Mia. Claire had said to feed her first if he wanted, but this was fine. They'd still be together, sharing a meal and a glass of wine. He'd never been on a date that included children and he didn't mind Mia's presence at all. There'd be times when it would be preferable for just the two of them to be together, but at this early stage in the relationship—if that was what it was becoming—all was good.

At the moment Mia was on the deck chomping into crisps, which meant she could wait a bit for dinner.

'Bring your wine and we'll sit in the shade on the deck.'

Claire looked completely at ease as she went outside to sit down, crossing those slim legs and sipping her wine as if she'd been coming here often. 'This is so relaxing.'

Something he doubted she got to do often. 'Any time you want to get away from people or town, feel free to drop by. I can't guarantee I won't be busy, but make yourself at home. There's a back door key under that pot with the fern growing in it.' Would she do it? Claire appeared to like laying things out, not going in blindly.

'I'll bring more brownie.'

'Then you can stay for ever. That was yum.' He'd sneaked a piece as he was crumbing the chicken. He hadn't got away with it. A certain little miss had demanded some too, and for some inexplicable reason that made him feel accepted. He also felt a tad guilty about giving Mia brownie so close to dinner, as if he was trying to win her over, but Claire had merely shrugged and said it was all right this time. It was all a bit familyish. Kind of cool. Definitely comfortable. Something he hadn't known since he was a kid, before the pressure started to be applied. Did Claire come from a close family? 'Do you have any siblings?'

'Not a one.' Her smile dipped, then she seemed to gather a breath and plaster it back on. 'It was just me and my mother. Dad left when I was four.'

He'd been far better off than her then. Even the daily grind of trying to prove he was as good as David didn't take away the fact he'd had parents and a brother to spend time with. There were good memories of going fishing with his father, and Mum teaching him to drive.

'I'm sorry to hear that. Did you see much of him?'

She looked sideways at him, her eyes narrowed. Debating how much to say?

'It's all right. Don't feel you have to tell me anything that makes you uncomfortable.'

Slowly her eyes widened back to normal and the tension in her body eased off. 'I've never seen or heard from him since.'

'What? That's dreadful.' How could any man do that to his child? Or any woman, for that. Insane, and selfish.

And hurtful beyond understanding. 'How did you cope growing up?'

'Some would say I didn't. I played up badly for a few years, demanding to be noticed, accepted, and even loved. When that didn't work and I got kept back at school as punishment I did a complete about-face and became engrossed in study and keeping my distance from people.'

'What about your mother? Where was she in all this?' Surely she'd have gone out of her way to keep Claire happy and knowing she had at least one loyal parent.

'Pretty much in her own little world, pretending Dad was going to walk back in the front door any day and we'd all carry on as though nothing had happened. I only existed to be fed and clothed—the mechanical chores that didn't involve Mum's heart.' The level in her glass lowered quickly as she took a big mouthful. Then she shook her head in astonishment. 'I can't believe I just told you all that.'

She'd surprised him too. 'I'm glad you told me. It means a lot to know more about you.' How could any mother do that? Claire was so loving with Mia. Of course she would be after her childhood, but she *knew* how to be the loving, exceptional woman that she was.

Placing his glass on the floor, he reached for her hand and squeezed. Doing that a lot today, he thought. Twice being a lot. 'You certainly don't let Mia think she's missing out on love. It's there in everything you do for and with her, even if you're growling about something she's done.'

'I hope so.' She sniffed, and looked down at their joined hands. 'I've worked hard to be the mother I never had.'

His heart squeezed tight for her and the love she'd missed out on. Life was so bloody unfair at times. Could she ever make up for what she'd lost? Could he help her? He'd like to. Heck. This was getting out of hand.

'Here.' He tugged a serviette from the set table beside him and passed it to her, his hand pausing to touch the back of hers. 'Wipe your eyes. Can't have little one seeing Mum crying.'

'Why are you so understanding? I'm not used to it.'

'Could that be because you don't usually admit other people's acceptance of who you are?'

Now her eyes widened in shock. 'How can you know that?'

'I didn't until you just confirmed it.' But he tended to be good at reading other people's pain. Had enough of his own to have learned to tread carefully and understand no one got away without some hurt in this world.

Claire scrubbed at her eyes with the serviette, and stared out beyond the deck.

Looking around for Mia, he saw her sitting inside on the couch with a small laptop on her knees. A furrow marred her forehead as she studied whatever was on the screen. She looked happy, not peeved about not being the centre of attention. Turning back to Claire, he smiled. It was time to lighten the atmosphere or the evening would be ruined.

'I'll put the chicken on the barbecue and get things underway.'

'Sounds good. Shall I get the salads out of the fridge?'

'Go for it.' *And while you're at it, throw me another of those beautiful smiles.*

'Nicolas?'

He turned around, and wham, right in the gut. A smile so darned beautiful he must've died and woken up in Utopia.

'Thanks. For everything.'

'Come here.' He had to do this. He had to, or bust apart. Winding his arms around Claire, he stepped back out of sight of Mia and leaned in, placing his mouth on hers. Feeling her soft lips under his, her warm waist under his hands, her breasts pressing into his chest. He closed his eyes, breathed her in, then kissed her. Kissed and kissed, until he had to come up for air. She tugged him back, reaching up on her toes to find his mouth, and returned the kisses as deeply, as intensely, engaging him completely.

When Claire slowly pulled back he lifted his head and locked his gaze with hers. 'Claire,' he whispered, and stopped, no words coming to his tongue. Or his mind. She'd blown him away with those kisses.

Running her fingers down his cheek, she smiled ever so slowly and tantalisingly. 'I didn't expect this.'

'Me either.' He'd hoped they might get to kiss before she left to go home, but those kisses went way beyond a goodnight kiss. 'I don't know what's happening between us, but I'd like to spend more time with you to find out. How does that make you feel?' Might as well be blunt. If she wasn't happy then best he knew now and not a couple of weeks and more scintillating kisses down the track.

'Interested. Keen. And still wary.'

'So am I. But nothing ventured, eh?'

'Agreed. Now, we'd better get on with dinner before a little someone finds us and asks questions I have no answers for. Yet.'

Yet. Hopefully he'd manage to help her find all the answers she needed—and him—over the coming weeks. With a quick hug he stepped away and turned the barbecue grill on, before going to get the drumsticks and thighs he'd crumbed earlier. His day had gone from ordinary to fun to exciting. He couldn't wait for more.

CHAPTER FIVE

'CLAIRE, THERE'S A patient in the monitoring room requiring urgent attention. I think she should be in ED.'

Claire put aside her coffee and followed Nicolas out of the staffroom. A week had passed since she had been out to his place, and in that time they'd worked together two days. 'What've we got?'

'Josey Brown, thirty-one, fell off bike alongside Taylor River. Rapid heart rate, light head, bruising on the ribs. No history in her file of anything other than a fractured tibia four years ago, though that mightn't be up-to-date.'

'Why is she here and not ED already?'

'Her partner brought her in, and won't listen to Charlene telling her to go next door. The partner's not someone I'd argue with either.'

'I might be about to.' She stepped into the room and crossed to the only occupied bed, where another woman sat on a chair, looking ready to pounce. 'Hello, I'm Claire McAlpine, a doctor. Can you hear me, Josey?'

'Hmm.'

It was something, though not enough. 'I understand you came off your bike. Did something go wrong with your ride? Or did you have a medical incident that caused you to crash?'

'She wobbled after dodging a small rock and fell,' the

partner answered, glaring at her. 'We've told the nurse all this.'

'I'd like to hear what Josey has to say,' Claire said in her firm, I'm-the-doctor tone. 'Josey?'

'Was light-headed. Rock in the way. Lost control.' Her speech was a little slurred and disconnected.

'Pain anywhere else?'

'No.'

'Any history of headaches, high blood pressure?'

The partner interrupted. 'What's with all these questions? Why aren't you examining Josey?'

'I'll get there a lot quicker if you let me do my job,' Claire replied, and noted a glint of interest in Nicolas's eyes. Didn't think she could be tough when required? He had a lot to learn. 'Josey, answer me.'

'No.'

'No history, or no you won't answer me?' Pedantic maybe, but necessary if she was to make an informed decision about the woman's condition.

'No history.'

'She's very fit.' The partner added her bit.

Fitness didn't give everyone a clean bill of health all the time. 'What about family history of high blood pressure or strokes?' She read the monitor, noted the raised blood pressure.

'My mum.'

Again her partner interrupted. 'Her mother had a fatal brain haemorrhage at the age of fifty.'

You knew that and didn't go to ED?

There was a possibility Josey could be following in her mother's footsteps. 'Right, this is what we're doing. Josey, I am transferring you to the emergency department, where they have more equipment to monitor you. They can also admit you to hospital, and call on a specialist.'

'Why can't you do that from here?'

'Because we're a private centre, and all our cases go through either ED or back to a patient's GP.'

'This is wasting time.'

Nicolas was reading the heart monitor and said, 'Josey's getting excellent care right now. Taking her through to the hospital department will up the ante.' He flicked Claire a look of *What the hell?* and said aloud, 'I've got this,' with a small smile aimed directly at her.

Even here that smile got to her, touched her and said she wasn't on her own. He was efficient and understanding. A top-notch nurse in all respects.

Returning his smile with a soft one of her own, she said, 'I'll fill in the details for ED.'

'Josey, you're going for a ride,' Nicolas said.

'I'm coming with you.' The other woman stood up abruptly.

'Of course you are. It's always best when someone else is with the patient and hears what the doctors have to say,' he replied.

Claire smiled to herself. He was as annoyed with the partner as she was and still being respectful. The woman was no doubt very worried about Josey, and it was coming out in a rude way, but Josey was the one who was ill and who needed all their attention and care. 'I'll check to see how you're getting on later, Josey.'

At her desk, Claire typed up the notes while ringing ED to inform them of her patient's problems. Next she clicked on the list of patients waiting to be seen.

'Samuel Crowe.' Her gaze fell on a small boy curled up in his mother's lap, and presumed he was the two-year-old she was looking for. 'Mrs Crowe?' Receiving a quick nod, she said, 'Bring your son through. I'm Claire McAlpine, your doctor this morning.'

'I'm Sharon. Sorry to bother you, but I'm worried. Sam's not breathing properly.'

'Let's lie him on the bed. And you're not bothering us. If your child is unwell never think you shouldn't bring him in for a check-up. It's far better to be safe than find out later there was something seriously wrong.'

'I know, but I worry a lot over the smallest things going wrong.'

She knew that feeling all too well. 'As any good mother does. Tell me what made you bring him in, Sharon.'

'He's been over-tired and grizzly, and then he started crying and breathing funny. I put him to bed early, and kept checking on him all night, thinking the breathing would get better, but it's no different this morning.' Her fingers were rubbing her son's arm.

Sam was red in the face and his breathing was laboured and there was a distinct whistling sound. Getting a stethoscope, Claire smiled at the little boy. 'Sam, I'm going to put this on your chest. It might feel a bit cold at first, but it won't tickle. Okay?'

He stared as she placed the chest piece on his hot skin and, when he didn't react, she listened to his lungs with one ear and heard Sharon out with the other.

'Mummy?' The little guy's eyes had filled with fright.

'It's all right, love. This lady's going to make you better.'

No pressure. 'Sam, you're doing well. I can hear you breathe through this.' She held out the earpiece for him to see.

'Need a hand in here?' Nicolas had returned, and she hadn't noticed. Her Nicolas radar had failed.

'Sharon, this is Nicolas. He's a nurse. I'm going to get him to take Sam's temperature.'

'Hey, Sam, that's a cool shirt you've got on.' Nicolas grinned at the boy.

'Has Sam ever had breathing difficulties before?' she asked Sharon.

'Once or twice he's made funny wheezing noises but nothing like this.'

'This is an asthma attack. At the moment I don't know what brought it on. It could be an allergy or a viral infection. I'm going to prescribe an inhaler to start using immediately, and refer him back to your GP for ongoing tests to find the reason for this onset.'

'Temp is thirty-seven point seven,' Nicolas informed her.

'Slightly raised.' Filling in the prescription form on screen, Claire glanced at the cute little boy sitting up with Nicolas's help. His big eyes were fixed on the nurse, as if he had all the answers to his problems. Something she could understand, because he made her feel the same at times. 'Here you are. Take that to the pharmacy and get Sam started on the inhaler as soon as possible. You'll notice a difference quite quickly. If not, bring him straight back.'

'Hey, Sam, can I carry you out to the car?' Nicolas asked.

'Yes.'

'Thank you both. It's so worrying being a parent.' Sharon watched her son cling to Nicolas as they headed for the door.

He had a way with kids that was endearing, and something Claire trusted.

'I'm a mum, I know where you're coming from.'

'I hear doctors are far worse when it comes to their children needing medical help.' Finally there was a hint of a smile on Sharon's face.

'There's something in that. Take care, and go to your GP ASAP.'

'Yes, Doctor.' The smile improved, showing a lovely woman behind the worry for her son.

'Sharon's on the phone making an appointment already.' Nicolas stood in the doorway five minutes later. 'She was impressed with your calm approach.'

'Sam isn't my son. It's easier.'

Stepping into the room, he closed the door and leaned back against it. 'Would you like to go out for dinner tonight? I'm sure Michelle would be happy to babysit. She's always looking for extra money.'

So she couldn't use Mia as an excuse to say no. Did she want to? Nicolas's invitation had instantly made her glow on the inside. Going out for dinner wasn't rushing things between them. Instead it would give them time together away from here to relax and chat about anything and everything.

'I'd love to.'

He blinked. Hadn't expected her to accept so quickly? A wide smile lit up his face.

'Great. I'll make a booking. Want me to talk to Michelle?'

'I can do that.'

'I'll pick you up at six-thirty.' The door opened and he was gone, back to being a nurse, not her date for the night.

Grand. She was going on a date, dinner with the man who'd made her start changing her thinking about men and relationships almost before she'd learnt his name. Bring it on, said the buzz under her skin. Two dates without getting too deep too soon was new for her. Since she'd become a mother anyway.

Six-thirty. That would keep her moving. Pick up Mia, bath and feed her, have a shower and find the right dress to wear. Try not to get nervous. Work harder at not trying on every summer dress she owned before tossing them aside. Forget nervous. She was going with excited. Damn, but this move was turning out to be much more fun than she'd ever anticipated.

Picking up her phone, she texted Michelle.

'Hard to believe it's almost Christmas.' Claire pushed her dessert plate aside and leaned back in the chair in the restaurant. 'I could've sworn it was only a few months since last time.'

'You'd have been in Dunedin then.' Nicolas twirled his empty wine glass in his fingers. 'It's been a busy year for you, packing up and moving and starting a new job.'

'Most of that's happened in the last few months. Maybe that's why the year seems to have flown, it's all been about the second half. Come to think of it, the first six months were uninteresting.' Mostly packing up her mother's house and possessions, selling what she hadn't wanted to take with her, which turned out to be just about everything.

'Who did you spend Christmas with last year?'

'A friend and her family.' Thank goodness for Cheryl or it would've been a quiet day for two. Mia at least had other kids to unwrap presents and play with. 'My mother never did like celebrating Christmas or birthdays.'

'I'm sorry to hear that. It can't have been easy,' Nicolas said.

The night before her mother was due to fly to Australia had been the first and only time she'd ever told Claire the words she'd waited a lifetime to hear. Claire had been dozing when she sensed her mother approach and sit on the edge of her bed. It was unusual for her mother to come so near, let alone run her hand down Claire's arm before saying for the first time ever, 'I love you, Claire. I always have. I'm so proud of you and everything you've achieved, including Mia.' After a few silent minutes, she'd added, 'Don't make the same mistakes with your life I did with mine.' Then she'd left the room, leaving Claire gobsmacked. And finally at ease with her mother. She was loved, and that was all she'd ever wanted.

Next morning, when Claire had returned from dropping her mother off at the airport, she'd found the silver ring that had been her grandmother's and which her mother always wore on her bedside table. Claire had worn it ever since, accepting it as her mother's way of backing what she'd said the night before.

Now her mother's words resonated in her head. A bit like Mia's when she was sitting on Santa's knee, they came back to haunt her at the most inconvenient moments.

'That's Mum.' Phone calls were rare and stilted, as though she regretted what she'd said. But the words remained in Claire's heart.

'It's hard when people won't share their thoughts and emotions.' Nicolas was staring at the table as he spoke.

'Some people tend to show it in how they help each other, whether it's getting the car running when the engine died, or being there when their world is turning upside down.' Not when leaving their daughter behind, though. Bet Nicolas was always there when needed, by a friend, or his family, despite their expectations of him driving a wedge between them all. So far, it was hard to fault him over anything, but it would come. No one was perfect, and if she expected him to be she'd be in for a big disappointment.

'Where did you get to be so wise?' He was smiling now, looking at her and not the table.

'It must've rubbed off someone when I was standing in a crowded bus one day.' It paid to lighten the atmosphere further or she might get too deep about why she and her mother didn't spend much time together. Strange how right now she'd love to open up and talk about how her mother had kept her emotions locked down. However, while they were getting closer, she was still cautious about what made her hesitant. Her vulnerability was not for show.

'Which bus? I could do with gaining some wisdom over certain matters going on in my life.' He was still smiling so they couldn't be bad issues. Or was he good at hiding his true feelings? He *was* always friendly and cheerful.

Unless a patient's partner got stroppy about how the treatment was being arranged, Claire remembered. 'I'll buy you a ticket for Christmas.'

'Can't wait. Shall I pick up the kitchen set when I take you home?'

She still felt a little awkward about Nicolas taking over making the present for her, but it would save a lot of trouble.

'Good idea. It's locked in the boot of my car. I couldn't stow it anywhere in the house as Mia has a tendency to go looking through cupboards for no other reason than she wants to. Finding the kitchen box set would ruin the magical Christmas moment. It'll only be another year, maybe two, before the truth's out about Santa, and I want to keep her young and naïve for as long as possible.'

'Not for too long, or then you'll be wishing she'd hurry and grow up and get some sense in her head. Believe me, I've seen it all with Evelyn and Michelle.' Nicolas laughed. 'Evelyn worried about introducing another man into Michelle's life but Bodie handled it so well they got on well from day one. Evelyn was divorced and her ex moved away, but he does have Michelle to stay every school holidays. Then along came Kent, and Michelle's still as much a part of the family as she always was.' There was an intensity in Nicolas's face now, as though he was wondering how she would feel in the same situation.

Answer? Mia had to be happy with the man Claire settled down with. The man in front of her? Too soon to know, or to be thinking along those lines. Except he made her feel. Feel as in being alive and happy and excited.

'Sounds ideal. That's what I want for Mia if I find someone to share my life with.' Not saying anything else. That was too much.

'As you should. I can't imagine a man, or a woman come to that, not accepting their partner's children as part of the deal. There's so much to gain, and nothing to lose.'

Good answer.

'I agree. But then I'm on the other side of the picture.'

'Can I take your plates?' the waitress asked, reminding Claire they weren't alone.

'Thank you.' She moved her dish to the edge of the table.

'Is there anything else you'd like? Coffee, tea? Another wine?'

'Claire?' Nicolas raised one eyebrow.

'Not for me. Coffee would keep me awake half the night. But you go ahead.'

'No, think we'll hit the road.'

Walking out to his four-wheel drive, Nicolas slipped his hand around hers, and she leaned a little closer. 'I haven't enjoyed myself so much for a long time.' Since Saturday at his place.

'Funny you should say that because I feel the same.'

That had to be good. They were on the same page. But he must've been dating other women. He was good-looking, and had more good attributes other than the physical ones.

'You can't have been single for too long.'

'Depends what you mean by single. I've been out with

a few women, but there's been nothing serious going on for years.'

Why? A back story that made him wary? Or too busy with his work and vineyard to expend his leftover energy?

'I find that hard to believe.'

'Back at you.'

She hadn't told him how sparse her dating life had been. Was she so obvious? Probably if the way she got excited over being asked out to dinner was an indicator.

'Relax. I can't see you going overboard with anyone who didn't fit in with your position as a single mum.'

'I was in a bit of a rut before I moved here. Shifting homes, jobs and towns seems to have given me a boost. Getting out and about is fun, meeting new people and working in a different environment makes me feel pleased about the changes.'

'I'm glad you shifted this way.' They'd reached his four-wheel drive and he took her in his arms, gazed into her eyes. 'Very glad.' Leaning closer, his eyes still locked with hers, he said softly, 'Claire, thank you for coming out with me tonight.'

'More than glad I did.' *Please kiss me.* Would he? Wouldn't he? 'Nicolas?'

'Ahh, Claire.' Pulling her even closer, he leaned down to place his mouth on hers. Paused as though waiting for permission to continue.

Pressing her lips against his, she slipped her arms around his waist and relaxed into him.

Nicolas's mouth claimed hers as he began kissing her without restraint.

Desire swamped her, turning her body soft and limp, and stalled every thought, gave credit only to the sensations rolling throughout her. When Nicolas slipped his tongue between her lips, she held him tight. He knew what he was doing, and she had to have more. Holding that gorgeous, muscular body, she pressed more firmly against his mouth, kissed back as if she had no intention of ever stopping. Which she didn't.

Only one of them had to be sensible. Eventually. Soon.

Nicolas lifted his mouth from hers slowly, tantalisingly. 'We'd better go before the staff come out and send us packing like a couple of teenagers.'

Really? When she was having so much fun, and getting all wound up with desire. He was probably right, but at the moment she didn't want right, she wanted enjoyment. The heat of the moment had slain all her doubts and worries about getting involved.

She straightened, brushed her hands down the front of her dress. *Not wise to continue, Claire.* It was risky diving in when she wasn't certain Nicolas was the man for her. This was nothing like a quick fling. If she was to be intimate with him it had to be for the right reasons, and to be reciprocated. There'd be repercussions if they got it wrong. For her, and for Mia. Possibly for Nicolas, considering how seriously he seemed to be taking this.

'Take me home,' she said on a long sigh. Then hoped he didn't think that was an invitation to stay over. No, he was giving Michelle a lift back to her place. Damn it. All the same, she felt some relief that the rest of the evening was sorted.

Her head was all over the place. She wanted Nicolas, and everything he had to offer. She needed to be careful and look out for herself. *Steady does it.* Except, for once, steady wasn't in her vocabulary. She laughed, and felt free in an unusual way, all because of Nicolas. While that was a warning in itself, she carried on smiling. She was happy.

As Nicolas pulled out onto the road, she said, 'Let's go somewhere at the weekend. Take Mia to the beach and have a picnic.' Then she held her breath. He might not want to follow up on tonight. But how could he not when he'd just kissed her as if his life depended on it?

'You're on.'

She slumped into the seat, still smiling. 'I'll bring the picnic.'

'I'll bring the towels,' he joked.

'Sounds like fun.' And some.

What happened back there? Nicolas asked himself as he drove to Claire's house. She blew his socks off. With a kiss. A few kisses. Then minutes ago she'd suggested going out at the weekend, which had to be good, had to mean she wanted more kisses. Thank goodness, because he sure as anything needed more.

Easy does it. There'd be a little girl with them so kissing was out. They'd find a way round that. Mia would get tired at the beach with swimming and building sandcastles, then they'd head home. Wouldn't she? Fingers crossed she did.

Pulling into Claire's drive, he turned the ignition off and turned to her. Ran a finger over her arm, tried to ignore the heat that was rushing up *his* arm and deep inside. But he couldn't, so, unclicking their seat belts, he reached for her and hugged her tight. Then found her lips and began kissing her. Sinking into the heat filling his body, he knew wonder, and happiness. Something else was stirring through him too. A sense of homecoming, of having found someone who cared about what he felt.

His head shook abruptly to banish that thought. Might be reading too much into a few kisses.

'Nicolas?'

He'd broken their kiss. But that might be for the best after those thoughts. He wasn't ready for deep and committed. Would he ever be? He'd like to think so. He did want a future that included a loving and lovable wife, and a family. Over time the hurt of the past had gone, leaving him hollowed out, but since meeting Claire he was starting to feel whole again.

'Should I be going inside?'

No, damn it. 'I'm sorry. I was having a moment, that's all.' That was enough. His mouth covered hers before she could ask why. This was not the time to talk about his past. Not that he had a clue what constituted the *right* time. But now, kissing this amazing woman was all he wanted, and needed.

He kissed deeper, stroking Claire's mouth with his tongue, blotting out everything but the taste of her, the feel of her butt under his hands. It felt as if they were in their own space, where nothing could interrupt them. Except eventually they had to get out of the four-wheel drive and walk up to the house, where his friends' daughter waited to be driven home. His arms held Claire tighter, not wanting to let her go.

His lips brushed her cheek. 'I've had the best time.' He'd been going to say *night*, but there were plenty of hours left, hours that he wasn't getting to spend with her. Unless… No. He didn't think she'd be inviting him to come back after dropping off the babysitter. Claire kissed him like there was no tomorrow, but he already knew her better than that. She'd be cautious about inviting him to stay the night. She wouldn't want Mia waking up and finding him in her mother's bed when they weren't in a serious relationship.

'I'd better go in.' Her voice was clouded with disappointment.

At least that was his interpretation, but he might be looking for something that wasn't there. 'Fair enough.'

He held her hand as they walked to the door, only dropping it when she stepped inside. Following her, he had to laugh when he saw Michelle curled up on the couch watching something on her laptop. 'I bet you wouldn't hear Mia if she called out.'

Michelle jumped in shock. 'Hello. How long have you two been standing there?'

'Don't listen to him. We just arrived.' Claire's face had a red tint going on. A result of those kisses?

'Come on. You can finish watching whatever's so enthralling you didn't hear us come in when you get home.' Now he sounded like a father. Glancing at Claire, he wondered what lay ahead for them. She was right. It was time to head home. Lots to think about before he got too serious about a relationship with this woman. He didn't want to hurt Claire, or be hurt in the process.

Valerie had thought he wasn't good enough, and found another man while she was still with him. His family believed he hadn't done what he was capable of, thereby letting them down. He hadn't let himself down though. He didn't regret his career choices. Not often anyway. But what if he let Claire down? What if she walked away without looking over her shoulder? Found another man to flaunt in his face?

What if he didn't take a chance and never found love? That would almost be worse than falling in love and losing her later.

'Nicolas, are you still on for the picnic?' Concern radiated out at him from those beautiful brown eyes locked on him.

'Try stopping me. I'll talk to you later and we can arrange times.' He wasn't working at the medical centre tomorrow. It was a vineyard work day. Fresh air and no hassles with difficult patients. No sensuous woman distracting him at every turn.

He brushed a light kiss on her cheek. 'Take care, and thanks again for a great night out.'

'You too.' Her eyes lit up. 'Talk soon.'

Now there was a thought.

At home, Nicolas slipped between the sheets and pressed Claire's number on his phone. 'Hey, you tucked up yet?' Blanking that image from his mind took effort, mostly a failure at that.

'Been here for ten minutes.' Her voice sounded husky.

Which stirred him, made him hard. What was she wearing? He opened his mouth. Closed it again. Then, 'You looked stunning in that dress tonight.' She'd worn a fitted turquoise number that showed every curve to perfection. No wonder he'd kissed her as if all his Christmases had come at once. He was getting harder thinking about it.

'Thought I might've gone over the top, but I love getting dressed up.'

It didn't happen often—was that what she was saying?

'Then wear something fancy to the beach for our picnic.' He'd never be able to stand up or play games on the beach with Mia. He'd be rock-hard. Already was. Phone sex would help. Most likely kill the relationship for ever if he suggested it. Of course he wouldn't. He wasn't that stupid. Close, but not so close he'd finish something that every day was growing into a special connection he hadn't known since Valerie.

She giggled like a kid. 'I'll wear something appropriate for swimming.'

Oh, great. That'll cause just as much trouble if she wears a bikini. He could already picture that lithe body covered in little more than handkerchiefs. Did she have a wetsuit by any chance?

'You do that.' Go to the charity shop and buy a swimsuit

his grandmother would've worn. No, that wouldn't work. He'd seen photos of his grandmother in her twenties, sunbathing on the beach in a bikini. Only saying bikinis were the thing even back then.

Claire cleared her throat. Was he getting to her as much as she did him? He hoped so.

'I might see if Kent wants to join us on Saturday. He and Mia could play together.'

'Good idea.' They could lie in the sun and talk, or... Nothing else. Two children would be a bucket of cold water when he got too interested in Claire. This dating a woman with a child was different. It came with handbrakes. Not that he was worried. Mia was fine and he had no issues with her being around. They wouldn't be going to the beach in the first place if not for her. But it did mean being aware he and Claire weren't alone when he felt frisky. Or just wanted to kiss her.

Which brought him right back to those decimating kisses they'd shared earlier. They were heating his body in all sorts of ways he didn't need if he was going to get any sleep tonight.

'I'd better grab some shut-eye. Sleep tight. See you on Saturday.' He finished the call before she said anything else in that sexy voice that'd screw with his head.

CHAPTER SIX

'CLAIRE, WOULD YOU and Mia like to join us for Christmas Day?' Evelyn asked during their snatched tea break at the medical centre the next day. 'I should've asked earlier. It's not a lot of notice, I know. Nicolas will be there too,' she added.

For a carrot, it wasn't bad, Claire thought.

'We'd love to.' It was as simple as that. Her new friends were fun to be with. Nicolas was more than a friend, but not yet a serious contender for the rest of her life. Getting closer by the day though.

'Come for breakfast, which is usually around nine, followed by a late and large Christmas lunch.'

'What can I bring? And don't say nothing. I've made a Christmas cake, which I have yet to ice.' It was a recipe handed down from one generation to the next on her mother's side, and absolutely delicious. She'd made it out of habit, thinking she'd bring it into work for everyone to enjoy.

'Bring that, please. I haven't made one this year. Actually I never make one.' Evelyn grinned. 'Not my thing.'

'What else?' She wasn't going empty-handed, which in her book meant more than a cake. 'I can get a salmon if you like.'

'Done.'

Claire sipped her tea and waited. She knew this woman well enough to know there was more to come and it wouldn't be about Christmas. Usually she'd dive straight in to bring up some uninteresting topic to cut Evelyn off but she didn't feel the need today. She was open to people knowing Nicolas was a part of her life and talking about weekend plans. Very different for her. It brought a sense of relief, as though a load had been lifted.

'So how is it going with Nicolas? You must be getting on well to be going on a picnic and taking my boy.'

See? Got that right. 'He's great.' At a lot of things.

'Come on. That can't be all.'

Claire ran two fingers across her mouth. 'My lips are sealed.'

'So are Nicolas's. Which tells me more than you realise. He's not a blabbermouth but he usually drops a few hints when he's been out with someone. Mind you, I haven't known him to date anyone quite like you.' When Claire lifted an eyebrow, she continued. 'He's taking his time, as if he really wants to get to know you well.'

'Much the same as I'm doing,' she admitted. 'I'm scared of making similar mistakes to past ones. Not that I see Nicolas as the type to hurt me.' Been wrong before though, so the closer she got to Nicolas the more afraid of commitment she became.

'There's a lot at stake. I get that, and I suspect Nicolas does too. Be aware he's very loyal to those he cares about. He's had his knocks, and won't be leaping in like there's no tomorrow.' Evelyn stood to rinse her cup. 'That's all I'm saying, apart from I'm glad you're getting along. I'd like to see him settled. He deserves it, and I think the same might apply to you.'

'It is the first time I've felt so hopeful. And happy,' she

added on a deep breath, unusually fine talking to Evelyn about this. 'Thanks for inviting us to Christmas.' It was shaping up to be another great day.

What would the New Year bring? More magic? In the form of Nicolas? For the first time since she'd been with Anthony, she was looking forward, not backwards. Hank didn't count. He should be around for Mia, not her. New Year was supposed to bring new promises. Would next year come with all she suddenly wanted? What she was prepared to believe in because everything felt possible these days. Love, more family, happiness, trust, to name a few of her wishes.

New Year. A new life. Bring it all on.

The happiness factor was still there the next afternoon as she sat on the beach watching Mia and her little friend running in and out of the water with Nicolas chasing them, arms spread like a plane. He was as much a kid at heart as the two he was playing with.

'I'll be tucking you all in early if you keep this up.'

'Really?' he said, laughing. 'Does that come with a goodnight kiss?'

She'd walked into that one. 'Depends on how well-behaved you are.'

'That means I'll be out of luck, I guess.' He dropped onto the beach towel beside her and reached for a bottle of water in the cooler. 'They're energetic little blighters, aren't they?'

'What? You can't keep up?' She nudged a honed arm with her elbow.

'No comment.' Stretching out on his side, his head in his hand, he watched as she flicked her gaze between him and the kids, who were building a sandcastle nearly as high as Mia. 'How about you spend the evening at my place? I can rustle up a barbecue and the kids can catch a video. We could watch the sunset from the deck.'

He pressed the right buttons. It sounded like the perfect end to a wonderful afternoon. 'You're on. Drop me at my place first and I'll have a shower, make a salad and drive to your place so you don't have to take us home later.'

A hint of disappointment flashed across his face, before being replaced with a lopsided smile. 'If that's what you want. I can take Mia home with Kent. He can stay for a while if his parents agree. They might even join us.'

Touching his hand, she said softly, 'Thanks.'

Turning his hand over, he wrapped his fingers around hers. 'It's all right. I think I get it. Slowly does it. Part of me is on the same page, but then there are times I just want to leap in and see what happens.'

She opened her mouth to reply, but he held his hand up, palm out.

'We agreed the other night to go easy, and nothing's changed. Not much, anyway.'

'Meaning?' Had she done something wrong? Read him wrong?

'You kiss like the devil.'

Laughter burst through her concern. 'Same back at you.'

'Phew. I hate coming second.'

'Why does that not surprise me?' Leaning in, she placed a teasing kiss on his lips.

The next moment she was flat on her back with Nicolas on his elbows looking down at her with his eyes shining. 'You're not getting away with that, Claire McAlpine.'

'Careful, kids present,' she warned as she choked with laughter.

'They're busy.' His mouth claimed hers, and his tongue slid inside.

Her world went still. Everything about her focused on the sensations swamping her, driving her crazy with need. Slowly she breathed deep, smelt the salt and sun on his skin. Damn, she was gone. He had her in the palm of his hand.

Then he stopped, lifting his head and glancing around. Sitting up, he stared down the beach. 'They're heading this way.'

'Well timed,' she muttered through the desire pushing at her inside and everywhere.

'Call it luck. I was very distracted, yet knew I had to stop.'

Just as well, or she'd have lost all reason and given in to the bone-melting sensations filling her everywhere.

'I hate that you're right,' she admitted. Probably shouldn't be telling Nicolas how she felt, but he was being open and she wanted any relationship they might have to be open and honest.

'So do I,' he said ruefully. 'Only on this occasion,' he added with a shrug. 'Hey, guys, ready to go home?'

'No.'

'Do we have to?'

'We could stop for burgers and chips on the way,' he tempted.

'Yes!' Kent leapt into the air. 'My favourite dinner.'

'Can we, Mummy?' Mia asked. It would be a treat for her.

'Of course we can.' Though it was only five o'clock, not her dinner hour by a long time.

'I thought I'd cook something for you and me later, unless you're into burgers?' Nicolas asked.

'I don't mind a quick take-out occasionally when I can't be bothered preparing a meal, but honestly, right now it doesn't sound appealing.'

'Good answer. Right, guys, let's pick up our gear and hit the road.' He was folding his towel to put in the bag. 'Kent, you've left your sandals down by the water.'

'So?'

'So do you want a burger and chips?'

The boy trotted away in an instant.

'You'll make a great dad,' Claire said, laughing. 'You know which buttons to push.'

'The ones my parents used,' he replied with a grin.

'Mia, where's your bucket and spade?' she asked.

'Behind you, Mummy. They're wet and sandy. Too yukky to go in the bag.'

'Rinse them in the sea. I'll come with you.' To create a space between her and that seductive grin. Nicolas had a way about him that drew her in without any thought about where it might lead, and the more time they spent together the more she was concerned about where she was heading. He was turning out to be everything she wanted in a lifelong partner. Steady, kind, loving, and capable of turning her on in a blink. Almost as if she could leap in and take a chance. Trust Nicolas and her instincts. Mia sprang to mind, and her breath stalled. If Nicolas wasn't for ever then Mia would face rejection, which didn't just hurt. It stayed with a person for ever.

Glancing over her shoulder, she felt her stomach tighten when she saw him watching her with a similar longing in his expression. Impossible to ignore. Trouble was brewing. 'Good trouble, me thinks,' she whispered. 'Or hopes.' To go with it, or not? He'd invited her to join him for dinner, and they'd no doubt share a drink on his deck, and a moment or two without children interrupting. Go with it. There could be lots to gain. Her smile spread from ear to ear. She liked it.

* * *

'Comfy?' Nicolas asked Claire as he settled into a cane chair on his deck.

'Couldn't be better,' she acknowledged before sipping her wine.

Dinner had been a success and now they were having a second small drink to finish the day with. 'Give Mia another five minutes and I reckon she'll be sound asleep. Her head keeps nodding forward and she's slumped sideways over the cushions.' The little cutie hadn't even heard him say goodnight quietly, she was so close to being out to it.

'It's been a big day for her, playing for hours on the beach and swimming, then more playing with Kent here. Thank you for letting him join her.'

'No problem. It makes it easier for you, and fun for the kids. I think Evelyn and Bodie were grabbing the opportunity for some adult time.' Lucky buggers, he thought, and laughed at himself for cutting his own chances of adult time by having the kids here. But where Claire went, so did Mia. Most of the time. Today had felt like they were a family, and he'd loved every moment. He'd invite Claire out on another date, adults only.

'Who'd believe it's Christmas next week? The year has flown past.' Especially in the weeks since Claire came into his life.

'Did Evelyn mention we're coming out to their place for the day?'

'She did.' He paused as an idea struck. Nicolas drew a breath. Did he put it out there?

Claire hadn't finished. 'It's going to be a great day, being with others. Hopefully young lady will be so busy she won't remember what she asked you for and raising the point about a certain man's hug. I have no answer for her.' Claire's voice was wobbly, as if she was about to cry. 'Not one I'm ready to tell her yet. Not until she's older and hopefully able to understand a little. If I recognise that time and don't wait too long so it comes back to bite me on the backside. I'm sure you'd hug her if she asked, but that's putting a lot on you and could raise her expectations.'

Expectations Claire obviously wasn't ready for. Not sure if he was either. Reaching for her hand, he felt the shivers and held tight.

'You're a good mum. You understand your daughter and I can't see you mucking this up. And, for the record, I would hug Mia any time she asked. I also see where you're coming from. None of it is easy.' To hell with it. He wanted to be there for her, to support her, and enjoy her company as often as possible. 'What would you say to you and Mia spending the night here? I have two spare rooms,' he added hastily, in case she was getting the wrong idea.

Not that he wouldn't mind sharing his bed with Claire, but he didn't know if she was ready for such intimacy. Or if she'd ever be. Though she'd been fast to kiss him back the other night, so he might be overthinking her reactions. Fast and mind-blowing. Yeah, he still felt the heat pinging through his blood now. Would he ever be the same again? It was one thing to have sex with a lovely-looking woman he liked, quite another to be intimate with a woman beautiful on the inside and out.

Suddenly he realised how quiet Claire had gone. 'It's all right. You can say no and I won't get upset about it.' Disappointed and sorry, but not cross.

Her fingers squeezed his, reminding him they were still holding hands, so not everything was off the table after his suggestion.

'I like the idea. As long as you're prepared for an early rising.'

His heart pounded as he replied. 'I'm used to getting up with the sun, so no surprises there. It might be you struggling to wake up, but I can remedy that with coffee or tea.' The pounding was still going on. He'd end up with sore ribs if it didn't slow soon. Claire was going to stay the night here next week. Maybe in the spare room, but definitely under his roof. It had to be a good sign of things to come.

'Tea that early in the day?' She withdrew her hand and clasped hers together on her lap, staring beyond the deck.

'Having second thoughts?' Better not be, because he was really happy about this, and the idea of her acceptance being retracted tightened his gut.

Twisting around, she faced him full-on. 'None at all. I admit to feeling a little cautious though. Every day we seem to move another step closer to each other, and that excites me. Until I stop and wonder what I'm doing.'

Instead of slowing, the pounding got harder. What was she about to say? Did she need some encouragement to see things his way? Or some time to think it through?

'Am I rushing you?' He'd put his hand up and take the blame, though in reality Claire was winding him up so fast and tight she had him in the palm of her hand.

'No more than I am. It's not something I'm used to.' She nibbled her bottom lip. 'I'm out of practice when it comes to relationships. Mia was the result of a short fling, not a long-term involvement.'

She'd said something about that the other day, and he'd been very surprised. She was so lovely that he'd have thought men would've been lining up to get her attention. That might mean she had reason to be ultra-cautious and therefore he'd made great inroads. Or he could be making it all up to justify the fact he cared one hell of a lot about her, and that was growing by the day.

'We could gain experience together. I like you a lot,

Claire, and I don't want to walk away. Certainly not before
I've given it everything I've got. I get that you're hesitant
due to your past. I too have insecurities when it comes to
trusting someone to accept me for who I am, and not who
I should be. I was married once. She left me for another
man and a job in another town when I believed we were
trying to have a family.'

He stopped. No more words to put out there. He'd
spilled his heart far too easily. Kind of said how much
she was coming to mean to him. He wanted her to know
he wasn't playing with her emotions, and that he had issues to work through as well. But it was hard. He didn't
need Claire feeling sorry for him. Support and understanding was enough.

Claire's head dipped in agreement. 'That's lousy, Nicolas. Now I can begin to understand your issues with trust.
The thing is, we're not twenty years old and full of expectations that everything love-wise will be a picnic.' She
smiled. 'We've had one of those and it was wonderful.'
Then the smile dipped. 'I wasn't making fun of it, I promise. I haven't had so much pleasure doing something so
ordinary in a long time. That's because you were with
me, with us.'

Us. Yes, Mia was a part of the picture, something that
didn't bother him at all. He'd never known Claire as a
solo act. Being a mother was part of who she was, and he
had no problem with that. Nor with being a father to her
daughter if they got that far.

'You couldn't have said it better. Thank you.'

'So, we're coming to stay here on Christmas Eve. I
haven't had a fun Christmas for a while. Spending a whole
day with you, and Evelyn, Bodie and Kent sounds wonderful. I can't wait.'

His muscles loosened as her words struck. Claire was

happy to be with him, and to stay the night. In one bedroom or another, he added optimistically. Might as well hope for the best, and not dwell on the negative.

'I'll have to get a tree and buy some decorations.' None in this house. There'd never been any need. It wasn't as if he'd put a present under it for himself.

Claire glanced inside. 'Mia's out for the count.'

He turned for a look. The wee girl was sprawled over the cushions, her eyes shut, and one hand touching Toby's head where he lay beside the couch. 'She fought it for a long time.'

'Nicolas,' Claire said softly.

He turned back to her. His breath caught in his throat. Her lovely face was so close he could see golden flecks in her eyes. And longing. For him. Yes, he knew it was for him. Because he felt the same for Claire. Longing, and tenderness, and a sense of love.

'Claire,' he whispered.

Leaning closer, her lips claimed his mouth.

And he was lost. In an instant. One touch of those sensuous lips and he had no way of stopping from kissing her. Kissing and wrapping his arms around her, bringing her as close as it was humanly possible for two people to get while sitting in chairs. And it still wasn't close enough. Without letting her go, he stood up, taking Claire with him, bringing her even nearer to his body. Still not near enough. There were clothes in the way. They needed to be one, melded together.

Her grip tightened around him, as though she felt the same need. His heart sang, and his head spun. This was beyond anything he'd experienced, or could remember experiencing. No, it was new. Claire had snagged his heart when he wasn't looking, and there was no way he was getting it back in a hurry, if he even wanted to. Which, right now, he doubted would ever come about.

She lifted her mouth, whispered, 'Nicolas,' in such a husky voice his toes curled, and then went back to kissing all reason out of him.

'Mummy... Where are you?' A tiny voice crept through the mist in his head.

He pulled away at the same moment as Claire jerked back. Looking around, he found Mia sitting up on the couch, staring around the room, her sleep-filled eyes wide open.

'I'm here, sweetheart.' With a wry smile, Claire headed into the lounge. 'What's up?'

'I want to go home.'

'We will shortly. Mummy and Nicolas are finishing their drinks and then I'll help clean up. Curl up and try to get some more sleep, sweetheart.'

'I want to go now.'

'Mia, lie down and close your eyes. I won't be long. Nicolas has been good to you and we don't just walk out without helping him.'

There was a don't-argue-with-me element to that voice Nicolas hadn't heard before. It made him smile. Claire wasn't too soft with her girl all the time.

'You can go. There's not a lot to be done in the way of cleaning up the kitchen.' But his body was calling out for another kiss. That wasn't happening tonight. 'As you said earlier, Mia's very tired.'

'We'll be home before eight and since it'll be Sunday she can sleep in tomorrow. She's not used to being out like this.'

Claire not having been dating or in a relationship recently saddened him, but it also made him happier to know she wasn't hankering after another man, and that she was free to date.

'We'll have to give her plenty of practice.' Was he rushing them both? Probably, but he couldn't help it. No doubt about it, his caution was easing. Claire was special, and the idea of walking away from her turned him cold. 'If you're willing,' he added, to show he was open to hearing how she felt.

Coming close, she brushed a quick kiss over his swollen lips. 'More than willing.'

And so ended a wonderful day, Nicolas sighed as he waved them off and closed the door. There'd be more to come. He just knew it. He might find an excuse to call around to Claire's tomorrow, just for the chance of seeing her.

Did he need an excuse? What was wrong with turning up and saying hi? It was what people did with family and friends, so why not turn up unannounced to see the woman who was changing his perspective on his future?

Done. Or it would be tomorrow. He would visit Claire. Spend some time together. Roll on tomorrow.

'How was your weekend, Claire?' Joachim asked on Monday morning.

'Fabulous. We went to the beach on Saturday, followed by a barbecue, and on Sunday we went to a vineyard for lunch. The sun shone all weekend and nothing could've been better.'

There was such a happy note in her voice that Nicolas found himself smiling as he perused the patient list in the triage office while the docs were yarning in the doorway to one of their rooms. Sounded to him like Claire had enjoyed their time together as much as he had.

'We? You have a partner?' Joachim asked. 'I thought

you were single and that's why Nicolas drove you to the work party.'

'We as in me and Mia, and Nicolas.' She still sounded happy, so she wasn't feeling under pressure about having been with someone she worked with.

'I'm not surprised. You and Nicolas were inseparable that night,' Joachim said.

Nicolas's smile widened as warmth snuck under his ribs. Claire wasn't afraid to put their friendship out there. They weren't quite at the partnership stage, and if pushed he wouldn't have called her his partner either. They were getting there. But he cared for Claire so much he couldn't imagine not seeing a lot of her outside work, or never kissing her again, or not sharing a meal on his deck.

They weren't rushing round madly like young people in love. There was seriousness to their burgeoning relationship, an understanding that they had things to consider about each other and their own pasts. There was also a lot of laughter and fun, and sharing anecdotes about their careers and lives outside work, and occasionally about their pasts without touching the bad stuff.

Claire was still talking to Joachim. 'Moving to Blenheim is turning out to be marvellous. I'm loving the area and the people I'm getting to know.'

Loving the people. That was better. Nicolas bit his bottom lip to stop the grin that was trying to take over his face. Clicking onto the list of patients, he opened the first one.

Jody White, thirty-two, itchy rash on back and abdomen.

He stepped into the waiting area. 'Jody?'

A tired-looking woman with a puffy red face stood up. 'That's me.'

'Come through. I'm Nicolas, the triage nurse.' As he

closed the door and pointed to the chair by the desk, he asked, 'Do you have a history of skin rashes or reactions to certain foods?'

'No, never.'

The day was underway. Nicolas found himself humming as he filled in patient details or when he was walking back from taking someone through to Radiology. He loved this job, but today it felt even better. There was a new spring in his step as he went about the clinic. When he wasn't behind a closed door assessing a patient he often heard Claire talking or laughing.

Everything kept coming back to Claire. She made him feel alive, and filled with hope. He hadn't been down or unhappy before he'd met her, but these days he felt like a new man.

'Nicolas, can you give me a hand with Archie?' Claire stood in the doorway, looking worried.

The little boy he'd prioritised minutes ago because of a high heart rate and flushed face.

'I don't like his heart rate and need help monitoring him. According to his father he has shortness of breath when he's moving around and isn't interested in eating very much.'

They were in a quiet spell with no one waiting to be triaged.

'Archie had a respiratory virus a couple of weeks ago.' Viruses could lead to myocarditis.

'I saw that. Can you set up the monitor while I listen to his lungs again?'

'Hey, Archie. Let's get you onto the bed, eh?'

The two-year-old pushed in against his father, his eyes lacklustre.

'Come on, Archie. Nicolas is going to help you find out why you didn't eat your favourite breakfast.' Dad laid his son on the bed and held his hand while Nicolas lifted his shirt and placed the monitor tabs on the tiny chest.

Claire stepped up. 'Archie, I'm going to listen to your heart.' She rubbed the end piece. 'I hope this won't be too cold on your skin.'

Archie's skin was hot as he gasped for air, not filling his lungs enough with such short breaths.

'Dad?'

'It's okay, Archie. Everyone's here to make you better.'

'How ill was Archie with the RSV?' Claire asked after she'd listened to the boy's chest.

'Tired, listless and grouchy, otherwise not too bad,' the father answered. 'He's been worse these past couple of days.'

Sitting at her desk, Claire added some notes to Archie's file. Then she faced the father. 'Len, I believe your son has myocarditis, which is an inflammation of the heart muscles, and likely a follow-on from the virus.'

Len went white. 'How serious is this? It's his heart, I mean, what the…?'

'Sit down and I'll explain. People with mild myocarditis are more often than not treated at home. But because of Archie's age and his general lethargy I am going to have him admitted to the hospital to be on the safe side.'

Len was taking deep breaths. 'Could I have done something earlier? Was there something I should've noticed?'

Claire shook her head firmly. 'I don't think so. Initially his symptoms would've been similar to recovering from the virus. It's only when the inflammation got worse would his breathing and listlessness have become more apparent. You said you brought him in here this morning because you noticed that when he woke up.'

'True, but what if I'd taken him to the emergency department last night? Would that have been better for him?'

'I can't answer that, except to say you hadn't noticed anything going on, and therefore had no reason to bring him out at night.' She paused, then smiled. 'Being a parent's hard, isn't it? Remember, you're not a doctor or nurse. You did your best, and Archie's no worse off for spending last night in his own bed.'

Nicolas felt his own heart tightening at her words. Claire was so good at this. She calmed patients, and treated people with respect. Turning back to Archie, he read the monitor. No changes to the heart rate. He hadn't expected any, but there was no such thing as too vigilant.

'Thanks, Doctor. You're not making me feel any better, but I'm grateful for your kindness, and your honesty.' Len returned to watching over his son.

Claire picked up the phone. 'Hi, Nola. It's Claire McAlpine from the Urgent Care medical centre. I'm sending you a two-year-old with myocarditis.'

Nicolas tuned out and focused on his patient. 'I'm going to take you for a ride on the bed, Archie. Dad's coming with us too.' But first he needed to let the other nurses know he would be away for a short while. Someone else could cover triage. This boy wasn't going anywhere without him. 'Be right back. You hang in there.'

Claire handed him a sheet of paper the moment he returned. 'Here's the admittance form. We're in luck. The paediatric heart specialist is visiting from Nelson right now.'

His mouth curved into a smile. 'The more on our side the better.' Not that Archie probably needed to see a specialist, but the kid was only two and didn't need to have any further heart problems to deal with in the coming years.

'You're onto it.' She smiled in return.

Did his smile make her stomach tighten and her blood heat as hers did to him? He hoped so.

CHAPTER SEVEN

Two days before Christmas and it was date night. Claire sighed happily as she studied herself in the full-length mirror. Once again she and Nicolas were going out for dinner and Michelle was babysitting Mia. This time the teen was driving herself here, and wouldn't need a lift home afterwards.

It shouldn't make any difference to how she felt about going out with Nicolas, but damn, it did. It meant they could share time together back here afterwards, away from other people. Could share some of those devastating kisses, or more. More? Yes, well, how was she to know how she'd feel when they returned from the restaurant?

Since you already seem to know, what's with the question?

Claire laughed to herself. The black lacy G-string and low-cut bra were new. The olive-green dress with string straps and a deep vee partially revealing her breasts and flowing over her hips had been hanging in the window of Blenheim's most upmarket shop when she'd gone into town in her lunch break to pick up a book she'd ordered. The moment she'd seen the dress, she'd had to have it. Thank goodness it fitted perfectly or she'd have been disappointed beyond reason.

She'd been twenty minutes late getting back to work,

but not even the annoyed look from Ryan had put a dent in her excitement. She worked extra time pretty much every day, and today had been the only time she'd ever taken longer for her break than she was meant to. Because it was date night. Nicolas did this to her. Making her toss caution to the breeze. Bring on more. She'd never felt like dancing so much. Her toes constantly tapping whenever she sat at her desk, hearing his voice as he talked to patients in his office.

Going out with Nicolas—again—got her adrenalin flowing and her head spinning. This was nothing like the flings she'd had. Nothing whatsoever. This was real, in that they were interested in getting to know each other. She grinned. Embracing how the other kissed, and how it felt to be held in one another's arms. Hopefully there'd be a lot more to experience very soon, because she didn't think she could hold out much longer. She didn't want to. She was ready to go further. Of course to have sex, but for her, with Nicolas, that meant a deeper, more personal knowledge of him.

Date night just got a whole lot more interesting and thrilling. Every time she thought about Nicolas her knees wobbled, her sex heated and her heart tripped.

'Mummy, Michelle's here.' Mia bounced into the bedroom looking as happy as her mother felt.

'Great. Tell her to come inside, will you?' The sound of another vehicle in the driveway had her heart revving. Nicolas had arrived. One last flick of her hair and she left the bedroom, ready for the evening, whatever it entailed. As long as it was fun, warned a little voice in the back of her head, causing her to trip. Why wouldn't they have fun? What could possibly go wrong? They got on so well.

'Hi, Claire.' Michelle stood inside the door.

'Come through, Michelle. Thanks for doing this. I really appreciate it.'

'Any time. Mia's fun, and I like looking after her.' The teen followed her bouncing charge into the lounge.

Turning back to the front door, her lungs stalled at the sight of him standing on her doorstep. Dressed in a cream open-necked shirt and tan trousers, his hair brushed away from his face, Nicolas looked breath-taking.

'Hi,' she managed in a quiet voice.

'Hello to you too. You look stunning,' he added, his face serious.

Money well spent, she decided. 'Th-thanks. Come in. Do you want a drink before we leave?'

'I don't think so. We're due at the restaurant in half an hour. I'll say hello to Mia and Michelle, then we should get on our way. It's a little way out of town, on the other side.'

'Nicolas!' Mia came racing out of the lounge, stopping directly in front of him.

'Hello, you. How was preschool?'

'Good. I drew a picture of what my new kitchen will look like. I'm going to leave it in the letterbox for Santa.'

First Claire had heard. Her girl was persistent, she'd give her that.

'I'm sure he'll find it, sweetheart.' As long as there wasn't a picture of a father giving her a hug.

Nicolas looked over to her, understanding in his eyes.

So he'd had the same thought, had he? They were in sync so often it was a little scary. What if he could read her mind on other topics when he was near? Like sex. She winced. It was all right. Those thoughts had occurred while she was in her bedroom and Nicolas hadn't arrived.

Mia spun around. 'It's on the table. Come on.'

Nicolas brushed Claire's hand as he walked past. 'Have you seen this?' he asked with a gentle smile.

'No. A great lookalike, for sure.'

'The right colour?'

'Sort of.' Now she was laughing, which had probably been his intention in the first place.

'Here. See?' Mia held up the picture that looked something like a storm with pots and plates in the air.

'It looks good.' Nicolas scuffed Mia's head. 'I can see you're an artist in the making.'

'I'm good, aren't I?'

'Yes, you are. Now, do I have your permission to take Mummy out for dinner?'

'I think so.'

Claire could see Mia's eyes lighting up with hope that there might be something in this for her.

'You can have one chocolate Santa before you go to bed in half an hour's time, missy. That's all.' Scooping her up into her arms, she kissed her girl on both cheeks. 'Be good for Michelle. I'll check up on you when I get home.'

'Have fun, Mummy.'

'I'm going to.'

'You seem certain about having fun,' Nicolas said as they settled at the table in the restaurant.

'Why wouldn't I be?' she replied, laughing. 'Unless you've got a hidden agenda of turning this into a night of torture and torment, I fully intend having a wonderful time.'

'You're safe.' He reached for her hand. 'Let's start with a glass of wine.'

'Perfect.' The restaurant was crowded, and the waiters were rushing around trying to keep up. More time to spend with this man. 'What have you been doing today?' It had been one of his days working in the vineyard, and she'd missed him at work. Something she'd keep to herself.

'Helped Bodie with some bud pruning. His grapes are coming on well. This is the quietest time of the year, more

a watching phase and hoping the weather doesn't go wrong
and we get too much rain.'

'When does harvest start?'

'Around the beginning of March, though there are some
varietals that get hand-picked before then. Neither Bodie
nor I have those.'

'So you'll be crazy busy come autumn?'

'You have no idea. Little sleep, lots of checking crops
and decision-making on when to pick. Crazy is the right
way to describe it. While my vineyard is small, I also work
with Bodie on his.'

'So you don't work at the medical centre at all during
harvest.' Hard to imagine the place without him. Even now,
the two days a week he worked on the vineyard seemed to
drag out. How would she survive a month or more?

'It's part of my contract to take weeks off at that time
of the year. Management find someone to take my place
so I don't have to feel bad about not being there.'

'Evelyn says she works fewer hours too because Bodie
doesn't have time to look after Kent when he's not at preschool.'

'I think you'll find a lot of the businesses in town jug-
gle their staff during harvest. It's the way of it, and no one
really complains as the industry brings so much wealth to
the area.' Nicolas looked over at the waiter approaching
their table. 'Chardonnay? Or something else?'

'Chardonnay, thanks.' They were dining at another
vineyard, and she wanted to try their wine. Picking up
the menu, she perused the options, and sighed. 'How am
I supposed to choose one dish when there are at least three
I'd like to try?'

After their orders had been taken, she relaxed back in
her seat and looked at Nicolas. He really was gorgeous.

'Did you ever see yourself being a wine grower when
you were training to be a nurse?'

'Not once. Though I admit to a restlessness that I didn't understand for a while. Then I realised as much as I enjoyed nursing I also enjoyed being outside doing physical work. I missed that from the fishing years. When Bodie said there was land up for grabs next to him, it was a no-brainer.'

'Now you have the best of both worlds. How many people can say that?'

'Not many, I guess. What about you? Why medicine? Was it something you always wanted to do?'

'Nope. I was going to be a vet. Nothing or nobody was going to change my mind. I adored animals, and in the school holidays I worked at the local animal care centre, looking after cats and dogs mostly.'

Didn't most teenage girls with an aptitude for science want to be a vet? She'd been one of four in her class at high school who had. Only one had gone on to follow her dream.

'What changed your mind?'

'Watching a vet put down the most beautiful dog I adored and was pestering my mother to let me adopt. It was attacked by another dog, which had managed to escape from its cage when one of the helpers didn't fasten the latch properly. The injuries were terrible. Both dogs were put down that day. I cried for hours, and the end result was I decided to be a doctor instead.'

His eyes widened and there was a bemused smile on those sexy lips.

She added, 'It's far worse losing patients, but somehow I've learned to cope. As do all medical staff or we wouldn't last very long in the job.'

His grin faded. 'You're right. It's the downside to our work.'

Thankfully the wine arrived just then, and they picked up their glasses at the same time.

Nicolas tapped his against hers. 'Here's to more dates, and less gloomy talk.'

'I agree.' To both. Sipping the Chardonnay, she sighed with delight. 'That's so good.'

'Isn't it? I haven't given you a sample of my Chardonnay yet.'

'Have you still got some over from last year?'

'There's a couple of bottles in my cellar to take to Christmas lunch. Be warned, Bodie will want you trying his wines too. You might be inundated with different wines on the day.'

'Not likely. I don't tend to get carried away with drinking.' Not with Mia to keep an eye on. Nor was having a hangover the next day her idea of fun. 'But I look forward to trying yours.'

'You'd better.' His laughter tickled her insides. As did a lot of things about him.

Until he asked, 'Have you ever been in a serious relationship? A long-term one?'

Her instant reaction was to say no and close down, but she was starting to think he was already a part of her life that she wasn't willing to let go. She cared about him, more than a lot. So much she could feel love on the horizon. Time to open up a little. Deep breath and, 'One. We lasted three years before he left. I tend to have trust issues after that and how my dad left me.'

He leaned back, his steady gaze not wavering, instead fixing on her more directly. 'Understandable. Can you see yourself moving past those issues?'

With Nicolas, yes, she could. But. There was always a but. What if he let her down? Walked away once she'd handed her heart over? Left without a glance over his shoulder, never to be heard from again? And broke Mia's heart as well? Talk to him. How was he going to understand if she didn't?

'I'd like to think so.' Her breast rose as her lungs filled.

His gaze softened and he slid her glass towards her. 'You worry about Mia. It's only natural.'

The wine was cool on her tongue and reminded her not everything was bad. Especially Nicolas.

'No, I couldn't face the idea of heartbreak again so I stuck to having the occasional fling, Mia being the result of one. The man who fathered her all but ran when he learned I was pregnant. I wasn't asking for anything more than he recognise his child and take part in her life in some way.'

Plates of food appeared in her line of vision. She wasn't sure she was ready to eat. Talking about those things always got her stomach roiling.

Nicolas picked up her free hand and kissed her palm. 'Thank you for telling me. It helps to understand how you must feel about relationships and putting Mia first.'

Hadn't she said he was good at reading her?

'Thanks,' she squeaked. 'I am wary about love. But I so want to have it all,' she added with an attempt at a smile. She had a feeling it didn't come off very well when Nicolas tightened his hand around hers.

'You can,' he said quietly, then sat back. Taking his hand with him. 'Let's enjoy our meals before they get cold. This is what we came out for. And making the most of each other's company.'

'True.' So why ask about her relationship history? Was he starting to think they might get together permanently? Wasn't it too soon for that? *Tell that to your heart, Claire. You mightn't be admitting to love, but what other word describes the emotions that fill you day in, day out?*

'Eat,' Nicolas said, before taking a mouthful of his steak.

The salmon was delicious, as was the company. They laughed and talked all the way through the meal, no more deep questions asked or answered. Nicolas appeared re-

laxed, and not scared off by her lack of commitment in the
past. Of course he saw her commitment to Mia, so possibly
that helped. Claire got on with enjoying herself, putting her
concerns aside. She could fall in love and have a great future. Yes, she could. And would, if she carried on like this.

'You coming in?' Claire asked Nicolas when he pulled up
outside the house.

'Yes.' But he didn't open his door, instead reached for
her and drew her close. 'After this.' He proceeded to kiss
her senseless. So easily.

She gave up all trace of resistance, let the wonder of
those lips on her mouth, his tongue teasing hers, take over.
She knew nothing other than Nicolas, his hands spread
across her back, his chest pressed against her breasts, his
outdoorsy scent, his strength and gentleness. His kiss went
on for ever, deepening with every passing moment. Taking
her on a ride of longing and love and wonder.

When he eventually pulled back and looked into her
eyes, she knew. It was time to let go the past and move
forward. To see where their relationship led. To make the
most of every opportunity that presented itself with Nicolas. To take a risk. She took his hands in hers, and brushed
a soft kiss over his lips.

'Come on. Inside and alone.' Apart from a hopefully
sleeping Mia. Michelle would hit the road as soon as she
went indoors. Then it would be her and Nicolas, free to
follow up on those kisses. She reached behind for the door
handle.

'Claire?' Nicolas ran a finger over her cheek. 'Are you
sure? I do not want to rush you.' His body was tense, and
if the front of his trousers was anything to go by he had a
hard-on that needed dealing with. Yet he was offering to
back off. What a man.

'I couldn't be more certain if I tried. Are you all right with that?'

'Ye-es.' He was out of the four-wheel drive and around to her door so fast her head spun keeping up.

Inside she became practical and talked to Michelle. 'Any problems with Mia?'

She got an eye-roll and a short reply. 'Are you kidding? She's never any trouble.'

'Just trying not to be the mother who thinks her child would never do anything wrong,' Claire said with a laugh as she paid Michelle. 'Thanks for looking after her.'

'Any time. See you on Christmas Day. Hey, Nicolas, catch you then too.'

'Right, kiddo.' He closed the door behind her and turned to Claire. 'You go check on Mia. I'll be waiting.'

Naturally that was the first thing she'd do. Nothing would be wrong with Mia, but she still had to see for herself, and give her a kiss and touch her baby.

'Back in a minute.'

'Don't rush.'

She looked him over and laughed. 'Really?'

Disappearing down to Mia's bedroom before he could come back with a wisecrack, she hugged herself. All was good in her world.

Very good, she corrected later. Nicolas had taken her in his arms and danced them down to her bedroom, kissing her all the way. Her throat, her shoulders, her arms. Sending the tingles heating her skin into overdrive.

Closing the door behind them, she began to unbutton his shirt, every button earning a kiss on his chest, his nipples, that flat, tight stomach. The gasps of passion as her tongue slid over his skin heightened her own awareness deep inside, filling her with desire and love. Tipping her over the edge into bliss. Holding him around the waist, she stepped backwards towards the bed, impatient to be naked and wound around him. Needing to know him completely.

'Claire.' Nicolas breathed her name as though it were gold. Looking at her with hunger, before his gaze drifted down to her cleavage and he leaned in to kiss and wind her even tighter. 'You are special.'

He made her feel special. Reaching behind, she fiddled with the zip on her dress.

'Let me.' His fingers brushed her hot skin, teasing, tantalising as he lowered the zip at an unbearably slow pace.

'Nicolas,' she whispered against his mouth. 'Come on. I can't bear this.'

'Oh, yes, you can.' His eyes lit up and his mouth curved into a heart-melting smile. 'We've got all the time it takes.'

She didn't need many seconds, let alone minutes. She was throbbing with need. So was Nicolas. When she undid the front of his trousers he was hard.

When he slid her dress off her shoulders and down her frame to her waist she briefly removed her hand from that heat to slip her arms free, then returned to holding him, rubbing up and down, and getting nearer to exploding with each caress.

Sinking onto the edge of the bed, she negotiated his trousers down those firm thighs to his knees and beyond. Then, leaning in to take him in her mouth, she felt his hands on her head, lifting her away.

'No, no, no. We'll do this together. I'm not coming before you, sweetheart.' Nicolas slid down onto the bed, wrapping her in his arms as he went and sprawling over the covers with her lying on top of him. His hands were between them, teasing her nipples until they were so hard she thought they'd explode.

'Don't stop,' she cried as she eased upward and crouched over his throbbing manhood, touching the tip, feeling the zing of heat that brought on in her core. Again and again, until she had to let go, to cramp around him, and bring him to his peak. Sliding down his length, she filled herself with his need, and lifted up, lowered again.

'Claire,' he cried. 'Claire.'

And then she came, exploding around him, falling into his arms, against his bucking body. Into a world she hadn't known before. A wonderful, exciting, loving place. Somewhere she would want to come back to again and again. She'd found what she hadn't believed possible. They'd made love, not had sex. She'd let go all restraints and been given so much in return.

Curling up around Nicolas, she sighed with pure happiness. Anything was possible when she felt so good, so comfortable with Nicolas.

He moved, stretching his legs and lifting his arm from around her.

She held her breath. He wasn't leaving already? He couldn't. Unless—unless this had only been a quick release for him and he wanted no more. Her heart started to flutter. Not this time. Not Nicolas. Not that.

Nicolas leaned up on one elbow and traced a finger down her cheek, over her chin, across her neck and down between her aching breasts that hadn't known such erotic tension in forever.

'Claire, I don't know what to say. That was amazing. You are amazing.'

Her lungs expelled a breath and her heart rate returned to a semblance of normal. 'No more than you.' She smiled through her relief. 'I can't believe what just happened. I've never known anything quite like what we shared.' Honesty paid dividends, didn't it? If he understood how much their lovemaking meant to her then he wouldn't let her down. Would he?

'Relax, sweetheart. I'm not walking away from this. From you. This is a beginning, not the end.'

See? He read her so well it was scary at times. But not now. She'd needed to hear that. There were no words to describe her feelings, unless she was prepared to sound gushy and stupid. Taking his face between her hands, she brought their mouths together and kissed him with an intensity that said it all for her.

What else could she do? He'd turned her life upside down within weeks, and now she was ready to take a chance on him, on them. She wanted more, a lot more, and she had plenty to give back. It was a freeing moment. She, Claire McAlpine, wanted to share her life with this wonderful man. So much so that she was prepared to put her heart out there and see where it led.

Lying down beside her again, Nicolas reached for her and drew her in close. 'Thank you,' he said so quietly she strained to hear his words.

'For what?'

'Trusting me. Giving yourself to me, accepting me without question.'

So she wasn't the only one with doubts. There'd been plenty of questions, but in the end, 'It was easy.'

His hug tightened, and he rested his head against hers. 'Very.'

CHAPTER EIGHT

'FINALLY…' CLAIRE SIGHED.

Mia was hyped to the max. Santa was coming.

'She's really asleep? At last?' Nicolas asked with hope widening his eyes.

Sinking onto the couch beside him, she dared to smile. 'Yes. But I'll check shortly to be absolutely certain. She's shattered.'

'She might sleep in a little later than expected.' The hope was increasing.

'Christmas Day and a stocking waiting at the end of her bed filled with surprises? Get over yourself.'

'Not forgetting the present she's waiting for. She hasn't forgotten for a moment that Santa's bringing it, has she?'

'Nope.' But so far it seemed she had forgotten the hug she'd asked for.

'Let's hope she's completely absorbed with it.' Nicolas dropped his arm over her shoulders and drew her nearer.

Claire mentally crossed her fingers. 'I have no idea what brought on that other request of Santa. She's never said anything like it before. She rarely mentions having a father and where hers might be.' Being more relaxed than ever with Nicolas had her opening up further about the things that bothered her. It was a new experience, and made her more comfortable with him and about herself and what she was looking for.

His hand was rubbing little circles on her shoulder. 'The questions will no doubt become more frequent as she gets older and understands most other kids have a father in their lives.'

'As long as she doesn't blame herself for Hank not being there for her.' The pain Mia would know would be very similar to what she'd experienced. Unless her mother fell in love and settled down with a man who adored her. Anyone come to mind?

She turned to Nicolas as he said, 'You still have a little time to think about how you're going to answer questions, and be as prepared as it's possible to get. She'll throw you some curve balls though.'

'No doubt at all.' Smiling at this man who was winning her heart all too easily with his understanding and care, she said, 'I can see you being a great hands-on dad. No walking away from the hard yards for you.'

'I'd like to think I'd do a good job.'

He most certainly would.

'How about some wine?' Before we go to bed. 'I hope you didn't make up the other spare bed for me.' Once upon a time she'd never have said that, but Nicolas made her so comfortable she found she often spoke from the heart and not the head.

'I didn't want to be presumptuous,' he said, laughing. 'But no, I took a chance and left it as it was.' He stood up. 'I'll get the wine. You stay there. You're looking exhausted.'

'It was busy at work today. Silly me thought it would be quieter with people out doing last-minute shopping for tomorrow.'

'Think about it. A lot of the patients we saw were older,

and alone, as though they weren't going to be busy with family or friends tomorrow.' The glasses clinked as he took a pair from the cabinet.

'I hadn't thought of that.' They'd admitted two serious cases to hospital though. Patients with family at their sides the whole time they were in the medical centre. 'I can't believe I've got four days off.' As one of the newest doctors working there, she'd been lucky when Ryan had said he was happy to work if she wanted to take a break. It'd only taken seconds to accept. Spending more time with Mia—and hopefully Nicolas when he was available—was right up there with the best way to spend her day.

'Lucky you. I'm on the roster for the twenty-seventh and eighth.'

She'd seen that. 'I can be on cooking duty then.'

'Here, try this.' He passed her a glass of Sauvignon Blanc. 'It's one of Bodie's, and I hate to say it, but it's damned good.'

'Exceptional.'

'Damn it, knew you'd say that.' He returned to sit beside her and rested his free hand on her thigh. 'This is cosy.'

'Very.' Having quiet time with Nicolas and looking forward to Christmas Day with him and friends lightened her heart in a way she hadn't known for a long time, if ever. 'Where were you this time last year?'

'Sitting here, a wine in hand, and watching some nonsense on TV.'

That was a clear memory. Similar to hers, apart from the wine. It would've been tea.

'You don't join your family at this time of year?'

'Dad's gone and Mum's in a rest home. My brother and his lot go to his wife's family and take Mum with them. There're plenty of them and they're into massive gatherings, which make me feel the odd one out. Probably my own doing, but I prefer to stay away. I fly up to see Mum every couple of months. It's hard as she's got dementia.'

How sad. The few times he'd mentioned his family he hadn't sounded close to any of them.

'Actually, if I remember correctly, I was a bit melancholy last year, and the TV wasn't distracting me from thinking about my life and being single and what might lie ahead.' He sipped his wine as he stared at the floor beyond his feet. 'Just saying, you know.'

Leaning her head on his shoulder, she said, 'Yes, I know. Even knowing feeling sorry for yourself is a waste of time, it's not always possible to ignore the sense of being alone and thinking about others who are with family or friends.'

'Yet I've got the best mates down the road and I can go join them whenever I want. But sometimes I like to stay away and be strong and even enjoy that solitary time.' And give them space.

'It's what makes you strong. Stronger,' she amended before tapping his glass with hers. 'Here's to a merry Christmas and a very happy New Year.' One week to go and then another year would be starting. This time, for the first time, a sense of anticipation filled her. There was lots to look forward to. Her hand tightened over Nicolas's. Lots. Hopefully.

'Back at you, Claire.' His smile went straight to her heart, warming her throughout like nothing else could. 'Drink up and let's go to bed.'

The warmth turned to full-on heat. Right between her legs, in her fingers, over her skin. Definitely a Christmas like no other.

If this was how the last week of the year was panning out, bring on the New Year. It had to be even better.

* * *

Nicolas rolled over and sat up in his bed. Excited giggles were coming from the room next door.

Beside him, Claire blinked open her eyes. 'What's the time?'

Checking his phone, he groaned. 'Five ten.'

'Great,' she groaned. 'I'd better get up before Mia comes looking for me.'

'Yes, we kind of messed up there.' They'd agreed last night that it was too soon for Mia to find them in bed together, even if she didn't understand what it really meant. Come to think of it, he wasn't one hundred percent certain what it meant either. He and Claire had become lovers very quickly, and deep down he knew there was a lot more to this than just getting together for sex. He didn't know how much more, and what he wanted. Apart from love and a long-term future. But was Claire the other half of that picture? He hoped so. Yet something was pulling at him, telling him to be careful. *Go slow, be certain, don't get hurt.*

'I'll go put the kettle on for a brew.'

'I'll go see what Santa's delivered.' Her grin was tired but still knocked him sideways.

'Go, Mum.' They'd moved the kitchen set into the lounge by the Christmas tree last night, but there were a couple of small parcels on the end of Mia's bed.

Slipping her satin robe over that sensational body, Claire shook her head. 'Any minute Mia'll be saying Santa's let her down. There isn't a kitchen.' Placing a kiss on his cheek, she smiled. 'Santa delivered a lot that I enjoyed during the night.'

Returning the kiss, he pulled on shorts and tee-shirt. 'He had a delightful helper.'

'Corny,' she groaned through her smile.

'Mummy!' Mia shrieked down the hallway. 'Santa forgot my kitchen.'

'Told you.' Claire laughed. 'Mia, it might've been too big to put in the bedroom. Have a look by the Christmas tree.'

Nicolas stepped out of the door. 'Merry Christmas, Mia. Santa won't have forgotten.'

'Coming, Mummy?'

'I wouldn't miss this for anything.' Claire grinned and snatched up her phone.

With Mia racing down the hall, he took Claire's hand and followed. Warmth and gentleness emanating from Claire caused his heart to melt. Mia's excitement got to him too. This was what having a family must feel like. Breathtaking wonder. If the rest of the day turned out to be boring, it didn't matter. This was the best it could be.

Wrong, it got better when Mia spied her present. All hell broke loose in the form of one small girl charging at the tree and the presents stacked around it. 'My kitchen's here! Mummy, look what Santa brought me.'

Tears were streaking down Claire's cheeks as she bit her bottom lip.

Nicolas had to blink back some of his own. This woman was such a loving mother. As well as a great big softie. He wound his arms around her and kissed the top of her head. 'You're special.'

Mia tore the wrapping paper off and giggled.

'Did you see that, Nicolas? Santa's cool.'

'Claire, give me your phone or there won't be any photos.'

She blinked, and handed it over. 'Take plenty. Then I'm going to make some tea.'

'Good idea. We're due over the fence at nine. On past experience, breakfast will be large, but right now a mug of tea sounds ideal.' Claire didn't sit around expecting to be waited on. She got stuck in with anything that needed to be done. Then again, she was used to living without a partner so no magical house fairy doing the chores.

'Does Evelyn go all-out for Christmas?'

'Breakfast, followed by presents and coffee, then mid-afternoon lunch. Usually one or two neighbours who have nowhere else to go drop in. Strays and waifs, Evelyn calls them.'

'Do Mia and I fit into that category?' she asked with a small smile.

'Hardly. You're her friend. And mine.' Friend? Yes, and now lover. 'A very special friend.'

'A friend with benefits?' Her smile was turning cheeky.

'Better.' And that, Nicolas told himself, was enough. He still didn't know where they were going with their re-lationship, only that he was loving every moment he spent with Claire. 'I take my tea black.'

'I think I've seen you make it often enough at work to know that.'

So she observed the most ordinary things about him. What else had she noted? Anything important? Like how he didn't care about trying to impress her around his house? He hadn't spent hours dusting and vacuuming yesterday. Not that there'd been time, but he did know of people who'd stay up half the night preparing for visitors. What a waste of sleep time.

'Do you want something to eat, Mia? Breakfast's a long time away.'

'Santa put some chocolate in my stocking. I'm going to eat that.'

Nicolas glanced at her mother, and had to laugh at the resignation on her face.

'Walked into that one, didn't I?' Claire said. 'Mia, don't eat all of it. Keep some to share with Kent.'

'Fat chance.' Nicolas went across to the small decorated tree he'd put up before going to work yesterday so that Mia didn't miss out. 'Let's see what's under here, shall we?'

'Are there more presents for me?' Mia bounced beside him, her kitchen momentarily forgotten.

'There might be.'

After she'd gone to sleep last night Claire had put a few parcels under the tree. From her friends for Mia, she'd said. He'd felt a little sad that there were none from family, because there wasn't a family other than her mum. And a grandmother in Perth, who didn't seem to have sent a parcel.

I want a cuddle from my daddy.

Those words rang loud in his head. Would he never forget them? Mia was such a happy kid, always laughing and talking, making her request even more shocking now he knew her a little.

'Let me see. What does this one say? Um…' He scratched his chin. '"To Mia, love from Mummy".' He held out the present, to have it snatched from his hand.

'Mia, don't snatch, and say thank you to Nicolas.' Stern mother on the job.

'Thanks, Nicolas.' The wrapping paper was flying in pieces, no delicate unwrapping going on.

'Wow, Mummy, this is cool.' Mia held up a pink bikini and pink beach towel. 'I love it.' Leaping at Claire, she wound her arms tight around her neck and plonked a kiss on her cheek. 'Thanks, Mummy.'

Nicolas picked up a small package. 'Merry Christmas, Claire.'

Locking beautiful toffee-brown eyes on him, she said,

'This really is Christmas, isn't it?' Her smile was tentative, as though she worried she'd said too much.

'It is indeed.' Glancing to see if Mia was distracted by her bikini, he leaned down to brush a light kiss on Claire's cheek. 'It's wonderful to be sharing the day with you both.'

'I can't imagine anything better.' Her fingers worked at the tape on the small package, first one piece then the next, then the wrapping paper was unfolded from around the small box. She looked from the jewellery box to him and back. Her breasts lifted as she drew a breath and opened the box to expose the delicate gold chain he'd chosen.

'Oh, Nicolas, it's beautiful.' Her fingers shook as she picked up the chain and laid it on her palm. 'Beautiful.' There was a hitch in her voice.

'I hope it's your sort of thing.' She'd worn a copper necklace when they'd gone out to dinner the first time, but he hadn't noted her wearing other jewellery, apart from that ring on her finger.

The look she gave him made his heart beat faster. 'It's absolutely my thing.' Holding the necklace out, the clasp undone, she said, 'Would you do the honours?'

'Try and stop me.' Her neck was warm against his clumsy fingers as he worked the tiny clasp. 'There.' The gold chain looked perfect against her lightly tanned skin. He wanted to swing her up in his arms and race down to the bedroom. Instead he drew a steadying breath and stepped back. The one drawback to having her daughter with them, one that didn't really bother him, apart from the tightness in his groin that wasn't going to be satisfied any time soon. He gave her a lopsided grin instead, and got one in reply.

'Mummy, can I see?' Mia pushed between them, her little face close to Claire. 'It's pretty, Nicolas.'

'I'm spoilt, aren't I?' Claire whispered something in

Mia's ear, who then raced to the tree. 'Thank you so much,' Claire said against his mouth before following up with a quick kiss.

'Nicolas, this is for you. From me and Mummy.'

Groaning inwardly at the interruption that was to be expected, he laughed and took the proffered present from Mia. 'What's this?'

'A surprise,' she told him.

It certainly was. A leather-bound copy of a book he'd been telling Claire about a couple of weeks back. He hadn't been able to track down a copy anywhere online or in the local second-hand stores.

'Where did you find this?' he asked in amazement.

Her forefinger tapped her nose. 'That's for me to know.'

'And me to find out,' he rejoined with a chuckle. Bending down, he touched Mia's shoulder lightly. 'Thank you very much for my present, little one.' Hugs were out of the question since the Santa debacle. He was too aware of upsetting Mia. But he could hug her mother. 'Thank you too. I can't believe you managed to track down a copy. I'll treasure this for ever.'

'You'd better.' She grinned. 'Now for that tea.'

The rest of the day continued in the same comfortable, happy way, with everyone having fun opening presents and eating too much salmon, ham and salads, along with pavlova and fresh fruit salads, and chocolate that seemed to disappear in a hurry, mainly gobbled up by two youngsters joined at the hip and their new toys to play with.

'It's been quite the day,' Nicolas said to Claire as they entered his house in the evening, trailed by an exhausted Mia.

'I don't remember a Christmas like it,' Claire admitted. 'Everyone was so relaxed. No arguments or grizzles. Definitely a first.'

He hated to think what that meant. Even in his family Christmas had always been a load of fun when he was a boy. They'd only got off-kilter when he and his brother became young adults with their own agendas, and his hadn't fitted the mould of perfect son.

'Here's to more like it.' If he had his way, they'd definitely be sharing more.

'Nicolas, I want a cuddle.' Mia stood right in front of him, leaning back, her big brown eyes staring up at him.

About to reach down to lift her up into his arms, Nicolas felt his heart thump hard. He paused, gazed down at Claire's daughter. Longing filled her eyes. Longing for something he wasn't sure he could deliver. A hug, yes, but what about what might be behind that hug? Would he be starting something that he wasn't ready for? None of them were ready for? If Mia saw it as more than a friendly gesture he could end up breaking her little heart. Something he had no intention of doing.

'Santa didn't bring me the one I asked for.'

Pain slammed his chest. His heart. Banging like crazy. He was not this kid's father. As much as he thought she was adorable, he was not taking on that role to make her happy. He wasn't even pretending to make up for the man missing in her life. Not until he and Claire knew where they were headed, and they had a way to go there, despite getting on so well together. He was falling for Claire but that didn't mean he was prepared to take a risk on his heart. Nor Claire's and Mia's.

'Come here, Mia. I've got a hug for you.' Claire held her arms out to her daughter, her face frozen with shock.

'I want one from Nicolas. He hugs you all the time. Why can't he hug me?'

Put like that, why was he hesitating? Because it felt wrong when this child longed for her father to pick her up and hold her. Because the look on Claire's face said she had a problem with what her girl wanted of him. Or was the shock because of Mia's request, not his delay in responding?

Mia stamped her foot. 'Don't you like me, Nicolas?'

He couldn't hold back any longer. 'Of course I do. Come here.' Sweeping her up, he held her close, and tried not to let the feel of her little arms winding around his bigger ones make him think he could step up to replace her father. He was not ready for that and, judging by Claire's face, neither was she. Mia certainly wasn't. What if he and her mother didn't last as a couple? Couple? They might be dating and spending quite a lot of time together, but were they even officially a couple yet? He had no idea. He wanted that, except now he doubted they would ever make the grade. Too much at stake. He'd known what the risks were but this was reality slamming into him, waking him up.

Claire reached for Mia, took her out of his arms and gave her a mummy hug, before saying, 'It's getting late and time we went home.' She didn't look at him as she put Mia down and headed down to his bedroom where her overnight bag was.

He followed. 'You don't have to go. You can stay the night.'

Tossing her few possessions into her bag, she said, 'I need some space. It's been a big day, Nicolas.'

Couldn't argue with that, but it had been a fantastic day. As had the night before. But… 'Nothing to do with the pain showing on your face?' Pain that said she didn't trust him enough to keep her and Mia safe. Or that she didn't love him and had realised she shouldn't be here?

* * *

Everything to do with what I'm feeling. She'd made a right mess of things.

'Nothing at all,' she lied. 'Mia did surprise me a little. Again. Which suggests to me she needs to be home catching up on sleep.'

Claire swallowed her panic. What now? Think everything through before she put her foot right in it. Keep quiet when she couldn't find a suitable answer, one that wouldn't tell Nicolas more than she was ready for. The day had followed on from such an intimate night she'd let go the brakes on her dreams and had a wonderful time with him. Hours of amazement, of fun, of sharing everything, of just being together. Hours when she'd forgotten to put Mia first.

All because she'd fallen in love with Nicolas when she hadn't been looking. Slam, bang, head over heels in love. It wasn't meant to happen, shouldn't have transpired, and yet her heart was full with love for him. She had to get away before any more damage was done. Before she said something she couldn't take back.

She wasn't ready, probably never would be. Nor was Mia. She wanted a father, but that wasn't Nicolas's role to fill. He wasn't ready for a full-on relationship with her, and therefore not with Mia either. He mightn't have meant anything by his hug than to make Mia happy, but her girl would see it as far more. Hope would start growing and she'd soon put more demands on him. It wasn't happening when there was no guarantee pain wouldn't follow.

Tugging at the zip on the bag, an ache formed in her chest. What had she done? Gone and hurt two people, all because she'd let her dreams get in the way of common sense. Because love had snuck in when she hadn't been looking.

Get me out of here.

'I'll put the doll's kitchen in your car.' Nicolas spoke softly, before striding away as though he suddenly couldn't wait to be shot of her.

Who could blame him? He was probably keen on a fling, and now the realisation of what that really meant was hitting home. Just as hard as the realisation she had fallen in love with Nicolas slammed her.

Talk about a double whammy. *I had no intention of loving him.* But she did. *Get out of here. Now. Fast. Go home and be safe.* Too late.

All she could hope was that it wasn't too late for Mia. Or was that being selfish? Was she using Mia as an excuse not to lay her heart on the line? To expose her vulnerability?

Damn, oh, damn. What now? How did she cope? She and Nicolas had to work together. Be calm around each other. Hardly going to act like a demented hen, was she? Possibly not. But how did she get through the days pretending to herself Nicolas meant nothing more than a nurse she'd had a few wonderful days with? Was there a self-help book to show her how to cope?

Claire buckled Mia into her car seat. 'Good night, Nicolas,' she said softly, meaning goodbye to more days and nights like those they'd just shared.

'Goodnight, Nicolas,' Mia shouted. 'I had fun today.'

He poked his head inside the car. 'Night-night, little one. I had fun too.' Then he straightened and locked his eyes on Claire. 'I mean it.'

'I'm sorry,' she repeated quietly. 'This is me being strong for my daughter.' That was an excuse, and she sensed he knew it. At least he'd never guess what she was really feeling, how she'd gone and fallen in love with him. That would be too much. It would never work.

'Mia is one very lucky girl,' he replied just as quietly. See? He wasn't as involved in this relationship as she was. He wasn't in love with her. They'd had a brief fling. Calling it quits had always been on the cards. Now it had happened. There was no returning to last night and the intimacy they'd shared, the warmth at being held in his arms as they lay naked in his bed. It was over—almost before it had started—but definitely over.

Claire headed around the car to her door, discreetly rubbing her cheeks with the back of her hand. 'I'll see you at work.' Should've taken that position in Auckland when it was on offer. But Blenheim had rung a lot of bells, and she couldn't in all honesty say she'd have preferred the large city. Her heart might still have been intact though.

Her hair swished across her face at her abrupt shake. Meeting Nicolas was the best thing to happen in a very long time. She couldn't deny it. Not even when the weeks and months ahead looked bleak.

Nicolas stood, hands on hips, watching Claire head down the long drive and out onto the road. All the time his body felt heavy and his head filled with longing. She had driven away with his heart in her hands, and no idea how much she meant to him.

Because you haven't had the guts to tell her.

He'd only really understood minutes ago. Right when she'd said she needed space. As though she'd had enough of him. Wanted to seek solitude, and didn't need him sitting beside her, sharing a wine or holding hands.

I'll see you at work. Claire's words rang in his ears, reminding him how he had not wanted a relationship in the first place. He'd believed they might share a few days and nights together and then it'd be over, no regrets. The regrets were already swamping his heart. Not once had he believed he could fall in love again, and yet here he was, his heart heavy with love. He trusted Claire more than he'd thought he'd ever trust again.

Now she was gone. Out of his life. She hadn't said as much, but he knew her well enough to know she had no intention of returning to what they'd had going. It had been there in the protective way she'd held Mia. They were done. Except at the medical centre. That was going to be painful. Could they still work as a team after this? They had to. It might be the way to get back on track and start over. *I wish.*

She had warned him she didn't do relationships. He'd be naïve to think that didn't matter. He could hope she'd talk about this when she'd had time to think it through, but he knew Claire better than that. The barriers were up, locked in place. It would take more than a few words to bring them down again. No, best he worked at locking down his feelings and moving forward, denying his love and not putting his vulnerability out there. He knew all too well how that went. It was like being chopped off at the ankles with nothing to save him.

Claire had been quick to head away. Did that mean she didn't trust *him*? It was possible, with her history. Did she think he wasn't good enough for her? Was he? What if he did get involved with Claire and then ended up leaving her? And her daughter? Yes, and what if they stayed together for the rest of their lives? How wonderful would that be? *I wish.*

He had a lot of wishes. Right now, after such a wonderful twenty-four hours, it was hard to believe none of them were coming true. The tail-lights on Claire's car as she disappeared around the corner rubbed it in. Gone for the night? Or out of his personal life for ever?

Was he really going to give up that easily? It wasn't in his nature to walk away from problems. He'd never avoided his father's insistence he do better at school. He'd merely reacted by showing how good he was at other things, which had so annoyed his parents they'd pressed down harder on him. When his ex had walked out on him, he'd shown her he wasn't hurting by getting on with his nursing training and buying the property he now lived on to forge a life on the land as well. He'd shown her he didn't need her to follow his dreams.

Did that mean Claire could drive away and he wouldn't do anything about the love he already felt for her?

No, it didn't.

This was something he wanted to fight for. Claire. Love. A life together. They'd only known each other for a short time but he knew she was the one for him. Might've known it the first time he'd seen her as she was aching for Mia, wanting to make it better for her daughter who was asking for a cuddle from her father.

The cuddle he'd been afraid to give tonight because he didn't want to hurt Mia, or Claire, or himself. His unconditional love for Mia had struck him hard. There'd been no compromise. When Claire had talked about the father and how he wanted nothing to do with his child even before she was born, the torment in her voice had cut through him like a knife through butter.

So, yes, he was going to fight for Claire.

But he'd go slowly, build up her trust, take it one long and slow day at a time. Somehow he'd manage to stay away from banging down her door and demanding they talk this through. Somehow he'd give her space and time to think about what they'd started. Hopefully she'd miss him as much as he was going to miss her. Working together would be hard—but doable. It had to be.

What if it wasn't? Claire might not feel the same about him. Then he'd be setting himself up for a big fall. But sitting back and doing nothing when his heart was so invested in her would be far worse.

Turning away from the view of the empty road, he headed inside, only to be met with the sight of the twinkling lights on the Christmas tree and screwed-up wrapping paper Mia had left behind a chair. He could hear her squeals of excitement and see Claire's laughter and relief as she tore the paper off the kitchen set. It had been fun putting that together last night, thinking about Mia's smile when she saw what Santa had brought. His heart beat faster as he remembered the morning, when he'd watched Claire open the box holding the gold chain he'd bought her, seeing her eyes light up and her delectable mouth curve into a soft, adorable smile directed at him.

I should never have let Nicolas get so close, Claire thought despondently as she tucked Mia into bed with her favourite doll. 'Goodnight, sweetheart.' She brushed stray strands of hair off Mia's face. Her girl was exhausted.

'Why didn't we stay with Nicolas?'

'We live here, sweetheart. We have to come home at the end of the day.' Did they though? She could've taken her time and not reacted instantly to protect her heart. Then who would? There was no one else for that job.

'We stayed there last night.'

'Because it was Christmas.'

Please don't throw a tantrum, kiddo. I'm about done for the day. No energy left in the tubes.

Admittedly, most of that had been used up enjoying herself with Nicolas and the others. It had been the best Christmas she'd ever experienced. She'd learned how special the day could be when spent with those who accepted her for who she was, and her heart had been fully focused on the people she'd shared it with, including Mia and Nicolas.

Funny how both names seemed almost linked in her heart now. Then it had all fallen to pieces. Because she'd let it. She'd panicked when Mia demanded that hug. She'd been afraid Nicolas would wake up to what he might be getting himself into. Because she'd suddenly realised how deeply in love with him she was, and that nothing was ever going to be the same. To give her heart away meant trusting him implicitly. Which she did. Or she thought she did. She was afraid to find out the true answer. Mia might be hurt. *She* would be.

'It's not fair,' Mia said through a big yawn.

Damn right it wasn't fair. Nicolas was *the* man. But he wasn't ready, and might never be.

'You can't always get what you want, little one.'

Nicolas had called Mia 'little one' earlier. As if he cared about her daughter. But that didn't mean he wanted the whole package. He had to love her for that and, despite how close they'd become, she couldn't say whether or not he felt that way about her. Or was she trying too hard to appease herself? Hard to deny her distrust of men though. Yet it hadn't taken long to fall in love with this particular one. He was everything she'd dreamed of, and more. Last night, lying in his bed against him, had been the best thing in a long time.

Bed. The idea of curling up under a sheet had seemed sublime an hour ago. Now she'd be alone, not tucked against Nicolas's hot, sexy body, caressing his skin, kissing his chest, making the most of being with the wonderful man who had opened her eyes to the possibility of a future where she wasn't raising Mia on her own but one where she gave her heart away and was loved deeply in return.

Filling the kettle, she stared out of the window onto the back yard. It was so small and ordinary after the wide green landscape that was Nicolas's vineyard. The kitchen was poky but practical, as was the rest of the house. Other homes surrounded the property on three sides. So close there wasn't a lot of privacy. At least it wasn't going to be her permanent abode. She'd rented so that she'd have time to get to know Blenheim better and decide where she'd like to live. Unfortunately so far she hadn't seen anything that compared with the rural location where Nicolas lived. Evelyn and Bodie's property was equally enchanting, which might suggest she'd like a house a little way out of town. Were there any houses out there that didn't come with acres of land requiring a lot of upkeep?

Get real, Claire.

She'd never lived anywhere but in a city, with neighbours all around, and a small lawn and few gardens to maintain. What would she know about the countryside? But there had to be some small properties, surely? It could be exciting living a little way out of town, with quieter roads and neighbours some distance away. What was she doing even thinking about this? A lot of her investments would be used in establishing her own practice later next year.

She poured boiling water over her tea bag. Stared as the water in the mug darkened. She was getting ahead of herself. It was a diversion from what had gone down between her and Nicolas at the end of a perfect day. Teach her for thinking her life had done a complete turnaround from how it usually ran. It went to show she was vulnerable when she wanted to find a new happiness involving a decent man, and a family life for her and Mia. When it started to look real, she'd done a runner.

I've only known Nicolas since the beginning of the month. What was I doing, thinking we might have a future?

How did she manage to fall in love so easily when she was so cautious? Not once did she stop and seriously think about what she was doing. It was too soon to be getting romantically involved. They didn't know each other well enough to be falling in love. Love was for ever, through the good and bad times, yet she'd wanted to go ahead. Nicolas had got to her in all sorts of ways, made her feel special and cared about, had her thinking about a better life and making her thankful for uprooting her life and moving here, but she wasn't ready to commit to for ever. She might want to, but it was so risky she was scared. It had been a brief interlude, exciting and sexy and had her waking up at night to pinch herself in case it was all a dream. Then her daughter had woken her up in a hurry by asking for a hug. No big deal really. It was normal. Except Claire knew it meant so much more, or could if she hung around too long. So she'd walked away before she could get badly hurt.

Too late, Claire. You're already hurting.

The idea that Nicolas mightn't care for her anywhere near as much as she did for him had her running for safety—aka these four walls. Brought on by memories of how the men in her past had all ignored her love, gone and left her to face life without them. Not that she'd loved Hank. Not at all, but he'd destroyed something huge for Mia, which was unforgivable.

She doubted Nicolas would ever do that, but he hadn't known them very long, and tonight had been a wake-up call for her. She couldn't risk waiting for him to fall for her because it might never happen. She had to protect their hearts. There was no one else who could do that.

Milk splashed on the bench as she poured.

Nicolas is the most amazing man I've known.

She didn't want to go days without seeing him, talking and sharing a joke, having a meal together.

She had to.

Great. They had to work together in the medical centre, discuss patients and treatment as though nothing was out of the ordinary. That was going to be hard—if not impossible. Every time she saw him she'd be remembering those arms around her, those lips on hers, his eyes filled with laughter as they talked.

Sitting on the tiny deck sipping her tea, her shoulders slumped as she sighed. This time next week would be New Year's Eve. A new year should bring wishes for the coming twelve months, wishes that included love and Nicolas. She'd dared to dream of a happy, fulfilled year. A year with him at her side, and the future opening up in front of them.

Now that seemed a stretch. A big one.

Her fingers ran along the chain around her neck. Nicolas had bought it for *her*. It was beautiful, special. It meant a lot. What was going on? Had the day been too good, and they'd both suddenly taken a step back, jolting each other mentally in the process?

It wasn't going to be easy not spending time with Nicolas. No making love, or kisses that were out of this world. In a very short time he'd given her so much she'd been missing for a long time. Had she ever known such enticing kisses or exciting sex? She must have. But she'd certainly forgotten all about them until Nicolas came along and stole into her heart.

But… She dragged oxygen into her lungs. Not one man she'd been close to had stuck with her in any way. The chances of Nicolas being any different were slight, if her track record was anything to go by.

Glancing at her finger, she saw her mother's ring. *I'm so proud of you.* Yes, she had to continue being strong. She couldn't succumb to her love for Nicolas. Not until she knew if he was interested in going further, and then it had to be the whole way. Mia wasn't getting hurt because her mother wanted to love and be loved by a wonderful man. Damn it, she didn't want to get hurt either.

So they were over. Finished.

CHAPTER NINE

CLAIRE SANK DOWN in front of her desk to type in the last notes for the day. First day back after Christmas and it had crawled by. Much like the days she'd been off work. Not even taking Mia to the beach every day had made the hours speed up. She'd missed Nicolas even more than she'd have believed possible, as if a piece of her was gone for good.

Until this morning they hadn't spoken since Christmas night, which had been hard to take. Too often she'd picked up her phone to call him, then put it down again. She wanted to see him, share time with him, but she was also afraid of where it might lead, if she was truly ready to take that final step. Full-on commitment would be wonderful—if she could let go the past rejections and move forward without worrying about what might happen.

Here at work, Nicolas was his usual friendly self, though the sexy smiles and occasional touch on her shoulder had disappeared. At one point he'd brought her a mug of coffee when she hadn't had a chance to take a five-minute break. 'Get that into you,' he'd said in the deep voice that had always melted her heart. Still did.

Damn him. It would be so easy—too easy—to tell him how she felt and not let the past get in the way.

But every time she'd thought they might be able to do just that, her chest would tighten with fear. What if she gave in and it all backfired? She should never have got so close to him. All her fault.

'You hanging around here all night?' Nicolas asked from the doorway.

'Not likely,' she muttered. 'Adding some notes about my last patient, is all.'

'See you tomorrow then.' Nicolas didn't move away, stood watching her with something like hope in those blue eyes she had recalled every night when she lay in bed with the light off and sleep taking its time to envelop her.

'I'll be here. Are you working every day this week?'

'Yes. It means others can spend time with their families.' And he didn't have one. Even so, that was kind.

Not that she was surprised. 'I'm baking brownies tonight to bring in tomorrow.' It was her birthday, but no one needed to know. She'd pretend it was for those who had to work between the two holiday weekends.

He licked his lips. Lips she could all too easily recall on her skin as they made out. 'Then there's nothing that'll keep me away.'

Watching him smile was undoing her resolve, making her flush with need.

Please go, Nicolas. I don't need you here, reminding me so clearly of what I'm missing out on.

Turning back to the screen, she finished with her last patient's notes and closed the computer down. She couldn't sit here staring at the blank screen for ever, though. Standing up, she reached for her keys and turned around.

Nicolas had gone.

Relief vied with disappointment. They'd not talked about anything except work, but she'd enjoyed every moment. Face it. Just sharing the same air as him turned her on, and made her feel she might be making a huge mistake trying to keep him at arm's length. Seeing his eyes lighten, his long fingers when he rubbed his wrist, the vee at the front of his scrubs, dragging her gaze downward to what she knew was behind his clothes—all added up to the love she wasn't ready to acknowledge openly. She needed more time to think about what she was prepared to take a chance on. Her emotions were taking a roller coaster ride—a ride with no end in sight.

Nicolas drove home with his head full of Claire.

Claire concentrating on helping the elderly lady who'd broken three fingers when she'd closed her car door with one hand still holding the framework.

Claire smiling tiredly as she stood up from her desk and rubbed her lower back before going to get her next patient.

Claire giving him a surprised smile when he placed a mug of coffee on her desk because she'd been too busy to get her own. Her surprise had stung, but then she wasn't used to people looking out for her. She'd once said it was one of the best things to come out of her move north so far. Everyone was friendly and caring. Her life in Dunedin must've been bleak. The little she'd mentioned about her mother suggested there hadn't been a lot of love going around.

Except for Mia. Claire loved that little girl so much. It was beautiful to witness. Could she love someone else half as much? Him? Because he loved her so much he ached twenty-four-seven.

The four-wheel drive slowed. His foot had slipped off the accelerator. He wanted Claire to love him. Of course he did. That was half the problem. He wanted her to share his life, and that meant she had to love him. She'd become remote at work, talking to him only when needed, smiling softly but not as whole-heartedly as she used to. He missed her so much it was as though his world had fallen apart.

The back wheels spun as he accelerated away, trying to outrun his thoughts. He did want Claire at his side. Long-term. Absolutely. For ever? That was the rub. How did anyone know the answer to that? He'd loved Valerie, believing it was for ever, and that had turned into a train wreck. Whatever he had going with Claire, they needed to talk. Not about patients but about themselves.

The entrance to his property appeared and he turned sharply. Hadn't seen it coming, been too deep in thought about Claire. Parking by the shed, he went to check the water metre and make sure the vines had had enough water during the particularly hot day.

A cold beer while he cooked a steak for dinner was next on his list. It had to be at least twenty-five degrees out here still. A hot night lay ahead. Not caused by Claire's gorgeous body lying entangled with his either.

Make that two cold beers. Something had to cool him down. If at all possible.

It was after midnight when he eventually managed to grab a few hours' sleep, and he was already hot under the collar within minutes of arriving at the emergency clinic next morning. Even hotter below the waistband of his uniform when he saw Claire talking to Ryan.

Claire. Filling out her version of the uniform with curves in all the right places. Wearing her hair loose for a change, curls tucked behind her ears. A tight smile appeared as she placed the container of brownies on the bench in the tearoom. Tiredness evident in her eyes.

Only Claire could make him feel this hot and flustered and wanting to scoop her into his arms and hug away her obvious exhaustion. Exhaustion similar to that dragging at his shoulders.

'Morning.' He nodded at the brownies. 'That looks delicious even this early in the day.'

'Do we have to wait until tea break?' Ryan took the lid off the container and inhaled the chocolate aroma. 'This beats what I had for breakfast.'

'Help yourself,' Claire replied with a small chuckle. 'But do leave some for everyone else.' As she made mugs of tea, she said, 'I hope we're not too busy today.'

He hoped they were flat-out and then the time would speed past.

'Here.' She handed him a mug and picked up one for herself before heading out of the room.

Nicolas watched her go, her back straight, and no doubt a forced smile on the face he couldn't see. She was trying too hard to fit in today. What had happened? A bad night trying to sleep? Or had Mia kept her awake? Or was she feeling confused and frustrated about him and them? Like he was? He followed her into the consultation room.

'You okay?'

'Why wouldn't I be?'

He should walk out of here, go back to the tearoom and drink his tea. Instead he continued. 'You seem tired and look like you don't want to be here.'

Her eyes widened. 'Great. Guess I went a little light on the make-up this morning.'

'Cut it out, Claire. I'm concerned that you're all right. That's all.' That wasn't the half of it but he wasn't saying any more here.

She dropped onto the chair in front of the computer, tea splashing onto her hand. 'Sorry. I could do with a little more sleep, but it's not happening so I'd better get on with my day.'

'Where's Mia today?'

'Jess and Joachim offered to look after her. She gets on

well with one of their daughters so they figure having Mia there gives them some free time.'

Didn't sound as though there were any problems with Mia then.

'It's good how she's making new friends so easily. But then she is a right little charmer.'

Finally a real smile appeared. 'She's always been like that. It does make life easier when it comes to taking up offers of staying with other people when I'm working.'

This from the woman who'd mentioned setting up her own general practice. There'd be even less free time to spend with her daughter. Not that he was mentioning that at the moment either. That smile was worth keeping in place.

'She's a lot like Michelle, very easy to get on with and happy to join in all the fun.'

'I won't mind if Mia is as good as Michelle when she's a teenager.'

'Think I said once before, don't even start worrying about those years. Make the most of this phase while you've got it.'

'Good idea.' Unfortunately Claire's smile dipped.

His suggestion not so easy to stick to? The sound of the front door being unlocked and people entering reached him. Saved him from further turmoil.

'Here we go.' He headed for the triage office, noting only three adults queuing at Reception. A quiet start to the day. Damn.

Twelve hours stretched ahead. Right now he'd prefer to be inundated with patients than sitting around, fully aware of Claire every second of those hours. His hand tightened, loosened. They had to talk, to get this out in the open and deal with their differences. Had to. Not at work though. There were other staff members who'd overhear them, and patients would still come through the door to interrupt when they least needed to be. Besides, the last thing Claire looked as if she might want to do was have a deep and meaningful conversation with him any time soon.

'I'm just calling into the medical centre to get my phone, Mia.' She'd left it behind last night and by the time she'd realised she was at home and couldn't be bothered going back to get it.

'Is Nicolas there? I want to see him.' Mia had got over her upsetting moment with him in a short time, as she had when Santa hadn't promised a hug. He hadn't turned into an ogre after all.

If only I could move on as easily.

'Yes, he is.' The car park was full. What was going on? It was New Year's Eve and the staff on duty hadn't expected to be busy. 'We'll have to walk a little way, Mia.'

They were barely in the front door when Ryan saw her and said, 'Claire, am I glad you're here.'

'What's going on?' The waiting room was over-full and a quick look to the room with beds and monitors showed the same.

'ED can't take any more patients. There was a multi car accident at the intersection of Jackson's and Rapaura Roads, with multiple patients in serious conditions. We're taking the backlog, and minutes ago a family was brought in needing urgent attention.'

'I'm available.' How could she walk out of here while everyone needed all the help they could get?

'I'll look after Mia,' Diane, the receptionist, called. 'Come on, Mia. You can help me in here.'

'Okay. Can I type on your computer?'

Claire laughed. 'Good luck, Diane. You've got your hands full.'

'So have you.'

'Where do you want me, Ryan?'

'In with the family that's just been brought in. Nicolas is already there. He'll fill you in. I've got a child with possible appendicitis in my room.'

'Claire, good to see you.' Nicolas stepped up the moment she entered the room, strain evident in his eyes. 'First, John Cooper.' He indicated the man writhing on a bed as a nurse tried to attach monitors to his bare chest. 'This family were out in their alloy dinghy when a rogue wave hit, tossing them all out. John took a hit on the shoulder and back, but managed to get to Troy.' Another nod at a small boy on another bed being cuddled by a woman, presumably his mother. 'Troy took in a lot of water and stopped breathing. Fortunately bystanders rushed to take over, forcing Troy to cough the water out and then got him breathing. This is Pip Cooper, and this little girl is Gina. She was very lucky and only got wet. And a big fright.'

Claire shook her head, trying to absorb everything while moving towards John. The woman looked shocked but in control, though she did wince when Troy moved. 'Where are you at with everyone?' she asked Nicolas.

'I'm checking Troy out. We've wrapped him in blankets to raise his temperature. He has mild hypothermia. Can you examine John? He's got an injury to his lower leg where he thinks the propeller might've hit.'

She shuddered at what might've happened. 'Why isn't there another doctor in here?'

'Ryan was, but then he got called to a more urgent case.'

More urgent? Then they were really up for an intense time. Claire snapped gloves on, and put a hand on John's chest. He was shivering from top to toe. 'You need blankets too. John, I'm Claire, a doctor.' She looked to Karen, the nurse. 'Need a hand?' They needed those monitors doing their job.

'Yep.'

'Leave me. Look after Troy. He needs you first. I'll be all right,' John growled. 'He's only little, he needs you.'

'Nicolas is doing everything I would do. We need to make you warm again, and to check you over for injuries.' Blood had soaked the bed from John's lower leg. 'And stop the bleeding and see what other damage has been done.'

'I don't care. See to Troy.'

'He's being looked after.'

'What about Gina? Is she all right?'

'She's fine,' Nicolas called.

Pip appeared beside Claire, her arms empty of her son. 'John, please calm down, darling. Troy is in good hands. Nicolas knows what he's doing, and Troy is alert now. You saved him. Now lie back and get patched up yourself.'

John locked his gaze on his wife, and slowly the tension left him. 'If you say so.'

Between them, Claire and Karen got the last of the wet clothes off John. While Karen dried him with a towel, Claire examined his leg. 'This needs a lot of sutures, but I think you've escaped serious damage.' She could see the bones and neither had been chipped. 'We'll get an X-ray to make sure there isn't a fracture but I think there'd be other damage if there was.' A spinning propeller wouldn't make a clean fracture.

The door kept opening and closing behind her as Karen came and went with blankets and other equipment.

Nicolas joined her. 'Karen will watch over Troy. I'll help you.'

'I need to look at his back where you mentioned he was struck by the boat.'

'You hear that, John?' Nicolas wasn't wasting any time. 'Claire and I are going to roll you onto your side. Don't try and help, or resist us. It will cause more pain.'

His tight nod obviously caused him pain as a groan escaped him. 'You sure Troy's all right?'

'Yes. He's going to need pampering for a day or two, and then he'll be charging around like nothing happened.' Nicolas's hands were firm on John's hip and leg while Claire held his shoulder. 'One, two, three.'

They had him where they wanted.

A massive bruise covered most of his back and neck. 'Why didn't someone put a neck brace on?'

'The family was brought in by those same bystanders who saved Troy. They went to ED but the orderly sent them across to us. By then John had been moving around a lot. I did suggest it but Ryan didn't think it necessary.'

'He's probably right.' Though she'd have erred on the side of caution. Then she did that all the time about most things. A quick glance at Nicolas. Including him. Mostly him. Then, inexplicably, she relaxed some.

Nicolas had things under control. He was applying the monitors that John had refused. He wasn't fazed by the trauma.

'Have any painkillers been administered?' she asked.

'A dose of Tramadol about two minutes before you arrived.'

'John, what's your pain level on a scale of one to ten?'

'Four.'

'I'll get something stronger,' she said, having seen the sharp spears of pain that hit John every time he moved. 'You're in more pain than you're letting on.'

'I'll get it. What do you want?' Nicolas asked.

Claire told him, and continued checking John for further injuries. Bruises and swelling were appearing all over his upper torso. 'Did the boat hit you more than once?'

'I can't answer that. I felt an almighty whack and don't

remember much afterwards other than the need to get to Troy. I could see Pip had Gina.'

'Is John going to be all right?' Pip asked, watching every touch Claire made, her face strained.

'He needs a scan and X-rays. His head has taken a hard knock, leaving the bone soft in one spot. His shoulder isn't moving in its socket. Whether it was dislocated then became wedged awkwardly in the socket will come to light in the X-ray.' She continued outlining the injuries and what would happen next.

Make that whenever Theatre and surgeons, plus Radiology were available. The people from the car crash were already in the queue. Blenheim Hospital was showing how small it really was.

Time dragged on. Claire and Nicolas treated John as much as possible. She stitched his calf muscle back together while Nicolas swabbed the site regularly and passed across whatever she needed. A team. Whatever happened between them, they had this. Which could mean a lot for the future if she toughened up and made a go for him.

Troy was moved to the paediatric ward. Pip went along to see him settled, then returned to her husband's side. 'Where's Gina?'

Claire took her arm gently. 'Come with me.' She led Pip to Reception. 'Look at her.'

'She's having fun,' Pip gasped, then swatted her face with the back of her hand.

Mia and Gina were on the floor, backs against the wall, playing a game on a tablet, giggling as they took turns tapping the screen to make something happen.

'Who's the other girl?'

'Mia. My daughter.' Her pride and joy was helping Gina get through a harrowing experience.

'She's lovely.' Tears were streaming down Pip's face.

The events of the day were finally catching up. 'Gina is John's daughter. I had Troy before I met him. But no one would know that. He treats him as his son, and today was no exception. He saved our boy. He put him first.'

Claire couldn't help herself. She wrapped her arms around Pip and hugged her. This woman had what she hoped for, love for herself and her children.

'He's one of a kind,' Pip sniffed as she stepped back.

No, there was another man like John. He just needed to accept she loved him enough for both of them. Of course she had to tell him first.

She took Pip's arm again. 'Right, everyone else is being taken care of, so now it's your turn to be examined.'

'You noticed?'

Hard not to. 'Your upper left arm. You can't lift it. You grimaced with pain every time you moved Troy. I suspect a fracture.'

'Two fractures within an inch of each other,' Nicolas read from the screen an hour later. 'I'll sort the cast when you've talked to her.' He stood up. 'Then you'd better take Mia and get out of here while you can.'

'As long as I'm not needed, I will.' Mia had been a champ but almost three hours was a long time. 'I think she deserves fried chicken and chips.'

'Don't we all?'

Which gave her an idea. 'Come on, Mia. You and I have something to do.' How many pieces of chicken would she need to order to feed all the staff?

'Thank goodness that's over.' Claire tossed her keys on the bench and opened all the windows to let the stifling air out. Working with Nicolas had been good for the first time since Christmas. Calming really. Rejuvenating. The last days she'd worked had been draining as she continuously fought the urge to wrap her arms around him and tell him he was special. Trying hard not to admit she was struggling with not sharing time together outside of the clinic had sucked what little energy she had out of her. Today had been different. Today they'd been connected, each knowing what was required for the patient without saying a word. Each knowing the other would give everything possible to help their patients.

How was she going to cope next year? A new year was beginning in less than eight hours. Fifty-two weeks to spend a lot of days working alongside Nicolas.

'Mummy, Nicolas is here.'

'What? Where?'

'His car's in the drive.'

How had she missed that?

'Hello, Nicolas. Have you come to see Mummy?' Mia had run to open the door.

'Yes, I have. And you too.' He was standing tall, tension in his shoulders and his face.

'I'm going to play with my kitchen. I'll make you some tea.'

Claire smiled. 'Come in, Nicolas,' she said.

A bottle hung from his hand. 'Would you like some wine?'

'I'd prefer to talk.'

Some of the tension relaxed. 'Yes, we need to, but a glass of wine with that won't hurt.'

Spinning around, Claire went into the kitchen and, for something to do with her suddenly tense hands, opened a cupboard for some glasses. She filled the glasses too much. Didn't care. They were going to talk. She sipped the wine, needing something to make her feel good.

Give over. Nicolas makes you feel good.

Even though she didn't know where they stood, he made

her feel she wasn't so alone any more. He set her heart racing and her blood warming. He made her realise she could put her heart out there and take a chance on him. She had to, or regret it for ever.

She passed him a glass. 'How's our family?' Work was not what she'd been about to mention. Nothing like it. Her self-protection mode was firmly in place.

'John's doing fine, but they're keeping him in overnight for monitoring. Troy's been shifted to the same room so he doesn't wake up frightened after what happened.'

'They're all very close.' *Go on. Ask him. Drop the façade, Claire. Be the woman you so want to be.* 'You understood John's relationship to Troy right from the get-go, didn't you?' This was going the long way round but something said it was the right way.

Those intense blue eyes locked on her. 'Yes.'

'You'd do the same for Mia.'

'Yes.'

Her head tipped back and she stared at the ceiling, willing the sudden rare tears not to drip down her face. Nicolas would've risked his life to save her daughter. He was the all or nothing kind of man, and she'd go for all with him.

Swiping at her face with her hand, she placed her glass on the counter and looked at him. 'Absolutely. I know that. It's one reason I can't live without you, Nicolas. The other is I love you. As in love everything about you. Enough to want a future together. More children with you.' When she finally let go, there was no stopping her. Because if she didn't get it all out there now she might not manage it.

The silence was deafening. He looked stunned.

Had she really got this so wrong? It was always going to be a risk, remember? She'd fronted up, and if she'd made a mistake then she'd live with it. She loved Nicolas. If he didn't love her, then so be it.

'Claire—'

'Nicolas—'

They stopped and locked eyes with each other.

He nodded. 'You were going to say?'

Again her lips trembled as she tried to smile. 'I…' Her breasts rose on a sharp intake of air and dropped slowly as she exhaled. 'I think I said it all. I love you.'

Claire loves me.

Nicolas stared at the glass in her shaking hand. She'd said she loved him. Showed she had a lot more guts than he did when there was a lot more for her to lose. But he wasn't surprised. Had known it all along. One of the reasons he loved her.

Moving beside her, he took the glass from her cold hands and wound his fingers around them. 'I've missed you these past days, even when we've been in the same building, working together on the same patient. Today not so much because we were as one.'

She didn't move, not a blink.

'You've come to mean so much to me it's been hard to focus on anything but what we've been missing out on.'

Teeth dug into her bottom lip.

Get on with it, man.

'But—'

Claire jerked backwards. Her hands slipped out of his.

Reaching for her, he said, 'Sorry. I'll start again.' This shouldn't be so hard. But it wasn't something he was used to saying, though the words were waiting, ready to spill from his lips and put his heart out there for whatever Claire wanted to do with it. 'I've told you I've been married and that it fell apart against my wishes. I have moved on, but there's been a certain amount of fear I might be hurt if I fell in love again. That has kept me wary, as I imagine your past has you.'

She blinked, nodded once.

'The thing is, Claire, from the moment I met you, no, make that from when I first laid eyes on you at the kids' Santa party, I've been fighting to hold onto the caution. I've wanted to let it go and fly high with you. I'd get in the car to come see you and then I'd remember what being dumped felt like and I'd go back home.'

'So why are you here now?' The hope was returning to her eyes.

'Simple. I've fallen in love with you, and I want to spend the rest of my life with you. Of course, Mia's a part of that picture. If you'll have me.'

She stared at him for so long he thought his heart was going to break into a million pieces.

Finally, 'How do you know it will be for ever?'

'I don't. Nor do you. But if we don't try, then we've definitely lost out. I'd prefer to get on with living and loving you, and do everything within my power to make it work right on into old age.' Had he made her see he did love her? That she was the most important person to him? 'Claire, I—'

Her finger pressed into his lips. 'My turn.' A smile lit up her face, and made him relax a teeny bit. 'I understand. I've struggled to accept a man will love me enough to be there for ever. Because of that, I probably hold back on my feelings too much. But when you came along there was no stopping me wanting to know more and more about you, to be with you. I have fallen in love with you. Nicolas, I love you so much I can't put it into words. I can't imagine the pain of not sharing my life with you.'

'Then you can stop worrying because I'm here for you, with you, for ever.' Only then did he do what he'd wanted to do for days. Taking her in his arms, he kissed her. And then some more.

When they finally came up for air, Claire laughed. 'I'd better check up on Mia.'

Taking her hand, he walked inside and stopped to grin at the sight of Mia busy making pretend tea. 'That's love. That's what we've got.'

'Only better.'

'Will you two move in with me?' he asked, surprising himself, since he hadn't thought this far ahead, fully expecting to have been walking down the path to his vehicle alone by now.

'I'd like that.' Claire grinned. 'Here's to the new year and new beginnings. Just what I'd wished for.'

It felt right. But not perfect. Turning to face her full-on, Nicolas reached for Claire's hands. 'Claire McAlpine, will you marry me? Have more children with me?'

A smile to remember for always took over her mouth, her face, her eyes. 'Yes to both, Nicolas Reid. Yes.' She leaned in to kiss him. 'Yes,' she whispered against his mouth. 'Yes.'

'Mummy, why are you kissing Nicolas?'

They leaned back in each other's arms and looked at Mia, her eyes wide as she stared at them.

'Because I love him, Mia.'

'Do you love Mummy, Nicolas?'

'Yes, little one, I do. So much that we're going to get married.'

Mia charged them, arms outstretched. 'Can I come too?'

'We wouldn't go without you,' he managed around the sudden lump in his throat.

'Can I have a cuddle, Nicolas?'

Tears spilled down his face. 'Oh, sweetheart. I've got so many hugs waiting for you, you won't believe it.' He swept Mia up into his arms. Then pulled Claire in to join them. 'I love you both.'

Claire whispered, 'Do you know what this means, Mia? We're going to live with Nicolas, and we're going to be a family.'

'Is he going to be my dad?' Serious eyes looked from Claire and fixed on him.

Nicolas felt his heart squeeze painfully. 'Yes, I am. Is that okay?'

'Give me another cuddle and I'll say yes.'

Tears slipped down his cheeks as he obliged this lovely little girl who'd once asked for something he hadn't thought he could deliver, and now found he could—easily.

'Cuddle number two.'

Claire hugged them both. 'Happy New Year.'

Yeah. Bring it on. Happy New Year.

* * * * *

COMING SOON!

We really hope you enjoyed reading this book.
If you're looking for more romance, be sure to
head to the shops when new books are
available on

Thursday 19th January

To see which titles are coming soon, please visit
millsandboon.co.uk/nextmonth

MILLS & BOON

MILLS & BOON ®

Coming next month

SINGLE DAD FOR THE HEART DOCTOR
Karin Baine

'Is this really necessary?' Lily batted away the heart-shaped helium balloons lining her path but managed to walk straight into the red and pink streamers hanging from the ceiling.

'I think they're keen to reiterate the purpose of this scheme. That it's for heart patients only and shouldn't be abused by those hoping for a lift to hospital appointments or who want us to pop round with a takeaway. Plus it's Valentine's Day so, you know...' Finn's soft voice in her ear caused the hairs on the back of her neck to stand to attention when he was so close she could feel his breath on her skin.

'Oh, I know. Let's bring in all the clichés we can to hammer the point home.' She rolled her eyes. Being deceived by the idea of love and romance wasn't an affliction she suffered from. She left it to naïve young couples who had forever to fool themselves into thinking it could solve everything. Life, and death, had taught her it only complicated things and made life so much harder. All the people she had ever loved had died and, as for romance, it had brought nothing but heartache when she couldn't give her partners what they needed— children and time.

'Something tells me you didn't get any cards in the post.'

'And I suppose you did?'

'Two, actually.'

More eye-rolling. Not only was he handsome but he knew it. One of the worst traits a man could have.

'Let me guess, one came from a grateful young woman who found herself locked out of her house in nothing but a towel and you came to the rescue? And the other…some impressionable schoolgirl whose class had a tour of the fire station?' Boasting about how many cards he'd received was juvenile, and clearly mentioned to get a rise out of her. He had, of course, succeeded.

Finn laughed so hard she actually felt the vibration through to her very bones. 'Actually, they were from my daughters, but it's good to know what you really think about me. You'll have to take my word for it that I'm not a ladies' man who would take advantage of vulnerable females.'

Continue reading
SINGLE DAD FOR THE HEART DOCTOR
Karin Baine

Available next month
www.millsandboon.co.uk

Copyright © 2023 Karin Baine

MILLS & BOON

THE HEART OF ROMANCE

A ROMANCE FOR EVERY READER

MODERN

Prepare to be swept off your feet by sophisticated, sexy and seductive heroes, in some of the world's most glamourous and romantic locations, where power and passion collide.

HISTORICAL

Escape with historical heroes from time gone by. Whether your passion is for wicked Regency Rakes, muscled Vikings or rugged Highlanders, awa the romance of the past.

MEDICAL

Set your pulse racing with dedicated, delectable doctors in the high-pressure world of medicine, where emotions run high and passion, comfort a love are the best medicine.

True Love

Celebrate true love with tender stories of heartfelt romance, from the rush of falling in love to the joy a new baby can bring, and a focus on th emotional heart of a relationship.

Desire

Indulge in secrets and scandal, intense drama and plenty of sizzling hot action with powerful and passionate heroes who have it all: wealth, statu good looks…everything but the right woman.

HEROES

Experience all the excitement of a gripping thriller, with an intense romance at its heart. Resourceful, true-to-life women and strong, fearless r face danger and desire - a killer combination!

To see which titles are coming soon, please visit

millsandboon.co.uk/nextmonth

MILLS & BOON
A ROMANCE FOR EVERY READER

FREE delivery direct to your door

EXCLUSIVE offers every month

SAVE up to 25% on pre-paid subscriptions

SUBSCRIBE AND SAVE

millsandboon.co.uk/Subscribe

OUT NOW!

Available at
millsandboon.co.uk

MILLS & BOON